Dreams of Verdure

Book One of Ndesa Series

David Pariseau

ISBN-13 (Paperback): 978-1-970791-00-6

First Wide Edition, 2025

Published by Dkp Books

Los Altos, California

www.dkp-books.com

david@dkp-books.com

For Janis. For everything.

Makers (n.)

Refers to an ancient species that seeded habitable planets throughout our galaxy. It is believed that intelligent life on Ancara and on other worlds was shaped by these beings, with species on each adapted to suit local conditions.

Though there are hundreds of worlds where their influence has been found, it is likely that many remain undiscovered.

They are known to others by many names: Creators, Ancestors, Prime, etc. Little is known of what befell them, and what is known has been obscured by time or clouded by lore or prophecy.

: source Ancaran Abridged Dictionary

Chapter 1

"You beady-eyed tunnel rat," Dashin cursed, sucking on the knuckle he'd just skinned on another stubborn bolt.

An amused chuckle drifted up to him from the opening below.

Twisting within the narrow confines of the air handler, he brought up a knee and wedged himself between the sheet metal walls of the air duct, trying to get a better angle on the bolt. The sheet metal walls popped and pinged, the tinny metallic twang echoing in the cramped space.

"Bet you're rethinking your life choices," Gralan quipped from the hallway below.

Dashin grumbled as he wiped his brow with a shirt sleeve and scratched the tip of a pointy ear with a fingernail. The gentle thrum of the ion engines resonated in the air duct, their vibrations felt in both his knee and back. This was the fourth air handler they'd serviced today, and the knuckles on both hands were bloodied. Whomever had designed this cursed model had certainly never had to service it. The newer models on the ship's port side were a breeze, but these older units... He grunted, reaching up for the retaining bolt with his wrench.

His headlamp lit up the duct, the blurry reflection of his short brown hair and green and yellow skin playing across the dull, silvery finish of the sheet-metal.

With a final stretch, the bolt slid into his tool. He flipped over the lever with his thumb, securing it. "Got it," he said, his voice echoing in the cramped space. After unscrewing it, he dropped the fastener into his shirt pocket and loosened the last clip at the top of the duct. Dashin wriggled from back down a body length and dropped to the ship's deck.

As his boots hit the floor, Gralan, his supervisor, shifted his bulk away from the wall. His work shirt rode up over his belly, revealing a light green sliver of skin dotted with yellow freckles.

"You need more shirt," Dashin said with a chuckle, wiping his sweaty hands on his pants.

"It's Mayra's fault. She's been trying out new recipes in the mess," Gralan beamed, patting his shirt down. "I've been helping her out."

Dashin grinned. "Seems to me you were well on your way before Mayra."

Gralan lifted one side of the air handler, freeing the lower clip. "Grab your side, youngster. You should have more respect for your elders," he said with a wink.

Dashin hoisted his side and took his share of the weight. They slid the bulky air handler module onto the floor and began removing the screws securing its access panel.

He reveled in the camaraderie he was developing with his supervisor. It was something he'd longed for on Ancara. In their short time together, Gralan had recounted countless tales of his life aboard a myriad of ships. He'd signed on as a lad, two Ancaran years younger than Dashin's eighteen, and had spent decades since in artificial gravity. Dashin drank in every tale, happily hearing them again and again.

"Bet you imagined space travel would be a lot more glamorous?" Gralan mused, dropping screws into the magnetic dish stuck to a wall panel.

This trip was everything Dashin had wished for. He smiled, remembering the day he'd met Gralan while interviewing for the junior engineering position on the Serendipity.

Dashin had been just one more candidate in a room filled with them. As they waited, a disheveled middle-aged man with dirty hands and a grease smudge on one cheek approached them. He wandered around with a perplexed expression, asking questions. Dashin watched bemused as the people he approached tried to avoid the man. They shifted away from him, answered curtly, corrected him dismissively, or became preoccupied with their vid-screens.

Dashin grew fond of the poor man, who was clearly out of his depth for this interview and yet strove to put his best foot forward. So when he approached Dashin, he did his best to answer the man's questions. As they spoke, the people the man had previously approached were called from the hall.

The disheveled man's questions had been straightforward at first, his confusion simple to correct. However, as numbers in the room dwindled, the questions grew more challenging. Dashin found himself straining to recall obscure details from his classes.

The other candidates around them fidgeted or scrolled anxiously on vid-screens, unsettled by the discussion. The questions were now far beyond anything Dashin had prepared for. His answers grew shorter and more tentative, and he frequently had to admit he had no idea what the answer might be. It dawned on him that the bumbling man had a prodigious command of ship systems.

When only the two of them remained in the room, Dashin apologized, stating that he should have been the one asking questions. Gralan roared, clapping him good-naturedly on the shoulder. Moments later, he'd taken Dashin into an adjoining lounge where the crew was seated and announced that they'd found their new junior engineer.

Some of the crew were laughing and needling others. A few of them had won a game they were playing and were collecting credits from the others. They'd all turned and greeted Dashin warmly. He'd smiled, anxious to make a good impression. It was then he noticed the wall-mounted vid-screen they were clustered around held an image of the now-empty waiting room. He'd blushed, his greenish skin going dark as he realized they'd been betting on the outcome of his interview. Gralan, noting his realization, mussed his hair. That gesture, coupled with the joyful banter and ease the crew had with each other, warmed his heart. He remembered how hopeful he'd felt to have finally found a home.

"Why so many screws?" Gralan grumbled next to him. "Have the geniuses who design these things ever been on a ship?" He added the last fastener to the magnetic dish.

Gralan popped open the service hatch and stuck his nose inside. He took a sniff and then poked around with a finger as he studied the contents. After only a few moments, he leaned back and grunted knowingly. He moved aside. "Okay, Mr. Academy, what's the problem with this unit?"

Dashin stepped up and looked. He tried to mimic Gralan, sniffing and pushing the wiring back and forth. He looked around at the circuit modules and components for burn marks or broken connections, but nothing appeared out of order, nor did he note any burnt or unexpected chemical smells. He probed around a bit more, growing frustrated. How was he supposed to determine the issue this way?

"The problem is right in front of your nose. Did you miss that day in class?"

"I could take some measurements," Dashin said defensively.

Gralan nodded. "Yes, you could do that. But air handlers are life-support, and you may not always have time to fetch equipment."

Dashin looked again. No revelations occurred to him.

Gralan chuckled at Dashin's frustration. "So, what do you know about these units? We already serviced a couple in this hallway. It was only preventive maintenance, but..." he paused, letting the words set in.

"The power couplers!" Dashin's face lit up. He leaned in and pushed aside the bundle of wires in front of the power entry module. And, sure enough, there was some discoloration and a thin crack on the power coupler. He looked up with a smile.

"We'll make a service rat out of you yet, Academy boy," Gralan said, reaching over and mussing his neatly combed hair.

Dashin feigned annoyance, but he enjoyed the easy contact. He was happy to be learning from Gralan, who'd been more of a father to him in these past few Ancaran lunar cycles than he'd known before.

"Can you handle replacing the coupler?"

Dashin nodded, reaching for it.

"Great." He sniffed. "I smell Mayra cooking up something new." He winked at him and turned. "Call me when you've fixed it, and I'll help you reinstall it."

Dashin thanked him, and Gralan waved back over his shoulder.

Dashin pulled the power entry module from the access panel and headed to engineering to fetch a replacement. As he walked, he ran his hand along the metal wall panels, loving their smooth feel beneath his fingers. He turned the corner and glanced through a viewport.

The asteroids around them were like a forest of shadows against the bright field of stars beyond. He hadn't tired of the view. On his desert world of Ancara, most cities were underground, and though the night sky offered amazing vistas, they didn't compare with being on a ship and immersed in an ocean of darkness.

The fact that this expedition was in uncharted space only made the feeling more wondrous. Their mining ship had been prospecting this particular sector for many Ancaran days now. They hadn't found anything worth their time yet, though he didn't understand much of the discussions regarding the cost-benefit of the sites they'd scouted. He'd listened to the mealtime discussions of the day's sensor logs, but he took his cue from Gralan, who enjoyed the food and kept out of those conversations.

Gralan's philosophy was that keeping your world small was the secret to a happy life. *"Just keep your world to what you can see and control in front of you, and don't let yourself worry about things outside that world. The ship you're on and those around you are all that matter. Everything else is noise."*

Dashin could see the sense in that. On Ancara, he'd longed for something other than the life he was living. Now he leapt out of bed each morning, eager for the day. He'd always been a tinkerer, taking things apart to see how they worked or to fix or improve them. He'd rarely been successful, but now he was learning real skills that would change that.

He passed another viewport, amazed at how far apart the asteroids were. He'd always imagined that they would be clustered together. To think that some of these might have riches beyond counting was exciting. As a crew member, he had a share of whatever they found. As a new junior member, his share was microscopic, but this didn't dampen his dreams.

As he stepped past the viewport, he caught a flash in his peripheral vision. It seemed to come from outside. A moment later, he was slammed into the wall and then hurled down the hallway. Time slowed down. His mind tried to work out what was happening. His body hit the ceiling, careened off a bulkhead, and tumbled down the hall as the ship lurched beneath him. He crashed into another wall, and Dashin's world went dark.

Alarms blared as Dashin came to, his vision blurry. Emergency lighting cast an anemic amber glow in the hallway, punctuated by bright strobed pulses in time with the alarm siren. His stomach dropped at the hissing sound of escaping atmosphere. The horrific scenarios they'd trained for at the academy sprang to mind. He pushed them away, trying to recall the proper response to an evacuation alarm.

Evacuation. He shuddered, the word eliciting desperation. It was the last possible step in a long chain of events that must have occurred while he was unconscious. Was everyone else gone? Had they left him? Was he alone on the ship? Ignoring his training, he rushed toward the bridge until he ran into an emergency door that had sealed off the corridor. He put his hand on it. It was ice-cold, confirming a lack of atmosphere beyond it. He tried another hallway and found another emergency door blocking that passage.

The ship lurched beneath him. Realizing he was cut off from the others, his training reasserted itself. He had to get to an escape pod. He scanned the halls frantically, trying to remember where the pods were in this section of the ship. His heart pounded in his chest as horrific images of explosive decompression crowded his mind. The ship bucked and slammed him against a girder. Gripping it, he closed his eyes and took a breath.

A pod, a pod, a pod, he repeated, forcing his mind to focus until he remembered the one tucked away in the back of engineering. The ship slid sideways beneath him. Clinging to the girder, he opened his eyes. The constant spin of the ship hesitated, gravity fragile and uncertain now. Hub rotation was failing. The attitude thrusters were either dead or missing.

His vision hazy, he rose and staggered down the hall toward engineering, using his hands on the wall to keep his balance. The door to engineering shuddered and then jerked open in response to his palm on the access pad. Standing on the gangway that ringed the cavernous space, he held his breath as smoke billowed past him into the hallway, engulfing him as it rushed by. The current sucked at him as the escaping atmosphere behind him grew to a terrifying whistle. He managed to get the door closed before being thrown into the gangway's safety rail as something large struck the door. The meshed walkway beneath his feet groaned, with the pings and pops of failed welds and projectile rivets as the ship flew apart beyond the door, seeking to take engineering with it.

Dashin pulled himself to his feet, taking shallow breaths of the smoky air, and surveyed the cavernous space below. There were small fires everywhere. The area around the ion engines was completely dark. Lights and systems all over engineering winked out as the fires below consumed them.

Dashin stumbled along the gangway, using the rail to steady himself. As he passed a bulkhead, his upper arm flared with pain. He jerked back, grabbing the scorched skin with his hand, his vision white from the pain. He closed his eyes and held his breath, fighting to stay conscious as the pain swept through him. Taking a breath, he glanced at the charred skin on his arm. The sight turned his stomach, and he doubled over and retched on the floor.

The air was acrid with toxic fumes and the smell of burning flesh. His lungs contracted, trying to expel the noxious mixture, even as they labored to take it in. And still, the sound of bulkheads being crushed beyond the door promised a greater horror still. The ship rocked beneath him, and he gripped the rail tighter, steadying himself. Time was running out.

Think. Work the problem. He looked carefully at the air in front of him. The smoke rushing past him shimmered faintly before him. The caution tape on the wall panel next to him marked the path of the ignition fuel lines. A ragged hole lay in the center of the tape. Shrapnel from an explosion must have punched through the panel and punctured the fuel lines. The escaping gas was pyrophoric, self-igniting in air and burning clear. He shuddered. Had he stepped fully into that stream, it would have roasted him alive.

The ship jerked beneath him, nearly throwing him forward into the jet of invisible fire. What attitude thrusters remained were trying in vain to correct for the collapsing bulkheads as the ship vented huge pockets of atmosphere into space. Struggling to breathe, he dropped to the floor, grabbed the gangway's bottom rail, and pulled himself forward, moving beneath the jet of flame toward the stairway. Once safely beyond, he crabbed and stumbled his way down the stairs and scrabbled over wreckage to the landing by the pod.

Both gravity and the emergency lighting gave out as he reached it. Despite the lack of both, he managed to clear the wreckage enough to get the pod door open and pull himself inside. Praying it was still functional, he pulled the door closed and yanked the ejection lever. The explosive thrust threw him against the door, slamming his cheek into the glass viewport as the pod hurtled away from the ship. Lying across the crash seats, he remembered being told to strap himself in before throwing the lever.

He coughed noxious fumes from his lungs as the air scrubber cycled, filling the pod with fresh air. Sitting up, he blinked back tears and scanned the space beyond the viewports, searching for other pods in the growing debris field. He didn't see any. Helpless, he watched his ship tear itself apart, praying that others had made it out.

He fumbled for the radio and pressed the transmit button, calling over and over as pieces of his ship streamed off into the dark. His heart sank when he glanced down through a viewport and noticed the antenna mount on the hull of his pod had been crushed and sheared from the pod. The mangled assembly dangled from a bundle of mostly broken wires at the edge of his field of view.

The overhead gantry he'd crawled over to get into the pod had likely sheared the antenna mount as it crashed onto the landing. Had it also compromised the hull?

He released the radio button. It would be useless without the antenna. Even if another pod had managed to escape, he had no way of contacting it. The same assembly also housed the emergency beacon. Without a beacon, no one would ever find him.

Dashin plopped down onto a crash seat, dejected. The tiny, egg-shaped space was his entire world now. A space that barely fit its two crash seats was all that remained of his ship. The pod thrusters fired, and he felt the press of acceleration push him back into the seat as the pod moved away on an unknown vector. His failure to plot a course for the pod had activated the automated navigation system. Without it, he wouldn't have known how to pilot this craft or even where to point it. The display on the instrument panel showed a planet, the chemical composition of its atmosphere appearing above it. The chemical signature was all in green, which he took as a good sign, but the transit time would take days.

His arm screaming from the burn, he shifted his weight in the seat and felt a sharp pain in his shoulder. He winced and coughed. The cough added a needle-like stab to his side. The initial impact with the wall, or the tumble down the hall, must have cracked some ribs. He ran his fingers gingerly down his side, and thankfully, nothing felt out of place.

Fishing through the onboard medical kit, he found a tube of antiseptic ointment and squirted a generous dollop on his arm before bandaging it. Tilting the lid of the medical kit back, he used the steel mirror embedded in the lid to inspect his head. His face was covered with drying blood from a gash over his eyebrow, which was still weeping. His cheek was bruised and tender to the touch. Slathering the rest of the ointment on the gash, he used some adhesive tape to close it.

At the bottom of the medical kit was a packet of trauma tablets. He washed two of them down with a sip from a water bottle from the meager supplies compartment. In the viewport over his shoulder, the wreckage of his ship receded. In moments, it had transformed from the ship he'd come to love into a rapidly expanding debris field. Tears ran down his cheeks. He was close to despair when Gralan's words came to him. *Narrow your focus. See what's in front of you.*

What was in front of him? He took stock. The air scrubbers had removed much of the smoke. His body was chilled, likely the result of shock. He dug out an emergency blanket and wrapped himself in it. The cabin was getting blurry, the trauma tablets taking effect. He fished around for the harnesses of his crash seat and strapped himself in. As he did so, he looked over at the seat next to him. The sight of it lying empty overwhelmed him. He took a deep breath, fighting the mounting panic. Letting the breath out slowly, he adjusted the tension on his harness in case he was unconscious when the pod arrived wherever it was taking him. Assuming the green signature on the display indicated that the planet had an atmosphere, he wanted to avoid being bounced around inside the pod on entry.

Dashin lay there, his body shaking as events caught up with him. He felt as though an immense hole had opened up within him. He tried to keep it from consuming him as he coughed, his lungs complaining from the smoke they'd been subjected to. Tears from both smoke and loss continued to pool in the corners of his eyes and run down his cheeks. The tablets, softening his despair, tucked it deep within him. His vision narrowed, and the last thing he saw before passing out was the small green dot in the center of the navigation display.

Chapter 2

Alina swung through the canopy, following the others. She loved the way light slanted through the foliage as evening approached, giving everything a dreamlike quality. The greens and browns of her jungle world were richer without the glare of the midday sun. Shocks of white molna moss abounded, the gossamer substance clinging in patches to branches and trunks. Beads of water from the day's rain still clung to the clefts and shaded surfaces of some leaves.

She noted the details of the trees she passed. Some had smooth, hard skin, while others had thick, ridged bark. One branch might be dotted with clusters of small leaves, another with broad leaves spread to catch slivers of sun. Some saw the forest as a single living thing, but to her, it was an immense collection of individuals.

This time of day always brought a pleasant breeze, as though the jungle itself were sighing after the heat of the day. The forest's breath carried the leafy smell of verdant growth, tinged with floral notes from the blossoms that dotted the upper canopy. And within that dreamy scent, she imagined subtle hints of the earthy forest floor.

Her friends had scoffed at this description, the forest floor too far below them to be visible. No one believed its smell was detectable from here. She glanced down through the foliage and the network of branches, trying to spy it. Distracted, she almost missed her next hold. Her lanyard barely grasped its target and threatened to slip free as it took her weight.

She adjusted her next throw, bringing her mind back to the motion while compensating for the sway of the trees in the breeze. The others had pulled ahead, but she wasn't concerned. They would have to wait for her. They would want her arm for the hunt.

The five of them were perched on branches, waiting for her as she came upon them. She'd spent every day of her seventeen sun cycles with them.

"Alina, we're always waiting for you," Aor said.

"Sorry, *Chief* Aor. I did not realize the urgency."

Aor bristled at the title, the way he always did when she used it. Kani and Hurza, her best friends, chuckled. Drur and Gamoc, his friends, looked away to hide their smiles.

He glared at her, and she watched the angry response forming on his lips. To his credit, he bit it back and said instead, "We were hoping to make it back in time for the evening meal, so others would not have to wait on us."

He was right, of course. She'd been so busy enjoying the forest that she'd lost track of time. Unless they picked up the pace, they might indeed be late.

"You're right, Aor. I'm sorry," she said, feeling so. "Where are the birds?"

Aor turned to Gamoc. Gamoc was a few sun cycles younger than the others and a full head shorter than the other two boys. The white freckles that marked TreeFolk had not yet reached prominence on his brow. He idolized Aor and was always eager to prove himself. "We're about halfway," he said.

"I thought you said they were close?" Aor grumbled.

Gamoc squirmed beneath his gaze. "They're pretty close," he said weakly.

"It's fine, Gamoc. Show us where they are." Kani said, smiling.

Gamoc leapt off his branch into the trees. The others leapt after him.

Alina adjusted her lanyards. They were ingenious devices, crucial for traveling any distance in the forest, and by far the most expensive goods the village traded for. She'd had hers since before her *becoming*, the ritual coming of age for all who were *of the tribe*.

She snugged the straps that secured them to her forearms so that the grips fell into her palms. The lanyards hung a little over a body length below the grips. They were made of rubber from local trees, with flower-like cups at the ends. These cups held metal fingers encased in rubber. The fingers would close together to grasp as one squeezed the grip in one's palm.

She leapt from her branch and cast one lanyard at a stout limb a short distance away. As it reached its target, she squeezed the grip, and the cup at the end of that lanyard grasped the branch. The lanyard took her weight as she swung toward it, the tension from her weight amplifying its hold. As she passed beneath it, she cast the next lanyard forward, setting it on a farther limb. As her weight came off the first lanyard, she released the grip, and it sprang loose. The rubber contracted, sending the cup sailing back at her. With practiced ease, she used its momentum to guide the cup forward to its next target.

She found her rhythm, letting her mind find the *TruePath* through the canopy, dropping or rising within it. Working with the forest and not against it, as she'd learned, letting the motion come naturally. She loved this feeling more than any other. She felt like a bird, threading her way through the branches as the breeze kissed her face. The others were ahead of her, but she kept up.

Aor had been right, which was frustrating since she knew how much he liked being right. He was the chief's son, and one day would be chief himself, though he often acted as though that day had already come. She didn't know why this angered her so. Perhaps it was just the assumption that it would come to pass because he said so. That the world would simply bend to his will.

Lately, Aor had been letting on that they would be mated. When he spoke of it to others as though it had already been decided, it lit a fire that took her reason. There wasn't anything objectionable about Aor. He was brave and intelligent, and she felt he would ultimately make a good chief. Also, in their village of fifty-five people, she was not spoiled for choices, nor had she met anyone in neighboring villages she preferred.

But with TreeFolk, women were meant to do the *choosing*. It was their way, and even had it not been so, she would have objected to his assuming their mating would come to pass simply because he desired it so.

Truthfully, she'd never fixated on a mate the way Kani and Hurza had. The traditional village roles they dreamed of didn't hold the same appeal for her. When they chatted about the homes they would build, the children they would raise, and the lives they would lead, Alina listened supportively and participated. But part of her longed for something more. What it was she could not say, but for her, wandering the forest held an appeal the traditional lives they spoke of lacked.

She attributed some of it to her upbringing. Her mother was the village seer, and her father was the healer. The demands on both her parents had meant that both were seldom involved in traditional chores. Alina assisted them with their duties, fetching herbs or medicines from the forest or helping otherwise as needed. The arrangement gave her a measure of freedom, one she was loath to lose. She wanted children, of course. She saw children clearly in her dreams, but her husband and the details of her life in the tribe had always been vague.

Kani, the sweetest amongst them, who'd never uttered a cross word in her life, had her heart set on Drur. Drur spoke little, but he was the fastest in the tribe. In the trees, he flowed like a river, seeming to float along without effort.

Hurza was ambitious and determined. She had her heart set on Aor. It didn't matter to her that Aor pursued Alina, though Alina thought he did so only at the direction of Hedrick, his grandfather, their previous chief. Hedrick had selected Alina as the future mother to his great-grandchildren. This was something she knew Hurza intended to change.

Oh, where were the others? Somehow, she'd lost them. She stopped and listened. Hearing rustling off to one side, she hurried in that direction. She was embarrassed now and sped up, racing along until she caught sight of Kani trailing behind. Alina was certain she did so to slow the others and allow her to catch up.

As she drew abreast of her, Alina smiled, and Kani returned it, crinkling her eyes. A short distance later, Gamoc alit on a large limb and waited. The others found perches around him. He pointed. "Just beyond that borka tree over there, the one with the fork on the side."

They craned to see the tree he indicated. It was a large tree loaded with borka. The red, pulpy fruit had a nasty husk from which they extracted the delicious nuts, a mainstay of their diet.

"The birds were up above in the branches of a dead tree just beyond it, eating grubs and insects when I saw them this morning," Gamoc said. "They were at the height of that crook."

Aor nodded and shrugged the small pack from his back. The others did the same. Alina adjusted her tunic, as it had bunched up at her shoulders. They were all dressed in the traditional clothes of TreeFolk, coarse-woven garments made from thread spun from Silas pods, dyed in the greens and browns of the forest to make them less evident to predators.

All TreeFolk wore pants and tunics with simple open collars. But the women wore their tunics longer, their hems ending just above the knee, though Hurza insisted on wearing hers a hand's width above that. The women also had brightly colored thread woven into their collars and cuffs. Alina smoothed her tunic and readjusted the small bags secured to her woven cloth belt. She liked them to sit just so.

Alina picked up the lanyards she'd removed, stuffed them into her pack, and fished around within it for her bag of stones. The others were ready and waiting on her.

"Did you bring your stones?" Aor asked, irritated.

She stopped and looked at him. "Oh, did you want me to bring them?" she answered, feigning ignorance.

Aor snorted and said nothing as she resumed fishing around. She found the bag, pulled it from beneath her lanyards, and slipped the neck of it through her belt. She wedged her pack in the crook of a tree like the others had and turned to them, "I'm ready."

"Finally," Aor mumbled, not expecting a reply. Alina considered supplying one, but seeing that the others were anxious to get on with it, she let it go.

"Drur, Gamoc, and I will set the nets here while the three of you see to the birds above," Aor said, which was the way they always did it and hadn't needed to be said, Alina thought. She took a breath and nodded. The boys moved off with the bundled nets into the trees. Alina, Kani, and Hurza climbed up higher into the canopy, where the branches grew more delicate.

"He means well," Kani said as they reached the spot Gamoc had indicated. "He is trying to learn to lead. His father and grandfather are daunting examples to live up to."

"I know," Alina said. "You're right, of course. I just can't help it for some reason."

"Is it because he's already been *chosen* for you?" Hurza chided.

"No, it's not that," Alina blurted, but it was the case, and they all knew it.

"Because if that's the issue," Hurza pressed, "I'd happily take him off your hands."

Hurza grinned as Kani chuckled. Alina felt the tension ebb away. Soon they were all laughing. They heard a hissing from below and looked down to see Aor glaring up at them, upset at the noise they were making. It made them laugh all the more, but they did so now with their hands over their mouths.

A few moments later, Hurza nudged Alina's shoulder and motioned below them with her chin. The boys had set up the large woven nets below, and each had a thin club in hand. Aor nodded up to them, and they nodded back.

Hurza directed the girls. "I'll take this side. Kani, you circle around the other side. Alina, you take the center as always. We'll wait for you to throw."

Kani and Hurza crept away, and Alina stole toward the borka tree. Since she couldn't see the birds, she assumed they were on the far side. She slipped through branches, avoiding the borka husks. She'd wondered why these rich and luscious nuts should live in such a nasty shell. Perhaps it was so creatures would avoid eating them, and the nuts could then fall to the forest floor and sprout into new trees.

She heard another hiss from below, and she bit her lip, feeling irritation well up within her. She took a breath and let it go. She needed a calm mind for the birds. She rounded the tree, staying within the branches to take cover in their leaves.

The nuxat were indeed still on the limbs of the dead tree, their little beaks burrowing and picking at what lay within the bark. There were eight of them that she could see, all of them grown and plump, each about the size of her head. Their gray and tan feathers blended in with the mottled bark. They hopped about on stout legs, their short wings and large breasts limiting their flight. Her mouth watered at the sight of them, and she felt her stomach rumble. It was getting late.

She took a breath and slid her bare feet across the branch until she found a stable position. Squatting, she found an unobstructed path through the limbs and leaves for her stones. She opened the bag she'd fastened to her belt and took out a handful of the eye-sized stones. The stones felt substantial in her palm. A lock of her short white hair tickled her brow. She brushed it aside and looked to make sure Kani and Hurza were in position. They met her gaze and nodded.

She took a final breath, letting the tension drain from her shoulders and letting her throwing arm hang loose for a moment with one of the stones held loosely between her fingers. She'd collected these river stones herself, testing the weight and feel of each between her fingers before she'd added them to her bag. She let herself feel the swaying of the tree beneath her feet, the wind on her cheek, and saw the gentle movement of the tree the birds were on. All her senses heightened. A calmness came over her, the feeling she always had before she threw.

The first stone was barely in the air before a second was also on its way. The two stones each struck their targets, stunning the birds and dropping them through the foliage to the nets below. A third stone, arriving close behind, dazed a third. The bird flapped and tried to right itself as it fell. Hopefully, the boys would get their clubs on that one before it recovered.

Stones from Kani and Hurza were in the air shortly after hers, and they each took a bird. Alina managed a fourth before the last two birds took flight. Hurza hooted from the far side of the dead tree. Six nuxat was an exceptionally good hunt. The village would be thrilled to have fresh game for the evening meal. She hoped the boys had secured them all below.

Alina slipped from the foliage of the borka tree and dropped down to join the boys. They were thrilled, slapping each other on the arm. She frowned. Surely, standing around down here while the birds fell into the net didn't warrant all that arm slapping.

"That was great, Alina," Aor said, genuinely pleased, as Drur and Gamoc joined in congratulating her.

She smiled, nodding, regretting her previous thought. I have to be more like Kani, she told herself.

Kani and Hurza arrived and were bubbling over. They'd indeed taken six of the eight birds. It was quite an accomplishment. They were still reliving it when the trees around them began to shake, an immense roar filling the forest. They each grabbed the nearest limb or trunk and held on. The roar intensified and grew unbearable. A ball of fire passed above their heads, scorching the area the birds had just occupied. She felt the fiery heat reach down for her through the canopy, the smell of burning leaves sharp in her nose and throat.

The ball of fire plunged into the forest beyond them, sending up an enormous column of steam and smoke. Trees swung violently in its wake. Massive branches and trunks snapped as it fell, the fall ending with a deafening crash.

Alina was horrified and frozen, unable to imagine what had just happened. Her heart thundered in her chest as she coughed and clung to her branch. She looked worriedly for her friends. She found them clinging to their own branches, her terror mirrored in their eyes.

Chapter 3

Alina looked up. The branches above them, where the birds had been, were scorched to stubs. Had the ball of fire arrived a few moments sooner, she, Kani, and Hurza would surely have perished. She coughed, her lungs stinging from the smoke that had trailed the ball of fire. Between bouts of hacking, she fished the water gourd from her pack and drank. The water soothed her throat, and she managed a complete breath.

"What was that?" Kani said, trembling, between coughs of her own.

Alina offered Kani her gourd.

"Is anyone hurt?" Alina asked her friends, her father's training rising within her. Her ears were ringing, and she had to repeat the question. Amazingly, they were all whole, though they were as scared and confused as she was.

"It's all gone," Hurza gasped as she looked up and then touched her forehead with her fingertips.

Her words prompted them to look up at the missing canopy above their heads, each of them mirroring Hurza's gesture as they did. It was a gesture common for TreeFolk, an obeisance made to the SkyGods for all manner of things.

Gamoc climbed up and whooped as his head breached the surface, his body pivoting in place to take in the full measure of it. "This is so *round*!"

"'Round?" Aor chuckled. "You sound like the children."

Gamoc tensed. "Come up and see. It's amazing."

They climbed up to join him. Alina gawked. It was as though a huge flaming hand had reached into the canopy and scooped out an enormous trench stretching as far as she could see behind them and then continuing for some distance beyond where they stood before dipping down into the forest. Wisps of smoke rose from charred branches and trunks along the entire length, with a thick column of smoke spiraling from where the trench disappeared.

"What could this be?" Drur wondered.

"Perhaps a SkyGod has fallen to the forest," Gamoc ventured.

Aor shifted uncomfortably. "That's ridiculous."

"What else could do this?" Hurza asked, turning to him.

"Perhaps it was lightning," Aor offered, trying to sound confident.

There was a pause as they considered this.

"I've never seen lightning like this," Drur said.

"Nor have I," Aor answered, warming to the idea. "But, what else could it be?"

"Perhaps we should go see," Alina said, regretting it as soon as she'd said it.

"Go see what?" Aor said, the derision in his tone making her spine go stiff.

"Go and see whatever it was that passed over us."

He scrunched his face. "Look around. Do you not see what it did?"

She dug in. "Yes, of course, I can *see*. I was suggesting we should find out what did this. We all know it wasn't lightning." She did not know any such thing, but she'd already charted her course.

Aor stiffened at her words. "This thing could have killed us. I'm not going to let any of you get hurt chasing after it."

Alina felt her face flush. "Well, then it's a good thing it's not up to you. I'm going to go and see. You can stay here where it's safe." She dropped down into the forest, grabbed her pack, fished out her lanyards, and put them on. Kani and Hurza hurried down after her. Aor grumbled above.

"What are we doing?" Kani whispered, terrified as she and Hurza dug through their packs for their lanyards.

"I have no idea," Alina admitted. "He just makes me so mad. Let's follow the path the thing left for a bit. Perhaps we'll see something. If not, we'll wait a while and come back. That way, they can sit here and feel foolish."

"Do you think they will?" Hurza said, arching an eyebrow.

"Probably not," Alina replied. "But it will feel better than climbing back up there now."

They leapt off into the trees, following the trench the fireball had carved. It was the most obvious trail she'd ever followed. They moved along it, the trail dropping into the forest as they went. Eventually, the trench became a vertical shaft plunging into the forest. Smoke rose from this shaft, and far below, wedged between some trees, lay a huge egg. The shell of the egg was cracked, a portion of the shell askew.

"What is that?" Kani asked. All three of them were perched on the edge of the shaft, looking down. Evening was approaching, the sun's fading rays coming horizontally through the trees now.

"I have no idea," Alina replied.

"We've seen it," Hurza said. "Can we go back now?"

Alina was about to agree when Aor and the others arrived.

"What did you find?" Gamoc asked, breathless.

"There's an egg down there," Hurza offered.

"That's stupid," Aor said, not yet near the edge.

Hurza flushed. Alina hid a smile. She knew that feeling well.

"Have a look for yourself," Hurza spat.

The boys moved to the edge and looked down the shaft.

"It does look like an egg," Drur said.

"I told you," Hurza replied.

They peered down at it. The smoke was lessening. The fact that the forest was still wet from the day's rain had stemmed the fire. Alina squinted. Soft light appeared to be coming from the crack in the shell. She could make no sense of it.

"There's a bird in there," Gamoc said.

"What do you mean?" Kani asked.

"I hear a bird calling."

They leaned forward, listening. Alina couldn't hear anything, her ears still ringing from the thing's roar. It seemed none of the others, save Gamoc, could hear it.

"Is there light coming from it?" Hurza asked.

"Yes," Alina said. "I see it too."

They stood there, all of them on the lip of the shaft, looking down at the egg. It was perhaps twenty body lengths below them. The fire it had wrapped itself in was gone now.

"Should we go and have a look?" Alina asked anxiously.

Aor paused, considering his reply, which Alina took kindly. After their previous exchange, he was being more thoughtful. The boys hadn't waited very long before coming after them.

"It does look quiet now," Aor said, more like the friend she'd grown up with. "What do you all think?"

"I still hear a bird," Gamoc said.

Aor nodded, putting a hand on Gamoc's shoulder. "You do have the best hearing. Maybe there's a bird down there near it."

Gamoc's face lit up, and Alina's feelings toward Aor softened further.

"We could drop down a bit closer and have a look," Drur ventured.

They turned to Aor. He took a breath. Alina could feel her pulse quicken. She wasn't sure she wanted to get closer. This thing had torn a hole through their forest. Was it a good idea to go down there?

"It might be *important* for us to see more of this thing," Aor said.

Alina tensed, and she felt the others do the same. For TreeFolk, *important* held many meanings, all of which were to be heeded. Alina's mother, their seer, used it only when an event would significantly impact a life.

"There may be others such as this one. It might be useful to the tribe for us to see more of it while it lies broken. It could be that others might not be so."

Alina listened attentively to Aor now. He took a breath, calmly assessing the situation and weighing it. Alina regretted the way she'd been earlier. He would be a good chief. She saw shades of his father in him, and Fodrick was a great chief.

"Drur, you stay here with Kani," Aor said, and when Drur went to object, he held up his hand. "If something happens and we need help, you'll be the fastest to fetch it. Kani can stay up here while you go. She will do what can be done while you get help." Aor did not elaborate further.

"We'll go carefully, dropping a couple of lanyard lengths at a time and watching and listening before going farther. We'll space ourselves evenly around the hole so that we can see all sides of this thing as we drop. If anyone sees anything that concerns them, speak up, and we'll leave."

Aor waited for any comments they might have, but no one had anything to say. Alina felt her senses sharpen the way they did before she threw. The world slowed down, and her vision narrowed on the target before her. The light was fading in the forest now, the light tending toward the pale red of unripe borka. They shed their packs. Alina opened hers and took her water gourd from it. She took a sip, the water a soothing balm on her raw throat. She passed it to Hurza, who sipped from it and passed it on. Her gourd made its way around their circle until Gamoc handed it back to her, empty. She stuffed it into her pack.

"Remember, just two lanyard lengths, and we wait," Aor said, making eye contact with each of them. "If I yell to run, do it at once. Don't look back until you are away."

Alina regretted having suggested they follow this thing. She would be devastated if something happened to her friends because of her decision. Why did she have to let her emotions guide her? Why couldn't she be more like her mother?

They took their places and dropped down along the shaft, stopping after two lanyard lengths. They sat for several moments, not seeing anything, though Gamoc swore he could still hear the bird.

They dropped down another two lengths and then two more, each time waiting before proceeding. The egg was clearer now. The shell was a dull grey, not the color of any egg she'd seen before. It was even in color, not speckled as eggs often were. There were marks on its surface, likely due to sap and crushed leaves, as it had crashed through the forest. It appeared that the forest near the egg wasn't charred. The fire had burned out before the egg had finished its descent.

When they were halfway to the egg, she heard the bird. It seemed an odd cry, unlike the call of a bird greeting the morning or warning of a predator. It was not a cry she'd heard from a bird before. It seemed annoyed and insistent, like a baby demanding food from its mother. And it was relentless. It never paused to listen or changed its call.

"What do you make of that?" Hurza whispered from her perch, partway across the circle.

"It sounds odd," Alina replied.

"Can anyone see the bird?" Aor whispered.

Alina scanned the trees around the egg but couldn't find a bird anywhere.

"It's coming from within the egg," Gamoc said.

Alina and the others looked over at him. He shifted on his branch.

They dropped down twice more. The egg was clearly visible now. It was wedged in the crook of a tree, still quite a distance above the forest floor. The light from it was more apparent in the growing gloom, and they could see slivers of the inside through holes that were not holes. Some portions of the shell could be seen through, like one might see through water.

"There is a creature inside," Hurza said.

"What? How can that be?" Aor asked, leaning forward but unable to see within from his vantage point.

They moved faster as they descended, growing more comfortable with the sight of it. Alina glanced up, and both Drur and Kani were seated on the lip and leaning way over it, peering down at them.

A few stops later, they were even with the egg and just three body lengths away. Alina could feel a slight heat from it. The bird was still calling loudly, and as Gamoc had noted, the sound was coming from within the egg. Though Alina could not see the bird, she could see the creature. It appeared to be tied to a strange bed, and shockingly, it did not seem to have been burned by the fire, though immense tracts of the forest above were still smoldering.

Aor had moved around to her side and studied the scene with her. "What do you suppose it is?" he asked.

The others joined them.

"I don't know," Alina said. "It seems similar to a TreePerson and yet..."

"It's ugly," Aor said.

"Is it dead?" Gamoc asked.

"It must be," Hurza said. "There is a lot of blood."

"Why is it tied down?" Gamoc asked.

They studied the creature, trying to understand what it might be and why it was bound inside the egg.

"We should go back," Hurza said. "It is well into the evening meal. The village will be concerned."

Aor nodded. "I think we've seen all that is to be seen."

They turned to leave, but Alina stayed.

"What is it?" Aor asked, noting she had not followed.

"I think it just moved," she said, waiting to see if it did so again.

"Are you sure?" Aor asked.

How could the creature have survived such an event? "I don't know. It seems impossible."

"Is it moving now?" Hurza asked.

"No," she replied. Then, without thinking, she moved toward the egg. She placed her hand on the warm shell. The feel of it beneath her hand jarred her. She had not planned on moving. Her body had felt the urge to act and did so. She tried to ascribe it to the training she'd received at her father's side, an instinct triggered at the sight of blood and injury. But, deep down, she sensed it was something else, something she could not name.

"What are you doing?" Aor said, his words hard, insistent.

"I'm going to have a look," she said without turning to him. Her heart pounded in her chest. She sensed the tension in her friends and felt their eyes upon her. Aor protested, telling her to come away from the egg, but she ignored him and leaned into the open sliver between the egg and the broken piece of shell, examining the space within.

The air in the egg smelled foul. Partially digested food was caked on the floor. She turned away, took a breath, and held it. She slid closer and slipped her hand inside. The bird was loud now, calling insistently, but as she craned to take in the whole of the inside, she still could not find it.

She leaned forward, curbing her gift reflexively, as she reached for the creature's wrist, her body tense and ready to pull back and flee should it move. Its skin was smooth, like hers, but hot to the touch. It was too hot for a TreePerson unless that person was very sick. She closed her eyes and focused on sensing the coursing of blood in its wrist. There seemed to be no indication of flow, and she was about to drop it when she felt a faint throb. She pulled back and let out the breath she'd been holding.

"It's still alive," she said, looking up at the others.

"Can we go now?" Aor asked.

"It is covered in blood and unconscious," Alina said. "We cannot leave it here like this. It is nearly night. Predators will be here soon."

"Where do you want to take it?" Aor asked, confused.

"To the village," she said. "Perhaps my father can heal it."

"Are you serious? Why would he do that?"

"You said earlier this might be *important*. Perhaps there is something we can learn from this creature. Perhaps there are others in eggs like this."

She could see the curt reply forming on his face, his eyes narrowing, his lips tightening, and then opening. But he paused before he shaped the words. She could see his mind working, a few steps behind his instincts, as he heard her words and weighed them. He was working out the details, imagining the conversation with his father and what reasoning he would use to justify this. She had known him her entire life, and she knew the face he wore now. It was her favorite.

She didn't know if this was the right decision. The creature seemed close to death. It might be a mercy to leave it here to pass in peace. Dragging it through the forest would be an arduous process and might ultimately serve no purpose. But she felt compelled to pursue this. A shiver ran down her spine. She swallowed and took a deep breath, trying to shake this feeling.

Drur and Kani had climbed part of the way down and called to them. Aor waved to them, beckoning them. When they arrived, Hurza explained to them what they'd found and what Alina had proposed.

"What is that smell?" Kani asked.

"I think it was sick on the floor of the egg," Alina replied.

They discussed it for a time, unable to agree on a course of action. Finally, Aor held up his hand. "It is getting late. The village will be worried, and predators will be here soon. The smell of blood will draw them. We'll take this creature with us. It seems too near death to be a danger. We'll let the elders decide its fate when we get to the village."

Now that the decision had been made, Alina knew Aor could see the shape of it in his mind. It was a skill that Alina had always admired.

"Drur and I will fashion a litter for it. Alina, Kani, and Hurza, untie it, clean it up, and prepare it for the trip. Gamoc, climb up, and keep watch. We'll all be busy. Alert us should anything approach."

He looked at each of them to ensure they understood. Then he and Drur moved off into the wreckage of branches and limbs, seeking materials for the litter. Alina moved toward the egg with Kani and Hurza as it began to rain.

Chapter 4

"Maybe the knots are behind it?" Kani offered as she leaned against the egg, holding the broken section of shell open for Alina and Hurza, who were inside trying to free the creature.

"The ropes are secured to this odd bed," Alina replied.

"Maybe if you pull on the ropes?" Kani suggested.

Hurza turned to look at her. "Perhaps you could show me. I could hold the shell."

Kani scrunched her nose and shook her head.

"What kind of ropes are these?" Hurza said, running her hands over the wide fabric. "They are woven flat, and the weave is so fine. I've never seen the like."

"Are you looking for knots?" Alina asked, with a huff.

Hurza stopped admiring the material. They fished behind the creature's shoulders and waist, but the ropes had no ties.

"Can you hurry up? It smells out here," Kani said.

Hurza grunted next to her and then, in a sweet voice, replied. "That's odd. It doesn't smell bad in here at all."

"Really?" Kani said.

"Yes, it's the oddest thing. It doesn't smell at all here by the bed."

"That can't be," Kani said, unsure.

"It's strange. I can't explain it. I'll hold the shell, and you can see for yourself."

Kani paused, considering it, which was all the encouragement Hurza needed. She stepped outside and urged Kani in. Kani stepped inside and gagged. "It smells terrible in here," she cried.

"Oh, that's strange," Hurza said, standing outside with a huge smile. Kani turned to leave, but Hurza blocked her way. Kani grumbled and knelt to help.

"You fall for it every time, Kani," Alina said, as her friend joined her.

"I know," she croaked, trying not to breathe.

"Help me find the knots so we can get out of here."

They searched some more before Kani pulled the flint blade from the sheath on her belt and placed it on a rope above the creature's shoulder. She began sawing at the tough fabric as the rain intensified.

"Perhaps they are behind this metal thing on its chest?" Alina mused. She slipped her fingers beneath it, but it felt smooth. Alina pulled and pushed at the metal piece on the creature's chest to see if she could loosen the ropes. They were too snug to work free, but a part of the metal piece moved beneath her fingers, and the entire thing came apart, all the ropes coming loose.

"What did you do?" Kani and Hurza asked simultaneously.

"I don't know. It just opened."

Kani pushed the ropes aside, muffling a gag.

Hurza chuckled.

They pulled the creature from the egg onto the nest of branches the egg had amassed as it had crashed through the forest.

Hurza let go of the shell, and it returned to its partially open position. The broken section of shell was a near-perfect rectangle as if cut with a very sharp knife. The edges fit together seamlessly when closed. It was remarkable how such a thing could be fashioned. In the background, the bird that was not a bird kept up its relentless complaint.

It grew dark, with the shell mostly closed and blocking the odd light from within. Alina wiped the rain from her eyes with her sleeve.

Hurza peered at the creature. "Kani, hold the shell open, and I'll help Alina clean the creature. We need light from the egg to see."

Kani opened the shell with an annoyed grunt, having been stuck again with the smell.

"You did that on purpose," Alina said with a chuckle.

"Of course not," she said, crinkling her eyes. "It's just luck that it worked out this way."

They worked in the rain. Alina stripped the tunic with the odd fasteners on it from the creature. She cut the sleeve away from the bandaged arm. Peeking beneath the bandage, she saw where the skin had been burned, the outline of it charred.

Hurza asked about the bandages on its feet. The feet were encased in close-fitting bandages with rubber, similar to that of their lanyards, on the soles. Alina shrugged and asked her to remove them.

Alina couldn't pull the pants over the hips. There was no belt, but the pants fit snugly. She slipped her knife into the waistband, slit it open, and pulled them down. The lower body had plenty of bruises, but nothing looked broken, and there were no open wounds.

Hurza had cut away the odd bandages from its feet, but the feet had no sores or bruises. "They are soft like a newborn's," Hurza said. "Perhaps it's crippled and cannot walk and must wear bandages upon its feet?"

Alina inspected the head wound above its eye, peeling back a corner of the bandage. It seemed serious. One whole side of its face was discolored, and there was much blood on its face and chest. She felt again for a pulse, the thread still impossibly weak.

They washed the body using its clothes as rags in the rain. The creature was shorter than a TreePerson. Standing, it might have come to her shoulder. However, it was far stockier, its body muscled, its bones sturdy.

Hurza reached up and opened an eyelid. "Its eyes are brown. What an odd color."

The creature was indeed odd. Its green skin had a tinge of brown to it, and there were splotches of yellow on its cheeks and nose instead of the white freckles of TreeFolk. Its hair was dark, while TreeFolk had white hair.

But aside from that, it had five fingers on each hand and the same number of toes on each foot, two eyes, two ears, and a nose, all of these things similar to those of a TreePerson. She had never heard of another like this.

Kani scrubbed herself with her soapstone. Hurza and Alina took out their own and did the same, taking advantage of the shower to clean themselves and their clothes.

"I'm glad to wash that filth from inside the egg off," Hurza said.

Alina washed the blood from her hands and scrubbed her clothes free of ash and filth. She added soap to the intact sleeve of the strange tunic the creature had been wearing and used it to clean its body as best she could in the poor light. As the rain eased, they quickly rinsed the soap from their bodies and clothes.

Aor and Drur returned with the litter they'd fabricated. It was a long, smooth pole with the netting they used for hunting wrapped around it, and some thin vines to reinforce it. It was well crafted for something they'd put together in such a short time.

They slipped the creature into it, all of them working together, eager to be off now that it was dark. Gamoc came down to report that the forest was stirring. There were two large nerape nearby. The large snake-like lizards with sharp teeth and claws would not typically attack adult TreeFolk. But the smell of blood could make them unpredictable, and if they were in the vicinity, other predators would be too.

They climbed up out of the shaft, Drur and Aor grunting as they hefted the awkward load between them. Alina helped Aor in the rear since most of the weight as they climbed was on that end of the pole. As they made their way up the *not-bird* called behind them, unrelenting. She wondered how long it would continue to call after them.

"This may not be the best decision we've ever made," Aor said, as they hefted their end of the pole up over a branch.

"It may not be," she agreed. It was kind of him to share the decision.

Once they reached the upper canopy and their travel leveled out, the going grew easier. Gamoc and Kani swept the trees in front of them while Hurza took up the rear. Alina walked alongside, keeping an eye on the creature. When they reached the trading path used by the village, Aor sent Gamoc ahead to let the village know they were all fine and to brief them on what had happened.

Gamoc disappeared, the sound of his passage through the trees fading as he raced ahead on a path they'd all covered countless times. These paths, formed by stout branches and log bridges, were cut through the canopy and maintained to facilitate trade or gather supplies.

"Where do you think it came from?" Aor asked.

"I have no idea," Alina answered.

"How could it have survived inside that ball of fire?"

Alina could not answer. It seemed impossible.

"Do you think it might have come from the SkyGods like Gamoc said?"

"Aor, I truly have no idea. Though I imagine if the SkyGods had sent us a messenger, they would have sent one that wasn't injured and clothed in its waste."

They moved silently along the path, Hurza walking close behind now, Alina aware of how much Hurza disliked the forest at night. Night blossoms opened, turning their faces toward the moon that had risen behind them. The soft breeze, rich with the scent of leaves and rain, added the scent of these moon flowers. Nocturnal creatures stirred, scurrying nearby.

They picked their way carefully until Aras and Narat met them on the path. The twins, adults from their village, were almost always smiling and were loved by all. Alina let out a breath, grateful for their presence. They explained that the village had been concerned and preparing to search for them when Gamoc arrived.

"Fodrick asked us to carry the load for you," Aras said.

Narat peered down at the creature. "What is it?"

"We have no idea," Aor said.

"Is it alive?" Aras asked.

"I think so," Alina replied. "Though only barely, I think."

Aras took the front of the pole from Drur, and Narat took Aor's end. "Oh, this thing is heavy," Narat said. "The two of you climbed up from below with this?"

"Alina helped," Aor said. "It was a long climb."

"We'll have you two carry our stoda on the next hunt," Aras teased.

Aor smiled at the compliment.

"Your father wants the two of you to go ahead. He has been questioning Gamoc, and the lad is so nervous that he's stepping on his tongue."

Aor thanked the twins as he and Drur hurried off.

"Alina, you should go too. Your father has been peppering Gamoc with healer questions, too. We have Kani and Hurza here to watch for us."

"Thanks, Aras," Alina said, and she hurried after Aor and Drur.

As Alina neared the village, they wove through the huts ringing the village's central platform, each hut built around the trunk of a tree. Oil lamps dotted the trees, illuminating the platform and the people gathered upon it. They crossed the last of the log bridges, Alina sensing the tension from those waiting. Clearly, they'd seen the ball of fire and feared the worst. How would they explain this? The whole thing was too odd for words.

Marna, her mother, was there as Alina stepped onto the central platform. She touched her forehead briefly to Alina's, a sign of affection among TreeFolk. The warmth of her mother's touch spread through her, filling her with joy.

"I was worried for you, Lina," her mother said, her hands firm on Alina's forearms.

"You saw it in the sky?"

"Yes, it passed above and shook the village as we were preparing the evening meal. It was terrifying."

Beyond them, Aor answered Fodrick's questions as the village sat listening. Aor seemed frustrated and kept glancing at Gamoc, who was seated with his parents, eating his evening meal and avoiding Aor's eyes.

"Gamoc said you found a creature in the ball of fire?" Fodrick prompted.

"Yes, there was an egg made of stone within the ball of fire, and within that egg there was the creature. It was wounded and may already be dead," Aor replied.

Enor, her father, strode up to them, his arms filled with the bags that held his healing remedies. They clattered and shifted as he tried to keep them from falling. "I could not get Gamoc to provide anything useful regarding this creature or its injuries," he said, exasperated. He looked at Alina, frowning, before remembering himself and leaning in to touch his forehead to hers. "Forgive me. How are you, daughter?"

"I am fine. We all are," she answered. "The creature seems very sick. The thread of blood within it was only a whisper." She closed her eyes, trying to picture the things she'd observed, knowing her father wanted details. When she opened them, she began relating its state, the way she'd been taught. "The creature seems similar to a TreePerson in most things, though it is shorter and stouter. It has a bandage on one arm covering a large burn. The bandage is strange."

"Strange?" Her father asked and then stopped. "Never mind. Please continue."

"There are what seem to be bruises over much of its body, though none of the bones appear broken. There is a large gash above one eye that is also bandaged. Half of its face is discolored around this gash. The creature's body was very hot. Its breathing was uncertain when we left. It may already have passed."

Her father gave a short grunt of acknowledgment and shifted his bags again. Alina reached over and took several of them. He thanked her, bidding her to be careful with them, though she already was. Her father was endlessly fascinated by the world around them, and she could see his excitement at the prospect of meeting this new creature.

They moved closer to the others to hear Aor's account. He'd reached the part where they'd decided to bring the creature here, considering that it might be *important* to the tribe. He spoke of it as though it was a consensus, not playing up his role in the decision nor singling her out for blame should it not prove to be the right one. His father listened attentively, probing for details as needed, but Aor was thorough, having often been asked to relate observations by his father.

When at last he was done, Fodrick asked. "You're certain this egg was the fireball we saw in the sky?"

"Yes, there is no question. It passed quite close to us, taking the roof of the forest above us with it as it went and leaving a trail of burnt branches behind. We followed the trail of destruction, and it had come to rest in a large nest of broken branches."

"It was no longer burning when you reached the egg?"

"No, the shell was still warm, but the charring of the forest ended midway down the shaft it created."

"Gamoc said it was a fallen SkyGod. Do you think this is so?"

Aor looked over at Gamoc, who was fixated on his food, then at the faces of the villagers, who all seemed very concerned over this description.

"No, I don't think so. The creature is similar to a TreePerson and is seriously injured."

Fodrick nodded, letting out a breath.

"Could it be a messenger?" Rigin asked. Alina saw the anxious look on her face. The elderly woman sat with her two young wards, a boy and a girl, their eyes wide at the developments.

Aor shrugged. "There is no way to know such a thing. The creature was barely alive."

"Eat something," Fodrick motioned to Aor first and then to Drur, who stood behind him. "Eat, and we will await the creature."

At the mention of eating, Alina noticed the delicious smell of fresh nuxat. Gamoc, who'd been carrying the other boys' packs, must have taken them out when he arrived earlier. She'd forgotten about the birds or her hunger. Her mother smiled and dashed off, returning with a plate of food moments later.

Alina placed the bags she was carrying on the floor and sat next to them as she ate. The cool night air was refreshing, the food delicious, spiced with peppers, the way she liked it best. The villagers were all speaking about the momentous events. There was much talk of the SkyGods and what this might mean.

Her parents sat next to her, speaking softly. As she ate, Alina looked out over her village and its people. Their tribe held just over fifty people, which was not uncommon for villages on this side of the mountains. The tribes here tended to be smaller and more isolated than those on the far side.

Fodrick and Hedrick were speaking off to one side. Hedrick seemed concerned, pointing and gesturing animatedly. Hedrick had been their chief until he could no longer been able to lead the hunt, at which point he'd ceded leadership to his son. However, he continued to act as though he was still chief, and Fodrick rarely made a decision that was not discussed with his father first.

She considered Hedrick. He'd arrived with Fodrick in their village before she was born. Fodrick, at the time, had been Aor's age now. Not much was known about where they'd come from or why they'd been without a tribe. This was a harsh world, and life alone in the forest was often short. Few TreeFolk were without tribes, and those that were sought desperately to find one.

Their tribe, the TreeKeepers, had been struggling at the time. They'd lost their chief in a hunting accident and had no one suited to leadership, though some had tried, including her father. Hedrick had offered to join them as their chief. It turned out Hedrick was an effective leader, and with him, their tribe had prospered. But there were mysteries surrounding him, things Alina had often wondered about. She'd asked Aor about these many times, but he didn't know either.

She did know that both Hedrick and Fodrick were talented hunters and very comfortable with both spear and knife, more so than any other TreePerson she'd ever met.

Although many villagers looked up to Hedrick, and Aor revered his grandfather, Alina no longer trusted the man. Several sun cycles ago, he'd approached her in the grove when they'd been alone and informed her of his plans for Aor and how he felt that they should be mated. She'd stood there, certain she'd misunderstood. Then, as she'd realized what he proposed, she'd been too shocked to respond. A young woman's *choosing* was a topic usually only broached with best friends or family. Afterward, it had left her enraged.

She'd spoken of it with her parents. Her father, though he believed her, found it difficult to reconcile Hedrick's actions. Unable to conceive ever doing such a thing himself, he could not conceive it in others. Her mother had said little but held her hand with that knowing look that had unsettled her so. Her mother often had glimpses of the future. Sometimes she spoke of them, but many times she refused to, fearing that doing so would occasion a worse outcome. It was frustrating to Alina that her mother knew things about her and yet was unwilling to share them.

Alina finished her plate and set it aside. Her mother had an odd look about her, and she'd gone pale, a thin sheen of perspiration on her brow.

"Are you feeling well?" Alina asked, reaching for her hand.

Her father, who'd been looking expectantly off into the forest, turned to his wife. He reached up and placed a hand on her brow. "What is it?"

"Truly, I do not know. This feeling of alarm just welled up within me."

Chapter 5

Aras and Narat arrived and placed the creature on a corner of the platform, sliding it from the litter and leaving it naked beneath the flickering lamplight. There were gasps from the villagers at the sight, many of them touching their fingertips to their foreheads.

Her father rushed over with Alina in tow. She placed the bags she carried next to it and took one of the oil lamps from its post, holding it over the creature to illuminate it. Her father was thrilled, his eyes alive with wonder. His hands slid expertly over the body, noting every detail as he probed it.

"Is it still alive?" Fodrick asked.

Her father leaned in, reaching for a wrist and closing his eyes as he felt for the thread within. The children started murmuring. Alina turned to see what was eliciting this response. She saw some of them pointing at the creature's exposed waist, whispering to their peers, giggling as they did. The adults shushed them as Alina pulled a towel from one of the bags and draped it over its hips.

"How is it?" Fodrick asked again.

Her father held up a hand without opening his eyes. The entire village grew quiet, everyone waiting to hear. Her father's body tensed, and then he opened his eyes. He turned to Fodrick. "The thread is faint, but still there."

"Will it recover?"

"I have only just laid my hands on this creature and have never seen its like."

"Yes, yes, but do you think it will recover?" Fodrick pressed him.

Her father snorted, annoyed. "I have no idea. If you want speculation, you'll have to ask my wife." He turned to her, and seeing her expression, he swallowed. "Sorry, Amani," he said, the term of endearment soft in his mouth.

Alina smiled. Her father was incapable of remaining annoyed, his softness emerging moments after any outburst. He was often lost in thought, his mind wandering and dwelling on the unknowable. She'd once found him in the forest musing as to why the leaves of one banda tree were a subtly different shade than the leaves of a nearby tree. But it was clear to everyone that his wife was the canopy beneath which his world unfolded.

Her mother smiled as she walked over and placed her hand on his shoulder. Alina wondered what such a love might feel like. Her parents had always been devoted to each other. She shared the world with them, but often felt there was a conversation going on to which she was not privy. Glances, touches, and words between them conveyed more than what she could discern.

Her father turned back to the creature. Her mother followed his gaze and froze, her hand going rigid on his shoulder. He and Alina looked up, her mother's face a mask of shock. The color drained from her, and Alina feared she would faint as she swayed in place.

"What's wrong?" Alina asked, leaping to her feet and steadying her.

Her mother stared, her mouth open. The village grew anxious, sensing that something was happening but unsure what it might be.

Her father stood and took his wife in his arms, though her eyes never left the creature.

"Amani," her father said, trying to get her attention. Unable to reach her, he moved his body between her and the creature. She looked up at him, blinking as if she'd just woken and found herself here on the platform with everyone.

She mumbled something into her father's shoulder that made him stiffen. He moved her away so he could see her face. She met his gaze and nodded.

"What is it?" Fodrick asked, frustrated at yet another mystery. Hedrick stood at his son's elbow, brow furrowed.

Her mother took a breath and turned to face the villagers. "I have seen this creature before," she said.

The words made no sense. Alina was certain she'd misheard.

"You've seen other such creatures before?" Fodrick corrected.

"No, it was this creature," her mother said.

"That's ridiculous," Hedrick snorted.

Her mother glared.

Hedrick stammered. "It's just... It can't be. We've just learned that this creature arrived in that ball of fire."

"And yet," her mother added. "I've seen this creature before."

The villagers mumbled, unaccustomed to having their seer's *sight* questioned by anyone, let alone their former chief. Fodrick stepped in, his tone even, the words measured. "Are you quite certain?"

"Yes. The creature I saw was just like this one with the same bandages."

The crowd gasped, fingers reaching for foreheads.

Alina, like the others, couldn't make sense of this. It was so far beyond the realm of possibility. She'd seen the ball of fire, had followed it to the egg, and found the creature within it. She remembered how she'd felt compelled in that moment. Her blood suddenly chilled within her. Her breathing grew shallow, and her senses heightened.

The village erupted in speculation, folks arguing with each other over what this could mean. Fodrick held up his hand, and, after a time, the crowd grew silent.

Fodrick turned back to her mother. He paused, choosing his words carefully. "You've seen this creature recently?" he pressed, trying to trace the shape of her words. It seemed he'd been planning on building from there, but her mother shook her head. He frowned.

"It was some time ago," she corrected him, her face going taut.

Fodrick's eyes searched her face, sensing something in the statement.

"I had the sense this creature would be *important*," she added.

The murmuring resumed, and Fodrick had to raise his hand again. He seemed like a man trying to keep his feet in a storm.

"When did you see this?" Fodrick asked.

"As I said, it was some time ago."

Fodrick sighed, unhappy with the vague answer. "When exactly?"

Her mother squirmed. "It was the day I gained my *sight*. This is the first thing I ever saw."

There was another gasp.

"This is ridiculous," Hedrick said. "You gained your *sight* when you were a girl. This would have been more than thirty suns ago. You must be mistaken."

"I wish it were so," her mother said, a worried look on her face.

"Perhaps your *sight* was wrong?" Hedrick replied with a huff.

Her mother narrowed her eyes at Hedrick. "You, of all people, know better."

Hedrick looked away, shaken by her words.

"What do you mean, *you wish it were so*?" Fodrick asked.

Her mother held up her hands, and they were shaking. "I do not know why, but I feel certain that we must choose wisely. That much depends on our choice."

"Marna, how can we make sense of this?" Fodrick replied, exasperated.

Her mother paused. It seemed as though she was about to add something, but then she shook her head. "I'm sorry, Fodrick. I cannot make sense of it either," she replied, crossing her arms and clutching her shoulders.

Fodrick turned to her father. "You must do what you can for this creature. All we have now are questions. Perhaps if it recovers, we will get some answers."

Her father nodded. "We'll need a place to tend to it."

"You can use Sneva's room," Rigin offered immediately.

The entire village turned to look at the elderly woman. Her son Sneva had been killed in a hunting accident several sun cycles ago. It had devastated her, and she'd kept his room as it was. A widow and now childless, she lived in her hut with her two wards, both of them orphans.

"Thank you, Rigin," Fodrick said.

"Aras, Narat, can you help move the creature there?"

The twins nodded and leapt up to carry it. They picked it up as Rigin hurried ahead, the two orphan children running along behind her. They crossed the narrow log from the platform into the trees and were gone.

Her father and Alina gathered up their supplies and followed, her father stopping to touch his forehead to his wife's. "How are you, Amani?" he asked.

"I'll be fine," she replied. "Go, I will join you soon."

The creature was installed in Sneva's room. The hut, like most in their village, had a common room with a counter for preparing food, a table with four chairs, and three separate rooms. Rigin slept in one room, another was shared by the children, and the last had been her son's room. That room was a little over a body length long and two body lengths wide. It had a bed along one wall and a table and chair beneath the window next to it. A chest of clothes sat next to the wall at the foot of the bed near the door, which was a simple opening with a cloth curtain slit down the center. Though the room had not been used for some time, it was spotless.

Her father began a more detailed exam of the creature as Alina assisted him. He wet the crusted bandages on its arm, and once they'd softened, he peeled them away, revealing the huge burn. Ugly yellow pus oozed from it. Likely this was the source of the infection, Alina thought.

Her father cleaned the wound, forcing pus from it with his fingers until he'd extracted as much of it as he could. He slathered balm from a gourd in his bag upon it. This particular ointment was used to fight infection in TreeFolk. Alina hoped it would do so for the creature as well. Her father then laid wet banda leaves over the arm, using thin twine to hold them in place.

He dressed the head wound, sewing it shut once he'd cleaned it, and then applied balm and covered it with leaves.

He checked the skin on the creature's good arm, pinching it with his fingers and watching it respond before frowning.

"What is it?" Alina asked, seeing the concern on his face.

"The creature has lost much moisture. Do you see the way the skin remains when I pinch it?"

Alina watched as he repeated the motion. The skin remained in the position he'd forced it into for a moment before going flat again. "What does it mean?"

"The creature will need water soon or its body will fail."

"How do we get it to drink if it is not awake?"

"I don't know," he said. "I'm not sure we can."

Rigin came in with the fresh towels and a bucket of water. The two children appeared in the doorway behind her, their eyes wide with excitement.

"Thank you, Rigin," her father said. "We'll try to be quiet."

She smiled, dismissing his concern, "I'm an old lady, Enor. I don't need much sleep. I am happy to help." She looked at the body on her son's bed. "That is a strange person," she said.

"Yes," her father agreed, "it is indeed an odd thing to fall from the sky."

"There are more blankets in the chest if you need them."

"Thank you, Rigin," Alina said.

She left them, taking the children with her. They peppered Rigin with questions as they went, their little voices warming Alina's heart.

Aras and Narat set up a sleeping pallet next to the small table and chair, leaving only a narrow space on the floor between the bed and the pallet.

Alina sat on the chair next to the bed as her father tended the creature, dragging a wet towel over its body to cool the fire within. They would take turns doing so, with one of them tending to the patient while the other slept, just as they had many times before when there was a fever in the village.

Staring at the creature, she wondered how her mother could have foreseen this when she was still a girl. If it had been fated to be, had Alina had any real choice at all in finding the creature and seeing it back? She sighed. Her mother had often tried to explain choices and possible paths, but these explanations had always left Alina more confused.

Chapter 6

Alina sat on the edge of the bed next to the creature. It was restless again, as it had been many times over the past two days. It mumbled words that were not words as it tossed weakly beneath the wet towel she drew across its body.

She slipped a corner of the wet towel in its mouth, and the mouth took it, instinctively sucking moisture from it. She poured water on that corner of the towel, letting it seep into its mouth. She'd discovered this yesterday during another feverish bout and had been amazed to see the creature respond to it. She'd shown her father. He'd been thrilled to see it and had praised her ingenuity.

When it stopped taking water and resumed mumbling, she leaned forward, straining to make sense of it. The words were puzzling, but she strove to determine their intent from the tone. The creature seemed to be afraid of something. It flinched and shrank weakly as if trying to escape or avoid something.

Moments later, the creature grew still, slipping once more into a deep sleep. She sighed. There was much the village wanted to know. Fodrick had stopped by several times a day, eager to hear of any progress, and leaving each time frustrated at the lack thereof. Fodrick's questions were important for the village, but Alina longed to learn of its life, to hear of its friends and family, to discover its wishes and dreams.

She'd memorized every detail of its body, fascinated by the differences but even more by the similarities. She'd decided that the creature must be near her age. Its hands were meaty, short, and strong. Its feet were impossibly soft, though after examining them, she didn't believe it was crippled. The bandages they'd found on its feet had been tailored for it. They must have been something the creature wore daily. Why this would be so was another mystery since it would spell disaster not to be able to feel the branches beneath one's feet.

The skin on its face was soft and smooth, with no lines on the brow or in the corners of its eyes. She decided it was a kind and gentle face. She knew she might well be mistaken in this. But it passed the time to imagine it, and she let her mind roam. The creature, she told herself, would be intelligent like TreeFolk, though it would be humble and would never presume. She smiled, amused, realizing these thoughts said more about her than they did about the creature.

"Any change, Lina?" her father asked, rubbing the sleep from his eyes as he sat up on the pallet next to her. It was morning, and soft light filtered through the leaves and branches of the canopy, slipping into the room through the window cutout, warming the room.

"None yet," she replied without looking. She turned and dipped the towel in the small bucket, soaking up more of the cool water. "You can sleep a little longer if you like. I still feel rested from the nap I took earlier."

"No, I'm fine too. I can sit up with you." He rose and turned the chair from the little table toward the bed where she was sitting and seated himself at her side.

"Where do you think he's from?" Alina asked.

"Only the SkyGods know. Though I keep thinking about that ball of fire in the sky."

"There must be others like him, don't you think? He wore strange clothes and wrappings on his feet. The egg he arrived in was made from the oddest material I've ever seen. It would take many people to make such things."

"Perhaps, but if there were a large tribe of such creatures, it seems we would have heard of them."

The creature stirred, tossing on the bed and mumbling strange words before going still again. "What did it say?" her father asked.

"I don't know. It sometimes speaks these words that are not words."

"Perhaps they are words from tribes beyond the mountains?" her father speculated.

"The TreeHand tribe lives beyond the mountains, and their words are similar to ours. These are so different. Could there be a tribe living on the forest floor somewhere?"

Her father scratched his short beard. "I don't see how any tribe could survive on the forest floor. And how then would they ride the fire in the sky?"

Alina shrugged. She paused, turning to her father. "What do you think Mother meant?"

Her father sighed. "You know your mother. She's a mystery, even to me," he chuckled.

Alina smiled. "Yes, but it seems impossible for Mother to have seen this creature when she was but a child. This creature does not seem much older than me."

"It does seem impossible. Your mother is trying to *see* now. Perhaps she'll find answers."

Alina was comforted by the thought of her mother unravelling the mystery. "Do you think the creature will live?" she asked as she dipped the towel in the bucket, soaking up more of the cool water and then running it over the fiery skin.

Her father touched the creature's forehead. "If the fever breaks, there is a chance. Were it a TreePerson, I would think the chance even, but there's no way to know with this creature."

"Fodrick came by again. I told him there was no change."

"Why don't you stretch your legs and take some time for yourself? I will sit with it," her father said.

Alina nodded. She stood, rolling her head in a circle, trying to loosen the knots in her shoulders. "I will be back soon and bring you something to eat," she said as she left the room.

She crossed the bridge, the log worn smooth and flat from daily use. The morning sun slanted in through the trees, the village abuzz with activity as villagers went about their day. She found Hurza and Kani by the nuxat pens. The village kept a flock of these birds in a netted enclosure. Her friends had just finished cleaning the enclosure, gathering eggs, and feeding the birds.

"Thank you both for seeing to my chores," Alina said.

"We're happy to do it," Kani said, a broad smile on her face.

"Yes, don't worry yourself," Hurza added. "At first, I thought it might be difficult to manage your tasks in addition to ours. But, as it turns out, you do very little, so it was no trouble at all."

Hurza skipped out of the way as Alina slapped at her shoulder. The slap missed as Hurza leapt to a branch, laughing and without dropping a single egg from her basket.

"You can be such a..." Alina said, leaving the last word hanging.

"A treasure?" Hurza offered, leaping back to join them and nudging Alina with her shoulder.

"Yes, that's what I was thinking."

"How is the creature?" Kani asked.

"The same," Alina sighed. "It hovers this side of passing."

"How are you?" Hurza asked, concerned.

"A little tired, but fine."

They dropped off the eggs in the communal kitchen. Milena, Fodrick's wife, was making bread with several other women. They were grinding borka nuts into a paste and then adding fruit and other tree nuts. They baked the mixture on braziers set in wooden trays filled with sand to insulate them from the heat.

"Try some," Milena urged the girls, a batch of freshly baked bread having just come from a brazier.

The smell was rich and nutty. They crowded in together and reached for thick slices. It was hot to the touch, and Alina blew on hers until she could take a bite. The luxurious feel of baked borka coated her tongue. The bread was delicious, with bursts of flavors from fruit and nutty nuggets in each bite.

"These are amazing," Alina exclaimed. "They are the best yet."

Milena smiled. To Alina, every batch was the best yet, but that didn't make it any less true.

She prepared a plate of fresh bread, along with some dried meat, for her father. Milena added more of the bread to the plate, knowing how much her father loved it. Alina hurried off with the food while the bread was still warm, her friends close on her heels. She stopped and greeted Rigin, who was feeding the children in the common room of the hut, before stepping into Sneva's room.

"Something smells amazing," her father said, turning to her.

Alina put the plate in his lap and he dug in. "Any change?"

"No, still the same," he replied, his mouth full.

"I'm going to work with Kani and Hurza some," Alina said as her friends craned over her shoulder, studying the creature on the bed. "Call for me if you need me or if you want me to sit with it."

"Go, go," he said, chewing.

They ran off, skipping across the bridges on their way to the grove.

When they arrived, Aor and Gamoc had just finished dumping a large pile of silas pods from their packs. The reddish-brown tubular pods lay in the center of the grove's circular platform. Drur arrived with two wooden buckets. He poured water from them into the large wooden tub they used to soak the fibers. Trees above the platform had been cleared out to let the sun in. Plants were affixed in baskets in the trees, ringing the platform. This farm provided much of the village's food.

Kani went over to the tub and peered inside. She bent over to pick up one of the empty wooden buckets, perhaps to fetch more water, just as Drur reached for it. Kani flushed as their hands touched on the handle, and she pulled hers away. Alina looked over at Hurza, who arched an eyebrow. Kani was shy, especially around Drur. Drur rarely said much. Alina and Hurza couldn't gauge his interest in their friend. They'd spoken of it when Kani wasn't around. Hurza felt things couldn't be left up to them. Alina wondered whether meddling might make things worse.

"Drur, why don't you help Kani rinse the fibers?" Hurza suggested. "The rest of us will remove the husks, and you can both rinse them."

Kani flushed and gave Hurza a dark glance. They'd both have their hands in the tub as they rinsed mucus from the fibers. There was bound to be a lot of touching. Alina didn't know whether it would have any impact on Drur, but she knew the contact would be charged for Kani.

Alina shook her head as Hurza smirked, pleased with herself. "Aor, perhaps you can help me here? I'm having difficulty with these husks. I think they are too green."

Aor sat down next to her and shucked a few. "They seem fine to me."

"Really? Try these over here."

So Alina and Gamoc were left to work together, shucking their pile as Hurza kept up a playful banter with Aor. Alina found it amusing that the boys seemed none the wiser as to how Hurza had orchestrated things. Though looking at Drur, she wondered if that was true. He was speaking softly with Kani as they worked, intent on her replies. Although the conversation was stilted, it nonetheless progressed.

Perhaps Hurza was right, and all they needed was a little help and opportunity. The soaking of the silas fibers took far longer than normal. Both ensured the fibers were well rinsed, their hands lingering diligently, if not energetically, within the tub.

Alina reached for another husk, her eyes on Kani, and grabbed Gamoc's hand by mistake. He shuddered under her touch and apologized. The brief touch jolted her, taking her by surprise. She shut down her senses as she'd taught herself to do. She smiled at him and told him it was her fault, but the brief contact had made him nervous. She was aware that Gamoc was awkward around her, Kani, and Hurza. He was especially uncomfortable with Hurza, who delighted in teasing him, but Alina had not realized the extent of it. The boy's face was a deep emerald, and he would not meet her eyes.

"Where did you find these pods?" she asked to get him talking.

He explained where they'd found them, which was no surprise since there were only a few groves of silas in the area. He began telling her about the family of corsol they'd found in one of the trees. The tiny creatures were always climbing about and would give annoyed screams when they perceived encroachment in their space. He grew more at ease as he spoke. She half-listened to his account, nodding as she shucked. The contact had surprised her. She was usually more careful.

Kani and Drur spread the rinsed fibers out in the sun to dry and went off to get fresh water from the cistern in the kitchen. The wet fibers were translucent, but they would dry to the tan color prevalent in the village, since the fibers were spun to make clothing, towels, blankets, and even ropes and belts. The fibers were soft to the touch. She loved the way new clothing felt on her skin.

Once they'd processed all the pods, she excused herself and returned to check on her father. Nothing had changed, and, as midday approached, she could see her father was anxious to make his rounds of the village. She took the chair at his side, taking in the body at rest before her. Her father shifted on the bed next to her and was about to speak when her mother arrived.

"How is the patient today?" her mother asked.

"The same," they both replied.

She smiled at them. "It is near midday, Amani. Shouldn't you be tending to your other patients?"

Her father brightened. "Yes, I suppose I should. There isn't much at the moment, but there are a few things I should see to," he turned to Alina. "I won't be long. Can you see to things here?"

"Take your time," Alina replied. "We'll be fine, and Mother is here to keep me company."

Her father leaned forward and touched Alina's forehead with his own. As he stood, he repeated the gesture with her mother, though he lingered several heartbeats with her. She smiled up at him and squeezed his arm. He beamed back and hurried from the room.

Alina took her place on the bed and dipped the towel in the now-warm water. Her mother took the chair beside her.

Alina wiped the creature's brow. It was still hot to the touch. "He is off to chat with the old men. What he finds enjoyable in having the same conversation every day, I do not see." The older men from the village gathered in the grove every day to discuss matters of importance, they claimed. The few such meetings she'd sat through had consisted of rambling accounts of the tired tales of glory she'd heard many times before and had no interest in hearing again.

"Perhaps that is what he finds enjoyable about it. It's a constant in a world of change."

Alina looked at her mother. "I'd never considered that."

"The conversation today may be different," her mother said, indicating the creature on the bed with her chin.

Alina wet the towel and wiped the creature's chest. There were so many questions bubbling within her. But, knowing her mother, if she asked them directly, she was likely to receive a cryptic answer. She sorted through her questions, wondering which to choose and how to phrase it in order to obtain a satisfying answer.

"Just ask me, Lina," her mother said.

Alina laughed. "None of us are mysteries to you, are we?"

Her mother looked at her and wrinkled her nose. "On occasion, I am surprised by those around me."

"Father said you were attempting to *see* last night?"

"I did try, but there was only darkness and vague feelings."

"What kind of feelings?"

"There was a feeling of great importance, as though something large was just out of view. A decision that would change many lives, but it was elusive. I could not chase it down, no matter how I tried."

"You said you knew this creature?"

"I saw the scene on the platform when I was a child. This image has stayed with me. The *sight* was accompanied by a feeling that this person would be *important* to my tribe and my family."

Alina noted that her mother had called the creature a person. And then there was the mention again that it would be *important*, not only to the tribe but somehow to their family. The latter was a further mystery that was even more unsettling. "How could it possibly be *important* to our family?"

"I do not know, daughter. It was an odd feeling then, sensing it would be *important* to a family I was yet to have. As I mentioned, I was only a girl at the time. I can only tell you what I saw and what I felt. After all this time, I still cannot make sense of it."

The creature tossed suddenly and mumbled something repeatedly. Her mother leaned in. The mumbling was more coherent. The words were better formed, but still nonsense to Alina. Its voice sounded panicked. Her mother placed a hand on its forehead and sang the lullaby Alina had grown up hearing nearly every night of her childhood. Alina felt her breathing growing deeper and more relaxed as the soft tones seeped into her. The creature reacted similarly, its body growing still and then its breathing deepening as it fell asleep.

"Did you understand any of its words?" Alina asked when her mother had finished singing.

Her mother shook her head.

By evening, the creature's condition had worsened. No longer able to take water, its skin was fiery to the touch. Its heartbeat was erratic, its breathing hesitant.

Alina sat on the chair as her father finished his examination. "I think the creature will soon pass beyond our world," he said, sitting back.

Her mother, seated on the chest, stared at the patient. "Is there then no hope left?"

Her father shook his head. "I don't think so. Its body is beginning to fail. I don't think it will last the night."

Chapter 7

Alina felt a deep sadness well up within her. There were so many things she'd longed to know. The creature had seemed on the mend yesterday. She'd imagined it would open its brown eyes, see her, and somehow share the song of its life. That dream fell away, leaving behind a hole.

"I don't understand how this could be," her mother said to herself.

"It was your first *sight*," her father offered.

"Yes, it was, and the experience was very confusing for me. But it was so compelling that it stayed with me all these suns later. I was certain there was meaning to it."

"I'm sorry, Amani. It was barely alive when it arrived. We did all we could."

"Oh, I did not mean to suggest that you could have done more. I know you both did what could be done."

The three of them sat staring at the creature. Its skin had grown paler, its ribs prominent.

"I would like to sit with the creature while it transitions," Alina said.

Her parents turned to her.

"Are you certain?" her mother said. "You've done enough. Your father and I can see it through."

Alina sat up. "I would like to. I found it in the forest and brought it here. I have come to know it, in a way, these past few days. I would like to be here as it begins its journey beyond this world."

Her father patted her hand. "Of course, if that is your wish."

Alina's eyes remained on the withered body.

"We will be nearby if you need us," her mother said with a sad smile.

"It's for the best," her father said. "It's suffered these past days. It will find peace beyond."

Alina nodded, her lips pressed together.

Her father stood and placed a hand on her shoulder, giving it a reassuring squeeze. "Have Rigin call for us if you need us."

He turned and took her mother's hand, helping her up from the chest before they left.

Alina moved to the bed, sitting in the spot her father had just occupied. The blanket was still warm from his body. She reached over and placed her hand on the creature's chest, searching for the heartbeat. It was weak, uncertain.

"I had so hoped to hear the song of your life," she said. "It must be an amazing tale for one so young. My song is short. I have not added much to mine yet." She spoke to it as she drew the wet cloth across its skin, wanting the creature to hear a friendly voice as it began its journey.

"I would have liked to tell you of my village, to have you meet my friends. I've known them since I was a child. Though I do get annoyed at times, they are the best friends I could hope for."

She dipped the cloth in the cool water and traced the contours of its body. It was no longer necessary to do so, but she'd acquired the habit over the past days. Something about the rhythm and the contact with its skin soothed her.

"One time when I was very sick as a child, Kani and Hurza created a potion to make me better. I could tell they had worked hard on it and were proud of it, so I felt compelled to drink it." She smiled. "It was the foulest thing I'd ever tasted, but I forced as much of it down as I could manage and disposed of the rest from my window once they were gone. When they returned the next day with more of it, I declared myself cured, which dismayed them. I joined them in the trees on shaky legs that day."

Alina felt again for a heartbeat. It took a few moments before she sensed it. The evening breeze came up, the initial gust setting the hut swaying.

"I wonder what your friends are like? There were two beds in your egg, and yet you were alone. Was that bed meant for another? Were they too frightened to ride the fire? I imagine it would be frightening. You must be very brave."

"I'm more stubborn than brave. If it weren't for my stubbornness, we might never have met. Not that we've formally met, but I've cleaned your body, so perhaps we've been introduced in a fashion."

Alina thought back to the fire in the sky and how she'd set off after it in defiance of Aor's words. If her mother's *sight* had shown her this creature so many sun cycles ago, had the decision to pursue the ball of fire truly been hers to make? She sighed. Her mother's visions always twisted her mind in knots.

"My friends tell me I ramble. But I don't imagine you mind. So, I'll tell you about my world. Maybe your spirit will enjoy the story. It can be a song you take with you when you pass beyond the world."

Alina continued to speak to the creature as she cared for it late into the evening. Outside, she heard the villagers sitting down for the evening meal. Rigin brought her a tray of food. As she ate, Alina explained the various dishes and how they were prepared. She described her favorites, detailing their subtleties of taste and texture.

As evening turned into night, Alina continued to share stories of her life, whispering so as not to disturb Rigin or the children in the other rooms. Rigin came for her tray and to see if she needed anything. Alina thanked her and declined. The children peeked into the room to wish her goodnight before going to bed. They'd often been near the door over the past few days. Alina suspected they'd been told not to enter or disturb anyone.

Both children were orphans found in the forest. Matse was perhaps eight sun cycles old now. Her parents were killed by a krax in front of her. Aras and Narat, out hunting far from the village, heard the noise and arrived to find her standing there alone, untouched. They'd brought her back to the village, and the child hadn't spoken a word since. Unable to learn her given name, someone in the village had named her. Alina didn't remember who. In addition to being mute, she was a shy girl and could often be found hiding behind Solvan or Rigin. But she had expressive eyes and kept her clothes meticulously clean.

Alina's father found Solvan a sun cycle later, stumbling upon the boy while collecting herbs near the forest floor. The boy had taken a tremendous fall through the canopy. He was severely injured and near death. Her father found no trace of the boy's family or others nearby. He'd carried the lad back to the village and helped nurse him back to health, repairing broken bones and sewing wounds closed.

In time, the boy recovered from his injuries, save for the one to his knee. That joint had been damaged beyond repair. The boy walked with a severe limp, favoring his good leg and dragging the other. Despite the injury and the unkind words she often heard from the other children, Solvan was a slice of sunshine. Though he was a head taller than Matse, and perhaps a sun cycle or two older, he only came to Alina's elbow. He had an unruly shock of short hair that she'd never seen tamed. He was fiercely protective of Matse and had scuffled in her defense on more than one occasion.

They stood there, anxious to see the creature that had been living just beyond the wall they shared. Alina asked them to come in. Solvan bounded into the room and was at her side in an instant, with Matse close behind.

"How is it?" Solvan asked.

"I'm afraid it is dying," Alina said. The life of TreeFolk was hard, and death was no stranger to any of them.

They stared at the body on the bed until Matse tugged at Solvan's sleeve. He turned to her, and she looked up at him, then at the creature. Solvan leaned over and whispered into her ear. She shook her head. He whispered some more, and she shook her head again. He did this several times until Matse nodded.

Alina was surprised. She hadn't had much contact with the two children before and had never given much thought to how the girl communicated complex thoughts. It seemed they'd evolved some scheme. Alina was curious to hear the girl's question.

Solvan turned to Alina. "Matse wants to know where his family is?"

"How do you know that's her question?" Alina asked.

"I just asked her," he replied, confused.

"Yes, I saw you whispering to her, but I didn't see her say anything to you."

"Oh, we speak every night, and this is one of our questions."

"She speaks to you at night?" Alina asked, shocked to hear it.

"Well, I do the speaking, but she listens and nods or shakes her head a lot, and that way, we discuss things. There were many things we wanted to know about the creature. I went through them until I found the one she wanted."

"So Matse wants to know where his family is?"

Solvan and Matse both nodded.

"Matse, that is a great question," Alina replied. The child's face lit up. "I have wondered the same thing myself." Alina reached over and cupped the girl's face. "I'm sorry. I don't think we'll learn the answer."

Rigin stepped into the room. At first, she seemed upset the children were disturbing her, but Alina shook her head. Alina could see the sadness on her face. Rigin had experienced more than her share of death.

"Come on, let's get to bed. The morning will be here soon," Rigin said. The children bade Alina goodnight again, and Rigin saw them out. Alina heard Rigin telling them to wash their faces and hands before bed. She heard Solvan grumble when she didn't accept that he'd already done so. Not much escaped Rigin.

She sat with the creature as the village grew quiet and everyone found their beds to put this day behind them. A few villagers would be posted in the trees to keep predators at bay, replaced by others once the moon had reached its peak and started its downard path to morning.

It was a peaceful time, Alina thought. If one had to choose a time to transition, then one could not choose a better one. It was said the GodLights in the night sky were the eyes of the SkyGods looking down upon them. What better company could there be for a newly freed spirit?

As the night grew late, she kept vigil, waiting for the moment when the creature let go of its body and left the world. Several times, she'd been certain that the creature's spirit had gone. But each time she checked, laying her hand on its chest, she found the tentative heartbeat.

The moon dipped back into the trees, having completed its transit through the sky. Alina could no longer keep her eyes open. She stretched out next to the body, laying her hand on its chest and closing her eyes. Though she meant to stay awake and only rest for a moment, she soon drifted off, her mind filled with thoughts of GodLights and balls of fire.

Chapter 8

Dashin stumbled through fire, reliving the moment endlessly. The voices of his crewmates called his name as he searched for them down unfamiliar halls. Everywhere he turned, and every door he opened was filled with fire. He waded through it. He breathed it. He raced through the flames, seeking but never finding them. His skin sloughed off from the heat. His heart raced. The metal floor beneath his bare feet scalded him. The world, an inferno, scorched him and consumed his flesh. The ship came apart around him, the vastness of space swallowing it up. The voices receded as debris sped away, leaving him alone and empty in the dark.

He floated, clinging to a tenuous thread within himself. He felt his grip weaken as his resolve slipped away. Emptiness reached for him, offering release from the pain and nightmares. He let go, seeking its numbing embrace. But as he did, he became aware of a new voice calling to him. It was soft and spoke strange words. It puzzled him, engaging his mind as he sought its source. He cast about in the darkness, following its sound as it led him away from the void.

The voice touched him in a way he could not explain. Though he was so tired and weak, he followed it until it went silent. He searched for it then, rising from the depths of himself toward the place where he'd last heard it.

He opened his eyes. It was dark, and things were blurry. It took a moment for his mind to reacquaint itself with his senses. It smelled fresh and rich with life in a way he'd only smelled once before while visiting the domed gardens of Altria, the Ancaran capital. He was in a small room, lying naked beneath a soft blanket. His heart skipped a beat when he saw the alien lying at his side, a delicate hand on his chest.

He regained his composure as he noted that the alien seemed to be asleep. He could feel its breath on his cheek. It was taller than he was, though slighter. It was a young woman, near his age, if he were to judge. Her hair was silvery white and short, a hand's length at most. The pointed tip of one ear extended from it. Her skin was varying shades of rich green, and she had white freckles on her cheeks and brow.

Given the biological similarities, hers was obviously a race seeded by the Makers, though not one he was familiar with. And, given this was uncharted space, it was likely not one the known galaxy had encountered before. He'd met students from other worlds in school and had always been fascinated by them, often preferring their company to that of his kind. Her skin felt warm against his arm, her breathing soft and easy in sleep.

The room swayed beneath him. The motion shocked him, and his mind went to his head injury. It all came flooding back. The accident, the loss of those he'd hoped would become family, the escape. The bandages on his arm were gone, replaced by large leaves wrapped in twine. He could still feel the burn beneath, but it was a faint sensation now. He reached up with his bandaged arm and felt a new bandage on his forehead as well, his fingers discerning its leafy texture.

Dashin tried to swallow, but there was no moisture in his mouth. His throat felt raw. The room swayed again, but this time, he noted shadows moving within the room. An opening in the wall above him, a window of sorts, let in a faint square of light that moved across the far wall with the swaying motion. It was the room that was moving. He couldn't imagine what kind of room it might be. Were they atop some type of vehicle? It didn't make sense. Then he felt the breeze through the window, and the room swayed again. They were suspended somehow and moving with the wind.

Part of one wall was the trunk of a tree, and parts of the other walls and ceiling had branches in them. The room was in a large tree. The walls were woven sheets of thick leaves. He was lying on a bed with a mattress of smooth fabric stuffed with what felt and smelled like spongy moss or greenery. There was a small wooden table and chair next to him, both of which were simply made but well-crafted. At the foot of the bed sat a wooden chest with an intricate inlay in the domed lid. An empty mattress lay on the floor on the other side of the chair. The door was a simple tan curtain with a basic geometric design along the borders.

It was quiet, except for the sound of wind in the leaves outside and the soft breathing of the young woman next to him. A bird outside made a tentative call. It was answered a moment later by another. Other birds joined as soft light from the window spilled into the room.

The young woman stirred next to him. Large emerald eyes blinked open, and she yawned. She moved her hand on his chest, searching for his heartbeat, and her eyes went wide. She looked up, and their eyes met. An electric jolt ran down his spine. She gasped, sat up, and shouted something, the words oddly melodic.

Beyond the curtain, Dashin heard noise, and an elderly woman of the same race peeked through the curtain. Her eyes widened. She reached up and brushed her fingertips across her forehead before running out.

The young woman spoke to him, her words rounded, like a stream rolling over stones. Her voice sounded familiar. It was, he realized, the voice that had called him back from the darkness. He shook his head, his eyes on hers, indicating her words were unknown to him. She seemed to understand.

She placed her hand on her chest and said, "Alina," several times, pausing between each instance and exaggerating each syllable.

"A-li-na," he ventured, the feel of the syllables odd in his mouth. Ancaran was a harsher language, sharper and more guttural. The smooth tones of this language took effort to form, and there was intonation in it that was absent from his language.

She smiled at his attempt and repeated it a few more times, correcting him until she was happy with the sound of it. Then she touched his chest expectantly, her eyes inquiring.

"Da-shin," he said, supplying his name.

Her brow wrinkled at the sound. He said it a few more times as she tried to repeat it, exaggerating the sounds until she had a reasonable approximation.

They smiled at each other. She appeared pleased at this development, but he wasn't certain what came next. It seemed that they had found him and nursed him to health, which gave him some confidence that they weren't planning on serving him for dinner.

How had they rescued him from the escape pod? Could they have broken into it somehow? And why was he naked? His clothes were nowhere in sight.

Alina kept smiling at him, glancing over her shoulder at the curtained doorway. She was waiting for others. He was too weak to stand and greet anyone, even if he'd been clothed. He was more exhausted and weaker than he ever remembered being. He coughed, then winced at the rawness in his throat.

Alina made an excited noise and grabbed the wooden cup from the table. She dunked the cup into a wooden bucket on the floor and filled it with water. He nodded, his eyes wide. He took a sip. The cool water soothed his throat, but inflamed his thirst. He gulped it down, and she refilled it. Another cupful, and he was anxious for more, but she shook her head.

Two more aliens strode into the room, a man and a woman, both older than Alina. She turned to them and began speaking animatedly. The words came so fast that the man motioned for her to slow down, which she did only marginally. As she spoke, the man glanced from her to Dashin, but the woman's eyes were locked on Dashin's face. There was an intensity in her gaze that was unsettling. He couldn't discern what she might be thinking, so he smiled at her, trying to seem friendly.

The man sat down next to him on the bed. He smiled and put his hand on Dashin's chest and neck before peering into his eyes. He checked the bandages, making mumbling noises before sitting back and saying something in that same melodic language. This must be the healer, Dashin thought, likely the man who'd saved his life.

Dashin put his fingers to his chest and said his name. The man nodded and frowned, turning and speaking to the woman, who was still staring, and then to

Alina. The three of them spoke for a time before Alina nodded and ran from the room.

Dashin continued to smile, unsure of what to do. He said his name a few more times, and the man repeated it. The man touched his chest and introduced himself as Enor. The older woman sat on the chair and said his name and then her own, Marna, several times. They nodded and smiled at each other now that they were all introduced. But none of them, it seemed, knew how to proceed from here.

Alina returned with a tray of deliciously fragrant food. She put it on the table. Enor fetched some pillows from the mattress on the floor. Apparently, someone had been sleeping in the room with him, perhaps caring for him. Enor tilted Dashin's torso forward, his hand pulling on a shoulder, and stuffed the pillows behind him. Marna tipped a bowl filled with a rich broth to his lips.

Dashin hesitated. Could he digest this? Images of flesh-eating parasites and toxic substances ingested by other races from his classes sprang to mind. But what choice did he have? His stomach growled, a ravenous hunger awakening at the rich scent. He opened his mouth and took a sip. The liquid was hearty, with layers of flavor and deftly spiced. He leaned into it, gulping it down until it was gone, his tongue reaching for the last drops.

The three aliens laughed at this, pleased at his delight. Marna fed him bites from some of the other dishes on the tray, every one of them delicious. But after the water, the broth, and a bit of food, his stomach felt full, even though his body wanted more. Enor said something, and Marna put the dish she'd been holding back on the tray. She said something to Dashin he didn't understand, but he felt the warmth and nourishment of the meal coursing through his body. He smiled up at her in reply.

The aliens spoke softly together, glancing at him often as his eyelids drooped. The light activity of the morning had exhausted him, and though he tried, he found he could not keep his eyes open. Marna pulled the extra pillows from behind him and laid him back on the bed. He smiled up at her, and she touched his forehead with her fingers. He felt a warm river flow through him and take him away into a deep sleep.

Chapter 9

"I don't understand the point," Hurza said, flicking a nest of insects from the trunk where she was weeding. "We brought the creature back with us..."

"Dashin," Alina corrected her again.

"We brought *Dashin*," Hurza continued, emphasizing his name for effect, "back to ask him questions. If we can't communicate with him, how can we learn anything?"

"He's learned a few words," Alina said.

"I don't think that *more* and *tastes good* rate as revelations."

"It's only been a few days," Kani offered, trying to ease the tension.

Alina didn't reply, Hurza's words echoing her own feelings.

Alina, Kani, and Hurza were weeding tree-beans, each of them on a branch, chatting as they cut away ivy to expose the beans to the sunlight they needed. Like borka, tree-beans had to be harvested in place. Unlike borka, whose unpleasant husks kept them free of both ivy and pests, the beans needed regular help.

Since her father was changing Dashin's bandages, and Rigin was altering some of Sneva's clothes to accommodate Dashin's stouter figure, Alina had taken the opportunity to help with chores and spend time with her friends.

Dashin was putting on weight. He was eating heartily, many meals a day now, and gaining strength. In comparison, trying to teach him their language was frustratingly slow.

The girls continued in silence until they finished weeding, then joined the boys in the grove. The boys were mending the hanging baskets they used to grow the various crops the village enjoyed. They were seated on the circular platform, ten body lengths across, with benches dotting the periphery. Trees surrounded the platform and were covered in woven baskets, each basket harboring one or more plants. Baskets had loosely woven covers that were soaked in juice from borka husks to admit sunlight but keep out pests.

A mound of dirt sat in the center of the platform, emptied from the baskets the boys were repairing. The plants from these had been removed and set aside. "We've already done most of the baskets," Gamoc said cheerfully as the girls joined them on the platform.

"That's wonderful," Kani said, gracing him with a smile.

Gamoc returned it, but then Hurza grinned at him and crinkled her eyes. He blushed a deep green and looked away. Hurza chuckled, and Alina shook her head. No wonder Gamoc was awkward around them.

"Those baskets are ready." Aor indicated the pile of repaired baskets.

The girls sat down next to the empty baskets, which were torso-sized cylinders with rounded bottoms. Packed with dirt and plants, these would be placed in the cradles already secured to the trees. They began packing dirt into the weaving at the bottom of each to establish a solid base for the plants.

"Make sure you pack them tightly," Aor said without looking over. "Otherwise, the rain will wash away the soil and rot the bottoms."

Hurza looked at Alina and Kani, arching an eyebrow.

Aor stopped working on the basket he had in his lap. "Did you hear me?"

"Yes, *Chief* Aor, we heard you fine," Alina said, looking back at him. "We've done this before."

Aor paused, his lips going taut.

Drur stepped in. "Most of the baskets we're repairing had rotted bottoms. Perhaps some of these didn't have the dirt packed in tightly enough."

Hurza stiffened next to her. "Is there a chance that the weaving might have been the issue?"

Drur's eyes narrowed. He was not one to take criticism well. Aor put his hand on Drur's arm. "We'll try to do a better job on the weaving. Can you also try to pack the dirt as tightly as you can?" Aor said evenly.

"Of course," Hurza replied, relenting.

They worked for a while in silence. The morning light filtered into the grove. It was warm and inviting. The birds sang as a wisp of breeze rustled the leaves.

"How is the creature doing?" Aor asked as they worked.

"It's recovering from its injuries," Alina replied. She'd had this discussion a few times now with Aor and his father.

"Have we learned anything useful?"

"We know that it's intelligent and has a language and is like us in many ways."

"It doesn't look much like us," Gamoc offered.

"There are differences," Alina agreed.

"I heard it speak while I was passing the hut. It sounds more like a Stoda than a TreePerson," Drur said. "It was all grunts and snorts."

The other boys laughed. Gamoc snorted like a stoda, looking at Aor and Drur as he did so. The boys laughed louder. Even Hurza and Kani chuckled.

"It's not that bad," Alina replied, annoyed.

She packed dirt in the bottom of the basket she was filling, pressing it extra firmly now, and then pounding it to compact it. It was disappointing they hadn't made more progress with Dashin. She'd taught him the words for various foods, some objects, and for his basic needs, but they'd been unable to discuss anything of substance. In a moment of insight, she'd fetched a nuxat egg and had run around the room with it above her head, pointing from it to him. After an agonizing amount of time, he seemed to understand that she'd been referring to the egg he'd arrived in, but then he'd merely nodded.

"I think we should take it back to its egg," Aor ventured.

Alina sat up, her pulse quickening. "It's only been a few days."

"My grandfather believes that it's unlikely we'll learn anything of value and that it may be dangerous to keep it here."

Alina tensed at the mention of Hedrick. "Why would it be dangerous?"

"Perhaps others from its tribe will come looking for it," Aor said. "It can't speak our language and has never lived in the trees. We don't know anything about it. Perhaps it has enemies. Perhaps it was fleeing from something."

"I can see you've given this some thought," Alina said dismissively, certain he was repeating things he'd heard from his grandfather. Her father had mentioned recent discussions here on the benches with the elder men during their midday meetings. Hedrick was making these same arguments. Her father had been unable to offer them any assurances that their fears or concerns were unfounded.

"So you would put Dashin out into the forest to die. Is that what you're saying?"

"What would you have us do?" Aor said. "Would you have it stay in Sneva's room and have us feed it and care for it like a nuxat that does not lay eggs or provide meat?"

"Of course not," Alina replied. But what were they going to do? As much as she didn't want to admit it, they had a point. They couldn't very well continue this way. She'd assumed they'd find a way to communicate once Dashin had woken and introduced himself. But it had become clear it would take a long time before they could have a meaningful conversation.

She felt Kani's and Hurza's eyes on her as they worked, her friends sensing the unease in her. Hurza picked up a pebble from the dirt before them and tossed it beyond the boys. It landed on the far edge of the platform. Their heads swiveled toward the sound, and they waited, watching the spot where the noise had come from while Hurza grinned. After a few moments, they turned back to their work, at which point Hurza picked up another pebble and repeated her throw.

The boys turned again, Drur saying something about birds. At the third pebble, Gamoc got up and walked over to the edge of the platform and peered over it. Aor asked if there was anything, but Gamoc straightened and shook his head. Gamoc had just regained his place when the next pebble hit. The boys looked over to where it landed, and Kani couldn't contain a chuckle. Aor spun around and saw them all grinning, with Hurza's arm already perched to throw the next pebble.

"You're worse than the children," Aor said, shaking his head and turning back to his work.

Hurza made a face at him, and the girls burst out laughing. The boys turned to them, Aor annoyed as she made another face at him. The girls laughed harder, and the boys finally joined in. Alina drank in the joy of the moment, reminded of the countless times they'd shared laughter together.

Once they'd finished packing dirt into the bottoms of the baskets, they filled them with looser dirt and then repotted the various plants, stacking the completed baskets to one side. The boys finished their repairs and began taking the completed baskets and reinstalling them in the trees, adding a woven cover to each.

"How are you doing?" Kani asked. Hurza leaned in.

"Fine, a little tired."

"You shouldn't get too attached to Dashin," Kani whispered, the name odd in her mouth.

Alina saw the earnest expression on the faces of her friends. She realized neither expected this to end well. She nodded and forced a smile to allay their concern, but she knew that for her, it was already too late.

Her parents were engrossed in conversation when she pushed aside the curtain to Sneva's room. Dashin was dressed in Sneva's clothes, incongruous in them somehow. Panels had been added to either side of his tunic and pants, each a different shade from the garment they altered. Both the tunic and pants had been shortened to fit his body. It was well crafted for the short time Rigin had worked on it, far beyond Alina's skill with needle and thread. Dashin was eating again, the tray in his lap filled with empty plates. Aor's comment about them feeding him like a kept nuxat popped into her mind. She pushed it away. Her mother sat on the chair with her father perched at the foot of the bed. Alina slid onto the chest behind her father and pulled her knees up before her, not wanting to interrupt.

"There is no time for that, Amani," her father said.

"But surely the others will see the progress..." her mother began.

Her father shook his head. "I do not believe they will. Hedrick is already gathering support. I believe he intends to bring it up soon and force a decision. And we've been unable to give Fodrick answers he might use in defense."

Her mother sighed. "I cannot find my way through the paths of this," she said. "They are hopelessly tangled, beyond my ability."

Her father reached over and patted her mother's hand. "We've done all we can, Amani."

Alina felt a stone settle in her stomach. She looked at Dashin, who seemed concerned now, having caught something in the tone of their conversation. How she longed to reach him, to explain to him what was at stake and get answers that would help them make a case for him. He cast her an inquiring look, and she tried to smile before looking away.

Her parents grew quiet, she assumed, each imagining what would come next. Alina remembered that Hedrick, as chief, had turned away several TreeFolk who'd come seeking to join their tribe. These had seemed able candidates to Alina, young and strong. However, Hedrick had denied them the opportunity of *becoming*, the rite all children or outsiders had to face to be considered *of the tribe* and find a place among them. She'd been confused then, but now she believed it had to do with things that had happened to Hedrick before his time here.

As chief, he had always responded aggressively to any perceived threat to his power or control. Both from outsiders seeking to join and from those within the tribe speaking up against him. The former he turned away. The latter he stood his ground against, even on trivial matters.

Once Hedrick could no longer lead the hunt, he'd been forced, as was their tradition, to abdicate his position as chief. But he'd then installed his son, Fodrick, in his stead and thus continued to influence village life through him. It seemed he intended to do the same again with Aor once Fodrick stepped down as chief. Though the prospect of that seemed a long way off.

If Hedrick was speaking out against Dashin and gathering support, then Dashin was running out of time. That Hedrick had waited this long was likely due to her mother's vision. Such a thing was not easily overcome, but with Dashin unable to communicate and with her mother unable to supply details, it might only be a matter of days.

"It may be the only way," her mother said, meeting her father's gaze.

Her father turned to look at Alina, shock on his face. Alina looked up. She'd been musing and had lost track of their conversation.

"What is it?" Alina said, her eyes darting between her mother and father.

He swallowed and paused, turning to face her. "Your mother thinks you should attempt to *touch* Dashin's mind."

The floor fell out from beneath Alina. The room spun as the terrifying suggestion struck her. Her heart raced, and she hugged her knees. Alina had been blessed with the gift of *touch* in the way her mother had the gift of *sight*. The gift of *touch* was unusual, though their songs spoke of it, she'd never known another with it. For Alina, this gift had always been a curse. She'd first experienced it as a girl when Kani grabbed her hand when Alina tripped on a branch. The experience had been jarring. Her mind had been flooded by Kani's memories, and her own had flowed into her friend's. The *touch* had only lasted moments, but it had left them both shaken. Kani had lost her father a short time before. He'd gone out into the forest and never come back. The depth of that loss and the nature of it had poured into Alina, who then had nightmares of losing her own father for days beyond the *touch*.

They'd been so close, best of friends their entire lives, and yet the shape of Kani's thoughts and memories had felt intrusive and unnatural. And revealing her own inner landscape had seemed a violation as well. It had taken time for them to feel comfortable with each other again, and longer still before Kani came into physical contact with her again.

Since that time, Alina had learned to consciously block off that sense whenever she was near another. There were times when inadvertent contact elicited the response, but she'd learned to sever the link whenever such a thing occurred. She spent her life afraid of it, trying to suppress it. The thought of opening herself to it with someone she knew nothing about and who was so different from her was unthinkable.

"How can you ask this of me?" Alina said, clutching her legs, a shiver running through her.

"I would not propose it if there were alternatives," her mother said.

"I'm sorry, Mother, but you don't know what you're asking."

"No, I have never experienced the *touching*."

"It alters one. The two who share the *touching* both come away changed."

"*Seeing* is similar," her mother said.

Alina looked at her, surprised.

"Did you think that one could *see* without being changed?" she asked with a smile.

Alina considered this. "I'm sorry. I had not imagined that to be the case."

"People imagine that seers remain apart from what they see. But that has never been the case for me."

Her father added softly. "There were some difficult times for your mother. Times I had to hold her for many nights after a difficult *sight*. It has been a burden for her, more than she shares with others."

Alina bowed her head. "I am sorry, Mother. I didn't know."

"It is my burden to bear, dear. If my *sight* helps the tribe, it is my duty to do so. I only share this now to explain that I do understand some of what I propose."

Alina considered it. She looked over at Dashin, who observed the conversation wearing a confused expression. "I am afraid of this," she said. "I haven't used this gift since I was a child. Then it was with Kani, who is like a sister to me, and the contact was so disturbing that I cannot imagine doing so with someone I do not know."

"I understand, daughter. No one will force you to do this. I only suggest it because we have no other choice."

"Why is he *important*?" Alina asked, with a quick glance at Dashin.

"I wish I knew," her mother said. "I've struggled to find the answer."

"But you believe it to be true," Alina said, her eyes intent on her mother's. She nodded. "I do."

Alina couldn't believe she was considering this. She looked at Dashin, who was staring at her. "I don't think I can do this."

"I may be able to help," her mother said.

"What do you mean?"

"I've learned to protect my mind over time. It will still be uncomfortable, and you will still feel the effects, but I think I can make it easier on both of you."

"You'll be here with me," Alina said, making certain.

"Of course. I'll watch over you both, and I will break the connection if things do not go well."

Alina took a deep breath, her chin on her knees as she hugged her legs to her. She closed her eyes and gave a little nod.

Her father reached over and put a hand on her shoulder. "I cannot do much for you in this, but I want you to know, daughter, that both your mother and I are very proud of you."

Alina opened her eyes and gave a weak smile, terrified of what was to come but resigned to see it through.

Chapter 10

Dashin stood at the window, leaning on the table beneath it for support. Light from the morning sun seemed to rain through the rustling leaves. Birds flitted about nearby, and he spied what looked like a family of small monkey-like creatures, like those common on Itagia, in the far distance. This was a beautiful world, filled with life, and such a contrast to the world he'd grown up in, with its vast deserts and underground cities.

He looked down but couldn't see the forest's floor. They were impossibly high. He hadn't adjusted to the hut's swaying. Each shift in direction felt uncannily like thruster compensation. He was startled whenever an unusual gust changed the regular pattern of motion. The unexpected motion reminded him of the accident and his lost friends, the memory of that loss, heartbreaking and visceral.

He wondered what catastrophic event had caused the ship's destruction, despite the numerous redundancies in place. He was grateful that none of the service work he'd done had dealt with the propulsion or navigation systems. Still, he did find himself reviewing his work with Gralan, questioning every decision he'd made, wondering if some mistake or inattention on his part could have been the cause of the accident.

The ship had been prospecting in a dense asteroid field, dense being a relative term since there was always plenty of room to navigate in such fields. Their mining ship had performed countless surveys in them long before he'd joined. The ship constantly scanned the field, mapping nearby objects and continually plotting courses around them.

It could have been a cascade event. An asteroid outside their field of view could have crashed into one or more of the nearby asteroids, dramatically altering their trajectories. If such an event occurred near enough, there might not have been enough time to react.

Or perhaps it was an avalanche failure in the propulsion system itself. Perhaps an entire subsystem had failed catastrophically, eliminating all the redundancies and precipitating a rapid series of subsequent failures throughout the ship. Such a catastrophic event would have required multi-point failures in their safety systems. Given that Gralan managed maintenance, this seemed highly unlikely. But unlikely events were not impossible events.

He was coming to accept that he would never know what had destroyed his ship and taken his friends. By now, their regular report to the relay station would have missed its window, and they would be presumed *missing*. His parents would be notified. A ship would be sent to investigate, or perhaps only probes.

Space was immense, and the Serendipity changed course often during surveys as sensors sought out likely prospects. It would take time for a ship or probes to transit out this far. It had taken the ship over a hundred Ancaran days to make the journey. Searchers would scan for beacons along the way, but with no clear idea of where the Serendipity was, Dashin's beaconless pod would be impossible to find.

Even if, by some chance, searchers also scanned and found this world with a habitable atmosphere, there would be no way of finding him within it. And, interstellar accords would preclude them from disturbing a world with sentient life on it without clear evidence of an emergency beacon.

And so, no matter how the events played out in the stars above him, the result for him would be the same. The crew would be presumed lost. No one would know he'd survived and was here on this uncharted world, living in the trees.

His parents would be sad, of course, but they would throw themselves into their work, as they had for most of his life. Both his parents were scientists, brilliant in their fields. He'd been conceived by accident. They'd never told him that, but he'd overheard it one night as they entertained colleagues and thought him asleep. He'd been raised by tutors and boarding schools. The best available, his parents had assured him. So he'd spent much of his youth alone with his studies, dreaming of adventures like the ones he read about in fantasy books.

He bit his lip as grief swelled within. All those years dreaming of adventure. The reality was so different than the fantasies he'd entertained. It was different losing real friends. He'd not had many of those in his life.

Outside, at the edge of his field of view, a group of children played in the trees. They ran without care across the branches, leaping from one to another effortlessly and fearlessly. He'd been shocked that parents would allow such a thing until he noticed the netting below that area yesterday.

A few huts were visible from the window, each built around a tree trunk with a woven platform for a floor and thatched roof. The platforms extended beyond the hut's walls to provide a walkway around the hut as well as around wooden cisterns to collect rainwater. Each hut had one or more logs lashed to it, leading from it to other huts, which created a network of pathways within the village.

A hollow drumming sound rang out from somewhere nearby. The children leapt up in response and raced from the play area, a line of them tearing across one of these tiny bridges with no railings or safety lines to the platform of one hut and then across another such bridge before racing out of sight. It was amazing to see how gracefully they moved and how sure-footed they were, even though the trees, platforms, and bridges swayed beneath them continually.

Dashin had been watching one of the huts in particular. It was a tiny building linked to his hut by a couple of bridges. The area below it had been cleared, creating an open chute beneath. He'd seen a few of the villagers use the hut to relieve themselves.

The desire to relieve himself with a measure of dignity had become a goal for him once he'd spied it and divined its purpose. Since he'd woken up a couple of days ago, he'd been forced to use a gourd to relieve himself. It took every ounce of concentration he had to urinate with a roomful of people watching him and providing what he imagined were helpful tips to that end.

Now that he was eating, waste removal of a more solid nature had become a pressing concern. He'd been pacing the tiny room, trying to get enough strength to attempt the transit to that hut.

Rigin, the older woman who lived in this hut with two small children, had made him the clothes he was now wearing. They were basic but well-crafted, and the fabric felt wonderful on his skin. She'd also fed him, bringing him trays of delicious food several times a day. Thanks to Maker engineering, he imagined, his body had adapted remarkably well to the new diet, although some of his fever on arrival might have been related to adaptation.

Ancaran cuisine wasn't much in demand anywhere, even on Ancara. Off-worlders quipped that the diet consisted of lizard and cactus. And, though the cuisine was more varied than that, it was still an apt characterization. This food, by comparison, was amazing. It was rich and diverse and loaded with fresh produce, something lacking on his world. There was a wealth of spices and textures, and aside from one dish with sour, fermented leaves that he didn't care for and hadn't seen again after he failed to finish it, he devoured everything else she brought him.

Rigin was thrilled each time she came back and found an empty tray. He'd learned to say *delicious*, or at least that's what he thought he was saying as he patted his stomach. Each time he said it as she took a tray, her face would light up, and she'd nod. The nodding was something Dashin had noted these people did when they conversed, a sort of small bow of acknowledgment or agreement.

The two small children living with her often peeked into his room from behind the curtain. Rigin would shoo them away, but they would soon return. The boy had a huge smile, but walked with a pronounced limp. The girl hung behind him, her huge eyes peering over his shoulder. He'd waved at them a few times, which had thrilled them both immensely, the boy repeating something over and over when he did.

The past couple of days had been filled with eating and sleeping. His body was so depleted that it took all nourishment greedily. His sleep was fitful, nightmares of his last moments on the ship replaying in his mind.

He took a deep breath and felt the familiar but improving twinge in his side. He doubtless had at least some bruised ribs, perhaps even some fractures. He rolled his injured shoulder. It was stiff and tender but still had a reasonable range of motion. The burn on his arm was still tender to the touch, but his body was healing.

He was working up the nerve to attempt to communicate his desire to use the private hut to Rigin when Enor arrived. Dashin sighed with relief, by far preferring to discuss this with the healer.

The healer greeted him with a smile, saying something as he did so. Dashin gave the customary short nod in reply. Enor checked his bandages, replacing them with fresh ones and applying more of the marvelous ointment that made his skin tingle wonderfully. The stuff was amazing. It had nearly healed the massive burn on his arm and the gash on his forehead.

Dashin squirmed as Enor worked, the matter of relief growing urgent within him. When Enor sat back and asked something akin to *where his discomfort was*, pointing to his head and his arm a few times, Dashin shook his head and patted his stomach. This confused Enor, who might have thought he had a stomachache. Dashin thought about how to explain and then pointed to the gourd he used for urination and then to his backside.

Enor seemed to understand and disappeared into the common area of the hut, reappearing with a shallow husk. Dashin felt his face flush. There was no way he was going to squat here in the room and do that. He got up and walked to the window, motioning for Enor to join him. He pointed at the outdoor latrine and then to himself. Enor understood and nodded, saying things he didn't understand. However, the issue had become so pressing that understanding no longer mattered. Enor took his arm.

The path to the small hut was treacherous, and his legs were still shaky and weak. With all the huts and bridges moving in the wind, it seemed an impossible journey, but the urge was so strong it gave him a singular focus. Somehow, with Enor's help, he stumbled his way to his goal and reached the hut. When he stepped within it and saw it was a simple seat with a hole in it, with a large pile of broad leaves next to it, he felt deflated. He wasn't sure what he imagined it would be, but that didn't matter. This was infinitely better than doing this in a husk on the floor of his room.

The walk back to his room was different. The entire forest had stopped to watch him, villagers and birds alike fixated on his awkward progress. The village was larger than he'd imagined. A crowd of villagers, forty or fifty of them, were gathered on a large platform, all of their eyes on him as they tracked his progress. In the distance, he heard the monkey-like creatures cackling and imagined they did so at him. Now that he wasn't so pressed, he struggled to keep his feet. When he reached the edge of the hut's platform and looked down, he had a spell of vertigo and staggered.

On his world, he'd done some climbing and was comfortable with ropes and heights. But the mountains he'd climbed had always been immobile beneath him, and he'd had gear and boots. The soles of his feet were sore from the burs and uneven footing on the bridges, and from the rough weave of the platforms. He glanced back at the trail of bloody smudges he'd left on the platform. Without shoes, his feet would have to toughen up.

Enor squeezed his arm and said something to him, pointing straight ahead. Dashin guessed it was something akin to *don't look down*, which he thought was great advice given the situation. Together, with Enor supporting him, they made it back to the room. By then, Dashin was sweating profusely and exhausted. He plopped down on the bed and laid back on the pillow, spent but feeling delightfully relieved. He'd never imagined such a simple thing could bring such a feeling of satisfaction.

He was stranded on an alien world with no prospects of ever leaving. Assuming the escape pod had survived the trip, its meager engines were likely depleted. The transit to and from the hut had given Dashin a sense of the lesser gravity on this world. He estimated it at perhaps half that of Ancara. But even fully charged, the pod's engines wouldn't have the power to escape the gravity well of a planet.

The beacon and communications array on his pod had been ripped away by the explosion of the ship, so no one would know he was here. He'd lost everything and everyone he'd ever known. The grief welled up within him again, but he forced it down, trying to find something to keep it at bay.

He had been fortunate. He could have died on the ship or in the pod, or here on this world, overcome by infection or stumbling around in the forest. Somehow, against all odds, he was alive, fed, clothed, and among other people. There was still so much he didn't understand about this world. Gralan's words swept into his mind. *Focus on what's in front of you.* It wasn't something he'd been particularly good at.

Marna arrived and greeted him. He nodded to her. She took the chair next to him, and Enor sat at the foot of his bed. They began speaking to each other, and it seemed that they were discussing something serious. Their tone was different today. Rigin arrived with another tray of food. She paused at the door and asked them something. They waved her forward. She set the tray in his lap. He didn't know how to thank her, so he nodded, and she nodded, and he nodded again, and so did she until they both laughed. She smiled at him as she left.

Dashin offered some of the food to Marna and Enor, lifting the tray toward them, and they both smiled and shook their heads, Marna saying something that he imagined meant that *he should go ahead and eat*, which was fine with him now that he had space again to do so. He dug into the delicious food as they continued speaking. When he finished and was enjoying the warm glow of it in his body, Alina came in and sat on the chest at the foot of his bed.

She listened to her parents and then became involved in the discussion. She cast a few anxious glances his way, and there was something about the tone of this conversation now that disturbed him. Their words were strained. They were speaking more quickly. Their faces had lost the openness he'd come to know, frowns and worry now gracing their brows. Alina hugged her knees to her chest. She seemed afraid of something and was avoiding looking at him now.

They spoke for a time and seemed to come to some conclusion that none of them was happy with. Marna then turned to him. She gave him a weak smile and squeezed his shoulder.

Chapter 11

Alina greeted Rigin at the door to the hut where she'd set up a chair and was working on mending clothes from the basket at her feet. It was midday and she'd sent the children off to play. The older woman smiled up at her and gave her an encouraging nod, which made Alina's stomach clench.

She smiled in return and stepped into the common room. She took a deep breath, laying a trembling hand on the counter. What was she thinking? How could she have agreed to this? It wasn't too late to change her mind. She would explain to her mother that she couldn't do this. Her mother would understand.

She pushed aside the curtain and stepped into the room, which felt so much smaller. Her mother was at the table where she'd placed the head-sized brazier on the tray filled with sand and was now lighting it with a firestick. She spun the stick between her palms in its cradle until an ember formed and then pushed that into the dry tinder in the base of the brazier. A wisp of smoke curled up from the brazier, and her mother blew on it until it ignited. She fed a tiny flame with slivers of wood until it blossomed.

Adding a mound of hardwood chips over the nest of tinder, she sat down on the chair to wait for these to burn down into coals. As they did, the room filled with the scent of the fragrant wood. Her mother smiled at her.

Alina's mouth worked, trying to form words to stop this.

"Come, sit down," her mother said, patting the bed next to Dashin, who was seated with his back to the wall. "Are you having second thoughts?"

Alina nodded, looking down, embarrassed.

Her mother raised her chin with a finger. "There is nothing to regret in this," she said. "I would be shocked if it weren't the case."

"Really?" Alina said, hopeful.

"Of course, as I said, you do not have to do this thing."

Her shoulders relaxed a touch. She glanced over at Dashin, who watched the exchange with a curious expression on his face. "What will we do about him?" she asked, not wanting to use his name.

"I don't know," her mother said, "perhaps I can prevail on the village to give him more time."

Alina sensed such a request had little chance of succeeding. "Do you think Fodrick would agree?" she asked.

Her mother shrugged. "There is a chance."

Alina knew in her heart that there was no real chance. Her mother was simply taking the responsibility from Alina's shoulders. Would it be that bad to try? Her mother was there. She would watch over her. Perhaps it would only take a moment to retrieve thoughts that might save him. Her mother had said that Dashin was *important* to the tribe. Surely, a few moments were worth the risk.

"I'll do it," Alina said, setting her jaw.

"Are you sure?" her mother pressed. "As I said, you do not have to."

"Maybe I can capture a few thoughts or images that will make a difference," she said, frightened but determined.

"Very well," her mother said, reaching over and squeezing Alina's hand. "I will be here the entire time. I will sense if you struggle and put an end to it."

Her mother's words were reassuring. She nodded and met her mother's eyes, stoking her resolve. Her mother smiled and then turned to Dashin. "Alina is going to attempt to *touch* your mind. It is a rare gift she has. It may help us to understand each other."

Alina saw the confusion on his face. "He doesn't understand your words."

Her mother nodded but continued to look at Dashin. "Yes, I know, daughter, but some part of him may sense the meaning behind the words." She smiled at Dashin and resumed. "It will feel unusual and perhaps frightening, but Alina will be gentle, and I will be here to see to you both." She placed a hand on his shoulder and squeezed it. He smiled in return.

Her father stepped into the room, out of breath, his arms filled with bags. "Oh, good. I had hoped to be here before you began." Seeing that they were already underway, he stopped at the entrance. "I'll just sit here in case you..." he paused, hesitating. "Just in case," he said, piling the bags on the far side of the chest and then sliding up onto it.

Her mother smiled at him and turned to Alina. "I will watch over you both." She stirred the coals that had formed in the brazier and dropped moss and herbs from her bag onto them. "Just close your eyes and let the smoke soothe you. It should help your mind stand apart from what you see. My touch will help me sense the state of your minds so that I can watch over you. I will squeeze your shoulder when I sense you are both ready."

Alina closed her eyes and took a breath, centering herself. Her mother put a hand on her shoulder. A warmth flowed from it into her, relaxing her. She felt her mother's body reach forward for Dashin, and a moment later, she felt him take a deep breath too. She was surprised he accepted this so easily. Here he was among strangers in a world he knew nothing of, and he was trusting them with something he had no concept of. She doubted she could do the same were she in his place.

The room filled with a thick, rich incense that seeped into her. It wrapped her in a warm blanket of fragrance, her mind calming as tension drained from her body. A warm numbness spread through her. It was delicious in a way she hadn't experienced before. Her anxiety receded, yet her mind remained alert and detached from her body. It was as though she were floating above herself, aware of the room but separate from it.

Her mother began singing the song of their tribe. It was a comforting sound, one Alina had grown up with. The song was the oral history of their people, and it chronicled events through time. Each generation learned the song that had come before and added to it the tale of their own experiences. Usually, only parts of the song were sung, since the entire song took days to sing. But her mother started at the beginning.

Alina was floating, immersed in the warm, rich smells, the song in her ears, when she felt her mother squeeze her shoulder. It came as a surprise. She'd been so relaxed she'd forgotten why she was there. A wave of anxiety rippled through her at the signal, but it flowed through her, and she let it go.

Alina felt safe and secure. She reached down and placed her hand on Dashin's forearm next to her hip. The skin was warm to her touch, no longer feverish. Her fingers remembered the feel of this arm, though it was plumper than it had been. She felt Dashin tense briefly at her touch, but then his muscles went slack beneath her fingers.

Something about his trust moved her and reassured her. And it was this that allowed her to open her mind and reach out. She had to fight her natural reflex, the conditioning she'd built up over so many sun cycles. She let the aversion within her settle. She took a deep breath and eased the barrier she'd built around her mind, letting it slowly dissipate. Tentatively, she reached through it, touching the edges of his mind.

The song carried her along on its current. She floated above, the senses in her body vague impressions. As the barrier between their minds dissolved, their memories swirled together.

There was sand, lots of sand, sand everywhere, and no trees, none at all. The sight was jarring, and she felt the connection slip as Dashin's body grew tense beneath her fingers. Her mother's calm reassurance flowed into her. She took a breath and stilled her heart. She felt Dashin do the same. Then she stepped into that world.

The barren landscape was stark. Cliffs of stone rose from rolling hills of sand. All of it was devoid of vegetation except for the wiry bushes hiding in crevices and canyons. Alina felt exposed in the openness of this strange world. But somehow it also felt familiar. There was an odd feeling of home. She looked up and saw holes in the cliff face, knowing instinctively that these holes served as windows funneling light and air to the city within.

Dashin was a boy. A young boy, growing up within that city, a thriving mass of people within a mountain. There were so many people living in shiny tunnels and rooms with GodLights on the walls and ceilings, and no visible food sources anywhere. How was this possible? she wondered, falling so deep into the memory that she lost herself in it and became it, as though she'd lived it herself.

She sensed that supplies arrived from outside the city and that the city traded something intangible for these goods. Dashin lived in a home of smooth, gleaming stone with two parents and no siblings. His parents were occupied with endeavors outside the home and were inattentive to him. He spent his days learning the songs of his tribe with children his age.

Many songs, from many singers. Some of the songs he saw on clear tablets. These captured the spirit of people within them, their faces and voices appearing at will. There were many magical devices within the city. The songs were strange and spoke of things Alina struggled to follow, but Dashin grasped their essence easily.

He changed from tribe to tribe as he learned their songs. Continually, he was surrounded by people, and yet he remained alone. He yearned to make friends, but his pace within the tribes was unusually fast. There was seldom time for him to get to know others before he moved to another tribe. The songs became his world, and he drank them in as others around him struggled to do so.

His parents, encouraged by his abilities, provided adults to help him learn more difficult songs. This sped his progress further so that soon he was the youngest in each tribe. The other children saw him as different. They were anxious around him. When he attempted to join them in their activities, they were cruel, a few of them pretending to be friends and then embarrassing him in front of the others.

When he was not learning songs, he filled his days with activities. His parents were seldom home. They traveled much in their lives outside the family. He learned to climb the cliffs of the mountain and roamed the sands nearby, learning to recognize the life that hid in the cool recesses of the terrain. He brought home treasures he found wandering in the areas where people discarded broken things. He tinkered with them, trying to repair or improve them. His efforts were seldom successful, but he enjoyed taking them apart to see their hidden hearts and dreamed of the day when he would understand the magic within these things.

When he was almost grown, he left his home and traveled far away, where he joined a larger tribe. Within this tribe, he found others near his age with similar interests and circumstances. For the first time in his life, he felt like he belonged, that he was in a place where he could speak his heart. He and his friends were excited by the complicated songs they learned and spoke of them often. These songs spoke of the nature of the world, revealing secrets he had longed to know.

Before, alone, he had looked to the life yet to come. But now new friendships had captured his heart. There was one friend in particular, Krixa, whom he wished to walk with, but his experiences in his earlier tribes made reaching out frightening. He sensed a similar reticence in her, so by the time he had worked up the courage to reach out, it was too late.

Suddenly, they were celebrating the completion of this tribe's journey. Having learned the required songs, they had to leave yet again to find new tribes to belong to. It was a sad parting this time, as he was now leaving behind friends he might never see again. He traveled a long distance to a city situated above the ground, next to an immense body of water.

In this new city, he met with many people seeking to be accepted into their tribe. These tribes lived in sky homes that moved among the GodLights far above the world. The songs he'd learned explained how they did so, though he didn't yet understand many of the details.

He was accepted aboard such a sky home by a tribe he prayed would become his family. As they sailed into the realm of the SkyGods, he found deep happiness in the days he spent with Gralan, who became the father he never had. They worked together, repairing and maintaining the sky home, the tribe taking meals together, and enjoying each other's company. It was a harmonious tribe, and it felt the way he imagined family should feel. There was much laughter and hard work. Everyone had responsibilities they saw to, and the days went smoothly.

He felt a sense of fulfillment as he learned new things each day and applied the songs he'd learned to solve the problems he encountered. He fell asleep at night feeling fulfilled and eager for the next day.

The sky home ventured on a trip, seeking materials to trade for things the tribe needed. There was much talk during meals as to what the sky home was tasting in the sky around them. Decisions were made regarding which direction seemed most promising and whether gathering materials from a particular stone in the sky was worth the effort. He had little to contribute in that regard but listened attentively, happy to be included in the discussions.

Then the sky home was destroyed. He was battered and burned as his home was ripped apart around him. He scrambled toward an egg and managed to save myself before his home tore itself to pieces. He searched in vain through the window for other eggs with family members in them, but didn't see any. He shouted into the wall, sending his voice from the egg, hoping others might answer. But no answers came, and he realized he was the last of this tribe. Once more, he was alone, this time more so than ever before. In complete despair, he took medicine to make him sleep.

He awoke to find the kind face of a young woman he found beautiful in a way he couldn't describe.

The last thought was so arresting that it sent her mind spinning, breaking the link. Alina floated amid an ocean of images, her mind seeking to escape them and find itself. Struggling and exhausted from the *touching*, her body pitched forward as the world blurred and went dark.

Chapter 12

Dashin closed his eyes and took a breath. Rich, moist smoke filled his lungs. Marna placed a hand on his shoulder, and he felt a warmth flow into him. It was a delicious feeling. He sat there, his back against the wall, at peace and drifting.

Marna began to sing a song. It was an odd song, one without a chorus or refrain. It went on and on, the words changing, but there was a cadence to it, a rhythm that carried him along.

A few moments later, Alina placed a hand on his forearm. He opened his eyes to see if there was something she wanted, but she had hers closed, so he did so as well.

He was thinking of how odd this world was, how utterly different it was from his own. It was so... A crisp image of trees flashed into his mind. He was leaping from one branch to another. He opened his eyes, his pulse racing, to find he was still in the room.

Marna smiled at him and nodded. He didn't know what to make of it. Apparently, they'd expected this. She squeezed his shoulder, and he felt more of the warmth flow into him. He closed his eyes. The song continued, carrying him deeper.

The scene shifted and sharpened, the world now vivid around him. Somehow, he felt images, feelings, and thoughts flow into his mind through this connection with Alina. It was unsettling and yet compelling. He took a breath of the rich smoke and leaned into it. As the memory formed within him, Alina was a girl, a young girl.

She was a child running through the trees, her feet jumping from branch to branch. And, though it should have been frightening since the ground was nowhere in sight, she was at home in this place. She was filled with joy as she played with her friends. Someone chased her, and she squealed with glee, dashing away. The sun filtered through the branches and leaves around her. She chased another friend who tripped and fell into the rope netting below. She burst out laughing with the other children as their friend scrambled back up to join them, grinning.

Some sun cycles later, she was sitting in her father's lap as he extracted a long sliver of wood from her knee. She bit her lip, trying not to cry as he dug it out, and then bandaged the wound. He kissed her forehead and then wiped away her tears.

Then she was seated with Irina and Kani during the evening meal, chatting about the new nuxat that had just hatched. The new chicks were so cute, and they'd each brought one to the table to cuddle and pet, feeding them bits from the table as they named them. Each of them was certain that their chick would lay the most and best eggs. The chicks nipped at their fingers, taking the bits of rough bread hungrily. They laughed, and her father ruffled her hair. It was a warm evening, late in the hot season, when evenings were welcome after the day's heat.

She tried to feed her sour rusna to her chick, but even the chick wouldn't eat the foul leaves. Her mother reached over and put the dish back in front of her, telling her that she had to finish it before she could have borka cake. She wore her best pout in response, crossing her arms and shaking her head sternly. Her mother laughed, which made Alina furious, but her mother didn't relent, so she picked at the rusna, choking it down in little bits and making all kinds of disgusted sounds until it was gone. Her mother then placed a big slice of borka cake in front of her. All was forgotten as she ate every last crumb, licking her fingers to get all of the sticky juice binding it.

Later that sun cycle was a sad day for the tribe. Her best friend Irina went to gather borka with her family, and none of them returned. The adults in the tribe looked for them until nightfall and then again all the next day. Alina sat with Kani and Hurza on the edge of the platform, gazing down into the trees for many hours in the evening and the next day. They sat waiting for news of their safe return, but it never came. Only Irina's small beaded waist bag was ever found. It was a bag her mother had made for her, and it was worse to find that than to find nothing at all. Alina carried that beaded bag at her waist for many sun cycles, until it wore away. That night, there was a stone in her chest she'd never felt before. She cried in her bed until her mother came and sat with her, stroking her back until she fell asleep.

Dashin took a breath, his mind reasserting itself as the memories swirled and then seeped within him. The singing continued. The words were still odd, but they began to summon vague images within him. The words evoked images of people climbing into the trees and building crude shelters. These started near the ground, but over time, they ascended high into the canopy of this verdant world. The images were vague, not real memories, more like memories constructed from stories told and retold. He was amazed at the words themselves, at how they formed these thoughts and images. At the melodious sound of them. At the subtle intonation and inflection.

Then, Alina was twelve sun cycles old and traveling to the TreeHands tribe to trade. They were the nearest tribe beyond the mountains, and it was the first time she'd been allowed to go. Hurza was with her, but Kani stayed home with her mother. Since they'd lost her father, her mother had kept her close. It was sad for Kani, and she wanted to feel sad with her, but she was so excited to be going that she could not manage it. Alina and Hurza walked along together through the trees in the middle of the party, chatting about all the things they hoped to see.

Hurza talked about boys. She was always interested in hearing about the boys in other villages. Alina joined in, but truly, she was more interested in the adventure and seeing many new things. The tribe they were to trade with made the lanyards they used daily, and much of the fabrics, dyes, leathers, and foods their tribe made were used in trading for these. The lanyards were magical devices. The secrets of their construction were so closely held that she imagined their village must be filled with all sorts of wonders. Each member of her party carried a pack filled with the goods their village had to trade. The heavy packs the adults wore were cumbersome, but the pack Alina wore was so light she barely noticed it.

On the journey, they slept by a waterfall, with some of the adults keeping watch. It was frightening not having the walls of a room around her, but eventually she slept, though not soundly. The arduous climb through the mountain pass was exhilarating, the terrain so new and foreign to her.

The TreeHands village was exciting. It was twice the size of hers, with a much larger central platform and something called a forge, which she found fascinating. The artisan who worked it showed her some of its magic and gave her a small bracelet made from a shiny substance she'd never seen. She thanked him repeatedly, cherishing it and playing with it on her wrist continually. Hurza made friends and introduced her, and they sat around talking about life in the trees.

On the way home, she was heartbroken when she noticed she'd lost the new bracelet she'd been given. It had likely become caught on a branch and pulled from her wrist. She chastised herself the entire trip back for not putting it away in her bag like her mother had advised.

Kani was waiting for them with a smile when they arrived. She was thrilled with the sweets they'd brought her and eager to hear their tale. Alina and Hurza recounted every detail of the trip, Kani hanging on their every word, so that it brought them joy to share it with her.

When she was thirteen, she developed feelings for Aras, one of the twins in the village. He had always been kind to her, and though he was that way with everyone, she came to imagine he had special feelings for her. That he was ten sun cycles older, she didn't see as an issue, and for the first time in her life, she saw herself as a mate and mother. She began acting as though they were walking together. Her friends tried to make her see reality, but she would not hear them, for she was certain of these feelings.

When Aras began to walk with Nyan a few moons later, she ignored it, telling herself it was no more than a friendship. When Nyan tried to speak to Alina one day, she imagined her jealous and ignored her words. So, when the *choosing* came, and Aras and Nyan were mated, she was unprepared. The blow was like none she had known before. Alina had believed she'd found what her friends spoke of so often, but which she'd never felt. She'd become so convinced of it that when her eyes were opened to the truth, she was inconsolable, though her friends did try. She felt foolish, her heart cast adrift, but more than this, she doubted the feelings others spoke of would ever be hers.

When she was fifteen, she began training for her *becoming*. These were the trials that would make her *of the tribe,* not just in the tribe. She trained with Kani and Hurza every day. Various adults took them through the trials, preparing them to meet these challenges. They were exhausted at the end of each day and often fell into bed after only a bite or two of the evening meal. And then each morning they rose to repeat the training until it became a part of them.

The *becoming* involved a *trial of the forest*, where they needed to spend a night alone on the forest floor, where many dangerous predators prowled. It also involved a *trial of the hunt*, which for girls involved capturing a mating pair of wild nuxat, which were extremely skittish and difficult to approach. They hunted the birds often with throwing stones, but capturing them was especially challenging. Finally, there was the *trial of the trees*, which involved a race through a course high up in the canopy with an adult chaser.

Of the three, the *trial of the forest* scared her most. She felt comfortable in the trees, having spent her life playing and running through them. And the adults who chased candidates in that trial sought only to make it exciting. Unless someone made a serious mistake, they would all return ahead of the chaser. Catching the nuxat might be a challenge, but they'd been watching flocks of the wild birds for several moon cycles and knew where several nested. The forest floor, however, was terrifying even in the day. To spend an entire day and night on the floor of the forest had put a stone in her stomach that no amount of training could dislodge.

When that trial came, she built a shelter on the forest floor with Hurza and Kani. They sharpened short sticks and planted them around the perimeter of the shelter, then placed thornweed all around it, their arms cut up and bloody from the work. They built a fire in the center of the shelter and awaited the night, having gathered enough wood to keep it burning throughout. They heard all manner of sounds, including the chilling screams of unfortunate creatures. Some of the creatures that approached their shelter were merely curious. A few stoda, the snout-faced creatures, came close, rooting in the nearby brush with their huge tusks while lodra, small furry animals, scurried by, their eyes red dots in the glow of the fire.

But as she stepped outside the shelter to relieve herself, she felt a presence at her shoulder. She turned to see a huge krax not ten paces from her. It was like a desert cat, but huge. Its fur was black as night with short white stripes along its spine, enormous fangs, claws like knives, and a long tail that whipped back and forth. It was the thing of every child's nightmares. She'd grown up with tales of these beasts killing even the fiercest of hunters. The beast fixed her with intense yellow-gold eyes. She froze, helpless, unable to speak, her friends within the shelter unaware of its presence. She stood so for many heartbeats, certain that death had come for her. Then, inexplicably, the creature turned away and melted into the forest.

She staggered to the shelter, shaking like a leaf in the winter wind. Her friends asked her what had happened, but she was still unable to speak. They pressed their bodies against her, holding her as she shook. They huddled like that together until the trial was over, and they could once again climb into the trees. She had nightmares of that krax for many nights afterward, her mother sitting up with her and rubbing her back until they receded.

The rest of the trials went smoothly. The ceremony of acceptance, accompanied by the ensuing feast, was one of the happiest moments in her life. She was now an adult and *of the tribe*. She reveled in the feeling and began helping her father with his medicine and taking on more of the responsibility of gathering food and preparing it. She enjoyed being part of the tribe and trying to find ways she could help others who were unable to do things for themselves. It was a happy transition in her life.

There was talk of her someday taking her mother's place. It would have been a big honor to care for the spirit of the tribe, but she did not have the *sight*. Her mother was a figure beyond measure in Alina's life. She could not imagine filling the space her mother occupied, so she paid this talk no mind. None of the plans others had for her future spoke to her heart.

There was talk that she and Aor would be wed. Aor would likely be the next chief, and some felt Alina, as the daughter of the village seer and healer, would be a *suitable* choice as a life partner. She bristled at the thought, certain Aor or Hedrick was responsible for starting these rumors. That others should decide such a thing for her was like rusna in her mouth.

Then one day, when she had seen seventeen sun cycles, a ball of fire passed through the sky above her while she was hunting. She followed the path of that ball to an egg, in which she found an injured creature that they brought back to their village. She spent time nursing the creature back to health. The creature had a kind face... The image of the face was jarring, at odds with Dashin's sense of self.

Dashin lost touch with the image and found himself floating again, his mind confused and adrift, his body exhausted. A soft hand brushed his forehead, removing the crease that had formed and flooding him with warmth. The tension within him eased, and moments later, sleep took him.

Chapter 13

Dashin rose up from the dark, his mind remade, fragile. The old self he'd always known was still present, but it was confused and uncertain. Next to it, something new dwelt, something not quite him, but not quite apart. He now had memories that were not his own, despite how real they felt.

The song that had served as an anchor for him now spoke of a momentous hunt that combined two tribes. The words were still foreign, but now their meaning percolated up from somewhere deep inside him. The more he listened to them, the easier the process became. He lay there listening to the song, reveling in the images it conjured within him. Somehow, he knew this song. He also knew that they were high above the ground in a tribe that called themselves the TreeKeepers. Other tribes like theirs lived in the trees all over the surface of Ndesa.

The world had one sun and one moon. The solar cycle took two hundred and fifty-six days, and the lunar cycle took thirty-two days. Each year began at FirstLight, the moment after the solar eclipse that occurred once each solar cycle. A feast was prepared with thanks given to the SkyGods over several days as the song of the tribe was sung.

He was sifting through his newfound trove of memories, wondering how such a change to his mind was possible, when he heard children speaking in the outer room. He could make out some of the words. The young boy was asking Rigin when Alina and the *not-man* would wake up. Rigin replied by telling him and his *part-sister* to eat their food while it was still soft. Dashin smiled at the familiarity. Children were apparently the same everywhere.

He opened his eyes. Marna stopped chanting and smiled down at him from the chair. The room was dimly lit, an oil lamp on the table painting one side of Marna's body in a warm glow. Outside, tree frogs croaked and insects chittered as the sky lightened toward morning. Enor was asleep on the chest at his feet, his slender body wedged into the corner and surrounded by his bags. Alina lay asleep on the mattress behind Marna.

"Welcome, Dashin," Marna said. She seemed tired but composed, rolling a shoulder as she spoke.

"It is good to be with you, Marna," he said, dredging up the formal greeting from somewhere deep within. He put his hands to his mouth, amazed at being able to speak in this language. Though the words came fully formed in his mind, they were crafted slowly in his mouth. His tongue struggled to make the soft, melodious sounds, unfamiliar with their shape and feel.

Her face went wide with a huge grin. "It is good to be with you, Dashin," she completed the formal response with a giggle.

Enor blinked open his eyes, yawned, stretched, and then, realizing Dashin had just spoken, he let out an excited squeak. Rigin hurried into the room.

"It is good to see all of you," Dashin said, beaming, giddy to be forming these words.

Rigin's eyes went wide, and she touched her fingertips to her forehead and grinned. The children tumbled into the room behind her, Solvan's shock of unruly hair appearing at Rigin's side with Matse peeking beyond the boy's shoulder.

Dashin looked over at Alina, lying motionless nearby, and it concerned him. He looked at Marna. "Is she...?"

Marna nodded. "Alina is fine. The *touching* can be difficult on those involved, even in normal times, and yours was long, the longest I have ever heard of. She may sleep for a time."

Dashin understood. Having just woken, he still felt exhausted. His mind felt sore in a way that was difficult to explain. It seemed like a muscle that had been overused and now ached.

"My mind is," he sought words to describe the feeling. "Not me entirely," was all he could manage.

Marna chuckled. "Yes, it takes some adjustment."

"You've done this?"

Marna shook her head. "Not this, but something similar."

It came to Dashin that she was a seer. Memories of things Alina had seen her mother do throughout her life sprang to mind. "Oh, you have the *sight*," he said, his tongue finding its way among the round sounds of Ndesan.

Marna nodded. "Yes, since I was a girl, near Matse's age." She smiled at the young girl, who beamed but ducked behind Solvan's shoulder.

"I was preparing food for the children. I could bring a tray in for all of you," Rigin offered. Seeing eagerness on their faces, she ducked back through the curtain. She called the children to join her, which they did reluctantly.

Dashin rubbed his scalp. He had a throbbing headache and nausea.

Marna handed him a cup of water. "Drink some water. It will help."

He took a long drink, and Enor shifted on the chest and began rummaging around in his bags, full of who knew what, until he pulled out a dried root. "Here, chew on this while you drink."

Dashin took it uncertainly. It was a dirty, crusty piece of wood. He gave it a tentative bite, forcing a smile for Enor as he did. He'd intended to give it a few chews to placate him and then put it aside, but after chewing on it a few times and swallowing a tiny bit of the juice, he felt a soothing flush throughout his body. Surprised, he chewed more vigorously. He sucked the juice, and the throbbing eased, though it left the taste of dirt in his mouth.

Marna laughed at his expression. "It doesn't look very appetizing, but it works wonders." She reached over and patted her husband's hand. He squeezed hers in return.

Rigin came into the room with a tray full of food. Dashin sat up and crossed his legs. Marna slipped onto the bed next to Enor, leaving a space in the center of the bed, upon which Rigin placed the tray. Rigin took the chair as the children knelt on the floor next to the bed.

"The food is delicious, Rigin. It is far better than that of my tribe." Dashin said, teaching his mouth to form the entire sentence. Rigin applauded his effort. He smiled, pleased with himself.

Alina slept soundly, undisturbed by the clamor in the room. Dashin watched the aliens as they ate, since this was the first meal he'd shared with them. He'd been tilting the dishes up to his mouth and pushing the food in with his fingers. He watched as each of them picked a salted leaf from a pile on the table. He'd tasted these leaves. They were fine, but he hadn't known what to do with them. Creating a small pocket in a leaf, they used it to pinch food from the dishes. They repeated the process along the leaf until they'd assembled a desired mixture. Rolling the leaf and tucking in the ends, they then bit into it.

Dashin imitated them. It took him a few tries to get the sense of it. Both Rigin and Marna helped him with the finer points of holding the leaf, making the pockets, and rolling it up without tearing it. Assembled this way, it was even more delicious, the various dishes melding together in his mouth mixed with the salty crunch of the banda leaves, the same leaf he wore on his arm.

Both Marna and Rigin made rolls for him to try, and he obliged them, exclaiming how each one was the best thing he'd eaten. The children laughed and giggled initially as he fumbled with his leaves, but slapped the bed enthusiastically when he managed his first. The slapping he knew was their equivalent of applause.

Dashin smiled at the boy grinning up at him.

The boy beamed even wider.

"He's our little corsol," Marna said, combing her fingers through his hair.

He giggled and mussed it back into a mess.

"Oh, what is that behind your ear?" Dashin asked, leaning forward to look.

Solvan reached up and ran a hand through his hair, not finding anything.

"No, not there," Dashin said, reaching forward and then plucking a large berry from behind Solvan's ear and popping it into his mouth. He chewed it, the sweet juice a bit tart on his tongue. Dashin had spent a lot of time alone as a child, and one of the things he'd done to amuse himself was to learn some basic sleight-of-hand. Nothing elaborate, but he was moderately good at making objects appear and disappear. He'd practiced with Ancaran coins, but apparently, the technique applied to berries, too.

Solvan exclaimed, running his hand through his hair and looking between the adults who were all looking at Dashin now, with concerned expressions.

Dashin chuckled. "Did you not see the berry behind that ear?" They looked at him, confused. "There's another next to it." He moved his open hand toward Solvan's head and plucked another berry from it.

Rigin reached up and touched her forehead with her fingertips, and Marna and Enor paled.

Dashin, seeing their discomfort, exclaimed, "Oh, it's just a trick." Dashin performed the motion for them slowly this time, showing them how the berry was manipulated in his hand.

The adults relaxed, laughing as he demonstrated.

"Do it again," Solvan squealed, leaning forward so Dashin could more easily reach his ear.

Dashin pulled another berry, and Solvan bounced in place, unable to contain his excitement. He turned and, cupping his hand, whispered excitedly into Matse's ear. The little girl grinned and nodded to him, her eyes sparkling.

Solvan asked Dashin to do it again and again, squealing each time he did, Matse's eyes wide next to him. When Dashin pulled a berry from behind Matse's ear, she put a hand to her mouth, and there was the tiniest of giggles.

"It's remarkable," Enor said. "When you do it quickly, it seems to appear in your hand. This is quite a skill. It must have taken time to master."

Dashin nodded. "Yes, I had time as a child to learn many things of doubtful value."

Rigin smiled at the children. "It seems the children believe it to be of great value."

Solvan kept saying how *round* this was. Dashin repeated the trick for them until there were no berries left on the tray.

Dashin thought perhaps he was misunderstanding the word. "Why is this *round*?" Dashin asked. "Is there another meaning to the word?"

Marna shrugged. "When we were children, all things of interest were *weighty*. These days they are *round*. I do not know why."

After urging the children to finish their meals, Rigin sent them out to play. Dawn had broken, and the sun was streaming horizontally through the branches outside the window.

Dashin watched them go, Solvan pounding across the floor with his odd gait, full of joy, Matse running close behind him.

"I believe you have made a friend," Marna said. "He'll be eager to tell the other children of his good fortune."

Dashin frowned, not understanding.

Marna smiled. "Did you not hear? You are *round*, Dashin. Very *round*. There is much talk of you beyond these walls. There will be many ears among his peers eager for news. It is not often that Solvan commands an audience. His peers have not always treated him kindly."

"That is sad," Dashin said, looking at the curtain where the children had disappeared.

Marna shrugged. "It is life in the trees. Life here can be hard. There is much peril, and facts must be faced. Children repeat what they hear or comment on what they see with little thought as to the effect. But, it is true that with limited mobility, he will not be able to face the *becoming*. He is destined to be in the tribe, but not *of the tribe*. I think he has resigned himself to it. He carries it well, but it must be difficult for him."

"What happened to him?"

"We do not know. He took a great fall in the forest. Enor came upon him, alone and unconscious. Whether something befell the others with him is not known. But Enor brought him here, and he has been with us since. Enor did what could for him, healing bruises and fractures, but the knee was damaged beyond what could be healed."

Dashin felt sad for the boy, though it was amazing how much joy that small body contained. "Does Matse speak?" Dashin asked.

"No, she was also found in the forest, some time before Solvan. Her parents were taken by a krax. Some of our villagers found her, and she hasn't spoken since she came to live with us."

"Do you have memories of the children?" Marna asked.

"I have fragments of memories, but there are many holes."

"You must give it time. If the *touching* is like the *seeing,* then new pathways must be formed within your mind. It will take some time for them to settle and for you to get used to them. Your command of language is impressive."

"Thank you," Dashin said, "though my tongue trips over making these sounds."

"Your speech is remarkably good, Dashin. Most Ndesans would understand you with only a little effort."

"Who is Sneva?" Dashin asked. He had a fragment of memory that this person was somehow linked to this room, a smiling and good-natured lad that Rigin doted on. Dashin did not want to put anyone out.

The others went quiet, and after a pause, Rigin answered. "Sneva was my son. He was killed during a hunt a few sun cycles ago."

"Oh, I'm sorry," Dashin said. "I didn't mean to... I'm sorry."

"It is fine. I'm glad to have someone in this room again. It was time."

They sat in silence for a few moments.

"Dashin, perhaps you could answer some questions?" Marna asked.

"Of course, anything," Dashin said.

"How was it that you came to be tied inside a stone egg within a ball of fire?"

The image of Alina running around the room with the egg a few days ago flashed into Dashin's mind. They were asking about the escape pod and its fiery entry into their atmosphere.

"I come from a place a long way from here. The egg you saw was a part of a home I journeyed in." Dashin used the words egg and home since this language had no words for escape pod or spaceship.

"Where is your tribe?" Enor asked.

"A very long way from here, up there among the GodLights, as you call them."

Rigin gasped, her fingers touching her forehead and her eyes misting. Marna and Enor both looked at each other, concern on their faces.

"The SkyGods sent you?" Marna asked, awed, her words a whisper.

Dashin shook his head. "No, my tribe was created a long time ago by your SkyGods, but no one that I know of has ever met them."

Marna let out a breath.

"Your tribe travels among the GodLights, and yet you have never met the SkyGods?" Enor asked, frowning.

Dashin sighed. How was he going to explain space, cosmic distances, other worlds, the makers, or his spaceship? The subject also seemed to make them all anxious. Something was going on he didn't understand.

"Are others chasing you? Will they be coming here looking for you?" Marna asked.

Ah, they were worried others might come. "No, I'm afraid not, those I was with were all lost in a great fire. I was the only one to survive. My tribe no doubt believes me lost as well. I am like Solvan in the forest. I took a great fall from my home. They believe me dead and will not come looking for me."

Enor sat back, relieved.

"What do you know of our tribe?" Marna asked.

Another confusing question. "I don't understand. Until I woke up a few days ago, I knew nothing of your tribe or any other tribe on your world."

"Why do you say your world?" Enor asked. "Is it not the world?"

Dashin shook his head. They hadn't grasped that he'd come from space or that other worlds such as this existed. He glanced at Alina, wondering if perhaps she might have more luck explaining things since she'd seen his world and his ship, but she was still fast asleep. "My tribe lives on another world, like your moon."

"How can that be? You would fall from the moon. There is no floor to stand on, it hangs suspended."

They imagined their world to be flat and not a planet. This was getting confusing. "Why did you ask if I knew of your tribe?" he asked Marna.

"I had a *sight* that you would be *important* to our tribe," she answered.

"You had a vision of me in your tribe?" Dashin asked. It seemed an oddly specific vision. Perhaps it was a nightmare occasioned by a strange being appearing in their village.

"Yes, I saw you as you were when you arrived in our village."

"You saw this before I arrived?" Dashin asked, certain he'd misunderstood.

Marna nodded.

Perhaps reports of his arrival had reached her before they carried him back, and she'd formed some mental picture before he arrived?

"She saw your arrival when she was still a girl," Enor said, holding his eyes.

"It was over thirty sun cycles ago," Marna confirmed.

This stopped him. He had no explanation for this. He didn't have to calculate the relative lengths of solar years between Ancara and Ndesa. "How can that be? I would not yet have been born."

"I have no idea, Dashin. It is the strangest *sight* I have ever had, and it stayed with me all these sun cycles. I have always associated great *importance* with this vision."

Outside, the tribe was awake and active. Through the open window, they heard adults discussing the day's chores. Children raced by, shrill screams echoed as they played, receding as they drew away.

Dashin shrugged. "Until yesterday, I had no idea that *touching* was possible. So, today I find that I'm open to things I might have dismissed yesterday. Perhaps, this will make sense in time."

"That is the issue," Enor said, "we may not have much time left."

Chapter 14

Alina stirred and groaned. Her head pounded. She was unsure of where she was or who she was. Fragments of another were scattered about within her.

Her pulse quickened as she feared that she was lost, her mind adrift. She felt a hand on her shoulder, and warmth flowed into her. She blinked her eyes open and saw both her parents above her, her mother smiling, with a hand on her shoulder, and her father, his fingers on her wrist, sensing the pulsing of her heart.

He offered her a stick of valagy root. Her mother took it and, using her knife, peeled it before handing it to her. She bit down on the bitter root and sucked at the liquid. She closed her eyes, waiting for the effect to suffuse through her, and sighed as it did.

When she opened her eyes, her mother offered her a cup of water. She sat up and drank from it as Rigin hurried in with a tray laden with food. As the headache transitioned from nauseating to insistent, she realized she was famished.

She glanced over at Dashin, who was sitting on the bed looking at her. She flushed. Her mother moved into her line of sight, blocking him from her view. "Eat first," she urged.

Alina nodded as the tray was put before her. She quickly stuffed a banda leaf with bits of dried meat and fruit and bit into it. She devoured half the tray before the mental fog lifted.

Looking up from the tray, Alina voiced her concern for the state of her mind.

"Give it time," her mother said, patting her hand. "It will take time for these new memories to make a home."

Alina studied her mother's face, wondering how she could know this.

"It will be fine, truly. It is this way with the *seeing* too."

Her mother's words eased her mounting panic. She exhaled, her mind sluggish as memory fragments swirled within her. It had been an intense experience, and at times she'd feared losing herself in the strangeness of it. Had her mother not been there, she feared she would have been lost to it. She tried to sift through the memory fragments to find the answers they sought, but there were so many, most of them with aspects too confusing to understand.

"Give it time," her mother repeated, seeing the clouds on her face.

Alina peered around her mother at Dashin, who was still staring. She pulled back and shivered.

"I think the two of you should speak," her mother said. "It may help settle your minds."

The thought of speaking to Dashin mortified her. He'd seen parts of her she'd never shared. As intense as the *touching* had been with Kani, it was nothing compared to what she'd just experienced with Dashin. She felt naked and exposed.

Then she realized what her mother had just said. "He's speaking?" she whispered, leaning in.

Her mother smiled. "Yes, quite well too. We had a nice conversation over our morning meal."

"Did we learn what we needed?" she whispered.

"Not yet. Some of what he said was confusing. I was hoping you could make better sense of it."

Alina nodded. So many of the things she'd seen were unimaginable. It would be difficult enough for her to describe and impossible, she imagined, for Dashin.

"I know the thought of speaking is uncomfortable," her mother said.

"I can't speak of these things with everyone else here," she whispered. Her face flushed as she imagined having to discuss private things while others watched.

"Of course, we will leave. Call us when you're done."

Alina nodded. She turned her attention to the rest of her meal, pointedly ignoring Dashin. Her mother rose and had to pull up her father, who was asking why they couldn't stay. She felt her face flush. Her mother insisted, and her father relented, grabbing his bags and continuing to protest as they left.

Once they were gone and the hut had grown quiet, she pushed the tray away from her, gathering her reserves to speak.

"Did you see any sand?" Dashin said, grinning awkwardly.

His words caught her by surprise. They were ill-formed, but Ndesan. She gaped at him, amazed. He shifted, his face flushed, apparently as uncomfortable as she was. And yet he'd sought to put her at ease.

She couldn't help it, but a laugh bubbled up within her. "So much sand," she said, smiling gratefully.

"We don't have to speak of the personal things. They are raw for me, too. Perhaps we can put them aside?"

She nodded, biting her lip to contain her relief.

"I tried to explain where I was from to your parents. I could not make them understand."

Alina nodded. "Had I not seen it, I could not have imagined it. It was a wonder to behold. But there was so much loneliness among all those people."

Dashin's face fell as though she'd struck him. He looked away. Without thinking, she'd hurt him and spoken that which was personal despite their agreement.

She felt terrible. "Dashin, I'm sorry," she said. But he did not respond. She went to him, sat down next to him on the bed, and placed her hand on his knee. "Dashin," she said, waiting. He turned, his eyes tentative.

She held his gaze. "I'm sorry, Dashin. I should not have said that. I spoke without thinking. I have seen your heart and was touched by the person you became, given the world you came from."

She saw a glimmer of relief in his eyes. She nodded. "The *touching* has always terrified me. It's a gift that I've avoided, and I was frightened of attempting this with you, not knowing the shape of your heart and what this contact would do to me. But it wasn't..." her words trailed off, her feelings at the moment like leaves in the wind.

"It was amazing for me too, Alina," he said, meeting her eyes. "I've never experienced anything that compares. You're right. I was lonely." Alina went to apologize, but he continued. "And finding myself here on this world alone, unable to communicate, I was disheartened. But, by doing this selfless thing for me, you've transformed me."

Alina shifted on the bed next to him. "It wasn't completely selfless."

Dashin frowned.

"The previous chief of our tribe is gathering support to have you sent from the tribe."

Dashin's mind brought up shards of memories regarding Hedrick, his intransigence, and the mysteries surrounding the man. "Why would he do that?"

Alina shrugged. "He has always been protective of his place and his family's within the tribe. He must feel threatened by your presence."

"Threatened by me? I was near death a few days ago. I know nothing of your world. How could I be a threat?"

Alina smiled at him. "You arrived from the sky wrapped in a ball of fire."

"Oh, well, there's that," Dashin smiled. "Maybe I could explain it to him?"

"Explain what? That you are from another world among the GodLights, where people in your tribe fly through the sky in balls of fire and command immense power? You think that will help?"

"If you put it that way, perhaps not," Dashin sighed.

They sat for a moment, Dashin's memories still fluttering around in her mind.

"I'm sorry you lost your tribe, Dashin. It was a terrifying memory, the destruction of your home, and a wonder you survived it."

"Thank you," he said, his eyes misting. "It was a close thing getting out alive, and were it not for you, I would have perished in the forest."

They sat in silence for a time. Outside, the birds sang their morning songs, urging villagers to see to their chores, as her father liked to say.

"Your mother stated she saw me here when she was a child," Dashin said. "Is that possible? Could she be mistaken?"

"She has been known to misinterpret the things she sees, but I have not known her visions to fail her."

Dashin nodded. "That is the memory I have of her, too."

"This is so odd. I know the memory you have of her is mine."

"It is odd and yet kind of wonderful. I feel as though I know you in a way I've not known another."

Alina blushed.

Dashin stammered. "I don't mean that I know private things. Well, we both know... I mean that I have a deeper sense of who you are than I have of anyone else before. It's like gaining a lifelong friend overnight."

Alina smiled, her face brightening. "Yes, it's as though we grew up together. And, in a way, we did."

The memories of her life and her regard for others were still fresh in his mind. "You are a remarkable young woman, Alina," he said, his words tumbling from his lips.

Alina shifted on the bed, uncomfortable with this turn in the conversation. Even though they'd shared this intense connection, he was a stranger to their world. He might have some of her memories, but he hadn't lived them. He had never truly lived among them. She had no illusions that, simply because she had memories of travelling among the GodLights, she was prepared to do so.

"I have my faults like everyone," she said.

"Yes, I didn't mean... I'm sorry, I spoke without thinking."

They were silent for a time.

"What are we going to do?" Dashin asked.

"*We*? What *we*?" Alina replied, a smile on her lips.

Dashin felt a knot form in his stomach. Of course. He wasn't her problem. She'd already saved him once, then risked herself again with the *touching*. Feeling ungrateful, he chided himself for presuming she owed him anything.

Alina burst out laughing. "That is an adorable face."

Dashin looked at her, confused.

"Of course, we will do what we can. I was teasing."

He shook his head and smiled. "That was mean."

She crinkled her eyes. "I'm not the perfect person you imagined."

"I see that I was mistaken," he responded.

"Hey," she said, punching his arm. Her fist glanced off his bandaged burn.

He squealed in pain, folding over it, clutching it as he rocked and moaned.

Alina leapt forward, apologizing and trying to pry his hand away from it to check the damage. Why did she always act so rashly? He'd been near death a few days ago, and his body was still fragile.

Dashin started laughing. She punched him again.

Her parents and Rigin joined them when Alina called for them. She tried to explain the concept of other worlds among the GodLights. She told them that their world was round like the moon. She tried to explain that the GodLights were like their sun, but seen from a great distance, and so appeared tiny.

Dashin sat there smiling as she struggled to answer their questions and explain these concepts. He'd told her he'd tried without success, but she'd believed she could make them understand. And now he was sitting there smugly. She wanted to punch him again.

"I don't think trying to explain where I'm from will help," Dashin suggested. "I think the villagers will become confused, and they won't hear what else there is to say."

"How do we explain where you're from?" Alina asked.

"Can we just say I'm from a tribe a long way from here? That is the case."

"What about the ball of fire and the egg?" Alina asked.

"Could we say that for my tribe, these eggs are like your lanyards?"

"That's ridiculous," her father said.

"More so than flying here from the GodLights?" Dashin asked.

Her father frowned. "Perhaps not."

"You're certain no one will come looking for you?" her mother asked.

Dashin nodded. "A piece of my egg was damaged when my home was destroyed. It was the thing that would tell others where I am. Without it, they will be unable to find me and will assume I perished with the others. And, since the egg was damaged, there is no way for me to use it to return."

"Do you think this will convince Hedrick to let Dashin stay?" Alina asked.

She shook her head. "I don't believe so."

"What more can we offer?" Alina asked.

"Have him stand for the *becoming*," Rigin said. They all turned to her. She shrugged. "If he stands for the *becoming*, they cannot banish him until after the trials."

"But the *becoming* is not for another five moons," Alina said.

"Yes," Rigin agreed, her shoulders falling. "They will send him away until that moon."

"Why can't I go live in the forest for a few moons?" Dashin asked.

Her father shook his head. "The forest is treacherous. Even those who grew up in it would find it difficult to survive alone, even for a few days. A few moons would be impossible without others to share the load."

Dashin sat back, and Alina could see the hope draining from him. There had to be a way to save him. A few days ago, she had no concept of the man before her, and yet today it was as though she'd always known him, as familiar to her as Kani or Hurza. In a way she didn't understand, he felt even closer. She could not let him be sent away to his death.

"What if Dashin stands this next moon?" Alina said without thinking.

"There is no hunt until the official *becoming* five lunar cycles from now," her father replied, "and there would be no other candidates to help with the trial of the forest. Even if he trained for the next five months, he might not survive the *becoming*. Alone and without an organized hunt, such a thing is impossible."

Her father was right. It was a ridiculous idea. Alina's heart pounded in her chest. There had to be some other way. Dashin put his hand on hers, his touch gentle, reassuring. She felt the panic recede, though she could not meet his eyes.

"But if Marna saw him..." Rigin pressed.

Her mother opened her mouth to object, but no words came.

"He cannot walk and has no knowledge of the trees," her father said. "How can we be considering such a thing?"

"I also feel that Dashin was sent here," Rigin said.

"You had a vision too?" her father asked, rubbing his scraggly beard.

"No, nothing like that," Rigin answered, looking down, embarrassed. "I have not the gift," her words trailed off, "but I had a feeling when Dashin arrived. I cannot explain it. It was as though a familiar wind blew through me."

"A what?" her father asked.

Rigin blushed, "I do not have other words for it."

"Where are we in the moon cycle?" her father asked.

"Twenty-eight days, till the new moon," Rigin offered.

Her father shook his head. "We're discussing whether Dashin here, who could not walk to the cleansing hut without me carrying him, will stand the trials in twenty-eight days. Is that what we're proposing?"

Alina looked at Dashin and bit her lip.

Chapter 15

"You don't expect us to believe this ridiculous tale?" Hedrick spat.

"I'm afraid it's all we have," Enor said. "Dashin was injured when his tribe was destroyed. He does not remember anything of his travel before awakening here in our village."

"Where is this mysterious tribe?" Hedrick asked, "I've never seen such as he or of these mysterious eggs, and I've traveled far."

"How could he know such a thing? His village was burned, and he was unconscious within the egg when he was found."

Dashin cringed but tried to keep his emotions from touching his face. It was a ridiculous story, but one Enor told remarkably well. Given his outward demeanor, Dashin saw that it would be easy to underestimate the keen mind within.

Hedrick had taken over the questioning as Enor told his story. He'd asked his son's permission but hadn't awaited approval. As the tale drew on, Hedrick seemed to be at a loss as to how to proceed. Dashin, fleeing the destruction of his village, hadn't played into Hedrick's plans.

"You say the creature speaks our language?" Hedrick said.

"Yes, after a fashion, though his words have an odd sound. It must be that his village is a long way from here."

The villagers watched the exchange, their eyes darting between the speakers and Dashin. The entire village was gathered on the communal platform. Short tables were spread about with everyone seated on the platform for the evening meal. Dashin had arrived with Marna, Enor, and Alina once the villagers were done eating.

Dashin had found the walk from the hut to the platform treacherous. He'd leaned heavily on Enor, wondering how these people moved so easily with the constant swaying of the world beneath their feet. He'd been relieved to finally sit, although since he was a full head shorter than most adults, he found he couldn't see above the heads of those around him. Alina had fetched him a stool like the ones the children used. His face had flushed as chuckles rippled through the crowd.

The tension was palpable, Hedrick's words hard and harsh. He clearly didn't believe the story, and Dashin couldn't fault him. Hedrick peppered Enor with probing questions once Enor finished the tale they'd decided on. But Enor had sounded so disarming that it seemed most villagers took it as fact.

"Enor says you speak our language?" Hedrick said, addressing Dashin.

"Yes, I do," Dashin answered.

There was a collective gasp from the assembled.

"Can you share the tale of how you came to be with us?" Hedrick asked.

"It's as Enor has described."

"Yes, we've heard it from Enor," Hedrick griped, waving his hand dismissively, "but it would be helpful to hear it from you."

"There was a great fire in my village that took all the others in my tribe. I was bruised and burned and barely made it to one of the eggs we use for travel. The egg had just begun its flight when I lost consciousness. I woke here in your village."

"We heard that on waking, you didn't speak our language and were making odd grunting sounds instead."

Dashin swallowed. "Yes, our language is different. Alina *touched* my mind and helped me see the shape of yours."

The village gasped, and all eyes turned to Alina. He could see her color darken, though she did not move or look away.

Hedrick screwed up his face. It was clear he didn't like how this was going. Dashin imagined that having Marna's earlier words coupled with Alina's *touch* would make it more difficult for Hedrick to discount the story.

"Why was Marna singing our song then?"

"She was setting the way for Alina," Dashin said. "The *touching* was difficult. Our tribes have different songs. Yours is one to be proud of."

A round of appreciative murmurs arose, some of the villagers nodding and looking more sympathetic than they'd been moments before.

Hedrick looked around, frowning, his lips tight. He must have also sensed the change. "It is indeed an odd and unbelievable tale. It seems you were very lucky to survive."

"Yes, I was fortunate that your people found me and nursed me back to health. Without you, I would surely have perished," Dashin said, looking to Alina, Marna, and Enor as he spoke.

"It is unfortunate that you will not be able to remain with us," Hedrick announced, shaking his head as though he regretted saying it.

A wave of anxious whispers rippled through the village.

"You would turn him out into the forest like this?" Enor pled. Though Dashin had been told it was likely that Hedrick would press to have Dashin sent from them, it was still a shock to hear the words. The thought of being alone again, especially in the forest, where death was all but certain, was devastating. He glanced over at Alina. Her face was drawn, her fingers balled up into fists.

"Oh, not I," Hedrick said, "certainly the chief would have to decide this." He motioned to his son.

Fodrick looked as though he had bitten into something unpleasant, something he dared not spit out in front of guests.

"It is clear that this is not a TreePerson. He cannot even keep his feet. We are a small tribe. Those who join must earn their place. We do not have the luxury of providing for someone who is not *of the tribe*."

The village had gone quiet. Dashin had fragments of Alina's memories where similar meetings had turned away abler candidates. He'd been aware that this was tonight's goal for Hedrick, but it didn't make the words any easier to hear. Hedrick turned to his son, sitting next to him.

Fodrick shifted in his seat. "What Hedrick said is so. We are too small a village to care for an adult who cannot care for himself. It is sad that after this ordeal, we should have to turn him away."

Hedrick waited for his son to say more, but Fodrick stopped there. Hedrick frowned and picked up the thread. "It is as I suspected and, as I said, unfortunate. Life in the trees is hard," he noted, a phrase Dashin knew to be a common affirmation here. "It is a difficult decision," Hedrick concluded, "but we've had to make them in the past, and we'll have to make them in the future. Unfortunately, it is the way of things."

Marna stood up. "I call for Dashin to stand for the *becoming*." Marna had remained silent throughout, even as folks turned to her while the tale was being told. Now her words confused the villagers. Loud muttering arose, and Hedrick raised his hand to still the village.

"Marna, the *becoming* is not for many moons," Hedrick said, "we have not even decided who will stand this sun cycle."

"I understand," Marna replied.

"He could, of course, return to stand for it at that time," Hedrick added, explaining what everyone in the village already knew, a wary look on his face as he did so.

"I would have Dashin stand this coming moon," Marna corrected.

The village went quiet. All eyes turned to Hedrick, who was speechless. Dashin could see him trying to work out what she intended. Deep furrows gathered on his brow as he looked off into the trees. Finally, he turned back to Marna and shrugged. "You are aware that there is no hunt scheduled and that this would mean that he'd be alone for all the trials." It wasn't a question. As a villager, she would be aware of this.

Marna nodded.

Hedrick sighed. "Even though this has not occurred in our tribe for many generations, such a request is your right. But to stand for the *becoming* still requires three families to endorse him, and the three of you," he indicated, Enor, Marna, and Alina, "are only a single vote on this."

"I ask that Dashin stand for the *becoming* as well," Rigin blurted, standing up. Heads turned to see her standing there, a woman Dashin knew most pitied for her lot in life.

"This is still only two votes," Hedrick huffed. "I'm sorry, this is not sufficient."

"I ask that Dashin stand for the *becoming*," Hurza and Kani both said, nearly together, as they got to their feet.

Dashin had no idea if this had been arranged in advance. He didn't remember Alina stepping out to do so, but there'd been so much discussion and activity getting ready for this that she might have. He glanced at Alina. Her face held a mixture of emotions he could not place.

Hedrick's mouth hung open as though he might respond, but no sounds came out.

Fodrick stood. "Marna, it seems your request is endorsed, but I want to make sure the candidate understands what he's asking."

Marna nodded, and everyone but Fodrick sat.

Fodrick hesitated and leaned down to his wife, Milena. They exchanged a few words before he stood and cleared his throat. "Da-shin," he said, drawing out the name, "these trials are intended to test TreeFolk. We spend our youth training for these trials. These trials are dangerous. Candidates die on occasion. In your case, it seems likely. Is this something you truly want?"

Dashin nodded, grateful for Fodrick's tone. From the memories, he seemed a decent man, though he lived in the shadow of his father. He wondered at the immense scar that ran from one hip to the opposite shoulder, a sliver of which was just visible at the neck of his tunic. Alina had a memory of it, having seen it as a child. She had never learned the story of it. Whatever had caused it had occurred before Fodrick arrived in their village.

"Did you understand my words?" Fodrick said, concerned at Dashin's pause.

"Yes, I would stand for the *becoming*," Dashin replied formally.

Fodrick nodded, a sad expression on his face. "The trials will end on the new moon. To be considered *of the tribe*, you must complete all three trials before then."

"I understand," Dashin replied.

"I'm not certain you do," Fodrick said, "but it is done regardless. Good luck, young man, though I fear you will need more than luck."

Fodrick sat down, and the platform erupted in conversation. Dashin felt the stares and glances and squirmed under the scrutiny. Now that it was done, or at least now that it had started, he was tired. This evening, on the heels of the *touching,* caught up with him. He felt himself nodding off.

Alina touched his elbow. "Dashin, let's get you back to the room."

Alina guided Dashin to the bed. His body, not yet recovered from the trauma of his escape, was exhausted. He leaned against her as she sat him down on the bed, exhaling as she did.

"This brings back memories of helping Aor carry you up from the egg," she said, plopping down on the chair.

Solvan came clomping in, beaming from ear to ear. "You get to stay with us," he exclaimed, Matse peeking out from behind his shoulder.

"Looks like you'll be stuck with me for a while," Dashin said, giving the lad a tired grin.

"I can show you all my favorite spots," he offered.

"There won't be time for that, I'm afraid," Marna said, pushing the curtain aside and stepping into the room. Enor and Rigin followed her in.

"We only have a handful of days," Marna stated, "and I'm afraid Dashin's training will fall upon you, Alina." Dashin felt Alina squirm next to him. "I've had odd and disturbing visions lately, and I fear that Dashin's arrival is tied to them somehow. I must seek answers in the seer cave and seek counsel from Karita. Both of these tasks will take time, but regardless of what I find, trust that I will be back in time for your *becoming*."

Dashin had a vague memory of Karita, an older seer in the tribe Alina had traveled to as a young girl. But the thought of losing one of the few friends he had here made him anxious. Marna reached over and squeezed his shoulder, smiling at him as she did so.

Enor knelt next to him and opened one of his ever-present bags. "Let me see to your feet. If you are to start training, you will need them."

"Thank you," Dashin said, sighing as the Enor applied cool balm to the soles of his feet and wrapped them in banda leaves.

Dashin glanced at Alina. She'd grown quite pale and had a strained expression. It seemed as though she'd just glimpsed something terrifying and could not shake the image.

"Can it be that hard?" Dashin asked.

Alina gave a strained laugh that didn't hide the fact she was on the verge of bursting into tears.

Chapter 16

Alina sat at the wooden table in the hut she shared with her parents. The moon dipped into the forest, having finished its nightly trek. It would soon be light, but the morning birds still dreamt of fat grubs. The GodLights cast a faint glow through the doorway into the room. Her mother sat across from her, a travel pack and lanyards on the floor next to her. Both had cups of cool tea before them. From her parents' room came the soft rumble of her father's snoring, a sound she found as soothing as a warm blanket during the rainy season.

"Must you go now?" Alina asked.

"I'm sorry to leave you with this daughter. I do not understand it, but I feel compelled to seek answers."

Alina sighed. Her mother was going to the cave seers in their tribe used to seek visions. Her mother had taken her there once when they passed near it during a trading trip. It had seemed a magical place at the time. At midday, light entered through a hole in the cave's dome and reflected off the crystal facets in the walls. It had made her mother's gift seem all the more wondrous. Her mother had assured her that untold hours spent seated in a damp cave chasing elusive visions was not as exciting an adventure as she imagined. The cave, her mother had explained, amplified and focused the *sight*. Things could sometimes be seen here that could not be seen elsewhere.

Her father snorted and shifted on the bed in the bedroom. The rumble of his snoring became the full-throated roar of an angry stoda. Alina's mother leaned back into the doorway of their room. "Amani," she said softly. The snoring stopped immediately. Her father shifted again, and the soft rumble resumed.

"It did not sound as though he woke, and yet he heard you with all that noise."

Her mother shrugged. "We've been mated for many sun cycles and have learned each other's rhythms."

"But he didn't wake."

"No, nor will he remember my calling to him in the morning."

Though she should have been used to her parents' relationship by now, she found herself still regularly surprised by little things she had never noticed before. "You will seek Karita?"

"Yes, she may have answers," her mother said, taking a sip of tea.

"If she has answers, could your trip be shortened?"

"Perhaps," her mother answered, but Alina could see the truth in her eyes.

"I don't know if I can do this thing," Alina managed, her eyes on the cup before her.

Her mother reached across, took her hand, and waited until Alina met her eyes. "I wish there were another way to do this. Your father rarely uses his lanyards, and he can become preoccupied. Rigin's days of training youth are far behind her, nor could we ask such a thing of her were it not. And, with me gone, I cannot think of another."

"You're right, I can't think of anyone else either. It's just that it..." Alina's words trailed off, unable to finish the thought.

"It's that you do not believe such a thing is possible?"

Alina looked up, shocked.

Her mother was smiling. "I cannot believe such a thing is possible either," she admitted. "And, yet..."

Alina probed her mother's face. "Yet, you believe somehow this will come to be."

Her mother nodded and then shrugged. "Yes, though I cannot explain how."

Alina sighed, gathering herself. If her mother believed that this might be possible, then she would have to trust that it would somehow be. She tried to chase away the doubt, telling herself they would find a way. "I will do all I can."

"I know you will," her mother said, squeezing her hand. "Your father and I have always been proud of you, but never more so than in these past days."

Her mother's eyes misted, and it was all Alina could do not to break into tears. Her mother patted her hand and stood. She slipped the pack onto her back, cinched the shoulder straps, and secured the chest strap. Moving her arms, she twisted one way and then the other to ensure she had a reasonable range of motion. She made a few minor adjustments to the straps before slipping her lanyards over her forearms and securing them.

She leaned in and touched her forehead to Alina's, the warmth of her mother's regard flowing through her. Alina reciprocated, letting her mother know she would do everything she could in her absence.

Her mother smiled one last time and then slipped through the door, her footsteps light on the bridge and then in the trees beyond. Within moments, Alina could no longer hear them amid the rumble of her father's sleep.

Alina hurried to Rigin's hut. If they were going to be ready in less than a moon, there was no time to waste. She crept into Dashin's room, his form dimly lit through the window. He tossed fitfully on the bed as he mumbled in the language of his tribe. Alina imagined he must be reliving the terrible events of the destruction of his SkyHome. She sat next to him and placed a hand on his shoulder.

He flinched, pulling away, his eyes wide, unfocused, his breathing short and ragged. "Dashin," she whispered, her fingertips finding his knee, "it's me, Alina."

His eyes found her. His breathing eased as he blinked and took a breath. She waited for his face to lose its tension. He gave her a weak smile and rubbed his face with his good hand. Alina peeled the blanket off him and checked his feet in the dim light. His skin had absorbed the balm, the thick banda leaves drying into a fibrous skin.

She turned to him. "Dashin, come with me," she whispered, rising from the bed and stealing from the room. She waited for him on the platform outside the hut, watching as he moved through the common room, a hand on the counter to keep his balance as he made his way to her.

She helped him cross the bridges to the central platform, his arm heavy on hers as she led the way. The sun kissed the upper branches of the canopy. A few birds stirred and announced the coming day.

"We have little time before the new moon," Alina said, "we'll be training long days." She watched his eyes to make sure he was hearing her. When he nodded, she asked him to walk across the platform. The tables they used for the evening meal had been stowed, so it was clear, which made it ideal for him to practice keeping his feet. He was unsteady, but made it across.

His legs were like those of an infant, tottering and unsteady beneath his body. "Do not stand so tall," she corrected, quietly so as not to wake the villagers. She bade him cross again. "Bend your knees more. Let them absorb the motion."

Her suggestions helped, but he seemed unable to feel the trees. She had him walk back and forth as the forest woke with a chorus of birds and the village stirred.

People made their way to the communal kitchen to get a bite to start the day. Most of them stopped to watch Dashin. Alina tried to ignore the expressions of disbelief and the inquisitive stares as she continued to direct him.

Rigin came over with two thick slabs of nutbread. "Perhaps the platform in the grove is smoother," she said, handing her the bread.

Alina frowned. The platform in the grove was rougher than this one. But Rigin kept her eyes, and it dawned on her that the grove would be much more private. She smiled at Rigin and thanked her, guiding Dashin toward the bridge to the grove. Solvan and Matse pounded up behind them, but Rigin called to them, saying something about chores, eliciting an exaggerated groan from Solvan. Alina chuckled.

Dashin's body tensed as they stepped onto the bridge, the morning light making the forest beneath visible now. He stumbled and almost fell, dragging her to him. "Look straight ahead, Dashin," she barked. His head snapped up. After a moment, he took a tentative step, then another, until they reached the grove.

Once they reached it, she led them to a bench and handed him one of the slabs of nutbread. He thanked her, distracted, his eyes taking in the grove and their vertical farm.

"This is beautiful. You grow all your food here?"

"Not all of it. Some of it we gather from the forest, and twice every sun cycle the men hunt stoda."

"Stoda. Those are the creatures with tusks?"

"Yes. They are large, hoofed creatures that live on the forest floor. They eat roots and plants. They are fearsome creatures, though they provide much of the meat that sustains us."

They chewed their slabs of nutbread, the fruit within adding delicious pops of flavor to the hearty fare.

"I have some of your memories from your *becoming*. There are three trials, correct?"

Alina nodded, chewing. She swallowed. "Yes, *the trial of the hunt, the trial of the forest,* and *the trial of the trees.*"

"The hunting involves netting birds. That doesn't seem too hard."

Alina bristled. "It involves netting a mated pair of nuxat. I assure you it is more difficult than you think."

"I'm sorry, I didn't mean to imply..."

She shook her head. "No matter, that is the hunt for women. The trial for men is different." The scope of the task overwhelmed her in the moment, and she had to take a breath. "Let's continue working on walking. We can chat about the trials later."

Dashin got up and stumbled back and forth across the platform some more. He was managing it when the swaying was regular, but even mild gusts took his feet out from under him.

"You can't think your way through it," Alina explained, "you have to let yourself feel the motion and get your body to respond without thinking."

"How do I do that?" Dashin griped, picking himself off the platform.

Alina opened her mouth to reply, but realized she didn't have an answer. TreeFolk grew up in the trees. They learned this without having to be taught.

"Have him close his eyes," Hurza said from behind her. Hurza and Kani had just stepped onto the platform from the bridge, large, empty baskets under their arms with which to gather vegetables.

Alina turned to her friends. Hurza went on. "When Regra took that fall and injured his ear, he had to learn to walk again. He told me the thing which helped him the most was walking with his eyes closed to allow his body to feel the motion."

The girls put down their baskets and perched on the bench next to Alina. Alina vaguely remembered Hurza's cousin, Regra, and the incident in question. He'd smacked his head on a branch obscured by foliage while using his lanyards. Stunned, he'd fallen a long way through the trees. Fractured bones and bruises had healed, but the blow to the head had taken the hearing in one ear and damaged his balance. It had taken him time to learn to move normally again.

"Try it with your eyes closed," Hurza suggested. Dashin looked to Alina, who shrugged. He closed his eyes and teetered and stumbled as he walked. He opened his eyes, exasperated.

"Keep doing it," Hurza said.

He kept at it. Alina shook her head as he wove and fell repeatedly. She was about to tell him to stop when his body sensed the motion of a gust, and he took a step to correct for it. It was a tiny gesture, but Hurza nudged her shoulder, grinning.

"That's it. Keep doing it," Hurza yelled, leaning forward.

"Listen to the wind," Kani suggested.

Of course, Alina thought. She'd forgotten that detail, the notion being so ingrained within her she'd failed to mention it.

Dashin opened his eyes, confused.

Kani explained, "If you listen, you can hear the changes in the wind as it rustles through the leaves. You can sense its progress through the trees and anticipate it. Just stand for a moment and listen." They waited, listening. A few moments later, the rustling changed subtly. "There, do you hear the breeze changing? Here it comes. Getting closer. Now," Kani said. The platform swayed as the breeze arrived.

Dashin's eyes grew wide. "Oh, that's great, thanks," he said, closing his eyes. He leaned forward, turning his head back and forth, gauging the sounds as he walked across the platform.

"Bend your knees more," Alina suggested, "let your knees absorb the motion." He made it all the way across, Hurza warning him when to open his eyes as he reached the edge of the platform. They were all overjoyed and laughing when Aor strode up with Drur and Gamoc.

"I don't see what there is to celebrate. Even infants manage that," Aor sniggered. Gamoc giggled. The boys had their packs on, lined with the waxed bags they used to gather borka.

Alina set her jaw. She felt her face flush and was about to lash out when Hurza beat her to it.

"I recall a lot of sniveling when Fodrick showed you how to fall," Hurza snapped.

Aor's body tensed, and his face darkened. The other two boys went quiet as the air grew electric. Aor had a rare but fearsome temper. Hurza shrank back toward Alina but continued to face him. The moment stretched on until Aor turned and strode across the platform and onto the far bridge. The other two boys hurried along after him.

Dashin turned to watch them as a gust sent him sprawling.

"That was not wise," Alina whispered to her friend.

"I know," Hurza replied, "I couldn't help it. He was standing there so smug, and it just came out." She tried to laugh it off. "Oh, I'll just crinkle my eyes at him the next time I see him. He'll forget all about it."

Kani shook her head. "That may not always work."

Hurza shrugged. "It's worked so far. Anyway, who else is going to choose him?"

Alina felt the blow, her friend's words exposing the uncertainty within. She had often shared her misgivings and ambivalence toward Aor with her friends, yet she had never said she would not choose him.

Hurza reached for her shoulder. "Oh, Alina, I'm sorry. I did not mean to. It's my mouth. You know me. I always speak nonsense without thinking."

Alina waved it away. Hurza opened her mouth to add something, but no words came.

"You're doing better," Kani said, speaking to Dashin. "How does it feel?"

Alina felt the tension ebb between them, Kani having found a way to ease it.

"It feels better," Dashin replied.

"We should use twine like we do for the children," Kani proposed.

"Yes," Alina agreed, "that's a great idea."

"You might want to do that on the village platform," Hurza suggested. "It's approaching midday."

Alina was confused for a moment until she realized Hedrick would soon be meeting with his group of followers here in the grove. She certainly didn't want to continue training with them looking over her shoulder and making comments or scoffing at their efforts.

She thanked her friends as they picked up their baskets.

Chapter 17

Dashin and Alina sat on a corner of the platform, eating their midday meal as the rest of the village went about their day. Solvan tried to join them, but Rigin called him away. The boy pretended he hadn't heard, but when Rigin called a second time, with an unmistakable tone in her voice, he relented and left, grumbling.

Dashin woke in a sweat this morning, having spent the night stumbling through the ship looking for his crewmates. So, it was a relief when Alina pulled him from bed. Over the past few days, his body had recovered much of its strength. Though the burn on his arm was still tender and the soles of his feet stung, the balm and leaves had worked wonders on both. And, multiple hearty meals a day had put some meat back on his bones.

Dashin spent the entire morning walking back and forth across the platform. What was trivial to TreeFolk he found daunting, and the reduced gravity of this world only added to the challenge.

"You must not get discouraged," Alina urged, after swallowing the banda leaf she'd stuffed from the bowls in front of them.

"I think my body is beginning to get used to it," Dashin said, trying to sound hopeful as he struggled to pinch his banda leaf closed without ripping it.

"Much better, but hold the end as you fold it over," Alina remarked, nodding to the leaf he'd stuffed. She watched as he tried another. "You seem more comfortable walking."

"Thanks," Dashin said, taking a bite and then stuffing the entire thing into his mouth as it came apart.

She arched an eyebrow. He shrugged, chewing.

Alina shook her head. "The *becoming* has three trials, and all three must be completed before the new moon."

Dashin had fragments of memories from Alina's trials. "One of them is on the ground?"

"Yes. The *trial of the forest* requires candidates to spend a day and a night on the forest floor. Normally, there are other candidates to help build the shelter and share guard duty."

"But, I'll have to do it alone," Dashin said, swallowing.

"Yes, and there is little time to teach you to make an appropriate shelter. The most fearsome predators live on the forest floor. We prepare from childhood to face this challenge."

Dashin remembered her trial and the nightmares that ensued. The thought of being eaten alive by some creature took what remained of his appetite. He put the banda leaf he'd just picked up back down on the plate. "I might be able to build a shelter that would last a day. That doesn't seem impossible."

"Have you built such a shelter before? You must choose the location wisely. You must gather the resources to build it. They can be scarce. It's not a simple task."

Dashin exhaled, putting that trial from his mind for the moment and hoping the next one might be more hopeful. "You mentioned the *trial of the hunt* was different for men?"

"For men, the *trial of the hunt* involves providing the killing blow to a creature that has a weight equal to or larger than your own and then carrying that creature to the village."

Dashin now understood the comments made during dinner about there being no hunt planned until the next formal becoming. "I imagine the other men herd the creatures into a position where the candidates can dispatch them."

"Yes, you have the measure of it," Alina said. "The creatures and the forest floor are dangerous. It takes all the men of the tribe to do this."

"I take it there are no large, slow-moving birds near my weight that I could hunt instead?"

"No, I'm afraid, given your weight, only a large stoda will suffice."

"So, I'll have to do this alone without ever having seen such a hunt."

"Yes, and if you achieve this, you will still have to carry the creature from the forest floor to the village by yourself to provide proof."

Dashin didn't like how this was shaping up. Solvan slid in next to him, putting Dashin's body between him and the kitchen. Dashin chuckled and nudged the lad's shoulder with his own.

The hunt was another task that seemed impossible. And there was still one more trial. "The last trial is a race of some sort?"

"Yes, the *trial of the trees* is a race through the forest. A course is laid in the trees, and the candidates must follow it and gather tokens along the way. A tribal member is sent out to chase the candidates once they are on the course. The candidates must return to the platform with their tokens before the chaser does."

Matse walked over and stood across the table from Dashin. Solvan, at his side, was shaking his head vigorously. She raised a tiny hand and pointed at him as she looked back at the kitchen. Dashin glanced over. Rigin was staring sternly this way. When Solvan peeked around him, she caught his eye. Solvan sagged against him and then stood and clomped back to the kitchen with Matse behind him, giggling.

Dashin watched them go and then turned to Alina. "I have memories of your race. It was incredibly fast and challenging. After trying to walk on the platform this morning, that trial seems the most out of reach."

"Candidates are normally children the village wants to see succeed. So the chaser affords them a healthy lead and then challenges them to make it exciting. Since your *becoming* was forced on the tribe, and Hedrick will likely be involved in selecting your chaser, this trial will be more difficult than normal."

Dashin looked out into the trees, trying to imagine himself moving through them at the speeds from Alina's memories. He shook his head. The task was impossible enough without an adverse chaser. "I don't understand what Hedrick has against me."

"I think he feels your presence is a threat to his power."

"Aren't you and Aor to be mated? Don't you have some influence?" Dashin asked. Confusing memory fragments hinted at this.

Alina stiffened next to him. "There is no such agreement, though some have spoken as though there were. I saw in your memories that things are different in your world, but in ours, it is the woman who chooses her mate. How it could be otherwise makes no sense to me."

"I'm sorry, I just assumed from the memories..."

"Yes, many have assumed as you did. I have not made my *choice*, and this is not something I wish to discuss with you."

"Alina, I'm sorry if I said something hurtful. I have these fragments, and I'm just trying to make sense of them."

Alina softened. "No, the fault is mine, Dashin. You did not mean to offend. I should not have reacted as I did."

They sat in silence for a time.

"When I was young, Hedrick sought to force my *choice*, believing I could be persuaded. When I told others, he denied it, saying I'd misunderstood the conversation, and that I was a silly girl."

Dashin felt a rush of anger, his face growing hot.

Alina turned and, seeing his reaction, placed a hand on his arm. "There is no need. It was a long time ago."

But, despite her words, he thought he saw gratitude in her eyes. He exhaled, letting the tension drain, but determined not to let anyone force Alina into anything. He wasn't sure what he might do, but he would do something.

All three trials seemed impossible. But he remembered the stories Gralan had told him of impossible situations he'd gotten himself out of. In each of those situations, Gralan had worked the problem before him, solving it before moving on to another. He decided he would do the same. First, he needed to learn how to walk. The other problems he would leave for later.

He'd just decided this when a memory floated to the surface. "Wasn't there also something about preparing food for a feast?"

Alina laughed. "Yes, at the end of the becoming, once all three trials have been completed, successful candidates each present a dish at the feast for the tribe to share. Although it is not required for the trials, much thought goes into preparing this dish. However, in your case, if you manage to survive all three trials, everyone will be so amazed you can serve a handful of nuts and no one will notice."

"Well, that's good to know, I guess." He brushed crumbs from their meal from his legs. "You mentioned something about training with string?"

She looked at him, frowning. "After the description of the trials, how can you be so calm? Did you not understand the seriousness of your situation?"

"Oh, no, you made it quite clear. I figure I can sit here and wait to die, or I can try to find a way to live. And, if I'm going to do the latter, I will need to train."

She sat there for a moment regarding him. She glanced at his burned arm and his bloody feet. An expression he couldn't place flashed across her features, and she stood. "Very well," she said, "let us be about it."

Alina had him run slowly around the platform. It was more challenging since the platform was often moving when his feet met it. He had to absorb the motion more aggressively in his knees and legs. Though every gust still made him stumble and reel, he was managing to keep his feet.

The children sat along one edge of the platform watching the entertainment. They'd giggled and laughed at first when he'd fallen, but Alina had curtailed that reaction with a stare. Now they whispered and chatted among themselves. Solvan and Matse sat in the middle, and some of the children leaned forward to ask Solvan questions as Dashin's training progressed. Solvan answered each with authority. As Dashin passed by at one point, he heard Solvan tell the child next to him that Dashin could breathe fire whenever he wanted to.

Solvan reveled in his sudden fame. Given how difficult his life had been, it warmed Dashin's heart to see it. Matse stuck close to his shoulder, her eyes darting between Dashin and Alina.

A group of women worked in the kitchen, preparing the vegetables Hurza and Kani delivered. It seemed as though they were pickling them, which made sense since once picked, the produce would not stay fresh for long in this hot, humid weather.

Dashin smiled at the women as he strode past, and there was a ripple of chuckling in his wake. "Bend your knees more," he heard Hurza call out, which was followed by more chuckling.

Dashin bent his knees, speeding up a little as his confidence grew.

"How do you feel?" Alina asked.

"I'm getting the feel of this," he answered, his mind on the task.

"Let's see how you do with this," she said, unrolling a length of twine across the platform and then laying another length next to it with the width of his foot between them. "Imagine this is a large flat branch and walk along it, staying between the two lengths of twine."

Dashin tried to walk along the imaginary branch but found himself struggling to stay on it. He concentrated on placing his feet between the lengths, but the platform was moving, and sometimes it moved before his foot reached it, so that he stepped off to one side or the other.

"Don't look down," Alina urged, "look ahead, beyond your feet. You must sense the motion before it comes, anticipate it, and then adjust for it without watching your feet."

"I don't understand. How can I keep my feet within the twine, if I don't look at where I'm placing them?"

"When you walk on the ground, do you look at where you place your feet?"

"Well, no..."

"Then why are you looking at them here? Your body knows where your feet are. If you assume this twine is a branch, you must trust that if you look ahead, your mind will remember where the branch is and find it as you move through the forest."

"I don't..." he began, but she cut him off.

"Now is not the time for discussion. Trust that I know what I speak of and do as I say."

He looked down, feeling embarrassed. She had lived her life in the trees, and he was letting his anxiety question her. He looked up again, determined. "I'm sorry. What should I do?"

She smiled and went to stand five or six body lengths ahead of him on the twine. "Look this far ahead as you walk. As the branch moves in the wind, let a mental picture of the path form within you, and let your feet find that path. The world moves too fast to think. You must let yourself feel the path."

He looked up and took a few steps, but he was stumbling and felt the twine often beneath his feet, certain also that he was often well outside it. Moments ago, he'd felt a level of confidence while jogging that he no longer enjoyed.

"Do not worry if at first you do not find the branch. It will come as you learn to feel the path."

She had him repeat this over and over for the rest of the day. As the day drew on, he did better, but he was still rarely within the lengths of twine for long.

By the time they stopped for the day, his legs felt like jelly. He staggered about on them as he tried to help set up the tables. He was stumbling so much that Rigin had him sit down for fear he'd hurt himself or someone else.

Solvan clomped over and fetched a stool for him, placing him at the table he shared with Rigin and Matse. Dashin thanked him. The lad beamed and ran off to fetch dishes for the table. He and Matse set the table, placing a tray of dishes in the center and a stack of salted banda leaves next to it, with a stone on top to keep the breeze from blowing them away. They brought a large gourd of water and some wooden cups. Dashin poured a cup of water and drank it in one gulp. As the village sat down for the evening meal, Enor and Alina joined him at Rigin's table.

"How are your feet?" Enor asked.

Dashin dared not look. They'd been burning most of the day, and he'd been trying to ignore them, so focused had he been on remaining upright.

Enor peeked at the soles beneath the table. He sat up, his lips a taut line. "I will see to them after the evening meal," he promised.

"Thanks, that would be wonderful."

"You are much improved from this morning," Rigin said, smiling.

"Thanks, it feels better. But it is humbling to see the children running and jumping and doing things without thought that I struggle to do despite being entirely focused on the task."

"We are bred to it," Rigin said. "From the time we are born, we feel the swaying of the trees in our bones."

"My bones, I'm afraid, only know sand and stone."

Rigin reached across and patted his hand. "The trees are within you, Dashin, I sense them."

Her words stopped Dashin, who was feeling a little deflated after the exercise with the string. He could see she believed her words, though it was an odd thing to say. He smiled at her, and she sat back. He picked up a banda leaf and filled it. This was an odd world with wonders beyond what he'd learned in schools he'd attended or texts he'd read. The *touching* had changed him. Alina's mother had seen images of him before his birth, and now others were sensing things within him. Perhaps there was something there he could draw from?

During the meal, the conversation at other tables was hushed and guarded, with many glances in his direction. But by the time the meal drew to a close, he hardly noticed it, as he struggled to keep his eyes open. He sat up and stretched his back, having to move over a bit to give himself room since Solvan was leaning against him. The lad grinned up at him. It touched his heart. He'd often dreamed of having a brother and of just such an exchange. The reality of it made his eyes mist so that he had to turn away.

"I think we should get you to bed before you fall asleep at the table," Enor said. He rose and helped Dashin up. Alina bid him good night. She'd been quiet throughout the meal. It seemed there was something on her mind. He yawned, and Enor took some of his weight as they left the platform and crossed the bridges to Rigin's hut.

Enor sat him on the bed and put his feet up. He shrugged his bag onto the bed and pulled a fist-sized leather bag from it. Undoing the ties, he slipped a banda leaf within it and scooped out a dollop of the wondrous balm. He applied it liberally to the bottom of Dashin's feet. It tingled deliciously, heralding the marvelous numbing to follow. Enor applied the leaves over the balm, tying them lightly in place with twine. As the burning in his feet subsided, Dashin exhaled, his body relaxing. Enor then applied balm to the burn on Dashin's forearm and covered it in fresh banda leaves.

Dashin tried to thank Enor properly, but he only managed to mumble something incoherent. He heard Enor chuckle before sleep took him.

Chapter 18

Alina tossed restlessly as memories of fire and destruction plagued her sleep. Near morning, she woke and lay there taking deep breaths, letting the tension ebb from her body. The night air was cool, and the fragrance of night blossoms carried on the breeze grounded her in this world. She pushed away Dashin's memories of the loss of his friends and the trauma of his escape. She couldn't imagine how one could awaken on a strange world, having lost all one knew, and manage to function. But somehow Dashin was doing so, even when faced with what promised to be certain death. That he had little choice didn't affect her opinion of it. He was a remarkable person, and the glimpses of his world had opened her mind to possibilities she hadn't known existed.

There were other worlds with people who had other songs. Though the loss of Dashin's family made her more grateful for her own and for her tribe, it also made her question the dreams others had for her. She didn't dismiss the traditional dreams of her friends, but for the first time, she felt that wanting something different was not unreasonable.

Yesterday, there'd been a moment when Dashin had been angry and protective of her in a way she'd not felt before. It had elicited feelings she could not name. Surely it was just the concern of a friend, being protective like Hurza had been. The *touching* had created a bond unlike any she'd known before. The threads of it reached deep within her.

She rolled out of bed and padded to the common area. The noise of her passing caused her father to shift, and the rumble of his sleep grew in intensity to a dull roar. She poured water from the wooden pitcher into the basin and washed her face. About to leave, she padded over to the curtain of her parents' room. The clamor washed over her as she leaned in. "Amani," she said in her best imitation of her mother's tone.

The snoring stopped immediately, and the bed shifted again. A moment later, the familiar rumble returned. Alina chuckled to herself, crinkling her eyes. She slipped out into the night and headed toward Rigin's hut. She came across Narat, posted at the far side of the village, standing watch. She waved to him, and he waved back, a curious look on his face as he watched her go by.

She woke Dashin from a deep, restful sleep. It seemed he'd been too exhausted from yesterday's training to have had energy for dreams. As he stirred, she pushed the blanket aside and checked his feet. The balm and leaves had worked wonders, closing the wounds and forming a protective skin over his soles.

"Is it morning already?" he croaked.

She placed her fingers over his lips so as not to wake the others. He nodded, and they made their way to the grove. She helped him with the bridges as they went. Once there, she had Dashin help her lay out the lengths of twine.

The morning breeze greeted them, bringing with it the rich scent of blooms from the upper canopy already touched by the sun. By the time the birds woke and announced the day, Dashin was walking back and forth on his imaginary branch, trying to stay within the twine.

"Bend your knees," Alina reminded him. He was making progress, but his movements were wooden and reactionary, lacking the smoothness he would need to move through the trees. "Feel the path ahead. Let your body seek it out."

They kept at it until his movements grew more fluid. Alina heard villagers in the distance on the communal platform chatting. As the sun licked the far end of the platform, Hurza and Kani stopped by to see how things were going.

"He's moving better today," Kani said.

"Still, he's barely walking," Alina whispered.

"It's like the nuxat egg you tried to make hatch more quickly," Hurza teased.

Kani choked back a laugh, and a moment later, Alina chuckled, remembering the egg. She'd been eight sun cycles at the time. She'd noted how eggs were kept warm by the hens, and she'd imagined that if they were kept warmer, they would hatch faster. She'd put one near a brazier and had watched it all day as it baked, awaiting the chick that never came.

Hurza was right. She had to push Dashin to ensure he had the best chance, but she couldn't force it. If he sensed she thought this was hopeless, he would soon think so too. "You're right. He has to believe he has a chance."

"But, Alina, is there a chance?" Kani asked.

"My mother believes there is," she said, leaving her doubts unvoiced.

"Could Marna be wrong?" Hurza asked.

The words struck at her core. She'd been trying to keep this thought at bay. What if her mother was wrong about this? It seemed even her mother didn't believe this was possible, and yet she had clung to the idea. Could it be she'd misinterpreted her feelings?

Her friends were silent for a moment. She felt them look at each other over her shoulders. Dashin moved across the platform, his entire body intent on the motion, his heart committed to the cause they had set him on. Something tugged deep within her. She could not imagine abandoning him. In that moment, she realized she would do everything she could for him. The SkyGods would ultimately decide the outcome, but she wouldn't let his failure be because of her lack of effort.

"I need to do this," Alina said. "I can't explain why."

Kani squeezed her shoulder. "If you need to, then we'll help, of course."

Hurza put her hand on her other shoulder.

Dashin hooted from the far end of the platform. He'd managed a successful transit along the imaginary branch.

Kani and Hurza slapped their hands on the bench, applauding his success.

"Well done, Dashin!" Hurza shouted.

"Yes, very good," Kani added.

Her heart swelled with gratitude for her friends. Moments earlier, she'd imagined herself alone with the weight of this. She felt embarrassed to have overlooked the two people who had always been there for her. Dabbing at her eyes, she reached for her friends' knees and gave them a grateful squeeze as she stood and walked to Dashin.

"That was very good, Dashin. Your body is learning." She leaned down and started to adjust the twine. Hurza and Kani joined her, and between them, they created a twisty path.

"Now, do the same thing, but imagine this path is the branch."

Dashin took a few steps, but his eyes were down again, watching his feet, so he teetered and lost his footing.

"Keep your eyes ahead of you like you were doing before," she corrected.

"But I can't tell where the branch is."

"Let your mind picture the branch and trust that your body will remember where it is and find it."

He opened his mouth to object, but Alina cut him off. "Try it."

He bit back his response and did as instructed. It went terribly, his feet straining to find the imaginary branch. But he set his jaw and continued, his brow furrowed, his fists tight with tension.

"Relax, Dashin," Kani said, reaching over and taking his hand and shaking his arm to drain the tension from it. "It is the same thing you were just doing. The path before was already moving with the wind. It is still moving in the same way."

Dashin forced his body to relax, his muscles losing their definition. He bent his knees as he walked, keeping his eyes up as he'd been told. Though he still missed the branch most of the time, his body was beginning to find a path close to the one he sought.

"That's it, Dashin, much better," Hurza said.

Alina walked backward ahead of him, drawing his eyes forward. He fixed his eyes on her, his expression intent and trusting. She felt herself flush strangely. She blinked it away, turning her mind to the task. "Better. Bend your knees. Hear the wind. Let yourself remember the path."

And then, as she walked past him to prepare for the next transit, her arm brushed his shoulder. She felt a jolt and gasped. He reached out to steady her. Her mind swam, and the platform spun. A river of energy flowed from her. His arm stiffened as it flowed into him. His eyes fluttered and blinked. She pulled away. It only lasted several moments, but it left Alina weak and unsteady on her feet.

When she met his eyes, they were different. His gaze held hers. She backed up a few steps, trying to make sense of what had just happened. Dashin followed her, his feet finding the branch as he did. Shocked, she shuffled unsteadily backward, her mind consumed by the contact. He crossed the entire platform, his feet finding the heart of the branch with every step, his motion smoother now. Her heart pounded in her chest, the experience so strange she could not look away.

When they reached the far end, she closed her eyes, her breathing ragged. When she opened them, her friends were frozen at the other end of the platform, shocked expressions on their faces. She looked away, embarrassed, as though she'd revealed an intimate part of herself.

Dashin was elated but also confused, glancing from the twine to her. "That was better," she said weakly, not able to speak of what had just happened. "Keep practicing," she said, returning to the bench. Her friends joined her, sitting on either side, both of them giving her space.

After a few moments, Hurza leaned in. "What just happened?"

Kani leaned in too.

"I don't know," Alina said.

She sat back, drained. She watched Dashin walking smoothly now, his feet finding the path, except for moments when he grew too confident and lost his focus. Kani and Hurza shouted encouragement, though their voices were tight and anxious. Alina sensed the unspoken questions in their bodies as they sat next to her. She had never felt anything like that. The suddenness and force of it frightened her. It was as though a new grove had just appeared in a familiar forest.

As midday approached, Kani and Hurza left to see to their chores. Alina watched them go, her friends speaking in the private tones that once would have included her.

Alina had Dashin help her gather the twine so they could return to the communal platform and leave the grove to Hedrick and his people. Her father would be here, she reminded herself, so they weren't all his people. Perhaps her father would have some sway in what was said.

As they gathered the twine, Dashin turned to her. "What happened earlier?"

"I don't know."

"It was like the *touching* but different."

She nodded, sitting down on the platform. "I've never felt this before. Perhaps it is something that remains from our *touching*." She fumbled with her hands. She had always been able to suppress it before. Now things were happening without warning. Could she have lost the ability to control it?

Dashin studied her face. "You're worried about it?"

Her eyes misted, and she nodded.

"I would never hurt you."

She looked up into his eyes and saw the truth in them. She had to bite her lip to stop it from trembling. Whatever it was that was between them, Dashin was on the other end of it, not some stranger or something fearsome. She took a breath, forcing the tension from her shoulders, and tried a smile, though it did not find its way to her eyes.

On the central platform, they ate the meal Rigin prepared for them in silence, both of them lost in their thoughts. Solvan, meanwhile, clomped around clowning for Dashin, who praised the young boy's every move. The simple moment touched Alina. This was Dashin. This was the person she was somehow linked to. He was kind. He was caring. She would be fine.

They set up the twine together, a long snaking pattern, as the children took their place along the edge of the platform. Dashin strode along it, finding the path as though born to it. His feet were still awkward, but he was not the bumbling and stumbling person he'd been yesterday. She was amazed by it and stared mutely. The children applauded each successful transit, slapping the platform, a flock of tiny hands taking flight.

She marveled at the transformation until she noticed the quiet. She looked over, and the adults working in the kitchen area were staring at Dashin, shocked expressions on their faces. She saw a few of them reach up and touch their foreheads with their fingertips.

Alina's heart sank. "Dashin, come here," she called, her heart pounding now. "That's enough for today."

"It's still early," he said. "I can practice some more."

"No, that's fine. We need to discuss your technique. You're still walking much too awkwardly," she said loudly, lying.

He looked at her, confused. She shook her head a tiny bit, but it was enough that he dropped it.

"Of course," he said, gathering the twine and rolling it into balls.

She took him back to Rigin's hut, turning Solvan away as he sought to follow.

Once they reached the hut, they sat down on the bed. Alina exhaled, composing herself.

"What is it?"

"You're scaring the villagers."

Dashin frowned. "What do you mean? They were clapping the whole time."

"Yes, the children were, but the adults were frightened."

"By me walking across the platform?"

"Yes."

"But even the children here manage this."

She turned and met his eyes. "Yes, but yesterday you could not walk at all, and today you've mastered the twisted twine. It's something that takes children moons to master."

"But I'm not a child."

"Nor are you a TreePerson."

He paused, considering her words. His brow furrowed.

"I don't understand. How am I supposed to meet these trials if I don't improve? And, since we only have one moon to do it, how do they think I'll pass the trials if I don't progress?"

"No one believes you will pass, Dashin."

His mouth fell open. He sat there for a moment before he could continue. "No one?"

"Well, perhaps a few do, but very few."

Dashin swallowed. "Do you believe?"

Alina looked away. This morning, she would have lied to him to keep his spirits up, but now she couldn't. "This morning I had doubts, but now I don't know."

"Now you believe I can do this thing?"

She shook her head and laughed at his earnestness. "No, now I have doubts about my doubts."

"Well, that's something, right?"

He smiled. She looked away, blinking back emotions that threatened to overwhelm her. A few days ago, little touched her this deeply, but now she found herself awash in emotions. Perhaps it was the *touching*? Could she have gained these feelings from him?

"Thanks for being honest. It would have been easy to lie to me."

She nodded, unable to meet his eyes.

"So, how do I train if I can't show people my progress?"

She looked up, amazed at him. He'd taken what seemed to her an impassible jungle and simply began seeking a path through it. She'd seen him do this in his memories while learning intricate songs in various tribes as a child, but those had been memories. She laughed, overcome with relief.

"What?"

"You are the wind in the leaves," she said, smiling.

"What?"

"You bring relief as on a hot day without wind," she explained.

"Oh," he said, smiling. "I like that."

"Me too."

It was a problem to solve. If the villagers became too frightened of Dashin, Hedrick would find a way to use it against him. They would have to be careful. Even her friends had been anxious. If they were, then others would be more so.

"At tonight's evening meal, stumble a bit, not too much so that it seems an act, but enough that those who witnessed this afternoon question what they saw and those who only heard of it dismiss it."

"I can do stumbling," Dashin said with a chuckle.

"Not too much."

"Got it, just one helping of stumbling."

Alina chuckled and nudged him with her shoulder.

The evening meal was tense. As they arrived on the platform, Hedrick was speaking to a group of villagers gathered around him. Her father provided counterpoint, interrupting him and arguing. Alina couldn't make out the words, but the tone of the exchange carried all she needed to know. As villagers noted their arrival, the platform fell silent, all eyes on Dashin.

Dashin did wonderfully, struggling to cross the bridge, although he managed it himself. He tripped and took a few stumbling steps as he reached the platform. He moved to Rigin's table, staggering as he went. His movements had improved from yesterday, but not greatly so.

Alina watched the villagers' eyes as they took this in, animated discussions rippling through the village as previous accounts were discussed and questioned.

Solvan had already set up Dashin's stool right next to his own. Dashin took it, mussing the lad's hair as he did so, to the delight of the boy. Her father came over and joined them as they sat down.

"It seems Dashin's progress has become the topic of conversation," he whispered.

"He had a good day," Alina said, squirming as she crossed her legs.

"I have good teachers," Dashin offered.

Rigin placed a stack of the roasted and salted banda leaves between Dashin and her. "Eat, you must both be hungry," she said, her eyes soft on them.

"Thank you," Dashin said, taking one of the leaves and filling it.

As they ate, the conversation around them drifted off. They would have to be more careful. She hadn't anticipated this, and she realized she should have foreseen it after seeing the effect the change had on Hurza and Kani.

The meal passed pleasantly. Solvan dominated much of the conversation with tales of his day, embellished, she was certain, for the current audience. As the meal drew to a close, she found that tonight it was she who struggled to remain awake. Rigin told her that she would see Dashin to his room. Alina agreed, and her father accompanied her home.

When they reached their common room, he touched her arm. "Are you unwell?"

"No, I'm fine. It's just that..." she hesitated, unsure how to explain it.

"You *touched* Dashin's mind again?"

Her eyes went wide, "How..."

"Hurza and Kani approached me after the grove. They were concerned."

Alina sighed. "I don't know how it happened. I just brushed his arm without thinking."

"Perhaps the connection from your *touching* is still close at hand."

"Perhaps."

"It frightens you?"

"Yes, since the first time with Kani, I've learned to control it. And now it seems I no longer can."

"Perhaps, you just need to adjust your control."

She shrugged.

"It seems that the *touching* yielded some impressive results, though."

"Yes," she agreed, struggling to keep her eyes open. "It did, though it drew upon me."

"Get some sleep. There is little a good night's sleep cannot improve."

She smiled. That maxim had been her father's preferred remedy for as long as she could remember.

Chapter 19

Dashin opened his eyes, his mind lingering on the edge of waking. The morning birds were singing, the features of his room growing sharper as night's cloak ebbed. He'd been climbing the red hills of Aerdra, the town he'd grown up in, his fingers searching the rough stone face for holds as he worked his way to the summit. He sat up with a groan, his muscles complaining. As the dream left him, he rubbed his face, worried that he'd somehow slept through Alina's attempts to wake him.

That didn't make sense. Alina would have shaken him awake. She hadn't had any qualms about doing so before. Perhaps she'd been delayed? She was exhausted last night. Maybe she was still sleeping.

Peeling back the blanket, he saw the fresh bandages on his feet and arm. Enor must have applied them as he slept. He couldn't imagine having slept through that, but there they were.

He stood up and was surprised when his knees automatically absorbed an unexpected sway of the room. He smiled, making a note to share this with Alina. He took a few tentative steps. His feet were sore, but not horribly so. Whatever was in that balm was potent.

He looked out the window. No one was about yet. In the distance, he could just make out the form of someone sitting in the trees, the tip of a spear outlined against the brightening forest. Dashin knew from memory fragments that villagers took turns standing watch against night predators.

These new not-memories, as he thought of them, had begun to settle within him. As the days passed, they grew more familiar. Though he knew it was not the case, they felt like they'd always been there and that the *touching* had somehow simply unlocked them. The *touching* had also forged a bond between him and Alina. When they were together, he had to remind himself that they'd only just met, not wanting to make her uncomfortable with the intensity of the connection he felt.

This was her home, her tribe, her family. She already had a plan for her life, one which didn't include him. He'd seen images of the children she planned to have, though the details beyond them were hazy. But these were memory fragments, and pieces were missing. And it felt uncomfortable sifting through them in search of personal details, though his mind called them up, unbidden, whenever he thought of her. What did she think of him? She'd seen details of his life and had commented on his loneliness. Did she pity him?

Assuming the impossible happened and he somehow survived these challenges, what would it be like to live here among these people? It wasn't like he had options. There was no way off this planet, and no one would be coming to look for him here. The entire planet was one huge jungle, and all the people lived as this tribe did. There was no advanced technology, though there were skilled craftsmen and artisans. All his training had prepared him to live in a space-faring world. He was like an infant in this world with few worthwhile skills.

He'd been lucky to have been rescued and taken in. Though Marna's words made him wonder if there had been more than luck involved. Could her *sight* be believed? It seemed impossible. And yet, he never would have believed the *touching* had he not experienced it.

He heard stirring in the common room. He left the window and stepped through the curtain.

"Good morning, Dashin," Rigin said as she tidied up the counter. It ran along the wall between the doorway to her room and that of Sneva's room, as Dashin still thought of it. A table with four chairs sat against the opposite wall next to the doorway to the children's room.

"Good morning," Dashin answered, walking to the basin on the counter to wash his face and hands. He poured water from a pitcher into the basin and reached in, splashing water onto his face. It was cool and invigorating. He wiped his face with the towel hanging on the hook above the counter.

"Perhaps you should see to more than your face," Rigin said, crinkling her nose.

Dashin took a breath and flushed, his skin growing hot. He stank. The past few days had been exhausting, but they'd been outside with the wind blowing, so it had been less noticeable. He'd caught whiffs of himself a few times, and each time he'd promised himself that he'd see to it as soon as they were done for the day, but the days were long, and by the time he'd gotten back to the hut, he'd fallen into bed. All the exercise and anxiety in this hot and humid weather just made it worse. "I'm sorry, Rigin. I meant to wash up, but I..."

She reached over and put her fingers on his lips. "You are not the first one who has needed to wash," she said, chuckling. "Come, it seems you have a few moments before Alina arrives." She stepped outside onto the platform.

Dashin followed her. As he stepped out, a small body clomped out after him. "Dashin, are you leaving?" Solvan asked, breathless.

"Not just yet. I'm going to wash up."

"Oh," Solvan said, hesitant to follow.

"Solvan, you come out too and bring some towels," Rigin said.

The boy groaned, and Matse, peeking out from behind him, smiled, amused at the wounded face he made.

A cistern located at the back of the hut collected rainwater that ran from the roof. The funneled water passed through a piece of loosely woven fabric stretched over a frame to form a lid that kept out leaves and debris. Next to the cistern sat a few wooden buckets. Rigin lifted the lid and dipped one of the buckets in, filling it before pulling it out and placing it at Dashin's feet. She reached into one of the other buckets and took out a couple of stones. She handed one to Dashin.

As Solvan trudged up, she handed him the other stone. "Show Dashin how TreeFolk wash," she said, cupping his chin. Solvan perked up, grinning at Dashin. Solvan dipped the stone into the bucket of water and then rubbed it between his palms. In a few moments, a rich lather developed, which he slapped on his clothes. He repeated the process until his tunic and pants were covered in the lather.

Dashin imitated the boy. The earthy scented lather was silky and thick in his hands, with a very fine mineral feel to it, almost like a mildly abrasive talc, he thought. He soaped up his clothes and watched as Solvan reached inside his tunic, rubbed his chest, pulled up his sleeves to do his arms, and then his pant legs to do his legs. Solvan reached for the bucket to rinse, but Rigin grabbed an ear and asked about his face and hair. The boy chuckled as she tickled his side. He grinned up at her and added two handfuls of lather to his hair and then scrubbed his face.

Solvan leaned over and splashed water onto his face, and then rubbed his eyes dry. He picked up the heavy bucket and poured it over himself, letting the water wash away the soap. It took two more buckets to rinse most of it away. Rigin poured a third bucket over his back to get the spots he'd missed.

Dashin reveled in the feelings of lather on his skin and in his hair. He felt delightfully clean and was embarrassed again that he'd let it go this long. He worried that folks in the village might have wondered at his hygiene.

He sat down on the platform to scrub his hair and face, not wanting to lose his balance and pitch off into the trees. He asked Solvan to rub his back, which the boy did with enthusiasm, scrubbing as he giggled. Rigin pulled a comb through Matse's short hair as the girl watched Dashin and Solvan.

Dashin poured a bucket of water over his head, wiping his eyes dry with his fingers afterward. "Solvan, can you get me more water to rinse with?"

Solvan grabbed the bucket and hobbled over to the cistern. Turning over the remaining bucket to give him something to stand on, he climbed up, lifted the cistern's lid, and filled it.

It seemed a precarious setup, and Dashin was concerned that the boy might fall or hurt himself managing the heavy bucket. He braced himself to catch the boy should things go awry, but he needn't have worried, for even balancing on one leg, Solvan was remarkably agile. He pulled the wooden bucket from the cistern, pivoted in place, and launched himself from the bucket to land on the platform. His good leg absorbed all the shock, some of the water sloshing over the rim and landing on Dashin. Solvan poured the bucket on Dashin's head. Dashin wiped his eyes as Solvan fetched another bucket and Rigin handed him a towel.

Solvan poured several more buckets of the cool water over him until the water ran clear. "Thanks, Solvan. Now people won't run away from us when we meet them."

Solvan roared with laughter as if this was the funniest thing he'd ever heard. Dashin reached over and tickled his side. The lad squirmed and danced away.

"Thank you, Dashin. You will be much more approachable now," Alina said, with a chuckle.

He hadn't heard her join them, and he blushed at her words. "I'm sorry. I hadn't realized..."

"Dashin, I was teasing," she said, laughing.

Rigin chuckled along with her, and then a curious expression appeared on her face as she looked at Alina, as though something had just occurred to her. Dashin glanced at Alina but didn't notice anything.

"Come on, you two," she said, taking Solvan by the collar, "Dashin and Alina have things to do, and the two of you have chores to see to."

Rigin crinkled her eyes at Dashin and Alina as Solvan groaned, a sound he'd perfected, Dashin thought.

Alina watched them go and then turned to Dashin. "Are you ready?"

"Yes, how are you feeling?"

"I am fine. Why do you ask?"

"You seemed tired last night, you know, after the..."

She waved it away. "Yes, some sleep has seen me right again. Let's go. There is much to do today."

"Of course," he said, standing up and rubbing the towel over his clothes to absorb some of the water. The sun had just slanted into the leaves above him, and the day was warming. Though his skin had bumps from the cool water and air now, he felt wonderfully clean. He would not let it go this long again.

He followed Alina toward the central platform, hurrying to catch up as he adjusted his tunic and pants. She stopped abruptly and turned to him, smiling. "What did you just do?"

He looked down at his wet clothes and then back at her. "What do you mean?"

"Did you notice the past three bridges we crossed?"

He looked back, trying to understand what it was about the bridges she was pointing out. She waited, smiling at him, and then he understood.

"I crossed them without thinking about them."

She nodded. "Yes, almost like a TreePerson," she patted his arm. "I think you have absorbed some of my sense of the trees from our connection. When you let it come, you move naturally. It is something to remember."

"It's amazing. This connection is... it's... I don't know..."

"It's beyond words," Alina said, her eyes serious.

"Yes. It is."

"Today, we will start working in the trees."

Dashin swallowed, anxious at the thought of trying to move as he'd seen the TreeFolk do.

"Don't worry, today we'll be staying near the village where we have netting for the children. So, there is no danger."

He exhaled, relieved. "Oh, good. Should I stumble a bit and make it look like I'm struggling?"

"I don't think you'll need to do that today," she said with a cryptic smile.

He soon learned the meaning behind the smile. The platform was a solid plane, even with the twine. But now the branches were round and uneven. And on either side of each branch, there was truly nothing to catch him, so every misstep resulted in a tumble through the branches into the netting below.

It seemed that each time he fell, he hit every possible branch there was on his way down. Well before midday, he was bruised from his ankles to his ears. Though he spent much less time on his feet, the surface of the branches had knots and rough patches of bark that he was not skilled enough to avoid, so the soles of his feet were torn up as well.

"Don't look at your feet," Alina cried out.

Dashin grumbled. Those words preceded every tumble he'd taken that morning. He tensed, his toes gripping the branch. The bark peeled beneath them as his arms flailed on either side of his body, trying to counteract his swaying. He took another step, the branch dipping with his weight before slipping out from beneath him. He pitched forward as the branch sprang back, smacking him in the jaw and shoulder and hurling him backward into the netting below.

"Are you hurt?" Alina called down to him, concerned.

He groaned, trying to untangle himself. "I'm fine," he answered. "Just a few more bruises for my collection."

"The idea is to move through the trees without collecting any."

Dashin scrambled back up. He steadied himself on the branch again and took a deep breath and then a step.

"Don't look at your feet," Alina cried out.

Dashin groaned.

By the time they returned to the central platform for a midday meal, his body was once again leaving bloody smudges on the platform behind him. He was beat and sweating, and this morning's delicious feeling of being clean and refreshed was a distant memory.

"You did miss one branch," Alina said as she took a bite of a thick slice of nutbread. They were seated in the shade on a corner of the central platform. Villagers went about their day around them.

"What?" Dashin asked, puzzled, looking up from the bread he was too tired to eat.

"You missed a branch," she repeated, chewing.

He didn't understand what branch she was referring to. He looked up and met her eyes.

She swallowed. "I think you managed to hit every branch this morning on your way into the netting, except for one. That's quite an accomplishment, and not at all easy to do."

He groaned. "Great," he said, realizing she was teasing him.

She chuckled and patted his arm. "Don't be so disheartened. I'm certain news of your prowess will allay any discomfort folks were having at your rapid progress." She crinkled her eyes at him.

"You knew it would go like this, right? That's why you didn't think I should try and appear less able." Dashin rubbed his shoulder, trying to loosen the knot of bruises clustered there.

"Yes, I knew this morning would be challenging."

"Challenging? There is not a part of my body that hasn't been battered. How old are TreeFolk when they start walking in the village trees?"

"Oh, a handful of sun cycles," she said, waving it away.

"Children do this?"

"Yes, TreeFolk learn the way of the trees at a young age. Though there are some areas with simpler branches and where the netting is closer."

"Really? We couldn't have started there?"

"Perhaps, but then we wouldn't have made as effective a statement," she said, motioning around at the villagers moving around the platform.

Dashin looked around. Many of them were chatting and casting glances his way as they did. He turned to her. She crinkled her eyes.

Dashin exhaled, exasperated. Well, at least they'd convinced folks he was inept again.

"It was not only to show the villagers," Alina said, catching his eyes. "As difficult as the morning was, your body is learning the way of it. I can see it even if you cannot."

Once they'd finished their meal, they returned to the trees and training. The rest of the day was even more brutal since he found it harder to move, given the bruises and his burning feet. His body grew tense with the anticipation of falling, which inevitably led to exactly that.

Kani and Hurza came by and added their voices to Alina's instructions, but as evening drew nearer, Dashin could barely function, let alone take direction. And yet he kept picking himself out of the netting and climbing back up to the branches they were training on. He thanked the Makers or the SkyGods or whoever had created this planet for having created it with less gravity than Ancara. That slight edge was the only thing that made the ordeal bearable. Some of his falls might well have been fatal on Ancara, and clawing his way up repeatedly from the netting to the branches would have been impossible without the advantage his body had in the lower gravity.

The children sat nearby watching, rapt, none of them chatting as he fell over and over. When Alina called an end to it, he was lying in the netting, too exhausted to look at her.

There was more discussion during the evening meal, though the tone was much different. The glances in his direction carried pity rather than anxiety or confusion. At his table, Enor and Rigin spoke, and Alina said something to her father that he acknowledged. But Dashin was so weary that it was all a blur. Even Solvan gave him more space tonight, perhaps not wanting to hurt him by accidentally bumping into him.

He found himself staring down at the banda leaf he'd wrapped and wondering what the object was in his hand. Enor helped him to his feet and led him to Sneva's room. He laid him down on the bed, pulled his tunic and pants off, slathered balm over his body, and then covered his limbs and torso with banda leaves. By the time Enor was done, he'd exhausted his supply of both.

"With you in the village, I see that I'll have to keep far more balm and banda leaves on hand. You have already consumed what should have lasted me a full sun cycle."

Dashin started to apologize, but Enor waved it away. The magic of Enor's balm seeped into his muscles, his entire body tingling now. He couldn't contain his gratitude, his eyes misting up at the relief. Enor patted him on the shoulder.

Chapter 20

"Don't look at your feet," Alina repeated, having lost track of how many times she'd said it. Dashin was caught up in the netting below. His leg had broken through a section of webbing and become tangled.

"If this keeps up, we'll have to replace the netting," Hurza said at her elbow as they looked down at Dashin thrashing around below. Kani and Hurza had stopped by to see if things were improving.

It was midday, and she and Dashin had been in the children's area for the past three days. He still couldn't manage more than a few steps before losing his footing. She couldn't understand how something TreeFolk found simple was so challenging for him. Thankfully, he was doing better about missing some of the branches on the way down now, and a few times he'd even caught himself before reaching the netting.

"He's doing better," Kani offered.

"Barely," Hurza said, shaking her head. "Children have better balance."

Alina sighed. When he reached them again and got back onto the branch, ready to try it again, she had him sit down across from them.

"Let's get something to eat. We'll work on it some more after you rest a bit."

Hurza and Kani left to see to their chores. Alina thanked them again for doing hers. Hurza didn't have a ready quip, which made it clear what Hurza felt their prospects were.

Dashin was famished. He swallowed an entire slice of nutbread and chased it with several glasses of water. They were seated in their quiet corner of the central platform, a shady place she preferred. The days were slipping by. He was making progress, but Hurza was right. It was too slow. At this rate, he might be able to walk through the trees, but he'd be unable to use lanyards and race through the trees as he would need to.

"How is your body?" she asked. His body was covered in bruises, and it seemed he winced with every move these days.

"I'm fine, better today," he lied, biting into another slice of nutbread.

Villagers went about their duties, avoiding them, with more pitying glances than not. Her father mentioned Hedrick had stopped pushing to have Dashin sent away, apparently content now to wait for things to play out, now that the outcome seemed certain. Even Solvan, Dashin's staunchest supporter, seemed increasingly concerned. Only Rigin still seemed certain that things would work out. She always had an encouraging word and ensured he had fresh clothes, and with Solvan's help, buckets ready for Dashin to wash at the end of each brutal day. Her father still ministered to him every night, commenting to her that few places on his body were not bruised.

Her friends had asked her this morning, while Dashin was climbing from the netting, why she was putting him through this. The unspoken assumption was that what he was attempting was impossible, and so it seemed cruel to put him through all this suffering. A part of her understood. She had her own doubts, which had only grown with his lack of progress. And yet, she'd promised herself that if they failed, it wouldn't be because of a lack of effort on her part.

She inhaled sharply, surprised at the thought. She'd just thought of the failure as something they would share, not something he would own. Who was he becoming to her? These feelings had crept up on her over the past few days as she watched him climb out of the netting over and over. His determination and his heart, as he strove to do as she asked, despite repeated falls, touched her. It had changed how she saw him. And, though they'd shared something intimate, this was something else. She pushed the thoughts from her mind. It would not serve either of them to dwell on this.

"I'm sorry I haven't made more progress," he said, not for the first time since they'd started in the trees. His eyes were on her. She flushed, certain he could sense her disappointment.

"Dashin, there's no need. You are doing your best."

"It's not enough, though, is it?"

She took a breath. "No, it's not." There she'd said it.

He looked off into the trees, considering her words, not angry at her as she'd feared he might be. "Thanks," he said.

"For what?"

"For being honest."

They sat eating in silence. She couldn't imagine what was in his mind. The stress of the past few days. The looming trials. His quiet acceptance. His thanks. It was too much. She had promised herself she'd do all she could for him so that when he failed, she would have nothing to regret. But now she realized this would be little consolation. The loss of this connection, still unnamed, would be unspeakable. Emotion welled up within. Her heart raced. Hopelessness threatened to swallow her. Her eyes misted. She looked away, blinking hard, then wiped the tears gathering in the corners.

"Oh," Dashin said, sitting up straighter, "it's not over yet." He reached over and placed a hand on her arm.

Her skin tingled at his touch, and a shiver rippled up her spine. She moved back, unable to contain her emotions with his hand on her. "What do you mean?"

"We still have time," he said, his voice soothing like that of her father's.

She nodded, noting how he'd said *we*. He was frowning as though looking at a complicated knot he was working to untie.

"I was just thinking," he began, taking a sip of water. "You said your mother thinks I'll be *important* to the tribe."

"Yes, though she doesn't know why."

Dashin's frown grew deeper. "Then, that must mean there is a way through this."

Alina tilted her head. "You believe in the *sight*?"

"It doesn't matter. I didn't believe in the *touching* either."

"Dashin, I don't understand what you're trying to say."

He turned to her, holding her eyes. "If we assume your mother's *sight* was right, then it means that there must be a way for me to succeed."

"But even my mother said it was impossible," she cried.

Dashin paused, frowning over this piece of information she'd kept from him. He considered it for a moment but then continued. "It doesn't matter whether she believes it or not. The fact that she saw it or sensed it is what matters. That she finds it impossible is understandable since everyone else feels that way. Why should she be different?"

Alina opened her mouth to argue, but then she closed it. It was true. Her mother's disbelief would be a normal reaction to the impossible *sight*, but it would not change the *sight* itself.

"So, if we assume a path to success exists. We simply have to discover it."

"How do we go about finding such a path?"

"I have no idea, but it's encouraging to believe that one does exist."

A warmth blossomed within her, a ray of light piercing through the cold darkness that had taken residence. She could not yet see the shape of the idea, but there was something in his words that spoke the truth she had been searching for. "For someone not of this world, you are putting a lot of faith in things you did not believe to be possible," she said warily, trying to follow his logic.

"Yes, but the alternative is less attractive," he replied with a grin.

She chuckled, "So, it's a practical decision?"

"Of course," he said with a wink, which she knew for him was like a crinkling of the eyes.

It felt odd for him to be consoling her, since he was the one who was facing death. But his words touched her. Up until now, she'd been focused on doing all she could to prepare him so that she would have no regrets when he failed. She was embarrassed to realize that she had never truly believed success was possible. She'd wanted to do everything she could for him so she wouldn't feel guilty when he failed. She hadn't done this consciously, but she'd done it nonetheless.

What if she chose to believe that her mother's *sight* was indeed correct? Her mother often saw many paths, and not all of them came to pass, but her mother believed that all the paths she saw were possible outcomes. So, as Dashin noted, it meant that there had to be a way for him to succeed. This was the thought she'd been searching for, and Dashin had led her to it.

"So how do we find this path?" she mused out loud.

"I've been wondering that too."

"Like you said. It helps to know that there is a path."

"How does it help?" Dashin asked, perplexed.

She smiled. "I haven't been looking for a different path. I didn't know there was one."

"Oh, so you were..."

She blushed, her face hot with the shame of her admission.

"Alina, you have nothing to regret."

She glanced at him, unable to hold his eyes.

"I understand," he said. "You didn't think it was possible. And yet, you've been trying as hard as you could to help. Truly, I could not have asked for more."

She exhaled, grateful for his words, trying to let go of her embarrassment and focus her mind. Now that she felt there was a way, she was determined to find it. But there were so many challenges in the trials, so many things to accomplish, that the scope overwhelmed her.

"What is it?" he asked.

"There are too many challenges. How are we to find the paths through all of them?"

"We start with the one before us and ignore the others for now. It seems to me that I need to learn to move through the trees for all three trials. So, let's solve that problem first. Once we do that, we can work on the others."

That was true. Without being able to move through the trees, nothing else mattered since this would be the foundation on which all the trials stood. And, though the task was daunting, she felt lighter and more hopeful than she'd been in days. There was something here she wouldn't name, but it was something she was determined to fight for.

"Are you sure?" Dashin asked again.

"No, I'm not sure. But it's the only solution I can think of at the moment."

"Will it work?"

"I have no idea, I've never tried anything like this. The only way we're going to know is if we try it."

They were on the far side of the village, behind the outermost huts, above the last stretches of netting before these gave way to sheer drops beyond. Alina had ensured there would be no eyes on them as they tried what she proposed. She had decided that since the inadvertent *touching* in the clearing had yielded significant results on the platform, perhaps she could help Dashin see the forest through her eyes in some way. The *touching* in the clearing had not been enough to give him the ability to shed his innate fear of falling or to see the branches as twine on the platform. So she'd decided to try and address that. The very thought of what she was about to try unsettled her, but she couldn't think of anything better.

She strapped on one of the lanyards that she'd retrieved from her room before coming out here and, with practiced ease, launched the cup into the branches above her, fixing it in place. She stood on a branch that ran parallel to the one Dashin stood on, his hands on the trunk of his tree. She studied her branch and then closed her eyes. She walked back and forth along it using the picture she'd made in her mind and using the lanyard above her to provide an anchor she could draw on.

When she was comfortable that her body knew the branch and could follow it without effort, she opened her eyes and looked at Dashin.

"That's amazing," he said, looking at her feet. "How did you do that with your eyes closed?"

"I made a picture of it in my mind for my feet to follow. Do you not do the same?"

"I have no idea what that means."

She frowned. "Let me see if I can help." She reached out and put her hand on his shoulder. She breathed, asserting control over her *touch* the way she had since childhood. She reached through it for Dashin, from her hand to the muscles in his shoulder, to the vibrations surrounding him that were unique to him and that she'd come to know. Slowly, she let them seep toward her, but she kept them at bay so that they didn't *touch* her mind. Instead, she crept into his.

She felt his shoulder stiffen as she reached for his mind, but he immediately relaxed, letting her in. His trust moved her so much that she nearly lost her focus. She took a cleansing breath, composed herself, and pressed. It was dark and calmer than she'd expected. She sensed an emotion touch her, something she could not name but which felt personal in a way that made her heart beat faster. She pushed it away, not wanting her presence to be intrusive, though something about the emotion made her long to explore it.

"Dashin, open your eyes," she said.

As he did, she saw the world through his eyes. The branch, the forest below, the leaves, the huts. They were all familiar, and yet they were different when seen through his eyes, which sorted the colors and textures differently than hers. She was so fascinated by it that she forgot what she was doing until he turned, and she saw herself through those strange eyes. "Don't look at me, look at the branch," she said.

The view of the branch returned, and she let the picture of the branch form within her. Once she had it, she pushed it gently into his mind. He stiffened and made a tiny sound of wonder, excited at the novelty of the image. He examined it, rotating it in his mind so that he viewed the picture from above, from below, from the far side. These were things she'd never attempted and doubted she could manage. It was fascinating to see his mind grasp the essence of the image in a way she had never tried and spin the world around it.

"Stop it," she said, growing dizzy. "See the branch as it is in the world."

"Sorry."

The world stopped spinning. The branch was once again before him, the image lying upon it, but moving ahead of the branch as it swayed.

"The picture is moving," he said with a start.

"Yes, of course. Don't the pictures you draw move?"

"No, my pictures don't move."

"Oh," she said, dropping her hand from his shoulder. She sat down, the shape of the problem coming into view. He sat next to her, one arm around the trunk to his side.

She explained. "We form these pictures in our minds as we move through the trees. They show the world as it will be, not as it is."

"You see the future?" he frowned, scratching the pointy tip of one ear.

"Yes... No... I mean, our minds form pictures of the changing forest around us so that we can move through it. When I form a picture, I see the branch, but as the wind blows and the tree sways, I see where the branch will be as my foot arrives so that I can meet it."

"Your mind does that without you thinking about it?"

"I have to think on it, of course, but no more than you would while walking on the ground, I imagine."

"And, if you couldn't do this? I imagine you might fall repeatedly into the netting and perhaps hit a lot of branches on the way down?"

Alina opened her mouth to answer, and then, seeing his eyes, realized what he was saying. "I am sorry, Dashin. I did not imagine that you could not see the pictures. I thought that you were simply inexperienced at using them."

He shook his head. "Now that every part of my body has gained *experience* doing it my way, perhaps I could learn to see these pictures and do it your way?"

She smiled. He had the most amazing way of speaking. The pain of the past few days dispelled in an instant, no blame or anger assigned, understanding immediately that she had not known and had done her best.

"Of course. Let's try it again. This time, when you see the picture, walk along it and trust that the branch will be there when your foot reaches it. Walk at a steady pace, so I can feel your rhythm and supply the pictures. Perhaps if we do this together for a time, your mind will learn to do it for itself."

They tried it again, and Dashin stumbled and staggered a bit, his mind unaccustomed to trusting a picture over what his eyes saw before him. But as he continued to practice, he grew more comfortable. By the evening, he was walking back and forth on that branch as though he'd been born to the trees. Though, of course, Alina was supplying the pictures. For this to be of use, his mind would have to learn to do this for him and at a greater speed than he was managing now. But it was a huge step.

As he reached the trunk, she broke contact and sat down, lowering herself to her branch with her lanyard. Her legs ached from the tension of having her body follow its rhythm to stay on her branch as she supplied the pictures for Dashin to manage his. She was exhausted, her head ached, and she felt nauseous from having to hold both sets of pictures in her head at once and having to push his into his mind. She opened a pouch on her belt and fished out a piece of valagy root. She peeled it, put it in her mouth, and chewed it, swallowing the bitter juice. She closed her eyes for a moment, waiting for the relief. As she felt it blossom, the headache and nausea receding, she exhaled.

She opened her eyes and looked over at Dashin. He was covered in sweat, his tunic and pants drenched despite the cooling air, but he was grinning. She returned the grin. Today had started out as a disappointment, but it was ending with a ray of hope. There was still so much to do, and there was no telling whether this idea would work, but she was excited to find out.

Chapter 21

Alina's pictures were a near-perfect representation of the world itself, a shimmering copy of it floating in space, with detail and texture to rival the original. Somehow, her mind allowed her to choose to see this near-future world, instead of the current one, which made it simple for her to move through the forest to be, rather than the forest forever in flux.

Dashin concentrated on the branches before him, letting the picture form in his mind the way Alina had shown him. His pictures, by comparison, were stick figures, crude lines superimposed in space upon the existing forest he could not suppress. The thicknesses of these lines roughly matched the branches, limbs, and twigs they represented, his mind omitting smaller branches that wouldn't bear his weight as well as twigs and leaves.

The fact that he could now create pictures, however crude, spoke of some residual effect from his contact with Alina. His mind had learned to create these pictures after his session with Alina. It was adjusting the pictures as the environment changed, and getting his mind to trust them, which was the challenge. Were it not for remnants of Alina's magic, he could not have managed it.

He stepped forward, taking light steps along the thick line of the main branch he was on and following that line instead of the branch moving beneath it. He was still as thrilled and surprised each time the branch moved beneath him to find his foot as it came to rest as he'd been the first time he'd taken his first such step yesterday.

"This is so much easier," he said, not for the first time today.

He caught the edge of the branch on the next step, his toes curling to grip the rough surface so that he gained enough purchase to find the heart of the branch with the following step.

His feet were toughening up. The many days of practice, followed each night by the balm and banda leaves, had thickened his soles. They'd been at it for three days since Alina had shown him the world as she saw it. That TreeFolk were able to see the world so differently than he could had been a revelation to them both.

"Well done. Now leap to that branch beyond and complete the circuit," Alina called to him.

He let the picture of this new branch form in his mind, the segments readily falling into place. His mind adjusted the image to accommodate the effort he intended to exert on his leap as well as the current sway of the trees and change in the breeze.

He marveled, as he leapt, at the calculations involved in creating such a model and all the variables that needed to be taken into account to make it dynamic. His thoughts broke his concentration, and the picture vanished, leaving only the real branch before him as he flew toward it. He moved his foot to reach for it, but as he did, it swayed away from beneath him, and his foot found only air. He managed to catch the branch with an arm as he slammed into it, his chin taking the brunt of the impact but avoiding a fall into the netting. Though he'd fallen several times today, he'd so far managed to stay among the branches.

"What happened?" Alina called out from behind him.

"I lost my concentration," he said, climbing back up onto the branch and dabbing at the scrape on his chin.

"Are you hurt?"

"Just a scratch," he said, exhaling and settling his thoughts as Alina had taught him, letting his mind form another picture. Alina was amazing to watch in the trees. All the TreeFolk were, but he loved watching her. She floated, it seemed, her feet dancing across the branches as she raced through them.

They kept at it until midday, Dashin so excited by his growing facility that he wanted to continue while things were flowing. They broke as Hurza and Kani arrived, each bearing a basket.

"Dashin, you are doing so much better!" Kani exclaimed.

"What have you been feeding him?" Hurza teased, looking at Alina.

They dropped the baskets on the back of the platform of the outermost hut, near where Alina and Dashin were training. Kani and Hurza set out the lunch they'd brought. Kani handed Dashin a large piece of nutbread, his favorite, and he tore into it, the morning's exertions having stoked his appetite.

"Thanks," he mumbled, his mouth full.

"Kani, watch your fingers," Hurza teased. "You may lose them if you get too close to its mouth."

They laughed. The air was hot now, but a morning shower had cooled the forest. The birds were flitting about, hunting for the grubs and insects that had come out to drink rain from the bark. Dashin sat with his back to the hut, his legs out on the platform, and his feet dangling over the edge. In that moment, the world felt perfect.

"How is it that he has made such progress?" Kani asked Alina.

Alina explained to her friends how Dashin's mind worked. Her friends gaped on hearing it.

"No wonder he kept falling," Kani said.

"It's a good thing he has those thick bones," Hurza offered. "A TreePerson would have broken many by now."

Alina omitted the *touching* or how she'd realized that he could not see the pictures, or how she taught him to see them. Hurza and Kani had been uncomfortable with the *touching* they'd seen on the platform and had approached Enor with it out of concern. She didn't want this to be something awkward between them, so she left it out of her account. Dashin listened, enjoying the banter. It was heartwarming to see such a friendship, one that had grown over a lifetime. He'd only had fleeting tastes of friendship and nothing he'd had compared to what he saw between them.

"What?" Hurza asked, looking at him.

"Sorry," he said, wiping the grin from his face. "I was just admiring the three of you speaking together."

"You've never seen people speaking together?" Hurza asked, quirking an eyebrow.

"I have not had much experience with friendship," he answered, his voice tentative. "And, none like this."

Hurza sat stunned, unsure whether he was serious. Kani reached over and patted his arm. "You have friends now, Dashin."

They were such simple words, but the feelings they precipitated overwhelmed him, and he had to look away. His emotions were close at hand these days. He wiped at his eyes and swallowed before turning back. "Thanks, Kani," he said, and then, including them all, "Thanks."

They ate in silence as the birds continued feeding. A lizard the length of his forearm crept along a branch before them, snatching bugs from the bark with its tongue.

"Your bruises are starting to fade," Hurza mused, looking at him.

"Yes, I'm falling less now."

"It may be useful for you to continue getting bruised," Hurza said.

"I'm not sure I agree," Dashin replied, frowning.

"What are you thinking?" Alina asked, turning to her.

"Talk in the village has moved on from Dashin. The resistance has dwindled, and folks see him now as a sad case that will soon be taken from us. Hedrick has stopped speaking against him."

"And if Dashin suddenly gets better and is moving through the trees..." Alina said, continuing her friend's thought.

"Yes, it may revive Hedrick's opposition."

"I think I'd rather have the opposition. Even my bruises have bruises now."

Alina and her friends ignored him.

"I could create a dye with this coloring," Kani said, leaning forward and poking at one of the bruises on Dashin's arm.

"Ouch," he cried.

"Oh, sorry," she said, reaching to pat it as he pulled it away.

"Do you think you could make it look real?" Alina asked.

"I'm sure she can," Hurza said. "She created some obscure color yesterday when we were dying fabric. She worked it for ages, even though it was suitable long before she was done."

"It was not suitable," Kani objected, then turned to Alina and Dashin to explain. "We were trying to match nuxat eggs, and the coloring and mottling were subtle and took effort."

"As I said," Hurza shrugged. "I'm certain that if she can match the subtle *mottling*," she stressed the word, "she can manage a bruise."

"Well, we have the perfect canvas for you to practice on," Alina said with a chuckle.

Dashin held his breath, trying not to squirm as Kani tickled his chest. She'd been rubbing and dabbing at it for ages.

"Are you almost finished?" he asked, grimacing.

"Almost. Stop moving and hold your tunic higher."

Dashin lifted his tunic as Kani brushed more of the dye into roundish circles on his chest. She'd already applied a base coat of a different color and was now brushing in another. When she was done, she blew on his chest to dry it.

"Stop that," he squirmed, "it tickles."

"Keep your tunic up or you'll smudge it," she said, pushing on his arm.

Dashin looked over to Alina, but she and Hurza had their backs to him as they waited for Kani to finish. Kani had spent days working at various formulas, staining his chest where other villagers wouldn't see, and comparing her work to the bruises on his body. She requested some fresh bruises from him to study, and though Dashin refused to fall on purpose to supply her with such, he was still falling enough by accident that she had a ready supply.

Kani blew on it some more as he squirmed and then dabbed at it with a cloth, blending it in until she was satisfied. "Ready!" she announced.

Alina and Hurza, who had been chatting, turned and walked over. Kani pointed at two bruises on Dashin's chest. "Which of them is the real one?"

Alina leaned in. "The coloring is amazing," she said, reaching to touch Dashin's skin.

Kani batted at her hand. "No, decide which is real without touching."

Alina leaned in closer to study them, and Kani pushed her away. "No, don't come any closer than an arm's length."

Alina shook her head. "I can't tell. No, wait, that one, that's the fake bruise."

Kani turned to Hurza, who was squinting. "Yes, it's definitely that one."

Kani grinned, delighted. "No, it's the other one."

Alina laughed. "You are a master at this."

"I told you she'd get the mottling," Hurza said.

"Can I put my tunic down now?" Dashin asked, feeling foolish as he stood there with the girls studying his chest.

"Yes," Kani said, satisfied. "I think we have suitable dyes."

"I hope so," he said. "I'm covered in splotches."

"We'll try some on your arms for the evening meal," Kani announced.

Solvan crowded up next to him as they ate on the platform, the village enjoying the evening meal.

"It was so *round*," the boy exclaimed, as he finished recounting a maneuver he'd perfected. He assured Dashin that Matse could verify his account. Dashin oohed at all the right places, commending the lad on his feat. He told the boy that he might soon be asking him to teach him these tricks. The boy beamed up at him.

Dashin had learned from Rigin that the two children were confined to the areas of the village with netting, while other children their age were already venturing out beyond the village daily. Solvan's inability to walk and Matse's inability to speak, coupled with the fact both were orphans, had set them aside.

That they might never venture beyond the village and so would never be able to stand for their own *becoming* and be accepted as *of the tribe*, saddened him. But Rigin had reminded him that life in the trees was hard. Rigin mentioned that most TreeFolk learned to live with loss. She'd lost a child shortly after being married, then her husband, and recently her son. Dashin was shocked to hear it, having only heard of Sneva, but she patted his arm, waving it away and saying that the SkyGods must have their reasons.

"How are your feet doing?" Enor asked, filling a banda leaf with marinated vegetables and dried meat.

"They are much better, thanks. That balm is amazing."

"Yes, it has served our tribe well."

"Where did you learn to heal?"

"My father shared it with me, as did his father before him."

"Will you pass this on to Alina?"

He felt her stiffen next to him at the question, and he glanced at her. She didn't look up from the leaf she was stuffing. He turned back to Enor.

"I see you have some new bruises," Enor said, changing the subject.

Dashin wasn't certain what had just happened or how to answer this question. They hadn't discussed whether they should inform Enor or Rigin about the bruise dye. But since there were others nearby, he didn't want to risk discussing it here.

"Ah, yes, a few new bruises," he answered, which was technically true, though he had more fake bruises than new bruises.

"How is the training going?" Rigin asked Alina.

"It is slow, but we're making progress," Alina answered.

"After the meal, I have something for Dashin, but I'd like you to be there if you have the time."

Alina nodded. "Of course." She turned to Dashin and gave him a querying glance. He shrugged.

Once they were done eating, they put the remaining food away, wiped down the tables, stowed them, and started toward Rigin's hut. As they were about to leave the platform, Enor pulled Dashin aside and whispered in his ear. Dashin flushed. Enor smiled and then walked away.

As they walked back to Rigin's hut, Alina leaned in. "What did my father say to you?"

"He said that we should apply the dye once the skin has cooled and I've stopped sweating."

Alina's eyes went to his arm, where tiny rivulets of dye had collected at the base of each fake bruise.

Rigin sent the children ahead to get ready for bed, and Solvan leapt ahead, clomping across the bridge with Matse close behind.

Rigin waited for Dashin and Alina to catch up to her, and as they drew near, she said. "You should wash before bed or you'll stain the bedding."

Dashin and Alina both opened their mouths to speak, and Rigin laughed, patting them both on the arm. "You must think me blind as well as simple."

"If you rinse it off tonight, I can help reapply it in the morning if Kani brings me the dyes and some brushes." She looked at them. "It was Kani that created them, right?"

Alina nodded.

"I thought so. It is good work, though there is a touch more yellow than needed, and if she used the drier brown pigment, it would run less."

Dashin laughed, and then Alina joined in. "Thank you, Rigin. We appreciate it."

Rigin waved it away.

"Is that what you wanted to tell us?" Alina asked.

"No, no. Come, let me show you." She turned and led them into the hut.

She lit the oil lamp with a firestick and put it on the counter in the common room. Solvan and Matse had just washed up, and Rigin inspected their efforts, picking up a towel and scrubbing behind the boy's ears as he squirmed in her grip. She turned to Alina and Dashin. "Sit, sit. I'll just be a moment."

She ducked into her room, and Dashin and Alina each took a chair at the table. Solvan and Matse shared a chair, leaving the other for Rigin.

Rigin emerged from her room with a leather belt. It had been freshly oiled and gleamed in the lamplight. The leather was braided in an intricate pattern, each strand masterfully placed. It was more than a belt. It was a work of art. A leather sheath hung from it, with a bone handle protruding from it. Several leather pouches hung from it, the pouches and sheath beautifully crafted. She held it for a moment, the item clearly having great value for her, and then handed it to Dashin.

"This was Sneva's. I want you to have it."

Dashin choked up. He'd never had anyone give him something like this before. He started to protest, but Rigin pressed it into his hands and then reached up and put her fingers to his lips.

"It is mine to give. I want you to have it."

"Rigin," Alina said. "Are you sure?"

She nodded. "I am."

"There's one more thing," she said, stepping into the room Dashin was using. He heard her open the chest at the foot of his bed, rummage through it, and then close the lid. She stepped back through the curtain carrying a set of lanyards. She placed the bundle on the table. "You are going to need lanyards. These were Sneva's."

She put up a hand before they could protest. "They are just gathering dust here," she said, though the lanyards were spotless.

Solvan reached up and touched them with his fingers, his eyes hungry at the sight.

"Thank you, Rigin. I don't have words to express what this means to me," Dashin said, choking back emotion.

Rigin leaned forward and touched her forehead to his. A warmth flowed into him. He leaned into it, trying to express, in his heart, the deep gratitude he felt.

She pulled back and smiled. "Now you'll look like a proper TreePerson."

Rigin gathered up the children and sent them to bed. Dashin ran his fingers over the belt. The craftsmanship was exquisite. It was beyond anything he'd seen here in the village and would have been prized anywhere. He'd never owned anything so fine before. He worried about what daily use might do to it or whether he was worthy of such a gift.

Chapter 22

Alina sat in her favorite corner of the central platform, sharing some nutbread and tree melon with Dashin as she discussed her plan for the day's training in the village.

"I want you to build some speed at creating the pictures in your mind so that you can run across the branches or change directions."

Dashin nodded, chewing and then swallowing another impressive slab of nutbread. Where he put all that food was beyond imagining. Even accounting for his stout and denser body, she was still perplexed at where it might be going.

Kani and Hurza joined them, dropping the packs they carried on the platform and seating themselves on the opposite side of the table.

"Show me your arm," Kani asked, reaching for it.

Dashin laid it on the table, and Kani began rubbing and scratching at a few of the fake bruises on his skin, marveling at the improvements Rigin had made to her formulation.

"How did she manage to dry it so evenly and still retain its color?" she mused.

Hurza rolled her eyes. "Did you not discuss it when you met with her to give her dye?"

Kani huffed. "She mentioned she had some ideas. She did not provide details." She leaned in, studying them. "I will have to ask her about it," she mumbled.

Hurza nudged Kani with her shoulder. "Leave his arm alone. Others are beginning to notice."

Kani dropped Dashin's arm and turned to look behind her.

Hurza nudged her again. "Don't look."

Kani turned to Hurza, her eyes narrowed. But her face grew confused as she noted Hurza's surprise.

"Is that Sneva's belt?" Hurza asked, leaning forward to get a better look at it beyond the edge of the table.

"Yes, Rigin gave it to Dashin last night," Alina said.

"Oooh," Kani exclaimed. "Can we see it?"

"Sure," Dashin said, unfastening it and then sweeping crumbs from the table before placing it on the surface.

"May I?" Kani asked, reaching for it.

Dashin nodded. "Of course."

"It is a remarkable thing," Kani said, brushing her fingers across the exquisite leather. "She truly is the finest leather-worker the tribe has ever had."

Hurza leaned forward and ran her fingers over the pattern woven in the sheath. "She made this for Sneva's *becoming*."

"Really?" Dashin asked, hungry to know more.

"There's never been another like this, and she has not made another since," Kani offered. She leaned closer to study it. "Why would she..." Kani began.

Hurza bumped her with a knee. Kani glanced at her, annoyed, but then her face went wide, and she turned to Dashin. "Oh, I'm sorry, Dashin. I did not mean to..."

Dashin waved it away. "It's fine. I wondered the same thing myself. I've never owned anything so fine."

"No one has," Kani said, continuing to admire it.

"Where are the two of you going?" Alina asked, changing the subject as she motioned to the packs on the platform behind them. Dashin took the belt and refastened it around his waist.

"Enor asked us to gather supplies for his medicines," Hurza said.

"Can you get some valagy root?" Alina asked.

"Yes, it's one of the things he wanted," Kani said.

"I think I saw some near the mouth of the river, by the nuxat-shaped stone." Hurza nodded. "Yes, I've seen it there too."

Aor, Drur, and Gamoc strode up. They wore packs on their backs, their lanyards fixed and coiled around their forearms. The cups from these dangled and swayed, the rubber-encased fingers waving as they stopped before the table.

"My mother mentioned you were going to collect herbs," Aor said, looking at Hurza.

She nodded. "Yes, for Enor."

"We are going to gather silas. If you are going that way."

Hurza stood, and then Kani did. "Yes, that would be nice." Hurza crinkled her eyes at him in plain view of everyone.

Aor flushed. He had not meant it as a personal invitation. Alina suppressed a smile as Aor looked at the other boys, who had all found other things to occupy their attention.

Hurza beamed, pleased with herself.

Aor looked at Dashin. "I see you're still falling in the child netting." He motioned, indicating the extensive bruising. "Perhaps by the time the trials arrive, you'll manage to fall into the netting without hitting every branch in your way."

She felt Dashin tense beside her, the muscles in his jaw bunching.

Alina stepped in before Dashin could respond. "We have only begun training," Alina said, searching for the words that would paint the story she sought. "He has improved some..." She let the words hang.

Aor snorted. "Even if the trials were for children, held here above the netting, it seems doubtful he'd even complete one transit of the village. I have no idea why my father agreed to such a thing."

"He did so because he is the chief of our tribe," Kani replied.

They all turned at Kani's unexpected outburst. She met their eyes.

Aor shrugged. "He was maneuvered into it by Marna, invoking some long unused verse of our song."

"Unused or not," Alina said, angry at the slight to her mother. "It is a verse of *our* song."

"It doesn't matter. In sixteen days this will be over," Aor said, motioning to Dashin with his chin.

"Then we'll do the best we can with what time remains," Alina replied.

"It might not even happen," Gamoc offered excitedly.

Aor turned to him, his eyes hard, and the boy paled and looked down.

"What do you mean?" Hurza asked Gamoc.

"He babbles like a child," Aor said, his voice curt. Gamoc did not look up or answer. Aor turned back to them. As his eyes found Dashin, his mouth gaped open, his eyes growing huge. He stepped closer to the table. "Where did you get that?" he shouted.

Dashin looked up, confused.

"The belt. Sneva's belt. Did you take that?" Aor demanded, enraged.

Dashin flushed, his skin going dark green, his face stone. Alina hadn't seen him mad before, but she sensed fury writhe up within him. She put a hand on his arm.

"Rigin gave it to him," Alina said, trying to draw Aor's eyes.

"She couldn't have," Aor announced, continuing to glare at Dashin, his fists tight.

The tension between them mounted. The wall she kept between herself and the world was breached momentarily as a wave of emotions swept through her *touch*. The air sizzled with it, like meat on a hot brazier. Drur stepped forward and took Aor's shoulder, whispering something to him.

Aor shrugged it off without looking back. "It was Sneva's." Aor spat, his body shaking with rage.

Sneva had been Aor's best friend. The two had been inseparable growing up. Alina had heard the tale of Sneva's death from several of the men who were there. A large stoda had turned on the younger men driving the herd and charged Aor, who'd stood frozen before the enormous beast. Sneva had leapt in and shoved Aor from its path and been gutted by the stoda's tusk in his stead. It had taken several men to bring down the beast. Aor pulled his friend's body free and held him as Sneva died in his arms. Aor was devastated, for many moons, he had to leave the platform whenever his friend's name was spoken.

"It was Rigin's to give," Alina said, trying to dispel the rage in the air around her.

Dashin boiled next to her, about to erupt, the muscles in his shoulders bulging dangerously. Aor's tone brought to mind confrontations Dashin had had with aggressive children in his youth. She sensed a terrible violence coming, something that threatened to consume them both. She slid her foot beneath the table and touched Dashin's knee. It took a moment, a long moment, but finally, he took a breath and looked away.

The tension left Aor much more slowly. He continued to glare for some time before he turned away and looked at Hurza. "Are you joining us?" he spat.

She swallowed and nodded. "Yes, we're ready." She and Kani picked up their packs and slipped them on. Aor stormed off, the other boys in tow. Kani adjusted her pack and followed. Before she left, Hurza bent down and whispered. "I will try to find out what Gamoc meant."

Hurza hurried after the others, fastening her lanyards as she went. Once they had passed out of sight, Alina allowed herself to exhale. Her hands were shaking. It had been close, so close.

"I don't want to train over the netting anymore," Dashin said, his jaw set, eyes on the path where the others had just disappeared. "He's right, there isn't much time left. We need to start training in the forest."

Alina nodded. It was too soon, but Aor and Dashin were right. There was too little time left. And that was without knowing what Gamoc alluded to. Somehow, Hedrick must still be maneuvering. They'd likely misjudged him, assuming he'd given up. She prayed they would not live to regret the oversight.

Alina took Dashin into the forest, out of sight from the village, well beyond the netting. She took her time, allowing Dashin to pick his way after her. As he followed her, he kept looking down, his gaze fixed beneath him. She called to him repeatedly, instructing him to look ahead and form the pictures in his mind. But he was so terrified at the empty space below that he forgot all they'd practiced. He moved stiffly, his hands grasping at twigs and branches to steady himself as he lurched about, his knuckles pale from the force of his grip. His breathing was shallow and labored, his eyes narrowed and locked on the branches beneath his feet.

When they reached an area of the forest thick with branches, she leapt across a small gap and waited for him to make the jump. He was reluctant, but he set his jaw and followed. The branch he landed on swayed wildly as it took his weight and swept out from under him. He tumbled from it and screamed as he did, flailing as he bounced from one branch and then another before latching onto a third. He wrapped his arms and legs around it.

Alina held her breath as he fell, willing him to react and exhaling as he found purchase. She dropped onto the limb next to him.

"Are you hurt?" she asked, seeing the fear in his eyes. She remembered her own fear when her mother had first taught her to fall, but she didn't remember it being this intense. She'd grown up in the trees and was suited to it. She couldn't imagine what this must be like for someone who had grown up on the ground.

"I don't think so," Dashin replied, still clutching the branch.

"Can you release that branch and climb upon it?"

"I don't think my body is ready to release it just yet. Perhaps when the visions of my death stop flashing before my eyes."

She stepped onto his branch and offered her hand, but the movement made him tighten his grip. "The forest floor is a long way below us."

"I am aware of that."

She chuckled. "Yes, I can see that it's a concern for you."

"Nothing gets by you," he grumbled.

She softened. "Climb up here and sit by me." She sat down, making space for him to join her.

Dashin relaxed his grip enough to throw a leg over the branch and pull himself up. He locked one of his legs between two other branches and kept his hands on the branch beneath him.

"Dashin, look below us and tell me what you see."

"A long drop to the forest floor."

"Yes, that is so, but what else do you see?"

"Lots of branches to hit on the way down?"

"Yes, exactly!" She said, smiling.

"Exactly? Breaking my neck when I hit the ground after having broken all my bones on branches on the way down doesn't sound like a good thing to me."

She took her pack off and wedged it between some branches. "Watch me," she said. She stood up, opened her arms, and let her body fall backward from the limb they were on, her eyes on his as she did. Dashin lunged to catch her, but her foot slipped through his fingers before he could get a grip.

She fell a body length, barely missing several branches. Then she spun in the air, glanced off one branch, and alit on another several body lengths below him. She crinkled her eyes at him and let herself fall backward again before catching herself several branches below that one. She repeated the process several more times before climbing back up and dropping onto the branch beside him.

"You have to think of the branches below us like the ropes in the netting of the village. As you can see, there are a great many of them between us and the forest floor. So, if you fall, you can use them to arrest your fall and regain your footing."

"You make it look easy, and it sounds easy, but it's..." is all he managed before Alina pushed him over backward from the branch he was sitting on. She watched him fall, praying to the SkyGods that this would work on him as it did for TreeFolk. She had chosen a section of forest with a lot of branches to make it as safe as possible for him to learn, but accidents did happen, and she held her breath as he fell.

He crashed through a thick cluster of branches. A rapid series of impacts accompanied by loud grunts rose in his wake before he slammed into and latched onto a large limb. He was cursing in Ancaran as Alina dropped down next to him. "I did learn some of your language, you know," she said, arching an eyebrow.

He pressed his lips together, biting back the stream of words she could see swirling within him.

"Dashin, that was a little inelegant and perhaps painful, but you see, you did stop your fall. Does your side hurt? Let me see, lift up your arm." He shifted on the tree next to her and reached up to show her the bruise. As he released the branch, she shoved him backward off that branch. He tumbled again, crashing through more of the canopy. He snagged an ankle in the crook of a branch, which stopped him. His body bounced up and down as the branch recovered from the strain, with him dangling upside down by a leg. He was swearing again.

"An unusual technique, but that was much better," she called from above.

They spent the rest of the morning with Dashin falling from branch to branch and then climbing up again. After the initial terror, he gradually relaxed. Over time, it became easier for him, and she breathed easier. By the time they broke for a midday meal, he was covered again in real bruises.

Alina found a comfortable branch for them to sit on and pulled a bag from her pack. She folded the bag back to reveal a stack of banda leaves already stuffed and rolled. She pulled the water gourd from her pack, unstopped it, and took a drink. The water was cool and fresh, with just a hint of the wood taste from her cistern. She offered him the gourd, and he pulled from it greedily, some of the water escaping from the corners of his mouth to run down his neck.

"Easy," she said. "That has to last us the rest of the day."

"Sorry," he replied, returning it and then rubbing his neck and shoulder.

"Let me see," she said, leaning forward.

He scooted back. "No chance," he said, putting up a hand.

"Dashin, I wasn't going to..." she paused, and seeing his face, she chuckled. She held up her hands and then pointed to the bag. "Have some banda leaves. Rigin made them for us."

They dug into the meal, both famished. Alina hadn't done much physically, but she was exhausted from the stress. She had never considered the strain her mother must have felt in pushing her child from the branches. It had been heartbreaking throwing Dashin's already battered body from them and praying he'd somehow catch himself. She remembered crying and screaming at her mother and saying so many ungrateful things in her terror. Her mother had been impassive through it all, calm and caring, Alina realized now. She wondered whether it had been the same for her mother when she'd learned to fall. She had never met her grandmother, but she had heard stories about how gifted a seer she was. She wondered, not for the first time, if her mother and grandmother, because of the *sight*, had shared a bond that she would never know.

"I'm starving," Dashin mumbled, swallowing a stuffed banda leaf and reaching for another.

"No wonder your body is so heavy," she quipped.

"Thankfully, the gravity on your world is much less than on mine, or I'd have broken my neck this morning."

"What is this *gra-vi-ty* you speak of? I have memories of the word from your songs, but I did not grasp its meaning."

Dashin tried to explain the concept of mass and attraction, but he found himself having to step backward to cover other concepts. Before long, the explanation became hopelessly tangled.

"I do not believe you know what this thing is any more than I do," she chuckled.

He shrugged. "Perhaps not. There are many things I thought I knew that I am no longer certain of."

"My mother says that it's a good thing not to know too much, that to learn anything new, there must be space for it to live within."

"That makes sense," he said, taking another bite and looking off into the trees where a distant group of corsols was screeching. Swallowing, he turned to her. "I'm sorry, Alina. I didn't mean those things I said while falling."

She laughed, leaning forward and patting him on the arm. "When I learned to fall, I said many things I later regretted." She quirked an eyebrow. "Though I was only five sun cycles at the time, so the things I said were much tamer."

Chapter 23

The morning had been one of the most terrifying experiences of his life. Only the destruction of his ship surpassed it. The idea of falling as he followed Alina out into the forest had filled him with dread, but the reality of falling was a terror beyond anything he'd imagined. A primal urge wrenched him, taking control of his body as he tumbled, his arms blindly grabbing at whatever came near.

That Alina had pushed him without warning had angered and frightened him. Words tumbled from him that he would never have believed lived within. It was only through the force of repetition that he began to feel able to take an active part in the process, to actively see the forest flashing by around him, and adjust his body to find a way to stop himself.

As Alina noted, his efforts weren't elegant, but they were proving more successful at arresting his falls. There was still plenty of crashing, but he was able to absorb the blows and not lose his focus.

As painful and horrifying as the morning had been, he grudgingly admitted that learning how to fall incrementally would have taken ages.

As they sat having their midday meal, he reflected on this morning's confrontation on the platform. Aor's accusation had lit a fire in him. He'd been angry plenty of times, but the white-hot fury he'd felt this morning was beyond anything he'd known before. Were it not for Alina, he didn't know what might have happened, for he'd seen the same rage in Aor's eyes.

It was the fact that Aor assumed Dashin had stolen the belt from Rigin, someone who had been nothing but kind to him, that galled him. Alina had explained Aor's relationship to Sneva and Sneva's sacrifice. He tried to see things from Aor's perspective, but could not find his way there.

He'd grown up the youngest person in his classes, the target for boys older and larger than him who were uncomfortable with his presence. As such, he'd taken an interest in combat training and pursued these classes diligently after a near altercation. The confidence he'd gained from the classes had been enough to give prospective tormentors pause. He'd come to think that he'd never have to use those skills. This morning had almost seen this belief undone.

They spent the rest of the day climbing and falling through the trees. By the end of the day, Dashin felt more comfortable. The dread he'd felt at the beginning of the day had lessened to mere anxiety. The climbing he did on Ancara and the reduced gravity here served him well as he scrambled up. Alina praised his ascents. It was the one asset he had at the moment.

"I don't imagine the course for the *trial of the trees* will be vertical?" Dashin mused, resting on a branch.

She shook her head. "No, it will be a long loop through the forest, with only a little climbing or falling."

"Should we perhaps practice moving in such a loop then?"

"We have been."

He was perplexed. "I don't understand. All we've done all day is go up and down."

She smiled. "Do you see that tree over there with the patch of bark peeled away?" She pointed to a large tree ten body-lengths or so from them.

"Yes."

"Make your way to that tree and then back to me."

Dashin stood up and did so. This morning, he'd been stumbling along, blinded by the deathly fear of falling. Now, without that debilitating fear, the pictures came freely to his mind. He followed them, his eyes on the branches instead of the space beneath them. It was like it had been in the village with the netting. He reached the tree and turned around. He could see her grinning at him, her grin growing larger as he made his way back to her. When he arrived, he sat down next to her. "You are pleased with yourself, I imagine?"

She beamed at him. "Can you tell?"

On their way back to the village, it began to pour. The sheer amount of rain was astounding. Alina found a few solid branches and fished out her soapstone from a pouch on her belt. She took advantage of the torrent to wash her clothes, limbs, hair, and face.

Dashin sat down on a branch and put his back to the trunk, finding other branches with his feet so he felt well anchored. He fished out the soapstone from the pouch on his belt. He soaped up as well, putting the stone back once he'd lathered himself up so as not to lose it. Once he was lathered, he scrubbed, and then as he began rinsing, the rain stopped. He groaned. Alina, already rinsed, turned and laughed.

"You must learn the rhythm of the rain, Dashin."

"You knew when it was going to stop?"

She nodded. "If you listen, you can hear the rain moving through the forest."

"The rain moves?"

"Of course it moves. What a strange question."

Dashin wiped soap from an eye, squinting at the mild stinging sensation. As he rubbed at that eye, soap dripped into the other. He wiped at that one, too.

"Stop rubbing your eyes. You'll irritate them," Alina said.

He felt her move close. "Keep your eyes closed for a moment," she said.

He felt her fingers on his face, wiping his forehead. She poured water over each eye and then wiped his face with a cloth from her pack.He blinked his eyes open to see her smiling at him.

After the brief shower, the late-day sun slanted in through the trees, making the beads of water dotting the leaves sparkle. As he looked up, the soft rays behind Alina cast her in a warm glow, making the dewy pearls she wore on her skin and hair scintillate. It took his breath away, and he gaped up at her.

"What?" Alina said, running her fingers through her hair and flicking rainwater from her shoulders. She looked down at her clothes, smoothing them down with her palms, before looking back at him. She ran her hands through her hair again. "Do I have soap in my hair?"

Dashin snapped out of it. "No, I'm sorry. I just..." he cleared his throat and looked away, letting his heart rate return to normal. *What am I doing?*

She gave him an appraising look and seemed about to say something, but dropped it. Instead, she stoppered her water gourd. "That was the last of our water."

"Thanks," he said, scratching his soapy head.

"Don't put that back in your eyes," she said. "Leave it alone. You can wash when we get back."

Dashin was extra careful as they made their way back to the village. There were a few small patches of slimy moss that were treacherous, but after slipping on them a few times, he learned to spot and avoid them. His feet were toughening up. He found he could increasingly rely on them to grip the branches as he moved. However, since all the branches were laden with rain, the trip back was one long, sparse shower. Every branch he grabbed to steady himself dumped its accumulated rainwater on him, drenching him further. The air and the rain were warm, so it was not unpleasant. Alina moved through it without a thought.

When they arrived at the platform, the village children were waiting. They were fascinated by his many bruises and asked to see them. Solvan, it turned out, had been chronicling his training in tales Dashin imagined he was inventing. He was about to protest when he saw Solvan's nervousness among them. He acquiesced then, nodding as the children pointed and discussed how each of these must have happened based on Solvan's accounts. He half-listened, having no idea what they were talking about, but from the sound of it, Dashin was performing prodigious feats. Once they were satisfied with his inventory of bruises, he mentioned that there had been a lot of falling today, but he hoped to do better tomorrow. Most of the children had already learned to fall and could relate. He received encouraging words from them as they clustered around him before the evening meal. It warmed his heart, and he received their words gratefully.

He washed up and changed into fresh clothes. As he walked back to the central platform, he looked out into the canopy. He was starting to see the forest differently. Not only was his mind learning to supply the pictures of the changing forest, but he was beginning to glimpse routes through the foliage. He'd been watching the paths Alina chose, trying to note how she navigated. There were patterns there he hadn't noted before. The forest had seemed a wild and unstructured place to him, but now he was seeing the way the limbs stretched out from their trunks and could predict, in some cases, where an unseen branch might be before he came upon it.

Once the meal was done, Dashin asked Rigin to show him how to care for the belt she'd given him. It had gotten wet today and had scuff marks on it from falling. He apologized for not having taken better care of it, but she put her fingers on his lips and mentioned that she'd made the belt to be worn. She brought some oil and a cloth and showed him how to oil the belt and remove smudges from it by rubbing it with the cloth. He worked at it diligently, the interaction a bittersweet reminder of his days working with Gralan.

They spent two days moving vertically, and then horizontally through the trees. The more he practiced, the more easily his mind created the images, and the more adept he became at arresting his falls.

Things in the village grew even more strained. Aor stared daggers at him whenever Dashin looked over. Aor and the other boys sat with Hedrick during the evening meals, hanging on his every word.

Alina had to watch the forest now, having caught Gamoc in the trees watching them. She'd sent him away, but feared he'd been sent to report on their progress. Fortunately, Dashin had not been having a good morning while Gamoc was there.

As midday approached, Aras and Narat stopped by on their way back to the village.

"You're making progress, Dashin," Aras said, as they came upon him and Alina. They were both wearing packs and carrying a hefty log on their shoulders. They put it down for a moment and fished out their water gourds.

"Thanks," Dashin said, unsure how to answer. He hadn't spoken much to the twins since arriving, but they were always smiling and laughing and seemed loved by all. "What is the log for?"

"We need to replace one of the bridges in the grove, and there's also been a request for a few more benches. It's become a popular place at midday, it seems."

Dashin felt Alina shift next to him. Midday was when Hedrick held court. Could this mean his influence was spreading? Dashin glanced at Alina, who seemed anxious at the news.

"Hey," Aras said, wiping his brow and then catching their eyes. "Not everyone is happy with what is being said."

"What is being said?" Dashin asked, unable to resist.

Aras looked to Narat, who shrugged. Aras turned back to them and seemed about to say something, but shook his head instead. "Never mind, it's just talk. And many believe in Marna's vision. We just want you to know that there are voices in opposition." Aras reached over and patted Dashin on the shoulder.

"Thanks," Dashin said. "It means a lot."

"Don't mention it," Narat said. "Perhaps we'll leave a few splinters on some of the new benches. You know, give them something else to talk about." He roared at the thought of it, and Aras chuckled. They picked up their log, sliding it onto their shoulders, and headed off.

Alina and Dashin watched them go.

"Do you feel like time is running out?" Dashin asked, watching the twins maneuver the large log through the canopy.

"I do," Alina said. "We'll start working with lanyards tomorrow."

The tension during the evening meal was palpable. The amiable mood Dashin had first encountered had given way to muttered conversations and hard looks.

"Pay it no mind," Enor said, pushing the stack of banda leaves toward Dashin.

"I feel sad to have brought such dissent to your village."

"Who knows what you brought? My wife thinks your presence here is *important*. Perhaps you bring hope?"

"Hope? How could that be?"

"I'm just a simple doctor. I do not pretend to meddle in the affairs of SkyGods."

"There is nothing simple about you," Alina said affectionately.

He smiled and shrugged.

"Alina says you will begin training with lanyards tomorrow?" Rigin said.

Enor's eyes snapped up, and Solvan bounced with joy next to Dashin.

"Do you think he's ready?" Enor asked, his voice low, leaning in.

"We are short on time. We must press ahead," Alina replied.

Enor nodded, though Dashin could see his uneasiness at the thought.

Alina leaned into the table and whispered. "Gamoc let slip the other day that the *becoming* might not occur. Hurza tried to press him on it, but he wouldn't say more."

Enor waved it away. "It is only talk. I do not believe it will go far enough for that."

Alina exhaled, sitting back.

"I'm sure you'll be *round* with the lanyards," Solvan said, bubbling next to him.

"I'll do my best," Dashin said, nudging him with his shoulder.

"You will be," the boy announced with authority.

Dashin felt something tugging at his tunic. He looked down, and there was a little hand holding the corner of it. Matse, seated next to Solvan, had her hand around the boy and was holding his tunic in her little fist.

He smiled down at her, and she looked away, blushing, but her little hand remained where it was. She was so quiet it was easy to overlook the girl, but she had clearly formed an attachment to him.

The past few days had been hard. He'd been bruised and battered. He'd felt discouraged at times, wondering whether he'd ever learn to move through the trees. But as he sat there, he realized that he carried the hopes of others with him, too. Others were looking to him, anxious for his success, their thoughts and hearts with him. He'd never felt that before. It was a fragile yet tremendous thing. It filled him with an even greater sense of determination. He wasn't only doing this for himself, nor for Alina, with whom he'd developed a connection he couldn't describe. There were others caught up in this, too, others he could not let down.

Chapter 24

"Feel the fingers of the cup on the branch before you squeeze the grip," Alina repeated.

The lanyard cup bounced off the branch, the cup already closed as it reached it. Dashin pulled it back and tried again. She watched his fingers as he swung the cup toward the branch, his fingers loose on the grip, and then squeezing it just a moment too late. The fingers had already kissed the branch, the lanyard pulling the cup away as the fingers tried to close, its grip insufficient as the lanyard retreated. Dashin groaned.

"There's something wrong with these lanyards," Dashin said, frustrated.

They'd been at it most of the morning, Dashin standing on a branch and launching the lanyard cup up at various branches ahead of him, trying to grab them. The exercise was to throw the lanyard at a branch, grab it, pull on the lanyard to ensure it was secure, then release it and repeat. It was a simple exercise, and yet he'd only made a handful of successful grabs.

"Are you seeing the pictures of the branches in your mind?"

"Yes, I'm seeing the pictures. I think there's something wrong with the lanyards."

Alina dropped down from her branch and walked over. "Let me see." She took them from Dashin, strapped them to her forearms, and leapt into space, throwing one of the cups before her. She snagged the branch Dashin had been practicing on and swung from there to another and another, moving up and down through the canopy with ease. She flew by him a few times, her body grazing him before returning and landing with a thump on the branch next to him, the lanyards dangling from her wrists. "They seem to be fine now," she said, studying them as though there might have been a problem.

"I get it," he said, "the problem is between my ears."

She crinkled her eyes at him. "I never said any such thing."

"You never *said* it," he agreed.

She crinkled her eyes again. "Do you want to try again?"

He sighed and presented his forearms. She slipped them off her arms and tied them to his. Once they were in position, she hopped back up onto the branch next to him and watched as he launched one of the cups. It bounced off the branch.

"Too soon," she said.

The next one slipped off.

"Too late."

And so it went until the midday break. As they moved toward her pack to take their meal, Alina wondered what the problem could be. It was painful to watch him struggle so. The past few days had been difficult, forcing him to learn to fall so soon after he had only just learned to walk in the trees. She couldn't look at the bruises on his body without feeling guilty. Her mind flitted back to the rain shower of a few days ago. She'd thought on it a few times since. There'd been something odd in the way he'd looked at her once it had passed. Something she couldn't quite describe. She'd dismissed it at first and told herself she'd imagined it, but now she was no longer certain.

They sat down on some broad branches to eat their meal. Alina wondered how to help him feel the rhythm of the lanyards. She tried to break down how she knew when to squeeze the grip. Like moving through the trees, this was something TreeFolk learned easily. She wondered whether this was something else Dashin experienced differently.

"What do you sense when you throw the lanyard cup?" she asked him.

"What do you mean?"

"What do you feel from the lanyard?"

"I still don't know what you mean. What is there to feel? It's a piece of rubber in my hand. I wait until I think the time is right and squeeze."

Alina put her hand on his arm. "You do not listen to the lanyard?"

"You might as well be speaking Itagian," he answered.

"What's that?"

"It's a language made up entirely of grunts and clicks. It's unintelligible to anyone not from that world."

"They have lanyards?"

"No, never mind. What do you mean, *listen to the lanyards?*"

"It's like a song as the lanyard reaches for the branch. When the song reaches its peak, you squeeze."

Dashin shook his head. "Is there any chance you can show me that?"

"You do not hear the song?"

"No, I don't hear the song."

"Then how do you know when to squeeze?"

Dashin groaned.

Alina stood behind Dashin and placed her hand on his shoulder. She closed her eyes. This would be simpler than having to hold two sets of pictures in her head while moving, she thought. She reached for him, and this time the connection was immediate. She slipped inside his mind, the space familiar now, like the hut of a friend you visited often.

The world had the same distorted view. The colors were the wrong shades, the textures oddly rendered. "Go ahead and throw the cup," she said. She did not extend her senses to reach for the lanyard. She listened instead for the song within him. And, as he'd claimed, there was no song at all. She had him repeat throwing several times, straining to hear a whisper of it, but the song remained absent.

She let go of his shoulder and opened her eyes. "I do not hear even a whisper of the lanyard's song within you."

"That's what I've been saying."

"How do your people fly through the sky with the GodLights if you cannot see the pictures or hear the songs of your world?"

Dashin shrugged. "I don't have an answer for that. Perhaps my people once saw and heard these things and, over time, have forgotten how."

"Why would your tribe forget such a thing?" Alina was horrified at the thought of being so disconnected from the world around her.

"I don't know. If it happened, it would have happened very early in the song of my people."

Alina felt sad for Dashin's people. Despite their amazing songs, to be bereft of such a thing was unthinkable.

"Dashin, try it again. This time, I will reach for the lanyard's song as you throw."

Dashin turned to face the branch, and she put her hand on his shoulder. She slipped into his mind, keeping hers separate and being careful to avoid peeking into corners she longed to explore. She took a deep breath and reached through him, searching for his lanyards. They were some distance away, their voices muffled, as though beneath many blankets. Dashin's head swiveled back and forth as though looking for the source of some new sound.

In a few moments, he settled, his head cocked, intent. When she was confident she had a grip on the sound, she squeezed his shoulder. He looked up and launched the cup. As soon as it took flight, the song grew, its voice rising in pitch, becoming more insistent as it flew toward the branch. Then, just as the fingers of the cup brushed the branch, there was the brief lower tone she sought, what she thought of as the *kissing tone*. It was followed by a sigh as the cup slipped back away from the branch and returned to Dashin.

Alina opened her eyes. "Did you hear it?"

"Yes, that's amazing. So you squeeze when you hear that bong sound?" he asked.

"Yes, squeeze when you hear the *kissing tone*."

"Kissing tone?" he asked.

She blushed. "It is just the way I think of it."

"There is kissing here?"

Alina felt her entire body flush in a way she had never felt before. It was both exciting and disconcerting. "Dashin," she said, taking a breath and fixing him with the best glare she could manage. "Do you want to try this or not?"

"I'm sorry. Of course," he answered, turning again to face the branch.

This time, when the tone sounded, he squeezed, and the cup grabbed the branch. They both whooped with joy and tried it again and again until he could do it without fail.

Amazingly, once he'd heard it enough times, he found that with the residual sense from Alina within him, he could find a faint echo of the song he could use. It wasn't as sharp, but he thought that, like the pictures that were becoming clearer with practice, the lanyard's song would also improve. He was excited now, throwing the cups one after the other into various branches, managing to grab them most of the time.

By dusk, Alina felt that a huge weight had been lifted from her. They still had not dealt with any of the specifics of any of the trials, but Dashin had made tremendous progress for one not *of the trees*.

Dashin was hanging upside down, all tangled up in a knot of branches with the leads from his lanyard forcing his left arm behind his back, his right arm dangling uselessly in empty space below him. They'd been working with the lanyards for a couple of days now, and he was making good progress now that he could hear the lanyard's song. He'd picked up the swinging motion readily, his body adept with physical motion. This had been a huge relief.

Alina alit on a nearby branch, but he couldn't turn himself enough to see more than her legs. "How did you manage that?" she asked.

"I'm just gifted, I guess," he said. "Any chance you could help me out?"

"I don't think so, Dashin. You won't have me there during the *trial of the trees*."

"Okay, thanks." He squirmed and flailed. Grunting, he managed to rotate his body so that he could use his captive hand to lift himself enough to bring his free hand to bear. He shimmied some more and managed a seated position. He then worked at unraveling the mess of leads wrapped around him.

"Impressive," she said, though it was anything but. "The lanyards do take a bit to get used to."

"Really?" he said, still trying to unravel them from the knot of branches beneath him. He was yanking on them, trying to pull them free.

"Stop, you're making it worse," she said, and then helped him unravel them.

"Do I need the lanyards? Couldn't I just complete the course without them?"

"If there wasn't a chaser, perhaps. But a chaser with lanyards would complete the entire course many times over in the time it would take you to navigate it once without them. Even if speed was not an issue, the course will be laid out so lanyards are necessary."

"But I'm slower with these than without them."

She nodded. "Yes, that is the case now. You will have to learn to be faster."

"Oh, well in that case..." he said with a chuckle.

Though he was still struggling, his progress had buoyed both their spirits. They broke for the midday meal, and as they ate, Alina discussed the finer points of using the lanyards.

The metal fingers wrapped in rubber within the cups also provided weight that could be used to throw the cups more accurately. And the force of the compressing rubber as a cup was released from behind could be redirected to aid in the next throw. A skilled TreePerson wasted very little energy moving through the trees, letting the lanyards do the work and only supplying a tiny bit of energy on each throw.

"You should watch Drur in the trees sometimes," Alina said. "He is by far the best of us. He flies through the trees like a bird. It's a joy to watch."

Dashin made a face. She knew he was still angry with Aor and the other boys. She didn't blame him. He'd just met them, and they had not shown him their more endearing sides. But they could be good friends. It was circumstances that had driven this wedge. She was certain that if conditions were different, they could be friends. Perhaps there was still hope for that.

After their meal, they worked again till evening, even moving together through the trees in a light rain. He still worked much too hard, using his muscles to compensate for his lack of technique, pulling and forcing his way through the forest. Plowing holes through thick knots of branches, he'd get tangled up and then rip himself free only to launch himself forward into another thicket. It was inspiring to watch the sheer will he exhibited. She had grown comfortable with his gentle side, but seeing this determination stirred something within her.

Her feelings had become complicated. She'd been trying to ignore them, to explain them away. They were sharing an intense experience, such an experience would bring any two people together. These weren't feelings that could endure a normal life. And yet, try as she might, she could not find a way to put them aside.

"Alina, did you hear me?"

"I'm sorry, what did you say?" she asked, flushing.

"It's getting dark. Should we be getting back?"

Alina looked up, and evening was indeed upon them. Folks would be sitting down for the evening meal. "Yes, I lost track of time. Let's hurry."

They rushed back, moving as fast as Dashin could, which was perhaps a tenth of the speed of a TreePerson, but twice the speed he'd started the day at. They dropped their gear in Rigin's hut and washed up. They didn't have to apply fake bruises, since he was still making new ones.

They joined Rigin's table midway through the meal, trying to slip in unnoticed but failing, of course, to do so. There was no hope that Dashin could go anywhere unnoticed in the village these days.

"Here," Rigin said, uncovering dishes she'd kept for them. "Eat. Both of you. You look famished."

They dug in. Solvan regaled Dashin with epic tales of the day he and Matse had led as Dashin chewed, nodded, and made appropriate sounds of amazement and encouragement for the young boy's tale.

Her father leaned across the table, and as he did, so did Rigin. "How does the training go?" he whispered.

"We are making progress," she whispered in reply. "Dashin is getting better with the lanyards. He's still very slow, but he's moving with them now."

"There are only ten days left," her father reminded her, though she didn't need reminding.

Rigin patted her hand. "Much can happen in ten days. The battle of Ansui in our song took only seven days."

The words were comforting, though the battle in question hadn't gone well for her tribe. It was not an example she cared to think on.

Chapter 25

"Find the rhythm," Alina called out to Dashin as she flew ahead of him, her motion fluid and almost silent.

Dashin grunted and groaned with each cast of his lanyards and the ensuing swing beneath them. He muscled through each throw, swing, and retrieval. His path through the forest was torturous, slamming into branches and trunks as he struggled to find a clear path ahead, and the elusive rhythm Alina kept on about. But, despite the struggle, he was excited. He was moving through the forest on lanyards, something he'd doubted he would be able to do a few days ago.

The pictures of the forest were still coming too slowly, and his grunts and groans masked the sound of the lanyards. However, the morning had seen a huge improvement in his ability, from his point of view at least. He wasn't as skilled as the children he'd seen using them near the village, but he was now confident that he'd improve.

He'd always been a quick study in his combat training classes. Once his body had a sense of the sequence of moves, he would soon develop muscle memory for it, so that it became instinctive. As he moved, the motion seeped into him. He sought to embed the feel of the lanyards in his hands, the force of the swing in his shoulders and back, the rhythm in his core, as he switched the load from one arm to the other.

For a moment, he felt the rhythm, his body suspended, weightless, poised between one lanyard and the next, moving smoothly in the trees. He whooped, grinning madly as he turned to share it with Alina and smacked right into a branch. The blow to his stomach took his wind and wrapped him around the limb.

Alina hurried up beside him. "Are you hurt?"

It was a familiar query these days. "Not really," he groaned. "I think I felt the rhythm for a moment," he gasped, trying to catch his breath.

"That's great," she replied, though he could see from her expression that she wasn't convinced.

Dashin was in awe of how effortless the motion was for her. In contrast, he struggled with each throw, still missing a fair amount of the time, so that the cup sped back at him. When the errant cup didn't smack him in the head for good measure, he'd find himself dangling suspended beneath the first anchor point, spinning in place and struggling to set his free cup to pull himself free.

And with his greater relative mass, the lanyards only gripped securely half the time. The rest of the time, they either shifted on the limb, threatening to slide free, or slipped off at the point of maximum force, launching him into space, so that he had to work on his falling skills in addition to his lanyard skills.

By midday, he had some new bruises, plenty of scratches, and a few lacerations from forcing his body through the forest. They sat on a branch, eating their midday meal. Alina seemed distant. He was afraid she was disappointed again in his progress. It broke his heart. He tried so hard to give her hope, but she seemed terrified of the coming trials. He knew she was trying to find a way for him to succeed now that she believed one must exist. He worried that by giving her hope that there must be a path, if he then failed, she would see it as her fault, for not finding it. It had not been his intention at all to put his failure on her.

Dashin looked over the lanyard mechanism, impressed with the overall design. It was an ingenious device, though it seemed better suited to the lighter and taller frames of TreeFolk than to his stockier and heavier body. The lanyard length was roughly three times the arm length of a TreePerson, and the cup fingers were designed to support their expected maximum weight at speed, neither of which was true in his case.

He heard a tiny whimper from Alina, who was looking away from him. He leaned over to see her face, and she turned away, her shoulders shaking from some emotion. When he touched her shoulder, she tensed and began to sob. It broke his heart. He squirmed, trying to understand what was going on.

He scoured the past few moments, searching for what he might have said or done to bring this on. He could only imagine that she was disappointed in his progress. "Alina, I'm sorry. Will you look at me? I'll try to work harder. I will."

She turned to him, her cheeks wet with tears, and put her fingers on his lips, stemming his words. "You are doing wonderfully, Dashin. It's not you."

He sat, uncertain as to what to say, confused and adrift.

"It's just that this challenge before you is like asking you to capture the moon."

"You don't believe I can succeed?" he said, wanting to put words he could understand to her despair.

She looked down, taking his hand. "I fear not."

He felt a measure of relief, not because her fears were unfounded but because he finally understood them. "Would it help if I had an idea for the *trial of the forest*?"

She looked at him. "How could you? You have not even learned to build a shelter."

"What if I made the shelter ahead of time?"

She shook her head. "The shelter is not permanent. The animals soon tear it apart and scatter it."

"But what if I had a shelter they could not break or shatter?"

She shrugged. "How would you build such a thing when we who live here have never managed to do so?"

He smiled. "Would it be helpful if I could?"

She wiped her eyes, curious now. "Yes, there would still be two insurmountable trials, but having two instead of three would be wonderful."

"I don't have any ideas for the *trial of the hunt* yet, but as I've been looking at the lanyards, I have an idea of how to make these work more effectively for me." She looked at him, perplexed.

"TreeFolk have been using lanyards for many generations. The song of these is old, and you've only had days with them?"

Dashin shrugged. "These are expertly made, and I won't be able to replicate the artistry, but I think I could modify them to better suit me."

Alina's eyes were intent on him now. "What are you thinking?"

"I don't think I'm going to be good enough in a short time to use the entire length of these leads. And these cups on the ends are too weak to take my weight, especially at the end of a long swing."

He'd been doing some calculations based on his relative mass to the average Ndesan who used these lanyards. He tried to explain all of this, but then said, "I either need more of these fingers or stronger fingers. I don't imagine I can make new fingers, but if I doubled up the cups and shortened the lanyards a little, I think they would work better for me."

She frowned, not following.

"If the leads were a little shorter, I would be more accurate with my throws and wouldn't get them tangled so much in the branches. It might mean that I have to skirt some of the gaps I couldn't traverse, but I could make up time by being more accurate."

She nodded. "Children use much shorter leads like this when they learn."

"And if I doubled up the leads and tied them together, the cups would be better able to take my weight, and the spring from the rubber leads would be increased. I have a stronger upper body than the TreeFolk, so I could use that strength more effectively to increase the force I get from each swing. And, if I move down into the lower canopy where the growth is sparser and the branches are stouter, it should make it simpler for me to travel. It will mean that I have to climb up and down more on the course, but it should still be faster than what I'm doing now."

Tears sprang from her eyes, and Dashin was about to apologize again when she said. "Oh, Dashin, it's me who should be sorry."

Dashin frowned, confused as to what she might have to be sorry about.

"I've been trying to find a path through the trials all alone. Trying to shield you from it, forgetting that the wealth of songs from your world might hold solutions that would not occur to me."

"Oh," Dashin said, shrugging. "I never expected you to shoulder this alone. That you've shouldered any of this burden is more than I could have asked for."

She dried her tears, a smile tugging at the corners of her mouth. Dashin felt terrible for not having involved himself more in seeking solutions. He'd been so focused on what was right in front of him that he'd failed to see the impact the strain was having on her. But his reaching out now had moved her. She leaned forward and touched her forehead gently against his. He felt a flood of warmth wash through his body as a great affection flowed between them. He tensed, his mind awhirl at the contact, and pulled back instinctively.

She gasped, pulled sharply from him, and turned away. "I'm sorry, Dashin," she said without looking back. "I was not thinking."

Dashin wasn't sure what had happened, but she was embarrassed. He sensed the moment had caught her unaware and that she'd acted impulsively. He hadn't been expecting it, and his shock had scared her, perhaps giving her the impression that the contact was unwelcome.

She stiffened as he touched her shoulder. "Alina," he said, waiting for her to soften. She turned, her eyes down, her face flushed. He said her name again, and she raised her eyes. They were uncharacteristically shy and tentative.

"You just took me by surprise," Dashin said, holding her eyes and taking her hands. He swallowed and leaned forward, touching his forehead to hers. She did not move to meet him, but she did not turn away. The warmth he'd only glimpsed a moment ago blossomed within them now.

It was different than the *touching*. This was an exchange of emotion rather than memories, a revelation of each other's internal landscapes. That which they'd felt but kept from each other coming to light. He felt her start to pull away as he glimpsed her growing feelings for him, but then she glimpsed his feelings for her, and her need to explore them overcame her reticence. She relaxed into it, letting their feelings flow into and around each other fully. Heartbeats later, she pulled away, squeezing his hands as she found his eyes.

"I've wanted to do that for some time," he said, overwhelmed. He looked upon her, beaming as his heart soared. She was the most beautiful thing he'd ever seen. That she could have feelings for him set his heart soaring through the trees.

"I had not planned to do this," she replied, though there was no regret in her tone. She was grinning too, her eyes misty, her lips pressed together as she held her emotions in check.

"I didn't know you shared these feelings," he said. Not only had he glimpsed her feelings for him, but his were laid bare for her.

She looked away for a moment and took a deep breath. "None of this will matter if you do not pass the trials." She squeezed his hand. "What do you need for these lanyards you want to make?"

He blinked, the question taking a moment to register. "I could use one more set like these, and then I'll take pieces from both and make a new set."

She thought for a moment. "Then I think you'll need two new sets."

"Why two? Aren't they scarce?"

She grinned. "Yes, but we'll want you to keep using these when you come and go from the village. That way, prospective chasers will see you continuing to struggle with these daily. We can hide the new set somewhere nearby. If we're lucky, they'll underestimate your skill and wait too long before starting to chase you."

"Is that possible?"

"It's unlikely if Drur is the chaser. He's not one who cares about impressing others, but if I can get Aor to chase you, he'll want to show others how adept he is, and that may serve us."

She looked off, and he could sense the plan forming in her mind. "We must arrive each night looking frustrated, with you looking bruised and awkward, even as you improve. Much will depend on how weak they believe you to be."

"How likely is it that Aor will be the chaser?"

Alina shrugged. "Typically, Drur is the chaser. He is by far the fastest, but he only pushes the candidates to make a show of it. In your case, we can expect that he'll be instructed to outpace you. However, Aor has taken a personal interest in you, so it's possible he can be goaded into it. And if we manage that, perhaps he can be encouraged to delay chasing to make a statement."

"Would such ruses be accepted in the *trial of the trees*?"

Alina nodded enthusiastically. "Oh yes. They are even encouraged. It is a part of the trials for candidates to use every means at their disposal to prevail. A victory is found even more worthy if the candidate has found some way to tilt the trial in their favor. The trial is meant to test a candidate for life in the trees. We believe that anyone who can find an innovative way to prevail will bring those skills to the tribe."

"So you can break the rules in order to win?"

"No. You cannot break the rules, but they can be bent," replied with a smile.

Dashin squinted, trying to imagine what else this bending might encompass.

Alina looked off, summoning the rules from memory. "You cannot remove the markings for the trail set for the course, nor can you move the baskets for the tokens, nor take more than one token. Candidates must visit every basket themselves, take a token from it, and return to the platform before the chaser does. The chaser must also visit every basket and take only one token from it."

She turned back to Dashin. "However, chasers have been delayed good-naturedly by families seeking to provide a bit more of a lead. Lanyards have been misplaced, or misadjusted, or the cups coated in grease, so the song differs, and the cups do not grip well. The candidates can work together so that the fastest among them finds the baskets for the others. There have even been times where a strong candidate has delayed a chaser on the course, though doing so is a risky proposition."

"It sounds like an odd trial, more suited for testing wits than speed."

"The *trial of the trees* is more of a celebration than a trial to exclude candidates. Those participating have grown up in the trees and have already completed the other trials. They've typically grown up in the village and have trained for many sun cycles for it, so by the time they stand for the *becoming,* the tribe is already invested in their success."

"And that won't be the case for me."

"No."

"Do people fail the trials?"

Alina shrugged. "Rarely, but it does happen, though it has not happened in my lifetime."

"You've never seen anyone fail?"

She shook her head. "No, Hedrick has always been very careful with whom he's allowed to stand. He has opposed many of the tribeless that have come to stand, making his wishes clear so that none in our village offered sponsorship."

"Why would he do that?"

"I do not know. It's a mystery many have speculated about, since it seemed that some of them might have been valuable additions to our tribe. A few believe it has to do with something that occurred in his previous tribe."

"What happened?"

"I have no idea. Hedrick and Fodrick never speak of their time before us. Even Aor has not heard tales of it, though he's pressed them for such."

"Well, I'm no challenge at the moment, and I'll do what I can to keep them thinking that."

"Yes, as you improve, we'll have to use more of the bruise dye, too," she said.

"I am looking forward to having my body covered in the painted-on variety of bruises rather than the ones I have now."

She chuckled. "I can imagine." She ran her fingers over a cluster of them on his arm, which sent a jolt through him. Not pain, something else. "There are so many of them," she mused, not having noted his reaction.

He put his hand gently on her fingers, his cheeks flushing at the contact.

She looked up, pulling her fingers free and blinking as she studied his face, her cheeks darkening in response. She looked away, swallowed, and took a breath. "Lanyards," she stammered, looking off into the forest. "They are dear to us, and there are few spares, but I can take my father's. He seldom uses his since he rarely ventures from the village, and when he does, he prefers to walk through the trees, collecting herbs as he goes. I think Rigin may also give you hers since she has not used them in some time."

"I will have to destroy them to make what I'm thinking of. I feel bad taking them. What if I don't pass? They will have lost their lanyards for nothing."

"Let's both stop thinking that you won't succeed," she said, her voice firm.

Dashin was about to object, but closed his mouth and nodded.

"What else will you need to make these lanyards?"

"I could use some tools to do the work. Can you take me to the craft you found me in?"

She inclined her head. "You mean the egg you arrived in?"

He nodded.

"It is some distance from here. At your current pace, it will take some time. We should go in the morning."

"That's fine. What will we do with the rest of the day?"

She smiled at him and then pushed him off the branch. His hands pinwheeled as he fell, though he managed to catch himself several branches below where he'd been sitting.

He looked up at her, his heart racing, and she grinned. "That's better, only two new bruises, that time."

He bit his tongue.

Chapter 26

Alina floated through the trees on their way back to the village, keeping a keen eye on Dashin, grunting and groaning in her wake. What he lacked in elegance, he made up for in effort and persistence. She'd never met anyone with this much resolve.

She'd made a mistake not including him in the process. She was moved by how her despair had affected him and how he'd responded to it.

It seemed a normal response from a friend, one Hurza or Kani might have had, but this was different. The connection she'd experienced touching his mind was unlike anything she'd known before. She'd been mortified to bare her feelings before him, but elated when she saw her affection for him mirrored in his heart. That two people could share such a thing was wondrous.

She thought of her parents and the connection they shared. A connection that revealed to others only the peak of a mountain above the trees while keeping the heart of the mountain beneath the canopy for themselves. Could it be that she had found something like that? Her heart soared at the thought. She stopped and waited for Dashin to catch up. She'd lost track of him. It wouldn't do to lose him now that she'd found him.

How odd that she'd reached for him without thought earlier. It had seemed the most natural of things until she felt his shock. But, the kind soul that he was, he'd eased her discomfort and opened himself to her.

Surely, this was a sign. And yet a part of her ached. He was not of this world. He still faced enormous obstacles and might die. No, she would not accept that as a possibility. But what would a life together hold? She'd dreamed of children for so long. Could she live a life without them? Could she watch her friends have children and raise them without ever experiencing that joy?

She took them to the tiny platform she and her friends had made as children when they had created their own *secret* tribe. She hadn't been here in ages. It was close to the village, but out of the way in a section of forest overgrown with ivy.

Most of the makeshift platform had fallen apart, but there remained, to her surprise, a corner that was still serviceable. She swept off the debris that had accumulated, and as Dashin came panting up to it, she asked him to help collect branches to shore it up.

"What are we doing?" he asked, shearing twigs from a branch with his knife.

"We need a place for you to work on your new lanyards and to keep them when we're not training. Also, someplace where I can apply the fake bruises."

"What is this place?" he asked, indicating the crude platform.

"We used to play here as children. Aor, Drur, Sneva, Hurza, Kani, and I created our own tribe, and this was our village. There used to be a couple of tiny huts over there. Most of it is gone, but this end of the platform is still usable."

As they worked on it, she remembered all the days she had spent playing here with her friends, taking turns assuming various roles, copying daily life, and inventing drama and adventure. She had no idea then how fondly she'd look back one day on all those carefree times. She ran her fingertips over the poorly woven matting.

She used the branches Dashin stripped to shore up the underside of the platform, weaving them between the supports below and the branches of surrounding trees. Once she was satisfied with its stability, she led them back to the village.

Dashin was right. His lanyards were not working for him. He was too tentative using them since he could not trust them to hold his weight. It seemed impossible that he could take these magical devices, evolved by many generations of artisans, and create something new overnight. But his people had built SkyHomes and traveled among the GodLights.

When they reached the village, Hurza and Kani pulled her aside as Dashin went on to Rigin's table. They found a quiet corner of the kitchen where they could still see the platform. Over Hurza's shoulder, she saw Solvan launch into the daily tale of his adventures. Alina smiled, watching them together. It was heartwarming to see Dashin with the children, interacting and sharing time with them despite how exhausted he must be. She felt a pang of sorrow at the sight.

"Have you heard a word we've said?" Hurza demanded.

Alina blinked and then fixed Hurza with a bashful look. "Sorry, I was..." she looked at her friend. "You were saying?"

"Something is going on. We don't know what, but there's a lot of muttering we're not privy to. The village is being split in two, those who follow Hedrick and those who follow Marna," Hurza said, scrunching her lips.

"And, since your mother is not here, we think Hedrick is converting some of those who were with your mother," Kani added.

"Do you know what they intend?" Alina asked.

Her friends both shook their heads. "We don't know if there are specific plans yet," Hurza replied. "It seems Hedrick is gathering support to do something."

Alina sighed. "Thanks." She took both their hands and squeezed them. "See if you can learn anything else. There isn't much we can do until we know more."

"How is the training going?" Kani asked, her tone concerned.

"He's making progress. There is still much to do, but today was a good day."

Her friends waited for her to say more, but she excused herself, not having the energy to elaborate. She stopped by her hut, dropped off her things, and washed up. That Hedrick was planning something was no surprise, though she didn't have the energy to think about it now.

As she was returning to the platform, Aor stepped out of the trees, startling her.

"Aor," she gasped, "I almost jumped out of my skin!"

"Sorry, I was hoping for a quiet word."

"Well, you could have asked for one instead of falling on me like a nerape."

"I said I was sorry," he grumbled.

She exhaled. "What is it? I haven't eaten yet."

"Why are you doing this?" he blurted.

"Why am I doing what?"

"Teaching the creature."

"If you're not going to be civil, then there's nothing to talk about." She made to push past him, but he held up his hand, asking her with that motion to stay.

She waited.

"Why are you teaching Dashin?" He said the name as though it were rusna in his mouth.

"He has to stand for the trials. My mother asked me to teach him."

"But he has no chance to pass them. It's ridiculous for him to even try."

"That is likely true," she answered, wondering where he was going with this. No doubt his grandfather was bending his ear. Was he looking for information from her to use against Dashin?

"Then why waste all this time?"

There was something odd in his tone and in his eyes. Something she couldn't place.

"Why do you want to know?" she asked, probing.

He looked off into the trees for a moment, searching for words.

"We've always been close," he began. "We grew up together, and we used to talk about everything. But lately, I feel like I don't understand you, that you're different in a way I can't grasp. I miss speaking with you. I don't have anyone I can confide in like we used to."

His words shocked her. They were close and had shared things, but she'd never imagined that what he shared was unique to her. She'd always imagined he had similar conversations with others. He seemed sincere, though. Perhaps as the heir to the chief, he was more alone than she knew.

"This is you asking, not your grandfather?" she asked, watching his eyes.

"Honest. It's not a secret my grandfather has strong views on the subject, views which I happen to agree with, but no, this is me asking."

There was too much at stake to share all the truth, given how close he was to his grandfather, but she felt compelled to offer him a measure of it. She sat on a branch, and he took one across from her as they had countless times before.

"What would you do if your father or grandfather asked you to do something you believed to be impossible?"

"I'd explain to them why it was impossible," he said with a shrug.

"But what if they then told you to trust them and do it anyway?"

He considered this for a moment. "I suppose I would try to do it."

"Yes, but how would you do it?"

"What do you mean?"

"Would you do it half-heartedly since you thought it was ridiculous, or would you put all your effort into it because they had asked it of you?"

A glimmer of understanding dawned behind his eyes. "I would put all my effort into it," he said.

"Why?"

"Because they asked me to."

"And, when the effort failed," she prompted.

"There would be no doubt that I had done all I could and that the task was indeed impossible."

She nodded. "My mother asked me to do this impossible thing. You know it's impossible. I know it's impossible. Everyone knows it's impossible. And yet I must still do it. So that when it becomes impossible to continue, I will know that I did all I could."

He let out a long breath, the words finding a place within him as he considered them. "But he comes to the village every night battered and bruised. If it is impossible, then wouldn't it be easier not to push him so?"

She shrugged. "What does it matter if you die bruised or whole? At least if you die bruised, you know you've done all you could."

"So, you're doing this because your mother asked it of you?"

"Yes, I've already said so."

The clouds that hung on his face cleared, and he stood. "Thank you for speaking with me. It clears things up for me. I'm sorry I wasn't able to see it myself. What you do is honorable and does you credit. Many do not understand, but I'm glad to have a sense of it now."

"Thank you for asking me about it. The others you refer to have not."

He nodded, turned, and melted back into the trees.

"You should speak to Hurza sometime," she called after him.

"About what?" his voice called back to her.

"Things like this. Your hopes and dreams, your fears and frustrations."

"Hurza?" There was a pause. "You mean Kani."

"No, I mean Hurza."

"She would laugh at me."

Alina chuckled. "Well, maybe at first, until she realized you were serious. But I think you'd be pleasantly surprised."

There was another pause, and Alina wondered if he had moved off.

"I will think on it," he replied, and then she did hear him move off.

She called after him. "It can't hurt to have another friend to speak with."

There was no reply. She made her way to the platform and ate the meal Rigin had left for her as the villagers put away the tables around her. The others had already gone. Dashin would be washing up. Rigin and the children would soon help him slather balm over his battered body, the children applying balm over his bare back, their little hands making small, gentle circles on the muscled expanse of it. She hoped most of the bruising was behind them.

In the morning, they made their way toward Dashin's egg. It was the farthest they'd ventured from the village together. They were able to follow the well-worn path to the mountains for a time, which helped, but since Dashin could barely use his lanyards, it took all morning. When they reached the borka tree where they had been hunting nuxat, when Dashin's egg arrived in their world, she stopped and looked out over the trench it had cut through the forest. The charred nubs of twigs and branches had been washed clean by the near-daily rains, and new growth was evident.

"Why is the forest so strange here?" Dashin asked, looking at the trough before them.

"This is your fault," she replied, smiling.

He looked from her to it and back, frowning for a moment before it came to him. "Ah, this is the path my pod made in the forest."

"Yes, had your egg arrived a few moments earlier, Kani, Hurza, and I would not have survived since we were up here in the canopy."

Dashin shuddered at the thought.

It felt like ages ago, and yet it had been less than a moon. She felt like a different person than the girl who'd been hunting nuxat with her friends.

They followed the trench to the edge of the shaft in the trees, and she peered over the edge. She could just make out part of the egg at the bottom. Leaves and branches had been washed down on it, covering most of it.

They picked their way down through the trees. She kept Dashin away from the shaft, concerned that a slip from his lanyards could mean an uncontrolled fall with no branches to arrest it.

A family of corsol had taken up residence inside, and she had to chase them away. They screamed and complained as they scurried away, and once they'd gone a safe distance, they turned and complained again loudly before moving off.

Dashin stepped inside and looked around as she sat on a branch waiting. The bird in the egg was quiet. She wondered how long it had sung before growing tired.

"It smells in there," Dashin said, reappearing.

"Yes, you were covered in filth when we found you. It was not pleasant. And having a family of corsol living in there has not improved things."

"It's amazing you didn't leave me here," he mused.

"It was a close thing," she replied with a chuckle.

He smiled and stepped back inside, and she saw him open parts of the walls, which was fascinating. She stepped closer to see how he did this, holding her breath as she did so. He pulled things from within the walls, a long coil of the finest rope she had ever seen. He brought it out with a large bag he pulled from another not-hole in the wall. She tested the rope in her hands. It was as slender as a finger but incredibly strong and flexible. She pulled and twisted it, marveling at the wonder of it.

The bag made an odd sound, like a mixture of stones and birdsong, when he put it down. He opened it, and inside were shiny, intricately wrought implements. There were so many wonders in his world. She worried if he could ever be satisfied with a simple life in the trees after having lived in such a place.

"These are the tools I spoke of," he said, picking one of them up and manipulating it so that a pair of tiny jaws opened and closed. Alina leaned forward to study it, running her fingers over its smooth surface. She rifled through the bag, examining the magical tools within as he studied the broken piece of the egg.

He opened and closed it, examining the place where it joined the egg. "I think this will work," he said, though what it was he was thinking escaped her. She was anxious to leave now that he'd retrieved the tools they'd come for. She stood up, carrying the bag over to her pack.

He turned to her. "If we lowered this to the forest floor and I fixed the door, could I use this for my trial of the forest?"

She tried to follow what he was saying, but it made no sense. The egg was so heavy that it would take many people to lift it. And that many people carrying it somehow to the forest floor was ridiculous. But perhaps it could be pushed from its perch? "Are you thinking of pushing it from here and letting it fall through the trees?"

"That might work if the door wasn't broken, but I think we'll have to lower it."

"Lower it? You mean you and I carry this enormous thing?"

"Yes, sort of. We can use the ropes and me-cha-ni-cal ad-van-tage to lower it."

He had spoken the new words in the grunting speech of Ancaran, and though she knew of the words from his songs and sensed they had something to do with the magic of his world, she could not form a picture of the idea in her mind.

"You'd best show me. Your words do not enlighten me."

He took the large coil of rope and used his knife to cut it in half. He tied one end to a ring at one end of the egg. He threaded the rope through many branches above them, and then back down to where they stood before securing it to the trunk of the tree next to the egg. Then he fished through the broken branches surrounding the egg until he found a long one. He cut away its smaller limbs until he had a stout pole. He wedged one end beneath the egg and pulled down on the other end, attempting to pry the egg loose from its nest. The egg moved, but his weight wasn't sufficient to roll it free.

He made another pole and stuck it near the one that was already there. "Alina, can you pull down on the end of this pole while I do the same on mine? I think together it should be enough to swing it free."

She took the end of her pole, and between the two of them, they pushed the egg free of its perch. As it rolled free and tumbled below them, the rope took the weight, going taut as branches above it bent and creaked. A few of them snapped, but it held, and the egg hung beneath them, spinning slowly from the rope. He said something about the rope's material and this *gravity* thing he was always going on about. She didn't follow his explanation, but it was amazing to see.

He untied the rope, and she gasped, certain that the weight of the egg would pull him from his feet and hurl him into space, but he held the weight with magic she could not understand. "Dashin, how are you able to do this?"

"The rope is rubbing against all these branches above, which creates *friction,* which the pod has to overcome, leaving only a small amount of force for me."

She shrugged, the explanation insufficient to clear up the matter. She was content to watch as he played out the rope and the egg sank through the hole they'd created in halting steps. When he ran out of rope, he tied it off and then fastened the other half to the ring, threaded it through more branches, and then released the first length until the new rope took up the weight. It was marvelous to watch him work and see him lower the massive egg by himself through the forest.

Once the new length of rope was spent, she took the original length and repeated the process she'd seen, adjusting it here and there according to his suggestions. It went much quicker with her *rigging* the rope, as he put it, since she moved more easily about the forest.

When they were halfway to the forest floor, it began to rain. Dashin grew excited. "Help me force the pod against these limbs and turn it."

She didn't understand, but then, seeing him pull at the door, she saw that the rain would run inside and wash out the interior. They shoved and pushed, managing to get it into place while the rain poured down upon them. Dashin began laughing as the torrent soaked them and filled the egg. His laughter was contagious, and she was soon laughing too, without knowing why, only that it felt great to share it.

They could not wash themselves as they stood on either end of the egg, securing it in place. Once the downpour passed, Dashin rolled the egg and let most of the foul water run free. He wedged it in place with some water still within it, and Alina took the cloth from her pack and scrubbed at the more stubborn stains within the egg while Dashin held the door and kept the egg secure. Once she'd done all she could, they poured out the rest of the rain and continued lowering it.

As they neared the forest floor, Alina had them stop as she studied the forest the way she'd been taught.

"What are you doing?" he asked.

"Be silent," she bade him, intent on the sounds beneath, her eyes probing for movement. She saw a few lodra scurrying about and a few lizards. Birds were foraging about in the ferns below. All of these were good signs. When she was satisfied, she turned to him. "You must always be careful that there are no predators before leaving the trees."

"How do you know if there are predators?"

"The forest goes quiet. Life below senses their presence and holds still."

"So, the birds and the rat-like creatures moving about are a good sign?"

"Yes, that is the way of it. Though you must still be wary, the forest floor is the most dangerous place for TreeFolk."

They lowered the egg the remainder of the way, and it settled amid tall ferns. They rolled it so the bed inside was upright, then rolled it back and forth to create a cradle for it in the dirt. Alina scrubbed at the inside some more with the cloth she carried, while Dashin worked on the door.

Having done what she could inside, she emerged to find Dashin gone. A stick had been placed against the door to prop it open.

"Dashin," she called out, though she didn't yell so as not to attract unwanted attention. There was no answer. She spun about, trying to determine where he'd gone off to. She looked at the ground, trying to find tracks, but they'd been milling about in the soft earth as they'd lowered the pod, and there were tracks everywhere.

Her heart raced, and she called again and again until he emerged from the forest some distance away, carrying some small sticks he was whittling with his knife. He was intent on the sticks, as though there was not a care in the world. She felt her blood go hot, her eyes narrowed, and she wanted to strangle him. "What are you doing wandering off like that?"

"What?" he said, looking about.

"Didn't I just tell you the forest floor was the most dangerous place and that predators live here?"

"Yes, but you said it was safe."

"No, it is never *safe*. I said that I thought we could safely lower the egg to the ground, not that you could go off exploring without me." She shivered as thoughts of what might have happened played through her mind.

"I'm sorry. I went to find some sticks I could shape to hold the door closed."

She took a breath. "Ask me in the future before you wander off."

He nodded and then had her hold the door closed as he fitted the sticks he'd been shaping into the mechanism to hold it closed. After a few attempts, he managed to jam them into a gap and wedge the door shut. They climbed back into the trees, though it took Dashin some time to find a branch he could reach that would take his weight. Branches near the forest floor were sparser, and many were brittle since only filtered light reached this far down, leaving many of these devoid of leaves.

When they climbed back up to where the egg had first lain, they sat down for a late midday meal. As she bit into her stuffed banda leaf, she felt the tension drain from her shoulders.

Chapter 27

Dashin's muscles ached from struggling with the lanyards and from lowering the pod. It was a pleasant feeling, one he was familiar with from the climbing and combat training he'd done on Ancara. He'd always equated it with progress, and that was true here too.

Less familiar were his feelings for Alina, and even stranger was the knowledge that they were reciprocated. He'd never had a friend like this before, and he'd been delighted to learn that she saw it as more than mere friendship, too. How this could be, he could not say. What would come of it, he did not know. But this was beyond anything he'd experienced before. And it was something he would strive to be worthy of.

When they were done eating, they made their way back to the village. It took time since the village was some distance from the pod, and he was still struggling with the lanyards. However, every motion with them only solidified the image of a more ideal set in his mind. He imagined how they would feel, how they would function, and how he would move with them. He let those thoughts percolate as he fought his way through the forest with the ones he now wore. The mechanisms were intricate, and he would only have two sets to work with, but he'd worked out a rough idea of how they functioned.

When they arrived at the new cache, he was drenched in sweat and panting. He sat upon the small platform, catching his breath.

"You are making progress," Alina offered, though Dashin sensed the concern behind the statement.

"Thanks, but I hope to do much better with the new lanyards."

She shed her pack, pulled out the heavy tool bag, and the two sets of lanyards. They'd left the rope in the pod. He shook his head. "You've been carrying these all day, plus the tools, and it seems as though you have nothing on your back when you fly through the trees."

"I try not to fight the forest," she said, motioning to him with her chin, referring to the many scrapes and bruises he'd gotten forcing his way through it.

"I have no idea how you manage to float along without so much as brushing against a twig."

"Oh, I brush twigs. There are too many to avoid. I'm just careful which twigs I brush against," she said with a smile.

"You choose them?"

"Of course. You must always seek the *TruePath*."

Dashin had a vague notion of the term from his not-memories but hadn't understood it. It seemed to crop up often in many unrelated contexts within the tribe. "What is that? My memories of it are confusing."

"The *TruePath* is the best path available for you at the moment."

"You see this best path when you look at the forest?"

"No, not like I see the pictures of the forest. I must search for the *TruePath* and let it come to me. It is seldom found, but always something to strive for."

"But, once you find the *TruePath* in a section of the forest, does that mean you can follow that path every time you pass through it in the future?"

"No. The TruePath is forever changing. The forest is alive, continually reshaping itself, so paths change constantly. Also, the TruePath encompasses your own abilities and conditions. Who you are today is not who you were yesterday or who you will be tomorrow."

"So, if I'm tired or sleepy or the wind is blowing a bit harder or softer, then the *TruePath* will change for me, perhaps every instant?"

"Precisely so," she grinned.

Her approval felt like a warm blanket. "So, when people use the term in their lives, they are describing the best path through some difficulty or challenge?"

"Yes, you have the measure of it. In your case, we must find the *TruePath* through your upcoming trials. And this is something that might be forever changing around us as conditions change, but yet we must strive for it."

It was an interesting concept that there could be an ideal path not only through the trees but through one's life. To find such a thing through the trees seemed a challenge, but it was something he could imagine. How would you seek such a thing in your life?

"Is there anything else you need?" she said, indicating the lanyards and tools next to him.

"I could use some twine or something like that to tie things together."

Alina reached into her pack and pulled out a stick with a healthy amount of twine wrapped around it.

"Is there anything that is not in your pack?" he said with a chuckle.

"No," she replied, crinkling her eyes.

Dashin picked up one of the lanyards and examined the grip. He'd already studied it as he'd come up with his plan, but he wanted to make sure not to damage it. When he was comfortable that he understood how it fit together, he took a calming breath and pried off the top and bottom rings holding it closed about the length of the lanyard lead. After some effort, they came loose, and the grip fell apart in his hand.

"You will be able to put this back together again?" Alina inquired, squirming.

He could hear the concern in her voice, and it unnerved him since he was worried about that too. He looked up at her. "Your hovering is not helpful," he said, as gently as he could.

She nodded. "Perhaps I should go and see if Hurza and Kani have learned anything, so you can work undisturbed?"

Dashin smiled, relieved. "Yes, that would be great."

She left. Dashin examined the internals of the grip mechanism, absorbing the details of its inner workings. There was both an inner rubber core and an outer rubber shroud. They functioned independently and yet stretched together. When the grip was held, the inner core moved along with the outer shroud, both acting like a large rubber band. But when the grip was squeezed, it exerted force on the inner core, which contracted, forcing the fingers of the cup closed.

With the grips removed, it would be simple to shorten the lanyard by sliding them up the leads, reattaching them, and then cutting off a length from the leads where they were attached to the forearm mounts. The challenge would be in combining the two lanyards into one device.

He was just considering how to do that when he heard Alina return. He was mildly annoyed that she'd returned so soon, but he pushed the emotion away and looked up. And, standing there at the hole in the wall of ivy they'd come through, was Fodrick.

Dashin's heart sank, and he started to stand, but Fodrick waved him down. He walked to the platform, glanced around, and sat down. Dashin's heart rate picked up, anxious at what this could mean.

Fodrick looked down at the disassembled lanyard and then up at Dashin. His eyes seemed to be appraising him, taking his measure as he spoke. "I take it you have plans for these?" he said, his face impassive.

Dashin didn't know how to answer. They had planned on keeping this a secret, but here he was sitting with them disassembled in his lap. The air was electric, and he sensed that a lie here would not serve him. "Yes, I have some ideas on how to modify them to better suit my body."

Fodrick considered this and frowned, scratching his head. "Though you haven't seen a device like this one before, you choose to spend precious time changing something that has taken our best craftsmen a great many sun cycles to develop?"

Dashin squirmed, uncomfortable with the question phrased this way, but he was committed now. "I am not planning on developing something new. I'm making some small changes to adapt it."

"What kind of changes do you have in mind?" he asked, his dismissive tone indicating that he thought this effort was madness.

Dashin exhaled. "I'm going to shorten them since I do not have time to develop enough accuracy with these long leads. I'm going to double the leads so the cups can better bear my weight and grip the branches more effectively. This should also provide more thrust for my heavier body."

Fodrick sat back, a look of surprise flitting across his features. The answer had given him pause, and he bit back what he was about to say as his mind worked on it, his eyes never leaving Dashin's.

"What is this *thrust* you speak of?" he asked.

Dashin swallowed. Beads of sweat formed on his brow. He ignored them. "It's how much the forward lanyard pulls on you when you release the rear lanyard."

"This is something you can adjust?" Fodrick asked, motioning to the lanyards with his chin.

"Well, not as they are, but I have some idea of how to do so," he shifted, unsure of how much to share.

Fodrick seemed to notice the equivocation but chose not to pursue it. "That seems like more than a minor adjustment."

Dashin shrugged.

"Dashin, you are a problem for me," he sighed. Dashin opened his mouth to speak, but Fodrick held up his hand, and Dashin closed it. "You are a problem I need to solve."

"I have been watching you on the platform, in the trees, and now here," he said, indicating the disassembled lanyards. Dashin was shocked. He had no idea Fodrick had taken a particular interest in him. And, if Fodrick had been watching them, Alina had been unaware of it.

Fodrick continued, his face more open now. "Ours was a quiet and harmonious tribe until you arrived. Now I find my tribe is at odds with itself. Part of it is convinced you will be our salvation, while the other part is certain you will be our doom."

"I'm afraid I cannot shed any light on either outcome, except to say that I have only the best of intentions for the village."

Fodrick held his eyes. He seemed to be considering how much to say or how much to share. Dashin felt transparent before this keen gaze. He swallowed but did not look away.

"Being chief is not what folks imagine it to be. People think being chief involves telling others what to do and then getting to do whatever you want. But that is not at all the case. Everyone expects the chief to solve every problem that arises, to have answers when none are apparent, and to somehow divine the future."

There was something strange about his tone. It had a confessional quality Dashin had not expected. Perhaps the chief did not have those he could confide in? Though why he would then choose him was a mystery. However, he sensed Fodrick had some goal in mind, so he waited to find out.

"My father has reasons for his actions. No one here knows our story. Even my son has not heard the tale. I will tell you some of it if you will keep it in confidence," he said, waiting for an answer.

"Of course," Dashin said. "I will keep your secret."

Fodrick nodded and sat back. Exhaling, he looked off into the trees as though remembering some faraway time. "My father was chief in the village I grew up in. He led wisely in those days, and our tribe prospered. Then one day, meaning well, he allowed someone to stand for the *becoming* who was not worthy to do so. Later on, he chose again to overlook a failing from this person that he should not have let stand. Though I will not share the details, these decisions proved disastrous for us."

"One day, while my father was away, this person destroyed the entire village, my mother included, leaving me for dead." Fodrick reached up reflexively and brushed the tip of the scar peeking from the collar of his tunic.

"My father returned to find all those he loved and cared for dead, except for me. Death was singing its song in my ear, but somehow my father managed to still it. The loss changed us both, but it changed my father most. He never forgave himself for that day."

Dashin swallowed, his skin tingling. He couldn't imagine why Fodrick was sharing this with him.

"My father saw to our dead and nursed me back to health. Once I could travel, we wandered tribeless for many suns. We stayed with many tribes for short periods but never sought to join them. We learned to make war with some, to hunt or build with others, until we happened on this tribe here. It was leaderless at the time and struggling."

He paused, the tale apparently at an end.

"I'm sorry to hear of your troubles," Dashin said, touched.

"I tell you this, in confidence, because I want you to know that as chief, I will do what needs to be done to protect my tribe. I do not know if you are to be our salvation or our doom, but regardless, I will follow our traditions. A part of me hopes that you will somehow prevail, even though I do not believe such a thing is possible. But I want you to know that I will have no choice but to turn you from us if you do not succeed, though I will do so with a stone in my heart."

It made sense to Dashin now. Fodrick had come to explain that he would have to follow tradition in order to maintain harmony in the tribe should Dashin not prevail. Fodrick wanted him to know it was not personal. And perhaps convey that Hedrick believed he was acting in the tribe's best interests.

He felt grateful Fodrick had sought him out to share this. It was a thoughtful gesture.

"Thank you for explaining this to me," Dashin began. "I realize that this was a courtesy and that you could have said nothing."

Fodrick nodded, apparently relieved to have said his piece. Fodrick stood up. "I am curious to see if you make something of those," he said, indicating the lanyards in Dashin's lap.

Dashin nodded. "Me too."

Fodrick smiled and left. As he slipped back through the hole in the ivy, he turned. "Do not forget to use your lower body with the lanyards. Much of your strength and control comes from the waist down. You are dragging the lower half of your body along as though it does not belong to you."

Dashin thanked him, shocked Fodrick was aware of details in his training and willing to offer advice. It was kind of him to have come forward. He sensed Fodrick would be as fair as possible, which was all he could ask for.

He sat for a time, rehashing the conversation, trying to imagine the impact of such a terrible loss, especially on someone who took responsibility for it. There was clearly much of the story Fodrick had not shared, but Dashin felt privileged to have heard this much.

He turned back to the lanyards and took apart the other set, putting all the loose parts inside compartments in the tool bag. It would not do to lose any of these pieces in the trees. Should any of them roll off the platform, they would never find them in the forest below.

He tried various ideas for combining the cups, linking the leads together, and integrating the grips. Many of the things he tried were impractical, but he eventually arrived at a few ideas that seemed promising. He was playing around with options for the grips when Alina startled him.

"How are things going?" she asked, already at his shoulder, though he had not heard her approach.

He started, dropping the grips as he turned to look up at her. "How did you sneak up without making a sound?"

"I did not sneak anywhere. I walked up. You were so occupied in your work that you did not hear me."

He ignored her annoyed tone. It had been deserved. "I'm making progress. I think I have something that should work, though I have to make the changes more permanent."

Alina looked at the cobbled-together prototype and seemed unimpressed. "This does not seem very sturdy," she said, kneeling down next to him and running her fingers over the loosely tied leads.

"I will make it more permanent once I've finalized the design."

"Perhaps Rigin could help."

"Oh, I had not considered that. Her leather work is amazing."

"We will ask her at the evening meal," Alina said. A deep bong sound rang out in the forest, the result of someone striking the large, wooden drum in the kitchen. "Speaking of which, it seems the meal is ready." She stood and brushed her hands over her clothes.

"Oh, Fodrick stopped by," Dashin said, just now remembering.

Alina stopped, gaping at him, frowning. "Fodrick stopped by, and you did not think to mention it?"

"I just did," Dashin said, putting the new lanyards into a bag.

"Yes, after we chatted about the lanyards and other such things." She sighed, putting a hand on his shoulder. "Never mind, what did he say?"

"He stopped by to explain that he would be fair but that he intended to follow tradition and would have no choice but to send me from the village if I did not pass the trials."

"That seems an odd thing for him to come here to say," she said, looking off into the trees, her eyes narrowed.

"Well, he explained what happened to him and his father before they came here."

"He what?" she replied, turning to him, stunned. "Why would he share that with you?"

"I think he wanted me to understand Hedrick's opposition," Dashin said with a shrug.

"Tell me," she pressed, sitting down.

"Sorry, I promised I would keep it in confidence."

"He told you this in secret?"

Dashin nodded. He could see the frustration lining her face, the desire in her eyes to press him for details.

She exhaled. "Was there anything else?"

"Yes, he said I should be using my lower body more."

"What?" Alina said, frowning.

"With the lanyards, he said that I'm not using my waist and legs enough."

"He's been watching us in the trees?"

Dashin nodded. "Yes, it seems so."

Alina gaped at him, her mouth haltingly forming words that failed to fall from her lips.

Chapter 28

Alina stretched, rolling her shoulders to loosen the knot that had formed in her sleep. She sat with Solvan and Matse on the makeshift platform of the cache in the cool air, watching Dashin discuss his thoughts on modifying the lanyards with Rigin.

Rigin had been thrilled to be asked to help when they'd mentioned it after the evening meal. She'd been ready to go before daybreak with two buckets and a pack filled to the brim.

Solvan and Matse had woken as they were preparing to leave, and Dashin had suggested they take them along. Rigin had been apprehensive at first, but seeing the joy the suggestion brought to their faces, she'd agreed. The five of them had slipped away into the false morning gloom.

Alina had carried Matse on her back and led Solvan by the hand. It was the first time the children had ventured beyond the netting, and both were thrilled. Solvan, his eyes enormous with excitement, could not even manage a single *round*. Matse had been hesitant but had settled upon Alina's back.

Rigin nodded and made appraising noises as Dashin explained his ideas. She offered suggestions that Dashin received enthusiastically. It was heartening to see them working together, their exchanges growing shorter and more excited as the discussion progressed.

Matse held Alina's hand, her tiny fingers gripping it firmly as they sat. Solvan bubbled next to her, his eyes glued to Dashin and Rigin as they worked. Alina reached over and ran the fingers of her free hand through Solvan's unruly mop. He turned and beamed at her. He was always so grateful for any affection. His open grin warmed her, but also tugged at her. Matse regarded her with huge eyes that missed nothing. She reached over and tapped the tip of her nose with a finger, eliciting a shy grin.

Dawn was just breaking in the foliage above them, casting faint mottled light about them. The birds began their morning song. A few of them nesting close by were particularly enthusiastic, filling the air with urgency.

Dashin picked up a piece of lanyard lead about as long as his hand and turned to her. "Could you find two sticks like this piece of lanyard here?"

"Certainly," Alina said, leaning over and taking the piece. She turned to Solvan and Matse, who were watching wide-eyed. "Can the two of you help me find sticks this size?"

Solvan jumped up and started pointing out nearby branches at random. None of his choices were close enough to even bother measuring. Matse crept close to Alina and studied the lead, her eyes sparkling as she did. Alina ran her fingers through her hair as Matse leaned against her and looked out into the forest, her lips moving as though mumbling to herself.

Solvan continued to point out unsuitable branches. Alina shook her head, smiling at him. Matse tugged her hand and pointed at a branch that was much too far away for Alina to believe it could be a contender. Alina dismissed it, but Matse tugged again, and Alina walked over to it to humor her, with Matse on her heels. Once she arrived at the branch, she was surprised to find it was very close. Matse reached up and ran her finger along one section of the branch, and Alina laid the lead against it, and it was a near exact match.

"This is perfect, Matse. How did you do that?"

The little girl grinned shyly. Alina squeezed the little body against her leg, praising her keen eye. Matse beamed and gave a tiny giggle. Moments later, Matse found another branch. Alina cut them both and returned them to Dashin.

He took them and then compared them to the lead he'd given her, which she found annoying. He looked up to tell her it would do, but then noticed the look on her face and smiled awkwardly instead. He turned back to the grip he was working on with Rigin.

Rigin had spread her tools about her. A brazier boiled some water and also warmed some lacquer. They all watched, fascinated, as Rigin cut up some stiff pieces of hide and slipped them into the water. She put a stone on top of them to ensure they were submerged and waited as the hide softened, poking it with a stick until it was pliant.

She gave Dashin a thick glove to wear and then fished out a piece of stoda hide with wooden tongs and handed it to him. She draped it over the two pieces of wood Alina had retrieved and had Dashin form the hide around them by squeezing it in place with the glove. She wrapped twine on either side of the glove to fix it in place.

"Hold it like that until the hide is cool beneath your fingers," Rigin said, adjusting his hand.

When Dashin eventually opened his hand, flexing fingers that had grown stiff, the hide had the imprint of his fingers upon it. He removed the glove and picked up the grip, sliding his fingers into the thick grooves. "This feels amazing," he said, grinning.

They repeated the process with another piece of hide and the other hand. Once they were done, the lanyards had custom grips formed to his hands, something regular lanyards never had. Rigin slit them to leave an open groove on the inside, allowing room to compress the lanyards when squeezed. She applied a coat of lacquer to them and put them aside to dry.

Dashin showed her how he intended to merge two cups to create one larger cup. The cups were like flowers with metal petals encased in rubber that could be pulled together by compression of the inner rubber core. The larger flower cup would have twice the petals in it and give him twice the surface to grip with. Alina's breath grew shallow as they slit the cups and folded them open to combine them, worried this operation might damage the lanyards beyond repair. They carefully fit the pieces together, and Rigin wove a cradle at the base to hold it in place.

Dashin had been thinking of adding leather ties at intervals along the leads to keep them from pulling apart, but Rigin had some glue she thought might work better. She put it on the brazier to warm, and Dashin tied the leads with twine to hold them in place every hand's width along their length. When the glue was soft, Rigin applied it along the entire length of the combined leads and the seam of the combined cups. Once she'd done one side, they flipped the lanyard over and Rigin filled the groove between the leads and cups on the other side.

As she did this, Dashin shortened the leads and reattached them to the forearm supports. He discussed with Rigin and Alina what length he should make them, and they decided he should keep them a bit longer than he intended at first, then shorten them as needed once he used them for a time.

As the glue cured, Rigin applied lacquer to the cradle beneath the cups and added another coat to the grips. She fashioned thick leather rings for the tops and bottoms of the new grips. Then, once the lacquer on the grips was tacky, she wrapped them in a thin leather coat.

When they were done, Alina examined the lanyards. "These are truly beyond words." She reached over and ran her fingers over the grips. "There have never been any such as these," she said.

"I can treat the leather once you've worn them in some," Rigin said, apparently seeing something Alina's eyes couldn't, since to her they looked perfect as they were.

"Thank you all so much for your help," Dashin said, picking up a grip in one hand and squeezing it. The petals in the large cup at the end of the lanyard pulled in. He worked the grip open and closed a few times and then tossed it at Solvan and squeezed, gently grabbing the boy's arm. Solvan shrieked with joy, giggling as he pulled against it, rolling on the platform. Dashin released it, sent it back, and grabbed a leg, tugging the boy back. The boy was laughing hard now, his face flushed with glee. Matse giggled, beaming as well. She put out her tiny arm, offering it. Dashin tossed it at her and softly grabbed it. She bounced in place beside herself as she looked at Solvan, who was slapping the platform with both hands in delight.

"We'll have to see if the new lanyards grab more than children," Alina said with a smile.

"The two of you are not to speak of this to anyone," Rigin said, turning to the children.

Matse nodded, though she had no need to, and Solvan gave a cursory nod, his eyes still on the new lanyards.

Rigin reached over and took his chin in her hand and turned his head so he met her eyes. Solvan swallowed and nodded again, more sedately this time.

It was near midday, and they ate a meal together as Dashin and Rigin checked over their work, discussing other changes they might make or things they might do should these not work as expected.

Alina was anxious to be moving. They had spent the entire morning on this. It was an enormous gamble to place the fate of the trials on a new lanyard design, one never before seen or tried. Alina touched her fingertips to her forehead, praying they would work.

Alina gaped as Dashin flung his body forward with yet another powerful tug on the new lanyards, amazed at the progress he'd made in the short time since they'd left the cache. He'd been tentative at first, stopping repeatedly to make small adjustments to how they fit his body, which she'd found increasingly frustrating. But then his confidence had grown, and he was now moving more smoothly through the trees with them.

His motion was different than the one she knew. Rather than the fluid motion of TreeFolk, his rhythm had a pause in the center where he was suspended between the lanyards. The pause was followed by rapid acceleration as he released the rear lanyard, and the doubled lead of the front lanyard yanked him forward. She resisted the urge to correct his motion, letting him develop a feel for this jerky rhythm he'd found.

As the day wore on, he continued to refine his technique and commit to it. He was growing more relaxed with the rhythm and beginning to move with some speed. His body, unfamiliar with the motion, still exerted considerable energy in each swing, far more than would be possible for a TreePerson. She felt that over time, his swings would become more efficient. In the meantime, he seemed quite capable of expending the energy, which perhaps explained his prodigious appetite.

Dashin crashed onto the branch next to her, his legs absorbing much of the impact as he reached for the branch above to settle himself. His face was alight with delight. "These are so much better!" he exclaimed. "I don't think the leads need to be shortened at all. I'm getting a sense of their length now, and I think they are perfect."

"That's wonderful, Dashin. You're looking more at home with them. Is it very tiring moving as you do?" she asked, anxious at the level of effort.

"No, I'm fine. It's a bit tiring, but it feels good to move. I think it will get easier with practice. Using my waist as Fodrick suggested is helpful."

Alina bristled. She'd been telling him to do so for days now. "That's good," she said instead.

"What's next?" he asked, beaming.

Alina arched an eyebrow. He seemed to think he'd mastered moving and was ready for something new. She was tickled by this newfound confidence. She pushed him from the branch, and though he fell backward, his arm reached out and grabbed the one behind him, and he found his feet quickly. Alina leapt into the trees and threw her lanyard, racing off from him. "See if you can catch me," she called out.

Moments later, she heard Dashin in the trees behind her, his odd rhythm ringing through the forest, punctuated by the grunts and groans of his physical effort. She slowed, keeping the sound behind her at a consistent distance to push him, and yet not lose him. They were moving in the lower canopy where the branches were stouter and a bit sparser, and where she would be easier to follow.

She listened to his cadence, noting the pauses due to missed tosses and the odd sound of these new lanyards. Gradually, she increased her speed, keeping him a comfortable distance behind. Grunting in her wake, he forged on, the branches rustling behind her from the strain.

She felt joy in her limbs at the sound of him. Tears of relief pooled in the corners of her eyes. He was still much slower than a TreePerson, but he was improving quickly. A glimmer of hope took root inside her. He would never beat Drur in the trees, but he would certainly surprise folks.

She skirted the tree with the mirha nest, giving the insects a wide berth, and sped up a bit, intent on pushing him harder. When she heard his path change, her heart sank. He'd moved to intercept her, moving toward the nest in an attempt to take the shorter path between them.

She stopped and yelled back to him, telling him to stop, but he didn't hear her in time. She saw the nest shake as the branch next to it was wrenched back from the pull of his lanyard. A swarm of the nasty insects appeared and was angrily searching for a target when he swept into their midst. She heard him cry out once and then again a few more times. The impacts unsettled him, and he lost focus. Both his lanyards came loose, and he tumbled through the trees. He arrested himself many branches lower. The fall saved him, taking him from the midst of the insects and their fiery stings.

She hurried to him and alit on a branch next to him. "How many times were you stung?" she asked, her heart pounding. Mirha hives had hundreds of the aggressive insects, and more than a handful of stings would make one seriously ill.

Dashin groaned, peeling himself from the branch and rubbing his stomach, which had taken the impact, and then his shoulder, side, and cheek. "Three, I think."

She exhaled. "I'm sorry, I did not think you would take the path by the nest."

"What were those things?" he said, rubbing the eye-sized welts forming on his skin.

"Don't rub them. It will make it worse," she admonished. She leaned in and puckered each sting with her fingers, trying to push out the toxin. He squirmed and protested. "Be still," she commanded.

When she had removed as much toxin as she could, she sat back and exhaled. "We call these delightful little creatures mirha. There was a reason I avoided that tree, as I'm sure you realize now. You are fortunate that more did not find you. If you're stung by many, you can become very ill. Some have even died from it."

"Well, I can't say I'm glad to meet them. These stings are incredibly painful. I can't imagine getting stung by an entire nest."

"You'll be the topic of conversation in the village tonight, Dashin. You are providing much material for discussion these days."

"I hope they find it entertaining. It will be a welcome change from the looks I've been receiving."

Alina brushed her fingers across the sting on his cheek. It was already swelling. "They are fearsome creatures, though the nectar in their nests is prized. For obvious reasons, it is rare. I have never tasted it, but it is said to be a unique experience."

"People collect nectar from those hives?"

She shook her head. "No, no one would attempt that, but on occasion, someone finds an abandoned nest with a bit of nectar still in it. It is much sought after, and few have tasted it." She brushed his forehead with the back of her fingers. "You will likely run a fever, and you may hallucinate. Their toxin is potent."

His eyes lost their focus, and she worried the toxin might be more potent for an Ancaran. He looked at her strangely as though he'd only just noticed her leaning over him.

"You're so beautiful," he said, grinning up at her.

His words stopped her, and she blushed. Then she laughed, realizing the toxin was already loosening his tongue. "We'll have to get you back while you can still move, and I'd advise you not to talk to others for a few hours."

She led him back to the cache, having to support him as they walked through the trees since he was too overcome to use his lanyards. He continued to babble about his feelings for her. She didn't attempt to dissuade him, enjoying the sound of it, curious as to how much of it might be true.

By the time they reached the village platform, he was staggering and muttering in Ancaran. As she'd predicted, there was much laughter as the villagers saw them arrive, noting the obvious stings on Dashin's body, and hearing his incoherent rambling. He sang in Ancaran through much of the meal and even acted out little bits of the songs, making silly faces as he did. It did much to lessen the tension in the tribe as villagers reminisced on their own experiences with the insects.

Chapter 29

Dashin slept restlessly, tossing and turning. He dreamt of being chased through the forest by unseen forces. He raced headlong, running into branches and trees, but the pursuers were always behind him, gaining on him. He woke, soaking wet before dawn, his fever broken. He crept out onto the landing and breathed in the fresh night air, trying to clear his head. He padded around to the cistern, filled a bucket with cool water, and dumped it over his head. The water was bracing but refreshing. He drew another bucket and washed up, dabbing at the swollen mirha bites on his body.

He put on fresh clothes and went to wait for Alina on the village platform. As he waited, he poked around in the larder for something to eat.

Rigin arrived out of the darkness. "Let me fix you something," she said. "You barely ate last night." She pulled out a few bags and gourds, slathered a thick paste on some nutbread, and dropped dried berries on it.

"Here," she said, handing him the bread.

His stomach growled in anticipation. He winced as he bit into it, the tension of chewing pulling at his swollen cheek. "This is delicious," he mumbled, his cheek making the rounded Ndesan speech awkward.

"How are the stings today?" she asked, probing the edge of his cheek gently with her fingers. "The next day is always the worst."

"They're fine," he lied, shying at her touch.

A few villagers arrived on the platform and greeted Rigin. Most of them also nodded to Dashin, smiling amusedly as they did. He blushed as he remembered regaling the village with renditions of Ancaran nursery school songs. That he still remembered those was bewildering. And the fact he'd sung several choruses of Ickby, the itsy-bitsy mouse was mortifying.

Nyan, Aras' wife, crinkled her eyes at him, giggling at his reaction and mentioning it would feel better tomorrow. She seemed about to say more, but her daughters joined her, both of them clamoring for something to eat. She gave him another smile and stepped into the kitchen with them.

Alina passed by, on her way to fetch him, he thought. He called out to her. She seemed surprised to see him up and strode over, greeting Rigin warmly as she neared them. She seemed anxious to be away, fidgeting with her lanyards. He thanked Rigin for the bread, and they hurried to his hut to fetch his old lanyards. After using the new ones yesterday, these were a pain to use. He'd only just set off with them when they slipped from a limb, and he took a fall. He was glad to trade them for his new lanyards when they reached the cache.

"How are you feeling?" Alina asked him as he strapped on his lanyards.

"I don't remember much after the stings," he said shyly. He did have some memories of saying several embarrassing things on the walk back to the village, but he chose to feign ignorance.

"That's a shame," Alina said, a slight smile tugging at the corners of her mouth. "You had so much to say yesterday."

He flushed, his skin growing hot as the particulars swam to the surface. He cringed, trying to think of a way to apologize.

"Your expression is adorable. I think this one is my favorite."

Dashin blushed darker, which made her chuckle. She nudged his shoulder with hers. "It was flattering," she continued.

"Do we have time for this?" he asked, squirming, desperate to change the subject.

"Oh, we always have time for this," she answered with another chuckle. After a pause, she relented. "But, I suppose we should train a bit today." She crinkled her eyes at him. "It will give us time to review the many things you said."

He reached for her, and she squealed, leaping into the trees. He chased her as she flitted ahead of him, giggling and enjoying his inability to reach her. His vision narrowed, his technique sharpening as he sought to catch her. Every fiber of his being was intent on at least touching some part of her. She wove in and out in front of him, always tantalizingly close and yet just out of reach.

He grunted, his chest heaving at the exertion, straining with each lanyard pull to rocket toward her, and yet she would dart to the side at the last instant, crinkling her eyes at him as he sailed by. After ages of struggling to catch her, he fetched up on a branch, panting, letting his heart rate settle, and wiping the sweat from his brow. All the exertion had inflamed the stings on his body, and he rubbed at them, which made them burn all the more.

Alina alit next to him. "You're getting much better."

He'd forgotten that he was meant to be training, so focused had he been on catching her. He blinked, realizing that she'd been pushing him and that he'd acted instinctively, his body moving without thought as he strove to catch her. It was amazing how much freer he felt in the trees now. He looked around at the forest, surprised to find how comfortable he felt sitting here so far above the ground.

"Do you see how smoothly you move when you're not thinking?"

"You did that on purpose?"

"Of course," she answered, crinkling her eyes. "Though it was delightful. I haven't had fun like that since I was Solvan's age."

Dashin frowned. He'd pushed himself to his physical limits, and she'd darted about as if it were child's play. He rubbed at the welt on his cheek.

"Are those stings still bothering you?"

"Yes, these bites are nasty. I can't imagine getting stung by an entire nest."

"Follow me," she said, leaping into the trees. He scrambled after her, struggling to keep her in sight. He followed her to a dun-colored tree with plump red berries hanging from its branches.

"These are borka," she said.

"Like the nuts in the paste we eat?"

"Yes, the same. The nuts are inside that outer husk."

He reached for one, but she caught his hand. She took a leaf from the tree and used it to pluck a fleshy fruit. She pressed it against his still-burning cheek. The area tingled, the pain growing dull. She pulled it away, handing him the leaf.

"That's amazing," he said. "It feels so much better." He took the leaf and pressed the pulpy husk against the other two stings. He closed his eyes and felt the soothing numbness spread.

"Yes, the outer flesh of the borka has that effect. It is good for wounds. My father uses it in that balm he treats you with. Be careful not to overuse it, or your entire arm will go numb. Rub it on your stings. The effect will last for a while."

He rubbed more of it against his stings, and they were soon completely numb.

"Try a small bite. The outer flesh has an interesting taste."

He took a bite, and it was so bitter he spat it out, gagging on it. "That's terrible."

"I didn't say it was a good taste, only that it was interesting. Wait a moment, and you'll see what I mean."

"I don't know-wo-wo," his mouth went numb, his tongue and lips losing sensation. He looked at her, and she was grinning, trying hard not to laugh. "Oh, worwowo," he said, moving toward her while holding out the borka.

She screeched and dove into the trees. He dropped the leaf and tore off after her, muttering incoherently and drooling as he chased her through the forest.

They took their midday meal together on a branch, the effect of the borka having worn off some by then. His stings, even after the numbness subsided, felt much better. The air was warm, and the sunlight reaching through the leaves was glorious. If it weren't for the looming trials, it would have been perfect.

"I've been thinking about the *trial of the hunt*," he said. "I'd like to go see if we can find some of those stoda creatures, just to have a look at them from above and see what I'm dealing with."

"We should be able to find some. Though they are nocturnal, you can sometimes find them bedded down at midday."

"Has anyone ever tried to trap them?"

"I don't know. The men are the ones who hunt them. From what I gather, the hunters drive them toward a narrow area where others wait to take them."

"I see. That won't work with just one person. It may be useful to see them, though. Perhaps I'll get an idea."

"Should you be successful, you'll also have to find a way to carry it back to the village. Since it must exceed your weight, it will be challenging to transport in one trip. Leaving part of a fresh kill behind for predators could prove disastrous."

Dashin frowned. "I hadn't considered that. First, I have to get one. Then I'll figure out how to get it back."

After their meal, they roamed above the forest floor looking for stoda. They covered a large area, not finding any before happening on a small herd bedded in some ferns, eschewing the midday heat. A large boar lay in the middle of the herd, its eyes half closed but with its head up, nose in the air.

Dashin studied it. The boar seemed at least three times his weight and fearsome to behold. It had a tree trunk for a neck and a massive chest behind razor-sharp tusks. It had short, powerful legs and a hide that was so thick Rigin used a mallet and awl to work it.

This would be a lot more difficult than he'd imagined. He dismissed the meager ideas he'd been toying with. Nothing short of dropping a tree on this beast was going to get its attention. He swallowed.

"TreeFolk hunt these beasts with spears?" he whispered, in awe of what it would take to face such a beast with only a pointy stick.

Alina nodded. "Yes, the men work together to bring them down. They do not attempt the larger ones. But TreeFolk are lighter, and so for their *becoming* one of the smaller sows is typical."

"That's not going to work for me," Dashin mused.

Alina bit her lip.

The boar's head snapped up, and it was instantly on its feet. The motion was a blur. One moment it had been dozing, and the next it was alert, its head turning from side to side, sniffing the air. It gave a quick snort, and the herd was up. It strode out in front of the herd, facing the forest as the sows gathered up their young and pushed them into the center, turning to face the forest once they were secure.

"What's happening?" Dashin asked.

Alina pointed to a section of forest below.

Dashin followed her finger and saw forms moving in the brush. They were creatures like the wild desert-dogs on Ancara, but bigger, nearly two-thirds his size, with huge mouths filled with recurved teeth, designed to grab and hold onto prey. Their necks were barely defined, just a thick bundle of muscles between the terrifying jaws and stout shoulders. All of this on muscled legs built for speed.

"What in the world are those?"

"Turga," Alina spat the word, touching her forehead with her fingertips.

The predators stopped some distance from the stoda, looking at the herd. Two groups of three turga broke off from the pack, moving around the herd, flanking it on either side. The boar pawed the ground, his hooves sounding like a drum and throwing up clods of dirt on the young who milled about behind it, their cries frightened and confused.

The flanking turga probed the herd, trying to find a weak spot while the remaining turga kept the boar engaged, staying just out of charging range. It was riveting to watch these predators working together. Then, all at once, things exploded. Three of the turga on one flank dove at the pack, attacking one of the smaller sows, while the four remaining turga charged the boar.

Those engaging the boar turned away as it charged to meet them. Their attack only intended to keep it distracted. But the boar was fast and took one of the turga in the hind quarter, its tusk slicing through flesh as though it were nut paste, dispatching it in one thrust and throwing the predator high into the air. The other three swept in, but the huge head came back and impaled another, goring it viciously. The gored turga howled and stumbled away, blood flowing freely from a wound it was unlikely to survive. But the others that had set upon the sow had injured her and taken a fat shoat from among the young. They dragged it back with them as they retreated.

The altercation was over in a flash, the turga melting back into the forest. The cries of the shoat ended long before those of the sow did.

Alina looked at him, her eyes concerned.

He tried to put on a confident face to find some way to tell her that he had a plan, but after watching this, he couldn't manage it.

Alina looked away for a moment and took a deep breath. When she turned back to him, she nudged him with her shoulder. "Let's take a break. Follow me."

She led him through the forest, dropping down lower and lower as she went. She moved at an easier pace, and he was gratified to notice that at this speed his motion was smoother than it had been. Pressing hard through the morning had significantly improved his skills.

She stopped at an opening in the forest. The midday sun was streaming through the gap. At ground level, before them, lay a large cenote, a pond with crystal-clear water. Alina surveyed the surrounding area, and once she was content that there were no dangers, she dropped to the ground next to it. She removed her lanyards and jumped in, clothes and all. Dashin followed her in.

The water felt amazing. It was cool and so clear. The lower gravity on this planet made him feel more buoyant. It took little energy to stay afloat or swim around. He reveled in the feel of the water against his skin as he paddled about, memories of swimming in the underground pool of his city on Ancara came to mind as he did.

"What do you think?" Alina asked, treading water.

"This feels amazing. It doesn't feel at all like the water on Ancara."

Alina smiled at his obvious pleasure while still keeping watch on the forest nearby. "The water is different there?"

"I don't notice it much when I drink it, but it feels much different to swim in."

Alina swam to the shore and climbed out. "We should not tarry long in the water. This is the water supply for many creatures, and it is best to use it cautiously. Midday is typically best because of the light and the heat. Most predators bed down in the day."

Alina was standing in the light, her homespun clothing wet and revealing in the midday sun. Dashin was taken by the sight and felt a stirring within him. He turned away, not wanting to be caught staring, though she didn't seem to notice. He swam to the opposite side of the pond before climbing out, worried that the stirring in his body might be noticeable. He heard her call out sharply as he pulled himself out onto the bank. At first, he thought perhaps she had seen him looking after all, but then he noticed he'd climbed out into a pool of a clear sticky substance. A memory fragment flashed up, and he knew that it was crollan.

"That is unfortunate," Alina said, laughing now.

Snippets of Alina's encounters popped into his mind. Crollan was a sticky and slippery digestive ooze, often found near water. It lived on the bugs and small animals that became trapped in it and digested these slowly over time. He stood up and tried to take a step away. His feet shot out from beneath him, and he crashed face-first into the dirt. The substance was on his hands, legs, and feet. He tried to brush it off, but it was so sticky that he just ended up spreading it around. He tried to brush the dirt from his chin and ended up smearing it on his face. Within a few moments, he was covered from head to toe.

The more he worked at removing it, the more he spread it, and the more he heard Alina laughing. She was doubled over a short distance away, shaking with laughter as she watched him struggle.

He tried to move toward her, and she squealed and leapt away. His foot found a stone and slid out from beneath him. He fell flat on his face again, this time in something that was not dirt. Many creatures came to this watering hole, and some left behind more than footprints. The animal scat he'd fallen in was disgustingly foul, and he fought not to gag as he tried to scrape it away from his face. It mixed with the crollan until he was entirely covered in a mixture of both.

The hoofprints near the scat assured him that he now knew exactly how stoda scat smelled and tasted.

This, of course, was a whole new dimension of hilarious for Alina. He tried to throw some at her, but the substance refused to leave his hand. He crawled to some broad-leafed ferns, pulled some up by the roots, and used them to wipe at the ooze. It worked to some extent, but the ooze stuck to the leaves, so he had to continually get new leaves so as not to smear it back on himself.

After clearing out an area the size of a hut, he'd removed the bulk of it. He jumped back into the water to remove the rest. It didn't come off with water alone, but he found that scrubbing with sand from the walls of the cenote did the trick. Sometime later, he crawled from the cenote, clean again. He was careful to avoid the substance he'd spread across much of the surroundings.

Alina appeared to be in pain. Tears were still running down her face from laughing so hard throughout the entire ordeal. Dashin bit his tongue and waited until her latest bout of laughter subsided. "I'm glad you enjoyed that."

"Enjoyed? It was a thing of songs, Dashin. It will be sung by generations of TreeFolk. Never has a warrior faced such a ferocious beast and battled it so bravely." She burst out laughing again, holding her stomach from having overtaxed those muscles.

"Come," she said, "we must not linger here." She slipped on her lanyards, climbed a small tree, and then leapt to a larger one. He followed her up until they were far above the forest floor, sitting on a broad branch together.

"You're not planning on sharing this with anyone else, are you?"

"Would you deny them this tale?" she asked, arching an eyebrow.

"Yes," he said earnestly.

She smiled and patted his arm. "I think not. I have come to know your generosity and kindness of spirit. I know your true heart in this matter."

"You do?" he said, arching an eyebrow.

"Yes, Dashin, I've come to know your heart," she said, her tone serious, her eyes soft on his.

Dashin swallowed, unsure what to say. "Alina, I..." words failed him.

She waited for him, her eyes earnest.

He stumbled and stammered, trying to put into words the confusing feelings that were roiling within him. He opened his mouth a few more times, about to continue, only to have nothing come out.

She smiled, crinkled her eyes, and then chuckled, "Your face just now was beyond delicious." She reached forward and brushed his cheek with her fingers.

He was still trying to speak when she put her fingers on his mouth. "There is no need, Dashin. I know, of course. Just as you do."

"I do? I mean, you do?"

"Dashin, I've seen your heart, and you've seen mine. What more is there to say?"

Her words blossomed inside his chest, filling him with a warm glow. "What do we do?"

"We make sure you win your trials and become *of the tribe*."

"That sounds like a good idea to me," he said, turning over the problem in his mind. "We have a plan for the *trial of the forest* and no solid ideas yet for the *trial of the hunt*. But the *trial of the trees* seems like the greatest risk."

"You work on the *trial of the hunt,*" she said. "Let me think on the *trial of the trees*."

"What about the dish for the feast?"

Alina laughed. "As I said before, if you survive these trials, everyone will be so amazed that you can just serve a handful of nuts and no one will notice."

"Okay," he said, wanting to address this tradition as well, but too overwhelmed at the moment to pursue it.

She reached over and took his hand.

His skin tingled at the contact. The feel of her hand in his was sublime. Her fingers were delicate but firm. He looked out at the forest. It felt perfect sitting here with her. He never would have imagined that sharing such a moment with someone could feel this way.

As the moment stretched on, a thought occurred to him. "Have you heard from your mother?"

"No. I have not."

"Are you concerned?"

She shrugged. "It has often been so with my mother."

"So, you don't know when she will return?"

She shrugged. "No, she will return when her *sight* tells her to, I imagine. Only six days remain until the *trial of the trees*. We must keep our minds on these trials. Much depends on a few days now, Dashin."

He swallowed, recalling that the trials were so near. "You're not going to recount the incident with the crollan, right?"

The village roared with laughter as Alina recounted the episode, giving a commendable performance of the events and describing every detail. He watched her giggle and smile as she related the tale, her eyes alight and sparkling with the joy of it.

When she reached the part where Dashin fell into the stoda excrement and smeared it all over himself, the village erupted in such gales of laughter that she had to wait many moments for it to die down enough before she could continue the account. There were still some who would not be drawn in by the tale, but many who had been cold toward him had warmed after the incident with the mirha and now again with the tale of the crollan. Very few of the villagers were dry-eyed now.

He leaned toward Alina. "You were not serious about this becoming a part of the song of the tribe, though, right?"

She shrugged and then crinkled her eyes at him. "I make no such promise. It would make an interesting verse to our song. Much of our song is serious and dry. This would give it some life, don't you think?"

He threw a crust of bread at her, and she laughed, prompting everyone around them to laugh until the entire village was in tears again.

The children were especially tickled. Solvan and Matse sat in the center of them, with Solvan holding court, regaling them with tales of fancy. Given Solvan's habit of spinning tales, if he ever let something slip that he shouldn't, Dashin thought that it might well go unnoticed.

He sat watching the village, enjoying the lack of tension on the platform at the moment. He nodded and shrugged as people looked at him and laughed or pointed, accepting their mirth gracefully and laughing along with them, which they appeared to appreciate. He even forgot the trials until the laughter died down as the evening meal broke up and folks cleaned up the platform and headed off to bed. As Dashin headed to Rigin's hut, he could still hear bursts of laughter rising into the night.

Chapter 30

The next morning, Alina set up a course similar to the one Dashin would face for the *trial of the trees*. The course was marked with splashes of red dye on the branches and trunks of trees along the route. She showed him the baskets that held the tokens he must collect during his transit, and how the baskets were sometimes hidden above or below the course itself, forcing the candidate to be vigilant in locating them.

It was far more challenging than anything he'd attempted thus far. Kani and Hurza stopped by to see how he was doing and swung along with Alina, shadowing Dashin as he traversed the course. They worked together, moving baskets and changing the markings so that Dashin navigated course after changing course. By midday, he was exhausted from the continuous effort with his lanyards. They sat together, Alina pulling out her banda leaves and adding them to the ones Kani and Hurza had brought.

"Dashin," Kani said. "I cannot believe how well you move in the trees with your lanyards. I've never seen anything like them." She leaned in and ran her fingers over them, admiring the workmanship.

"It was wise to continue arriving in the village with the other ones," Hurza said. "You are much clumsier with those."

"You're getting the sense of it," Alina said. "You're finding the baskets more quickly, learning to seek them above and below you on the course."

Dashin pulled the palm-sized wooden tokens he'd gathered on his last pass from his bag. "The tokens are all different," he noted, laying them out on top of Alina's pack.

"These are the tokens from our *becoming*," Alina said, indicating her friends. "The tokens are numbered, and each number also has a picture of something in the forest. Number one here has a corsol, number four has a banda tree, and so on. That way, when a candidate arrives at the platform, the village can see that they've visited all the baskets."

"Do they always have the same numbers and pictures?"

Alina nodded. "Normally, yes."

"Why wouldn't I put these in a bag and then wait a few moments in the forest and return and present these instead of the ones in the baskets?"

Hurza chuckled. "I like the way your mind works."

"What you suggest happened in our songs, long ago," Kani said. "The chief marks the backs of each token now."

Alina turned the tokens over. "See the markings on the backs?" She ran her finger over the scribbling painted on the backs.

"What do the scribbles mean?" Dashin asked, leaning over and studying them.

"It's the chief's markings for that *becoming*," Kani said.

"But even tokens with the same number are different?" he said, comparing two of the tokens.

"Yes," Hurza replied. "There is some pattern within it that the chief recognizes, so candidates can't make copies."

"Does such a thing happen?" Dashin asked, frowning.

"Not anymore, but our songs speak of it, which is why chiefs have grown crafty and do not share their secret markings," Alina said.

"I'm surprised at all these precautions," Dashin said.

"Bending the rules is encouraged, and the entire village looks forward to seeing it done. Though each time someone finds a creative way to win, that approach is eliminated in subsequent trials," Hurza said.

"If I'm going to win, I think I'm going to need to be creative," Dashin said.

"You focus on getting faster," Alina said. "We'll work on creative ideas."

They finished eating, Dashin polishing off the bulk of the stuffed leaves. Her friends pushed theirs toward him, grinning at his appetite. As he stuffed the last banda leaf into his mouth, Alina said. "Try the last course again, and Kani will wait a bit and then chase you, so you have a sense of what the chase sounds like in the trees."

Dashin nodded, still chewing. He uncoiled his lanyards from his forearms, letting them hang in preparation. He swallowed and then leapt from the branch he'd been sitting on, planted the cup of his lanyard solidly, and then swung from it to plant the next one. His body swung between them in the semi-fluid, semi-jerky rhythm he'd developed. Alina listened to his rhythm recede, smiling at the sound.

"He's so much better," Hurza said. "How did he progress so quickly?"

"I think it was the *touching*," Alina replied, feeling a bit awkward with Kani there since they'd never spoken of it since the incident in their childhood. But Kani didn't appear uncomfortable. Alina relaxed, happy to have shared this with her friends.

"Do you have feelings for him?" Kani asked instead.

Alina stiffened and paused, not having voiced such a thing to anyone aside from Dashin. What would her friends think?

"Of course she does," Hurza replied. "It's obvious to anyone with eyes."

Alina flushed, flustered by the turn the conversation had taken. Kani reached over and put her hand on Alina's. "We'll do everything we can to help."

Alina's eyes misted, and she blinked, trying to clear them as she swallowed. "Thanks," she whispered.

"Of course we will," Hurza said and then turned to Kani. "You might want to get chasing. I think he just reached the third basket."

Kani's head spun toward the forest. She took two quick steps and dove into the trees, her lanyard reaching out. She raced away, moving fast. Alina and Hurza watched her go.

"We have to make sure Aor does the chasing," Hurza said, still looking after Kani.

"Do you have any idea how we can manage that?"

"I have some thoughts," Hurza mused with a grin.

"I thought I might doctor some sweets," Alina offered. "Perhaps I could add a bit of soapstone. I always prepare sweets. I don't think they would suspect."

"Would the effect be quick enough?"

"I think so. If I added enough soapstone and extra berries to mask the taste."

"I have an idea or two as well," Hurza said, still grinning.

"What do you think?" Alina asked Dashin after her friends had gone. Kani had pushed Dashin but had let him win. Hurza, however, had passed him halfway through the course, flying past him so that she arrived well before him, letting him see how much work there was yet to do.

"I'm feeling better in the trees, but Kani and Hurza are fast. I wouldn't stand a chance in a race with either of them," he said as he arrived panting.

"No, not in the time we have remaining."

"Can I keep these tokens for a time?" Dashin asked.

"Certainly. What are you thinking?"

"I don't know yet, but I want to study them. Perhaps something will come to me."

Alina shrugged. She looked out into the trees. "Let's walk. I want to try something."

They walked for a bit until Alina stopped and pointed. "See that tree with the limb that looks like a bent arm?"

"Yes," Dashin replied, squinting in the direction she was pointing.

"What is the best path to it from here?"

Dashin studied the forest and outlined a path that seemed reasonable to him.

Alina nodded. "That's an acceptable path, but look up and down too. See the branch above us? If you take that one and then over to that one over there, and then down toward the tree by those two branches there instead, you will save two lanyard lengths."

"Oh," Dashin said, growing excited. "Yes, that's much better."

"Remember the *TruePath*. You must always be seeking it."

They walked through the forest, Alina pointing out various landmarks and Dashin attempting to discern his *TruePath* to each. Alina was impressed with how much he'd improved. She remembered some of the songs of his world where he learned to see objects in space and manipulate them on a transparent plate that sat on a table, the objects somehow suspended mysteriously above the plate. And, when he'd learned to see the pictures of the trees in his mind, he'd been able to somehow change his view of the forest within his mind, something she'd never heard of anyone doing.

Next, she had him find paths with his lanyards, moving through the forest, and finding his *TruePath* to the landmarks she called out. She had him move slowly at first, more intent on finding an efficient path than on speed. As he developed a feel for it, she had him increase the pace until he was doing it at nearly his full speed.

She led him back to her pack. As they alit next to it, she pulled out her water gourd, took a sip, and then handed it to him.

"That's so much better, Dashin. How does it feel?"

"I think I'm starting to see it. Sometimes I realize that there was a better path after I've already committed to one, but I'm now seeing better paths. Before, I was just trying to follow as straight a path as possible."

"I want to do the last course again. I'll go out and put a token in each basket as fast as I can, and you follow behind and take them. I'll make another transit after I finish and try to catch you before you reach my pack here."

"You're going to go around twice, and I only have to make it once?"

"Yes. You make it sound like I don't have a chance?" Alina said, arching an eyebrow.

"What do I get if I win?" Dashin said with a smile.

She laughed. "What do you want?"

He whispered in her ear. She narrowed her eyes at him, a tiny smile tugging at the corners of her mouth. Scooping up the bag of tokens, she leapt into the trees. Behind her, Dashin fumbled with his lanyards, grumbling. She chuckled.

She sped through the course, pushing herself, floating between the branches, and stopping only briefly to deposit a token in each basket. At first, she heard Dashin making his way in her wake, but soon the sound grew distant as she outpaced him. Completing the course, she alit for only a moment by her pack before launching herself in pursuit.

She was chasing now, flying through the trees, intent on catching him. She touched each basket as she flew past, pausing only long enough to ensure he'd taken the token.

As she neared the fourth basket, she heard him ahead. His jerky rhythm was confident and consistent, the way it ought to be. She was proud of him, of everything he'd endured to make it this far. There were still mountains ahead of them, but now there were also mountains behind. They had achieved much together.

She'd been startled by her friends' statements, surprised they were aware of the song in her heart, a song she'd only shared with Dashin. Though she'd have noticed if either of them had developed feelings for another. It touched her that she'd not had to reply and that her friends had rallied to her cause without her having to ask. She didn't appreciate what she had with them enough.

She gained on Dashin, spying him below her, swinging along, each aggressive swing propelling him forward in his oddly powerful way. There were only two baskets left. She hung back, watching him move. Planning on catching him at the last basket. She saw him twitch and glance back, aware now of her presence. He sped up, surging ahead. She smiled. So cute that he imagined he had a chance.

"That's it, Dashin," she yelled down to him, moving to overtake him.

He glanced up at her, his face flushed from exertion, but with a smile on his face for her. She watched it unfold, unable to stop or avert it. Turning to her, he hadn't seen the huge limb covered in leaves he accelerated toward. By the time he turned back, it was too late. Though he tried to duck, his head smacked right into it, the sound like an axe biting into wood.

She dropped toward him, but his body went slack. His hands came loose on the grips of his lanyards, releasing the cups, and his body plummeted through the forest. For a TreePerson, an uncontrolled fall was a terrifying thing, the stuff of nightmares, and often fatal.

She flew after him, hearing him hurtle through the branches beneath her, crashing through them, as his body careened, picking up speed. She lost sight of him, the sound receding. Then it disappeared altogether.

A stone formed in her stomach. She ignored caution, letting herself fall in his wake, tumbling after him in a barely-controlled fall of her own.

She slammed into the forest floor, the impact jarring every bone in her body. Next to her lay a mass of branches torn from the forest during Dashin's fall. She was certain he must be dead. But she heard a moan. She leapt at the nest of branches, digging through them frantically to reach him.

His lanyards were twisted and knotted in the mass of branches. She crawled within it to unstrap them from his arms. Dragging him free, she pulled him into her arms. Unable to breathe, she sent silent prayers to the SkyGods as her hands flew over his body. He was scratched up and bruised everywhere, but amazingly, nothing seemed broken. When he opened his eyes and looked at her, she broke down and cried, cradling his body against her. He moaned and mumbled something.

"You hit your head and fell," she said, her fingers light on the massive welt forming on his brow. He winced, squirming as he shifted, trying to sit up. She stood and stepped back to give him space.

The skin on the back of her neck prickled.

She hadn't stopped to check the forest floor before dropping to it. She heard movement behind her and turned. The nightmares following her *trial of the forest* flooded through her, and she could not move. There, not three body lengths from her, was an enormous krax, larger than any she'd ever seen or heard tell of. It was already crouched to spring, its ears flat against its head, its deadly fangs bared, gleaming white against its night black fur.

Chapter 31

Dashin moaned as he came too. His battered body screamed at him. He tried to move but couldn't. He opened his eyes, and all he could see were branches packed around him. His arms were pinned across his body, and he couldn't move his legs. Someone was calling his name. He tried to turn toward the voice, but his head throbbed and swam at the sudden motion.

The voice was insistent. Alina. It was Alina. She was behind him, her voice panicked. The nest of branches around him rocked as she tugged at it, burrowing toward him. He tried to turn to her, but managed only to shift a bit, his wits wrapped in a fog.

She tugged at him and dragged him from the mess of branches. Her hands flew over his body, and then she was crying and speaking to him as she cradled him. There was soft earth beneath him. They were on the forest floor. Somehow, he'd fallen from the canopy.

"What happened?" he mumbled. She said something about a fall and brushed his forehead with her fingertips. It stung. He looked over at the mess of branches with his lanyards entwined within them. He'd likely pulled it all down with him. That mess would have slowed his fall and probably saved his life.

He swallowed and shifted in her arms, trying to sit up. Everything hurt, but his fingers and toes moved, and he could move his shoulders and waist. Breathing was a bit tender. Likely, a rib or two were bruised, but he'd been incredibly lucky.

Alina stood and offered him a hand. Aside from a nasty bump on one shin, his legs seemed intact. He saw her turn and freeze and then begin to tremble.

He stood shakily, peered around her shoulder, and gasped. A terrible creature crouched, muscles bunched, ready to spring. The cat-like creature was at least twice his size and seemed comprised entirely of muscles, teeth, and claws. It was jet black with large golden eyes, white rings on its long tail, and short white stripes along its spine. Its triangular ears were flat against its head.

Alina was frozen before it, and the memory fragment of her trial sprang to mind. Instinctively, he reached down for a branch. It was a dead branch with a jagged end where it had split from the trunk as he'd crashed into it, but its other end was mired in the nest of foliage that surrounded him. He could not free it, but he pulled the entire mass forward enough to allow him to step in front of Alina and tuck it up under his arm.

"Alina, run!" he shouted as the immense cat sprang.

It leapt the entire distance between them in a single bound, powerful jaws and razor-sharp claws hurtling toward them. Rooted in place by the branch and with Alina immobile at his back, Dashin braced himself for the impact, leaning forward and planting his feet. The pitiful weapon exploded into a hail of splinters as the creature crashed into them. Alina was thrown clear, and Dashin was driven back, the air rushing from his lungs as the crushing weight of the beast slammed him to the ground, pinning him beneath it. It raised its head and roared.

Gasping for air, Dashin tried to wriggle free, his heart thundering in his chest as he thrashed in the soft earth. The beast opened its jaws and reached for him, its hot breath on his face, huge fangs on either side of its mouth glistening in the filtered light. Still pinned, he reached up, wrapping himself around the creature, cinching his arms around its neck and locking his legs around its torso in a desperate attempt to avoid those fangs.

The move took the creature by surprise, and it shook itself, trying to dislodge him so it could bring its jaws and claws to bear. Tossing its head from side to side, its claws scythed the air behind him. Powerful muscles rippled against his body as Dashin tightened his grip, pressing even closer to avoid both fang and claw. His hips, jammed between the beast's forelegs, prevented its claws from reaching his back, though one of them managed to slice open his tunic.

Enraged, the creature leapt into the air, coming down in a bed of ferns and rolling over and over with him still attached. The impact drove out the little air he'd managed to draw in, but he maintained his grip, knowing that as soon as he was dislodged, he would die horribly. Chemicals surged in his bloodstream. His heart thundered. He gritted his teeth and held on.

The cat shook itself furiously, repeatedly striving to shake Dashin free. He nearly lost his grip several times, barely managing to hang on. After the fifth or sixth attempt, hot blood ran down his thigh. Somehow, the cat must have found his leg with a claw when it had first leapt on him. The blood flowed freely, and he feared he would soon pass out. He held on tight, seeking now only to buy time for Alina to reach safety.

He yelled at Alina to climb, but his words were clipped and labored. He couldn't see anything, his face buried in the furry neck. He prayed she'd made it up into the trees. The strength ebbed from his muscles, limbs shaking and lungs heaving from the strain.

The creature roared repeatedly, the sound painfully loud and terrifying in his ear. Its huge lungs were a bellows against his chest, its heartbeat an urgent drum beating in both their bodies. It continued leaping about and throwing its head back and forth, its teeth snapping near his shoulder. Blood gushed from him, flowing down his leg. A few moments more, he told himself, a few moments more.

Suddenly, the beast stopped. It took a tottering step. Its chest still heaving, it tried to shake him again, but the motion was weaker. A flicker of hope rose within him, and he squeezed with every shred of energy he had left. This elicited another flurry of thrashing from the cat, but it was brief, and soon subsided into panting. And then, impossibly, it fell over on its side with Dashin still wrapped around it.

He felt the creature's muscles relax, its huge neck moving against him a few more times before going still. He couldn't make sense of what was happening. He risked a glance down the creature's body and saw a large shard from the broken branch he'd been holding, buried deep in the creature's torso. Blood flowed from the wound onto him. The creature's body went still beneath him. Its heartbeat stuttered and then faded. He waited a few moments until its muscles went slack and then wriggled free. He had to push hard with one leg to pull the other from beneath the beast.

He tried to stand but fell over, his body shaking. He slumped to the ground. He was covered in blood and mud. Looking around, he saw large furrows in the earth where the creature had tried to tear him loose. He lifted his hands before him, and they were shaking worse than his body. Tears streamed down his face. He felt apart from his body, as though observing it from a distance. Moments ago, he'd been certain he would die and had been focused only on surviving long enough for Alina to escape. *Alina!* he thought, trying to move, to find her, though his body was impossibly heavy.

And then she was on him, her hands searching his body as she shouted questions at him. He stared up at her, trying to make out the words through the ringing in his ears and the fog in his mind. He realized she was looking for a wound, for the source of the blood that covered him. He pointed with a shaky hand at the fatal gash in the creature's side. She followed his trembling finger and came undone.

She wrapped her arms around him and sobbed, her body shaking as she clutched him. He winced at the force of her embrace. She asked him something, her eyes on his. He stared blankly, trying to read the words on her lips.

She frowned, peering at him, and then leaned in, touching her forehead to his. A warmth flooded into him, and he heard her gasp as her mind joined his. Two breaths later, he heard her in his mind. *"Dashin! Can you hear me? Dashin!"*

"Alina?" he thought, confused at finding her thoughts in his mind.

"I couldn't reach you," the thought arrived, wrapped in frantic, anxious emotions that washed through him.

He blinked up at her, trying to make sense of what was happening. "Alina?" he croaked, pulling away as sound returned to his world and he craned his neck to look her over, worried she might have been injured in the original impact. "Are you hurt?"

She shook her head, pulling him close again. He could feel her heartbeat, a solid, insistent rhythm against his cheek. She ran her fingers through his hair, pushing it from his brow. "I'm fine. Thanks to you, Amani," she said, biting her lip, holding back emotion.

"I thought *Amani* was the name your parents used for each other?" Dashin whispered, his voice still weak.

"It is," she replied, letting out a breath. "It's a TreeFolk word used for a *particular person*, someone *important* above others."

"I see. Thanks for clearing that up, *Amani*," he replied, with a grin. It felt wonderful to say it. The word summed up his feelings perfectly.

"I thought I would die," he whispered.

She choked back a sob. "I was so afraid I'd lost you." She pulled him closer, his head on her shoulder, her arms gentle bands of iron wrapped around him. She held him, rocking them, her heartbeat as fast as his own.

"Do you think this will count?" Dashin asked.

She pulled her head back and peered at him. "What?"

"Do you think they will accept this?"

"Dashin, I don't understand what you're asking," she replied, frowning.

"For the *trial of the hunt*. Will this count?" he clarified, the thought having just occurred to him.

Alina gasped, her eyes going wide, and then she hugged him hard, too hard. "Oh, Amani," she wriggled, shaking him. "How could it not!"

She loosened her grip a fraction and looked over at the massive creature. "Hedrick will be beside himself." She giggled.

"Alina, I can't stop shaking," he said, holding up his hands.

"It's normal. I've heard my father speak of it. It will pass." She sat back and took his hands in hers, holding them as she gazed at him. "Give it time. You'll be fine. Everything will be fine," she commanded, her voice barely shaking at all.

"How am I going to carry it to the village?" Dashin mused, looking around her shoulder at the beast.

Alina followed his gaze. "I don't know. Perhaps we can just take the skin. It will be obvious to everyone that it was much heavier than you."

Dashin shook his head. "No, I don't want to give them the chance to dismiss this."

"But, Dashin, look at it. No one would expect you to carry this?"

The beast was gigantic. He doubted he could even lift it here on the ground, let alone carry it up through the trees. He glanced up, trying to get his mind to function again, to bring his thoughts into focus. "How far away is my pod?"

"Your egg?" she asked.

He nodded. "The ropes we used to lower it are in there. Perhaps I can use them to lift the creature."

"It is some distance from here," she looked off into the forest, considering it.

"Could you fetch them?"

"I can't leave you here alone," she replied, looking around.

"I'll climb up into the trees and wait for you."

She thought it over. "The smell of krax is everywhere and will be strong for a time. Perhaps, if you stay in the trees..."

"I will. But, I'll need help to climb," he said, holding up his shaking hands.

"Of course, Amani." She ran over to the nest of branches and untangled his lanyards from it, being careful not to damage them. She worked the mechanisms, ensuring they still functioned as they should.

Dashin exhaled. Losing his lanyards would have spelled his doom. He tried to stand, his legs rubbery from the altercation. Alina rushed over and took an arm, steadying him.

"My legs are cramping," he said, leaning on her.

"I have no idea how you withstood it, Amani. I was certain it would dislodge you."

"I was, too. I just wanted to hold on long enough for you to get to safety."

The words stopped her. She put her fingers on his lips, her face fighting not to cry. She pulled him close, holding his body tight against hers as a warm blanket of emotions surrounded him.

When she pulled away, she touched his forehead briefly with hers. Then, with some pushing and some pulling, she helped him climb into the trees, managing to get him to a lower bough just above the creature's body.

"Do not move from here," she said, turning his head so she could look into his eyes. "I will be back soon."

He nodded. "I'll wait right here," he said, wrapping an arm around the trunk and threading one leg between two branches to ensure he felt secure.

Alina took one last look at him and dove into the trees, racing away.

The light in the forest was fading fast now as evening approached. This close to the forest floor, it was difficult for Dashin to get a sense of time. It was always shady down here. He looked up, trying unsuccessfully to see the angle of the sun in the forest, but he sensed that dusk was near. Evening would soon be here.

He felt separate from his body, as though he'd been given a new life yet again. He'd survived the destruction of his ship, a fall through the forest, and now, this impossible confrontation. Every time, he'd opened his eyes to Alina's face above him.

He leaned against the tree, trying to slow his breathing to help his body flush the chemicals from his bloodstream, hoping the shaking in his hands would subside. Everything around him seemed new, sharper, and more alive somehow.

The tree bark was coarse on his fingertips and thighs. The deadened colors in the gloom took on more textures than normal. The sounds seemed more nuanced. He took a deep breath, and it smelled verdant and earthy. Even his battered and bruised body was a delight. It was a gift to be still inhabiting it. He flexed his fingers and moved his shaky free hand, marveling at the wonder of it. He had taken this marvelous vessel for granted, he thought. How amazing it was to be alive.

Even the stench of himself was a wonder. The scent of sweat mixed with earth and the musk and blood of the magnificent creature below. He peered down at it. It was a perfect predator. It had felt so primal in his arms, a true force of nature, wild beyond belief. He'd been so certain it would take him. Through it all, his only thought had been for Alina's safety and regret that he would never know what might have been between them.

In the wake of the creature's death, the entire forest had gone silent, but now he heard scurrying again in the distance. What a marvel life was. It went on, the remaining cast of this vast ensemble picking up the pieces and reshaping itself with the passing of one member.

An odd bird began calling out below him. He leaned forward, looking for it, but could not find it in the ferns. The call was demanding and yet plaintive in a way. Perhaps an impatient nestling awaiting an overdue meal? The call came and went. It seemed near, and yet he could not locate the source.

Without thinking, he slipped from his branch, first hanging from it before dropping the body length below him to the soft earth. Despite the modest distance, his legs folded beneath him, and he landed in a heap with a thump. The awkward landing restored a measure of caution. What was he doing? He'd told Alina that he would wait above. He looked up. Without his lanyards, which were sitting in the branches above him, he had no hope of regaining his perch, even had he been able to use them.

The odd bird call had stopped when he hit the ground, but it began again moments later. He felt strangely drawn to it, a mystery that tugged at him. Alina had mentioned it was unlikely predators would venture near for a time, and the call was so close. Perhaps he could take a peek.

Chapter 32

Dashin moved toward the sound, turning his head one way and then the other to pinpoint it each time it called. It seemed to be coming from the thicket of scraggly brush ahead. He pushed through the ferns, which sighed against his body as he passed, his bare feet soft on the rich, loamy earth.

He stopped at the edge and peered inside, expecting a bird. There, within a small bower of branches, sat a kitten, a krax kitten. It stopped calling and fixed him with curious eyes, sniffing the air as it did.

No doubt this was the offspring of the beast he'd just killed. He looked behind him at the nest of branches from his fall. He'd fallen nearly upon them both, eight body lengths away at most. Her mother had merely been defending her young, instinctively attacking a threat that took her by surprise.

He'd never killed anything before, and doing so had left him changed. He'd had no choice, of course, but finding the kitten, he now saw the events through different eyes. He sensed the tenuous web of life that bound all creatures, and the risks they all faced, predators and prey, every moment of their lives.

What would happen to this tiny creature, defenseless now in the world because of him?

Its mother had been at the very peak of the food chain on this world. Her body honed and sculpted, in the prime of her life, but the kitten was still soft and round, clumsy as it tried to stand, awkward in its body. It bounded forward gracelessly, falling over as it did.

Dashin smiled as it righted itself and looked up at him, cocking its head and sniffing as it did. It occurred to him that he must smell a lot like her mother. He'd been pressed up against her throughout their encounter.

He knelt before it. The kitten took a step closer, looked up at him, and gave the plaintive mewing sound he'd mistaken for a bird. It broke his heart to think of what was likely in store for it. Without thinking, he reached out and stroked the cat, feeling the delicate fur brush his fingers. As he did, the kitten pressed up against his hand. An intense jolt shook them, throwing them both to the ground.

The kitten cried out, its confusion and fear flowing through him. The world was black and far away. He could hear a voice in the distance, but there were no other sensations, only darkness. It felt like the darkness of space. He was floating untethered. He opened his eyes, and the world looked different. His stomach heaved as a wave of vertigo washed over him. He blinked, and the image stabilized. The colors were muted, but his vision was crisp and sharp. The scene swam before him as he took in the forest and then saw an odd body before him. It was an Ancaran, with a misshapen head, who seemed to have crawled out of the earth. It scared him, and he gasped, moving back as the Ancaran did the same, unable to make sense of it until he realized he was seeing himself.

He opened his eyes, his real eyes. The kitten sat there looking at him, and then, as the link between them wavered, it fell over. He rolled over, the urge to retch an imperative. He knelt in the earthy loam, with his eyes closed as his stomach roiled, his breathing shallow, his heart racing yet again.

As the urge abated, he glanced over at the prone kitten, mystified. Somehow, he'd touched the kitten's senses. It was similar to what he'd shared with Alina but different. He could still feel this contact pressing in his mind. It hadn't lapsed as it did when Alina broke physical contact. His head throbbed. Something was wrong with him. He felt as though his mind had become infected.

An echo of his name rang inside his head, as though from far away, and he worried this was some further side effect. It rang out over and over, getting louder, until he realized it was Alina calling his name in the trees above. He forced himself to sit up, and as he did, the vertigo overwhelmed him, and he leaned over and retched. Once he'd emptied his stomach, he coughed and spit, trying to clear the filth from his mouth.

Behind him, he heard a thump followed by the sound of running feet.

"What happened?" Alina shouted, her knees slamming into the dirt beside him, her hands soft on his back.

Dashin rocked back on his heels, closing his eyes, trying to stop the spinning. "I heard a bird," he mumbled.

"A bird? What are you talking about?" He heard her gasp as she looked over at the kitten lying prone a body length away.

"What happened?" she repeated, her voice cautious now, an edge of tension in it.

"I heard a bird, I mean, the kitten crying, and I went to look," he began.

"You were supposed to wait in the tree!" she spat.

"I know," he replied. "I don't know why I felt I had to look."

"What's wrong? Did you hurt yourself falling out of the tree?"

"No, I was fine until I touched it, then something happened."

He felt her go very still. "Tell me."

"I felt a jolt, and then it was like the *touching*, but not. The world looked different, and I saw myself through the kitten's eyes. I don't know. It's still in my mind somehow. It's making me dizzy."

Alina sat back, her hands leaving his body. He turned and saw two of her, his eyes seeing double now. He closed one eye, and one of the images vanished, some of the nausea abating. She had her face in her hands and was quietly sobbing.

"I'm so sorry. I should have waited," he pled, unable to bear seeing her so. "I feel a bit better now. If I close one eye, the dizziness is better," he said, trying to put her mind at ease.

She punched him in the arm.

It hurt a little, but he was happy for it, hoping it would turn the tide.

"I don't know why I did it. I was in a daze and wasn't thinking clearly."

She opened her eyes, shaking her head. "Do you know what you've done?"

He shook his head. "No, I just heard this cry and found the kitten. I felt so bad seeing it, realizing I'd just killed its mother. The krax had only been trying to defend her child."

"I don't mean that," she said, huffing. "You've *melded* with this creature."

"I've what?"

"*Melded.* You've *melded* with a krax," she said, distraught.

"I have no memories of that word," Dashin said, frowning.

She shook her head. "It's rare. No one in our tribe has this gift."

He sat waiting. She dabbed at her eyes and sniffled, trying to compose herself. He squirmed, feeling terrible at having done whatever this was.

She took his hand, took a deep breath, and found an even tone. "On rare occasions, some TreeFolk *meld* with forest animals. It typically occurs after an emotional event when their spirits *touch*. It's similar to my gift of *touch* but different. There are no memories exchanged. Instead, a link is forged between the two."

Dashin swallowed and blinked, switching eyes.

"From what I've heard, the depth of the link varies. Some get only vague sensations or impressions from their *melded* partner. For others, the connection is deeper. In rare cases, it includes being able to access the partner's mind and senses." She paused, unable to continue.

"How long does it last? Is it like *touching*?"

She shook her head. "The link lasts for life."

He looked at her, stunned, the words not making sense. "You mean I'll be linked to this kitten until it dies?"

She nodded her head. "Or until you do."

He sat back, looking at the little unconscious body, its breathing slow and regular. "And if I let the forest take it?" he asked haltingly.

"It's too late for that. From what I've heard, the severing is traumatic. Often the survivor doesn't outlive the severing. And those that do are altered."

"Altered? How?"

"I don't know," she said, shaking her head. "Little is spoken of it."

He leaned forward and picked up the small body, holding it in his arms. Its body was heavy, despite its size, with strong muscles evident beneath the thick fur. He stroked it gently. He tried to find words to explain his actions. He had been in a daze and not thinking straight, but it was more than that. Somehow, the sound had reached for him, drawn him in a way he couldn't explain.

Alina leaned against him, her eyes misty. "Oh, Dashin, the SkyGods have a terrible sense of humor. They gifted you an inconceivable victory with one hand and then doomed you with a disastrous *melding* with the other."

"Is it that bad to be linked to this kitten?" he wondered, looking at the defenseless creature.

"Dashin, this is just not any creature," Alina said. She reached down and took his chin, turning his face so he was looking into her eyes. There was an intensity there she wanted him to see. "This is a krax. This creature will grow to eat TreeFolk like me." She let the words sit for a moment. "It is our greatest fear."

Dashin swallowed, squirming at the thought. "Perhaps this one won't," he said, looking back at it. "Maybe those thoughts aren't there yet. Maybe it can be taught otherwise." He opened the other eye, and his vision swam for a moment before slowly settling. He exhaled. At least he could now use both eyes.

"Dashin, it would be like asking the sun to be the moon," she said with a sigh.

Alina's words sliced into him. He felt terrible at yet again being the source of her anguish. But, try as he might, now that he held that small body in his arms, he could not bring himself to regret the action itself. He cradled it against his muddy tunic, and as it squirmed and cuddled closer to him, he felt warmth bloom within him. There had to be a way through this, he told himself.

"What will we do?" Alina cried out. "How can I explain this? I wish my mother was here." She bit her lip, holding in a flood of emotion. She looked up into the trees in the direction of the village.

"Maybe your mother is home. Only a handful of days remain. Perhaps she arrived while we were away," Dashin said, one hand stroking the kitten in his arms. He yearned to breathe some hope into the situation. It was his fault they were in this predicament. Things had seemed so hopeful when Alina had set off for the ropes.

She turned to him, her eyes desperate. "She might be back," she said, pausing and then turning to look toward the village. "There are only five days left, three if you exclude the trial days."

"Only three days?" Dashin cried. "How can that be?" He wondered what had happened to the other two days.

She gave him an annoyed look. "The trial of the forest requires spending a day and night in the forest. And the trial of the trees occurs after that on the last day, which leaves us only three more days to prepare." She huffed, frowning.

"Oh," Dashin said. He'd somehow assumed the days they were counting were for the start of the last two trials. He swallowed. The shaking in his hands had become a tremor. His body felt like it had been beaten by a tribe of unruly Ancaran baboons armed with spiked clubs. But the vertigo had passed, and he thought he might stand unaided now, which was a huge improvement.

Dashin looked at the furry body nestled against him. "I feel responsible for this life, Alina."

She sighed, her face softening as she met his eyes. "Well, you are tied to it now. It's no use chasing an escaped nuxat."

"What?"

"You are tied to it," she said.

"No, the nuxat thing."

She shrugged. "Oh, occasionally nuxat escape their pens. They do not linger long when they do."

He smiled, relieved that she appeared to be moving beyond the shock of the *melding*.

Alina stood up. "We'd best get climbing. I don't know what you intend to do with the ropes, but night is upon us, and the smell of blood will attract the more desperate scavengers."

They walked over to the kitten's mother, and Dashin was surprised again at just how enormous the beast was. He couldn't imagine how he'd managed to survive the encounter.

He took one rope and lashed an end around the hind legs, and did the same for the front legs with the other rope. Once Alina had climbed up above him, he threw her the free ends of both ropes. She draped them over stout branches and threw down his lanyards. Tightening his belt, he pulled out his tunic to make a pocket of material near his stomach and slid the kitten into it. He had a moment of anxiety as he felt needle-sharp claws on his bare stomach, but the kitten twitched as it stuck him and moved them away from his flesh. It curled against him and began to snore.

He strapped on his lanyards and then managed to swing himself up into the lower branches. Once settled on a limb, he removed them and handed them to Alina. They would be of no use on the long climb up with the krax in tow.

He pulled on the rope with the hind legs, lifting the rear end of the cat until only the front half was still on the ground, and tied off that rope. He did the same with the other rope until the front half was well above the rear half, and then tied that rope off. Then he climbed up a few branches and repeated the process. Had it not been for the lesser gravity on this world and the fact that his body had yet to lose significant muscle mass, he'd never have managed it. But, even with that advantage, it took ages to pull the dead weight up through the trees this way.

As they went, Alina watched the forest for dangers and plotted a diagonal path toward the village. She cajoled, coaxed, and encouraged him, telling him he was almost there even though the village was still a long way off.

It became an interminable ordeal. Dashin collapsed several times along the way, his body shaking so much from the strain that he could no longer hold the rope. He cried out each time that he could go no farther. Alina gave him water and assured him he would not have to go on, that they would find some other way. But, once he'd rested enough, she would ask him if he might just do a tiny bit more.

Sometime in the middle of the night, they reached the back of Rigin's hut, Dashin slid the carcass next to the cistern, and collapsed next to it.

Alina leaned down and cupped his face. She was crying with relief. "You are truly a wonder, Amani. How you managed this is beyond words. Rest now. I'll go and prepare things."

Rigin came out and almost screamed, but Alina waved at her, and she slapped a hand over her open mouth and stifled the outburst.

She knelt close to them. "What happened?" she pled, her eyes wide and her hands on Dashin, until she noticed the enormous beast in the darkness behind him. Alina clamped her own hand over Rigin's mouth before she could loose that scream.

"It's dead," Alina said. "Dashin killed it."

Rigin's eyes went wide, and she looked back and forth between Dashin and Alina until Alina nodded again and removed her hand.

"How is this possible?" Rigin asked, touching her fingertips to her forehead.

"He saved my life," Alina replied. "It attacked me, and he met it with his body and killed it with his hands."

Rigin touched her forehead with her fingertips again and began to cry. She leaned in and touched her forehead to Dashin's. She pulled back when he flinched and leaned in and peered at the enormous lump on his forehead.

"Before he killed the krax with his hands, he struck a branch and was knocked out, and had an uncontrolled fall to the forest floor."

Rigin touched her fingers to her forehead a third time, her eyes on Dashin.

"It's been a busy day," he said, forcing a smile.

Rigin patted his hand, lingering on the contact as though to convince herself he was truly there.

"I'm going to go rouse the village," Alina said. "Can you see to Dashin while I do?"

"I'll help him wash and get some fresh clothes," Rigin said, getting up.

Alina turned from the bridge and came back. "No, wait," she said. "Leave him as he is."

Dashin couldn't imagine why she would suggest such a thing. He'd been dreaming of washing the filth from his body and crawling into bed the entire climb up. He'd even talked of it during the climb, and she'd assured him cool water and a warm bed were waiting for him.

"The story is impossible to believe as it stands. The way he is now will make it a bit more likely that some might consider it," she said to Rigin before turning to him. "Don't worry, Amani, you'll get to rest once we've met with the village."

"Why must you do it tonight?" Rigin asked. "Surely this will keep till the morning?"

"If it was just this, it might, but there is another matter that won't."

Rigin looked from one to the other, trying to guess what that might be.

"I'll let Dashin tell you about it," Alina said. "I find it difficult to believe myself, and I was there." She raced away silently through the night, disappearing around a hut.

He heard her speak with someone, the night sentry perhaps, and then it grew quiet.

"What is this mystery Alina spoke of?" Rigin asked, sitting down next to him.

"I made a friend," Dashin said, reaching into his tunic.

He pulled out the kitten by the scruff of its neck. It stretched and glanced about as he put it in his lap. The kitten had slept the entire climb up from the forest floor, nestled against him, even as it was jostled and bounced around. It had just repositioned itself each time, its little head warm against his stomach.

"Dashin, that's a krax kitten," Rigin said, shifting back and touching her fingertips to her forehead.

"I killed its mother."

"Why did you bring it here?" she said, with a shiver.

"It appears we've *melded*," Dashin said, scratching its chin and eliciting an appreciative purr.

Rigin put a hand over her mouth, her eyes going wide. Then she softened, her face growing sad as she put her hand on his knee. "Oh, Dashin. Oh no."

They sat in silence as the kitten looked around, studying the village, its large eyes fascinated and curious.

"I'm sorry about the belt," Dashin said, running a hand over it. It was caked in mud and blood and had no semblance of its former self. It had been a cherished treasure for her, a last trace of her son, and it hurt him to have ruined it.

"Dashin, do not speak nonsense," she huffed.

He looked up, surprised at the tone. He had never heard her speak this way.

"No object is more important to me than your life," she said, her gaze holding his.

Her words broke him. The tension built up from the day tumbled from him as fresh tears rolled down his cheeks. She ran her fingers through his hair, letting the emotion pour from him. The kitten looked up at him, its eyes going from his face to Rigin's.

When the flood within had slowed, he met the cat's eyes and sniffled. The kitten sniffed in response. "I've been thinking of a name for her," he said, still choked up.

"What have you come up with?" Rigin replied.

"Pritha," he said.

"Joy?" Rigin considered it. "That's a good name. We could all use more joy," she said, though he sensed she didn't feel the krax would bring it.

Rigin ducked into the hut and came back out with a few bowls of food on a tray. It was a beautiful sight, and Dashin's stomach growled in anticipation. He was filthy except for the palms of his hands and the soles of his feet, which had been rubbed clean and then raw from the rope and the branches.

He dug into one of the bowls, stuffing bits of dried fruit and meat into his mouth without bothering with the banda leaves. After a couple of mouthfuls, the kitten caught his hand with a tiny paw, her needle-like claws pinning it midway between the bowl and his mouth. He sensed her hunger and opened his hand so she could eat from it. She ate every last bit and then licked his palm clean.

They finished the bowls together.

Chapter 33

Narat, who was on guard duty, was concerned when he saw Alina covered in mud and blood. She assured him she was fine. That they were both fine.

"We were all so worried," he said. "We were planning on going out to search for you at dawn."

"It's been an eventful evening," she said, biting her lip. "I fear we'll have to get everyone up to discuss it."

"Can it wait till morning? People didn't get to bed till the moon passed its peak."

Alina winced. "Sorry, I don't think this tale can wait."

"There's going to be some griping," he said with a sigh.

"Thanks, Narat," she said. "Give me a few moments before you wake them," she said as she left.

She hurried to her hut, praying her mother was there. How could she explain this day? She'd never been more scared in her life, first for herself and then for Dashin. He'd stepped in front of her without hesitation. Struggling upright after that terrible fall, he'd grabbed a stick, a stick no less, and stepped in the path of that ferocious beast. And then, thinking he was dying, he'd held on, trying to give her time to get away.

After she'd been thrown from the impact, she'd found her feet but had been unable to flee, her eyes locked on the battle as it unfolded. Had he perished, she doubtless would have been next. She shivered at the thought and touched her fingertips to her forehead.

She stepped into the hut, certain she'd find her mother gone. Instead, her heart soared when she saw the figure seated at their table in the dark. But her spirits were quickly dashed when she realized it was her father.

Her father looked up at the sound, his face going from relief to shock in the moment he saw the blood on her clothes in the moonlight. "Lina, where are you hurt?" he asked, racing to her. His bags were piled on the table. He'd likely been sitting there the entire night, waiting for her to come home, expecting the worst.

"I'm fine," she said. "It's not my blood."

"Is it Dashin?" he asked, turning and reaching for his bags.

She put a hand on his arm. "No, Dashin is fine," she said. "Well, mostly fine," she corrected. There were too many factors to weigh in that pronouncement.

She sat down at the table. The kitchen drum sounded outside as Narat woke the village. Her father looked out the door, hearing voices from nearby huts as villagers woke.

"I was hoping Mother was back," she said, more to herself.

"She is still away," he replied, looking from the doorway to her and back.

"There is little time, and there is so much to tell," she said helplessly. "And I don't know how to tell it." She looked out the door. "I was so hoping Mother was home."

Her father sat next to her, taking her hand. "Perhaps I can help?" he asked softly.

Alina shrugged. Her father meant well, but it was her mother's counsel she'd been yearning for.

"Lina," her father said, waiting until she turned to face him. "I know I am not your mother. But do you not believe I would stand for you against the world?"

"Of course," she said dismissively. She loved her father dearly for his curious nature, but he was easily influenced by others. How could she expect him to stand for her in this? Tonight would be a battle he was ill-equipped to wage.

"Will you not trust me to hold your heart?"

The question stunned her. Those were words her mother had spoken to her a precious few times in her life. Times when the challenges in Alina's world had seemed insurmountable, after the loss of her friend Irina, and after her devastating crush on Aras. Each time her mother had come to her and spoken those words, before helping her climb those mountains. She looked at her father, mouth agape.

"Did you think those were your mother's words?"

She had believed precisely that. Her father had always been a source of wonder and warmth in her life. But her mother had been the one she'd always sought counsel from.

"Your mother trusted me with hers. Will you not do the same?"

She sat back, trying to recover from the shock. "I'm sorry, Father, forgive me," she said, feeling guilty at having dismissed him. "I could..." she corrected herself, "Dashin and I could use your help."

The kitchen drum sounded again.

Her father looked out the door. "The drum is for you?"

She nodded. She explained Dashin's fall and the terrible battle with the krax. His eyes grew wide, his fingers tight on her hand. She spoke quickly, giving him the barest outline, explaining that they needed to have it count as Dashin's *trial of the hunt*.

Outside, folks made their way to the platform, anxious voices asking for news.

He looked up. "Don't worry, Lina, we will find a way," he said, brushing tears from her cheek. "Go prepare what you must. I will settle the village to hear your tale."

She stood up and pressed her forehead to his, her heart swelling as she did. She thanked him again and dashed into her room to change her clothes, realizing she'd forgotten to tell him of the *melding*. How would they manage that? She put it from her mind. First, they had to deal with the *trial of the hunt.* She suspected Hedrick would put up a fight. She skirted the central platform, hurrying back to Rigin's hut, the sound of her father's voice calming the panic she heard through the trees.

Dashin was sitting next to the dead krax and playing with the kitten as Solvan and Matse looked on, their eyes as wide as the tokens in her bag. She shivered at the sight of the thing. Why had he left that tree, she asked herself, not for the first time tonight.

"Do it again," Solvan urged.

Dashin took another piece of dried meat from the few remaining in a bowl and showed it to the kitten. He put both hands behind his back and then brought out his closed fists, placing them in front of the kitten. She looked from one to the other, sniffed briskly, and then patted one of Dashin's hands with her tiny paw. He opened it to reveal the piece of meat, which she promptly ate. The children bubbled over at the feat, but the kitten seemed unimpressed at the game, though perfectly content to continue playing it.

The children giggled, entranced by the creature, Matse hiding her giggle behind a tiny hand. The sight of the Matse stopped Alina as she realized the girl seemed at ease with the kitten, even drawn to it, and oblivious of the dead beast at Dashin's side. She couldn't understand how this could be since the child had watched her parents being taken by a krax. Alina looked over at Rigin, who was watching too. Rigin met her eyes and shrugged.

Alina stepped up and crouched next to Dashin. "How are you feeling?"

He turned and looked at her. "Tired, but better," he said, rolling a shoulder. "I'll feel better after I wash and get some sleep."

"Soon," she said. "I will address the village and give a brief accounting of events, but I'll leave out some of the details." She was still piecing together the plan in her head. "When we're ready for you, I'll send Solvan to fetch you." Solvan was overjoyed at this news and bounced in place so much that the kitten turned to follow him, peering at the boy.

"Do you think you can carry the creature the rest of the way to the platform? You can drag it if you have to."

Dashin nodded. "Yes, I think I can drag it. It's a short distance."

"Let's go join the others," she said to Rigin and the children.

She turned back to Dashin. "Oh, do not speak unless you're asked. My father and I will try to manage things."

"Of course," he said. "Thanks, Amani. I'm sorry for all the trouble."

"That gust has already passed us by, Dashin. A new breeze is upon us now."

Dashin nodded. "I'll wait for Solvan," he said.

She smiled at him and left with the others.

The village was seated on the platform, oil lamps lighting the space, when Alina and the others joined them. They sat in the places they used for meals, though tables had not been laid out. Most of the children were absent. They'd likely been sent back to sleep, perhaps her father's doing. She hadn't thought of the effect the tale might have on them. The villagers muttered among themselves, trying to make sense of the odd summons. They looked from Fodrick and Hedrick, who were seated, as usual, at the head of the platform, and to her father, who was standing off to one side.

Hedrick spoke up. "We're waiting," he grumbled. "How long do we have to wait for this tale?"

Her father opened his mouth to answer as she stepped onto the platform. Hedrick turned to her. "What is this tale that could not wait till morning?"

Alina burned, angry words coming to mind. But her father spoke before she could form them, his voice thundering over the platform. "I have been dragged from my bed more nights than not to see to one or another of you over the many sun cycles I've been your healer. In all that time, I have never failed to come, nor have I grumbled and begrudged the call, even when such a call was not warranted."

He stood there seething, his face dark with rage. Alina and the entire village sat stunned at the outburst. The face he wore now was not one she'd seen before. The amiable spirit she had always known was gone.

He took a breath, gathering himself. "Tonight, I'm asking you all to listen to my daughter, who is *of the tribe*," he emphasized the last words. "She has something she feels warrants this meeting, and I, for one, will hear her." He looked out over the crowd, daring anyone to object. No one did.

"Thank you," Fodrick said, his tone appeasing. "Of course, we will hear Alina. As you say, she is *of the tribe*."

It seemed to take a moment for her father to hear the words, his body still rigid, ready for battle. Alina swallowed, touched by his effort on her behalf, despite having only heard glimpses of the tale. Once he realized that the tribe would hear his daughter, his shoulders relaxed, and he turned to her, a tiny twinkle flashing in his eyes. She felt tears well up, but took a breath and stepped forward into the lamplight.

She looked out over the village and began. "Earlier today, while I was working with Dashin in the forest, he struck a branch with his head." She felt the eyes upon her glance away, searching for Dashin. There was muttering as folks realized Dashin wasn't on the platform. Alina forged on. "The blow knocked him out, and he had an uncontrolled fall to the forest floor."

This elicited a collective gasp from the village. Such a fall was tantamount to a death sentence. She'd heard of only a few that had ever survived such a fall.

"I raced down to him as he fell, fearing the worst, but somehow he survived it."

"Are we here to listen to some tale of Dashin's incompetence?" Hedrick mumbled, almost loud enough for his father to take exception, but as her father turned to him, Hedrick looked off into the trees.

"I was so worried at what I might find that in my haste to reach him, I neglected to check the forest floor."

Those words glued all eyes to her. "Once I'd freed him from the branches he was tangled in, I turned to find the largest krax I've ever seen, not ten paces from me. It was crouched to spring, and I froze in place."

The entire village held its breath. "As it sprang, Dashin pushed ahead of me and took the impact." There was a loud collective gasp. "I was thrown clear, and when I stood, he and the krax were locked together."

Alina continued, and even though she spoke softly, no one missed a word. "He and the krax grappled for ages. It was a blur of teeth and claws as they struggled, and I feared many times that he was dead. Blood was pouring from them, and it went on and on until they both lay still."

"Dashin is dead?" someone from the crowd gasped.

"No, he survived. He slew the creature."

"With his hands? I knew this was going to be another crazy tale," Hedrick shouted, getting up. He looked over at her father. "And you got us all out of bed to hear this?"

Her father had remained standing to one side throughout. He stared Hedrick down now. "If you ever expect me to get out of bed for you ever again, you will listen to the tale in its entirety," her father said, his eyes making it clear he meant every word. Hedrick stared back, seemingly weighing the seriousness of the threat. Finally, he sat down in a huff. Her father turned to her and nodded, though she could see the concern in his eyes.

She nodded to Solvan, who leapt up and bounded across the platform with his awkward gait and disappeared into the trees. "I admit the tale sounds impossible, and had I not been there, I would be struggling to believe it as well. But perhaps this will give the tale more weight." She turned to look at the bridge where Solvan had disappeared, awaiting Dashin's arrival. She glanced back at the crowd. All eyes were fixed on the bridge except for those of Kani and Hurza, which went back and forth from the bridge to her. They gave her supportive smiles, though she could see the tension in their faces.

Dashin appeared out of the darkness a few moments later with the bulk of the enormous beast on his back. The front legs were on one shoulder, the huge head on the other, with the rest of its body trailing behind. He was a horrific apparition, a thing of nightmares. She heard villagers cry out as fingertips found foreheads, TreeFolk warding themselves.

Hedrick's face drained of color, and he shuddered. The reaction from the village was so extreme, she feared she had miscalculated the impact. Dashin seemed more a figure to be feared than one to be celebrated or pitied. He pulled the cat's body into the lamplight and let it fall onto the platform. The force of its body landing upon it shook them all. He knelt next to it, his body and clothes caked in mud and blood.

There was complete silence. Alina took a breath, trying to find words to recover the earlier mood. "The bump you see on his forehead was from the branch that sent him to the forest floor. Some of the scrapes on his body, which you can't see now, are from the fall. The rest," she motioned to him, "is from his fight with the krax."

The villagers leaned in as the initial shock passed, which Alina took as a good sign. She noted the bulge at the front of Dashin's tunic and swallowed. They would have to deal with that too, but first, they would have to deal with the *trial of the hunt*.

"This is an amazing tale, Alina," Fodrick began. "And one that even though my eyes see the proof of it, I find my mind has yet to drink in. But could this tale not have waited? Daylight might have made it less jarring to witness."

"Of course, Fodrick, what you say makes sense, though the tale is not yet finished."

He chuckled. "You're telling us there is more to this tale that is already fit to be a thing of songs?"

"I'm afraid so," she said.

He sat back, nodding at her to continue.

"Dashin would submit this as his *trial of the hunt*." She waited as muttered comments ran through the assembled.

"This was not a hunt," Hedrick spat, defiant. "And even if it were, the candidate is meant to carry his quarry from the forest floor alone. He cannot even lift it here on the platform."

"Granted, this was not a regular hunt," Alina replied. "Though I don't recall the rules specifying that the hunt be regular. I believe they only require that the animal be at least the weight of the candidate and that the candidate carry it to the village." She looked at Fodrick. "Is that not the case?"

Fodrick squirmed for a moment before leaning over to speak with his wife, Milena, who was the authority on details of their songs. They discussed things in hushed tones before he turned back to Alina. "I believe you have the sense of it, but it still requires the candidate to carry the animal to the village even if it takes several trips."

"Since we were alone and Dashin did not know the way to the village, he did not want to risk leaving any of it behind to be set upon by predators. So, he chose to carry it intact."

"You would have us believe Dashin carried this beast by himself from the forest floor?"

She nodded.

Fodrick opened his mouth to question her statement but closed it. He paused for a moment and then turned to Dashin.

"Young man, did you intend to hunt this creature?" he asked.

Alina's heart sank.

"No," Dashin answered, "I did not. I saw the creature about to spring at Alina, and I stood in front of her. I didn't think beyond that. As I grappled with the creature, I was only trying to stay alive long enough for her to get to safety."

His words, delivered honestly and without pause, had spoken volumes.

"So you didn't consider this a hunt?"

"No, not at the time, but once it was over and I found myself still alive, I couldn't imagine any real hunt demanding more."

A collective chuckle arose from the village. Alina beamed at him. She loved this man. The thought took her by surprise, not because she wasn't aware of the feeling but because she hadn't said it before, even to herself.

"And you carried that krax from the forest floor all by yourself?"

"Well, I didn't carry it," he admitted.

Alina's focus had drifted. It snapped back with this admission.

"I used ropes to lift one end and then the other and made it up that way."

"You did this alone, all the way from the forest floor, with ropes?" Fodrick asked, scratching his head.

Dashin looked around, confused at the question, then shrugged. "Yes, it was a long way."

Fodrick laughed, shaking his head. Others joined in.

Even now, Dashin didn't understand what an impossible achievement the past hours had been. That he could sit there so innocently and speak this way softened the hard lines she'd seen on some faces.

"It seems our rules do not prohibit this from qualifying as a *trial of the hunt*, given that the creature is certainly heavier than you are and that you did get it to the village on your own. However, it is different enough from what is traditional that I find myself wanting to know what others think we should do. I'd like a show of hands."

Hedrick leapt up at these words. It was clear he'd been planning for a moment like this. "This was not a hunt. It was pure luck. No skill at all was involved. The *trial of the hunt* is meant to select hunters who will provide food for the village. This *encounter* did no such thing." He thrust his open hand in the air, and a smattering of villagers looking at him did the same. Other open hands went up, but then some fists began appearing. Alina raised her fist in support of Dashin. She saw Hurza and Kani do the same, along with Rigin and the twins, Aras and Narat, and their wives.

She did a quick scan, and the glimmer of hope that had been building within her faltered. There were twice as many open hands as there were fists. Hedrick was grinning as he looked out over the village. It was apparent now he'd been preparing for a vote like this. The open hands had gone up as a group, as though on cue. She felt fury burning within her at his smug grin.

Fodrick began counting hands and then stopped. "Enor, do you want to vote?" he said, noting that her father's hands were still by his side.

"Thank you. I would like to, but I find myself confused," he said.

"What is it that perplexes you?" Fodrick asked, frowning.

"It seems to me the trials that are part of the *becoming* seek to select the best candidates for our village."

"Yes, that is my understanding as well," Fodrick said, though Alina noted a keenness in the chief's gaze.

"I wonder," her father mused, "if Aor or Drur had stood before such a beast to save the life of Hurza or Kani, would we be having this vote?" He looked around at the villagers and then selected one with an open hand. "For example, Norka, if it was your daughter Dashin had saved instead of mine, would you still have an open hand?"

There was a pause, and the villager faltered for a moment as her father kept looking at him, until his hand became a fist.

"He has already voted," Hedrick objected, standing up, his open hand in the air.

"Everyone has the right to change their vote until all votes are cast," Milena announced. "Such has always been the custom."

Her father made the rounds of the open hands, posing questions and framing hypothetical scenarios. Open hands slowly became fists. The stone that had formed in Alina's heart grew smaller. Hedrick's face grew dark. He glared at those on the platform, his hand still defiantly open. He was poised to step in once her father had finished speaking. Alina feared he would force many of those whom her father had convinced to reverse themselves. This would all be for naught.

Her father had covered the entire platform and returned to the place he'd begun. He scanned the platform as though accepting his fate, nodding to Fodrick that he was done. As he did, he raised his fist. Hedrick stormed onto the platform, heading for a knot of fists.

"Wait a moment, Hedrick," Milena called after him, smiling.

Her words angered him further, his face bunching up as he spun around.

"The vote has been cast," she said, indicating that all hands were now raised.

He spun about, realizing too late he'd been outmaneuvered. He turned to her father and glared, his jaw muscles flexing. Her father shrugged helplessly, as though he was as surprised as Hedrick at the development.

Hedrick protested, demanding his turn to speak, but Milena explained that, unfortunately, the time for speaking had passed since the vote was complete. Hedrick was furious, his eyes fixed on Dashin with an anger she had not seen before. Alina shivered at the sight, but her heart soared.

She felt embarrassed for having doubted her father. She beamed at him, wanting to convey just how much she loved him. He looked at her and crinkled his eyes.

"It seems the village feels that your encounter with the krax qualifies as your *trial of the hunt*, Dashin," Fodrick said. Alina detected the faintest trace of a smile.

"As is our custom," Fodrick continued, "the quarry is yours to do with as you choose. You may not be aware of it, but the animal next to you is worth a fortune in trade. I have never seen such as that, and its hide, teeth, and claws will fetch much."

"I'd like to give it to the village," Dashin replied, without hesitation.

The village gasped, Alina included. At Fodrick's words, she'd grown excited, imagining all the things they might trade for.

"Perhaps you want to think about this some," Fodrick suggested. "You have little, and you might want things this bounty could bring."

"This village saved my life, and since then it has done nothing but give to me." He looked around at all the faces before him. "This is certainly the least I can do. There is only one treasure from this encounter that I wish to keep."

The words confused Fodrick, and as Alina looked on, she saw the same confusion on all the faces before her. She swallowed. *Here we go,* she thought.

Chapter 34

Once Alina left for the platform with the others, Dashin sat petting the kitten and waiting for Alina's summons. Pritha had eaten a surprising amount of food for such a little thing. She was now curled up, asleep in his lap. Oddly, he could feel her contentment, her senses tucked away in a new part of his mind he could access when he focused on her. He envied her composure. She had taken the monumental changes in her life in stride. Her ability to accept this new reality epitomized Gralan's motto.

Discussion on the platform had begun with a heated exchange between Enor and Hedrick. Dashin hadn't been able to make out most of the words, but the tone had been clear enough. Thankfully, it had settled quickly, and Alina's sing-song voice had begun speaking. It floated to him through the trees, punctuated by gasps and muttering. Dashin assumed these coincided with his fall and subsequent battle with Pritha's mother.

He was starting to drift off when he heard Solvan's odd gate on the bridge. He stuffed Pritha into his tunic, nodding to the boy as he reached for the krax. He squatted next to it, grabbed the front legs, and slid under them, so its legs were on one shoulder and its head fell on the other. It was an awkward maneuver, and Pritha protested as she was squeezed between his stomach and knees. But he levered himself to his feet, staggering a few steps as the weight settled on his back.

He took a tentative step forward, and then another, the beast's rear claws dragging across the platform. He made his way across the bridges, dragging the oppressive load and grunting like a stoda. Muttering on the platform stopped he reached the bridge leading to it.

The fear he saw on the faces as he stepped into the lamplight with the beast on his back made him wonder if they'd made a mistake. Fingertips flew to foreheads, amid gasps and abject terror. They even seemed frightened of him. Though he imagined he must resemble something which had crawled from a fresh grave.

But as Alina began speaking again, the fear receded. As she'd predicted, Hedrick objected to this being considered his *trial of the hunt*. It seemed he might prevail until Enor swayed the vote in their favor. He missed most of the exchange, certain they'd lost when he saw all the open hands. He'd drifted off, feeling dejected at having carried the beast all this way for nothing. With only three days left, his prospects for a successful solo stoda hunt seemed remote.

So, he was startled when Hedrick began shouting, and he looked up to find that many of the previously open hands were now fists. Still, it wasn't until he met Alina's eyes that he realized they'd won.

Keeping the quarry for himself wasn't even a consideration. He'd been happy to finally be able to repay the village in a small way for what they'd done for him. He was delighted to see how elated the villagers were at the news. Discussions broke out in the wake of the announcement until Alina said something to Fodrick, and he put his hand up for quiet.

"There is something you wish to add?" Fodrick prompted.

Alina nodded. "There is another matter. The one I felt needed to be discussed tonight."

All eyes turned to her.

Fodrick looked from Alina to Dashin and back. "You mean to say the krax here on the platform was a prelude?"

"I'm afraid so," she said, swallowing.

"You're going to tell us that on his climb from the forest floor, Dashin reached up into the sky and captured the moon?" Fodrick said, scratching his chin.

There was reserved laughter from the village, though it was half-hearted, everyone already intent on her words.

Alina gave a small smile and exhaled. "After his encounter with the krax, Dashin *melded* with her offspring," she said, matter-of-fact.

There was a long pause, too long. There were no gasps or muttering. Dashin thought perhaps they hadn't heard her. But as the silence stretched on, he imagined they were too stunned to speak.

Dashin reached into his tunic and grabbed Pritha by the scruff and drew her out. As he did, she cried out, mewling loudly. All eyes turned to him as Dashin cradled her in his lap. She blinked open her eyes and rubbed her face with a paw, gave a wide yawn, and looked out over the village. She took in the sea of gaping faces staring at her. She sat back regarding them impassively, as if this were an everyday occurrence.

"Dashin, you have *melded* with this creature?" Fodrick asked, incredulous.

"I do not understand the details of it," Dashin replied. "But, yes, we share some kind of connection now that was not there before."

Muttering enveloped the platform, growing in intensity as villagers discussed and argued among themselves. Dashin looked on, noting Hedrick's silence. He'd grown pale, his eyes wide with fear.

Fodrick put up a hand and had to hold it there for some time before the platform stilled again. "You do realize the creature you hold is a predator that feeds on TreeFolk such as those before you?"

Dashin exhaled. He stilled his thoughts, searching for words to convey what he felt in his heart. "I was vaguely aware, but Alina explained it." He looked down at the kitten. "But I believe this will not be the case for Pritha."

"Pritha?" Fodrick furrowed his brow.

"Yes, I've named her," Dashin continued. "I feel like the *melding* altered us both. I don't think she'll be a threat."

Fodrick frowned, narrowing his eyes. "It does not matter whether you consider her to be a threat. It only matters if I believe she's a threat. And she is a krax, which by birth makes her one."

Dashin swallowed. "Are there not tales in your songs of *melded* creatures living among TreeFolk?"

Fodrick paused, his eyes intent on Dashin now. The rest of the village sat hushed, hanging on the exchange. "There are such songs, but none of these involve a krax."

But if animals lived with TreeFolk... He was grasping at the corner of an idea, trying to follow its thread as it bloomed in his mind. "Do animals that *meld* change at all?"

"I do not understand your question," Fodrick replied, narrowing his eyes, wondering where this might be going.

Dashin saw the shape of it now. "Has a TreePerson ever *melded* with, let's say, a corsol?"

"Yes," Fodrick replied tentatively. "There are such tales."

"In those tales, did the corsol live in the village and behave not as corsol but as something different, something other than its nature?"

Fodrick pursed his lips, his eyes relaxing as he glimpsed the shape of the argument.

Dashin's heart pounded, but he worked to keep his face calm.

"A corsol is not a krax," Fodrick answered evenly.

"But is a *melded* corsol, a corsol?" Dashin asked, pressing gently.

The trace of a smile appeared at the corners of Fodrick's mouth. "Perhaps, but perhaps not," he allowed with a short nod.

Dashin exhaled. "Would it be possible to give this matter a little time to see if a *melded* krax is still a krax?" Dashin pled, petting the kitten as he did. Pritha sat in his lap, doing her part to look as innocent as possible. He did not know whether she sensed this from him or if luck had chosen to make one final appearance tonight. He'd never believed *makers* would concern themselves with the cares of individuals, but in case he was wrong, he offered a prayer to them to spare the kitten.

"Very well, we will give this some time. So we can see if a *melded* krax is still a krax."

Hedrick shot to his feet. "You cannot be considering letting this creature remain here in the village!" he shouted at his son. "Let the village vote on this," he demanded.

Dashin froze. Somehow, through Enor's efforts, they had narrowly survived a vote on his *trial of the hunt*. From the conflicted faces he saw before him now, it was clear they would not be so lucky again. He was certain Hedrick would not allow himself to be outmaneuvered a second time. He looked over at Alina, who was staring at him, her face taut, her lips a thin line.

"I find that in this matter, I do not need the council of the village," Fodrick said to everyone's amazement. There were immediate objections from the villagers, protesting their lack of choice on the matter. Hedrick led the unrest, his voice strident above the others. Fodrick raised his hand, and it took some time for calm to return.

He continued, his voice firm. "The kitten is of no danger to anyone at the moment. The trials will be completed in a handful of days. At the end of those trials, if Dashin does not prevail, they'll both be sent away, which will settle the matter. If somehow the will of the SkyGods sees him succeed, then we can revisit the matter of the *melded* krax then."

Fodrick stood up. Hedrick rushed toward him, still fuming, but Milena stood and put a hand on Hedrick's chest, preventing him from accosting her husband. Hedrick stood shocked, not understanding what was preventing him from moving forward until he looked down and saw the hand. He sputtered and seemed about to push her aside when she glared at him. They stood nose to nose for a charged moment as the village looked on. Finally, seeing something in her eyes that he chose not to test, Hedrick turned and stalked off into the trees.

Fodrick ignored the sound of his father's muttering as he stormed off. He kept his eyes on the villagers before him. "It seems morning is upon us," he said, looking up into the canopy. "Dashin, the village thanks you for your gift. We will see to its processing." He turned to Milena, who nodded.

The water coursing over his body felt glorious. Dashin had rinsed off the outer layers of mud and blood before changing into a pair of short pants and repeating the process, scrubbing to remove the remaining grime. Pritha sat close by, grooming herself, the water from Dashin splashing onto her as she did. Each time it happened, the kitten shook herself, shedding the water, and resumed licking herself clean without seeking to move out of range of the gouts of water. Matse sat close to Pritha, watching her.

Solvan helped scrub Dashin's back, his little hands rough on Dashin's skin as he scrubbed diligently. Dashin bit his lip, not wanting to curb the lad's enthusiasm but feeling every bump and bruise on his body.

As morning dawned, Solvan began to count the bruises on his body. Alina and Rigin stood off to one side, watching them.

"Solvan, perhaps you should stop counting," Alina suggested. The lad looked up, not understanding. "I think Dashin already has a sense of how many he has." She reached down and brushed the lad's cheek.

Dashin caught Alina's eyes and held them. He tried to convey the mountain of emotion within him. She bit her lip, overwhelmed as well. There was so much he yearned to say.

Pritha finished her grooming and gave a loud yawn. All eyes turned to her as she rubbed her head with a paw. Matse was fixated on the kitten, and Dashin worried she might be reliving her trauma in some way. Though her face seemed to hold no trace of it, perhaps it was coming.

Pritha stopped rubbing her head. She looked from Dashin to Matse, cocking her head as she regarded the girl. Matse's eyes opened wide at the stare. Dashin tensed, preparing to intercede. He felt Alina next to him do the same.

The kitten and Matse studied each other. Dashin held his breath, the tension mounting. Then in an instant, Pritha leapt into Matse's lap. Dashin went to reach for her, but Rigin put a hand on his shoulder. He looked up, and she had her other hand on Alina's arm, her eyes still glued to the girl and the kitten.

The kitten stared up into Matse's eyes, her nose a hand's span from Matse's. And then Pritha curled up in her lap and lay down, her chin on the girl's knee. Matse let out a delighted giggle and reached down delicately to touch the small furry head. Pritha rubbed her ear against the little fingers. Matse's beamed, petting Pritha, her hand just skimming the fur. Solvan announced how *round* it all was.

Rigin let go of their arms, her lips tight, her eyes misty. They all watched as Matse stroked the kitten, her entire focus on the small treasure in her lap. Pritha lapped up the love and affection. Dashin wondered if the kitten had become sensitive to his emotions, and perhaps those of others, since the *melding*. Had she reacted to his concern for the girl?

Enor arrived in a huff, carrying bags in both arms. He stopped short as he spotted Pritha in Matse's lap. He dropped his bags on the platform and touched his fingertips to his forehead.

"This day keeps yielding surprises," he said, looking at Matse and the kitten. He glanced over at Dashin and gaped at the bruises covering his body.

"I think I may need more of your magic balm," Dashin said with a smile.

"There may not be enough balm in Ndesa for such as you, Dashin," he said with a chuckle.

"I'm sorry," Dashin replied, embarrassed at how much work he was for Enor.

Enor waved it away as he fished through a bag. He brought out an enormous gourd that Dashin had not seen before. Enor caught his gaze. "I've had to move my balm to a larger gourd of late," he said, crinkling his eyes.

Dashin blushed and gave an awkward chuckle. The others laughed, except for Matse, who was entirely focused on Pritha.

"Sorry, I was delayed," Enor said. "Hedrick wanted words with me after the meeting."

The adults looked at him with concern.

Enor noted the worry and waved it away as he took a leafful of balm from the gourd and slathered it on Dashin's chest. "We had a minor disagreement. It resolved itself."

"You resolved it," Alina said, shocked.

Enor looked up with a mischievous glint. "He disagreed. And I resolved not to care," he said, laughing at his joke.

The adults chuckled, but Solvan roared, as though this was the funniest thing ever spoken. He repeated it to himself several times, apparently committing it to memory for later use.

"There is much talk of you in the village, Dashin," Enor said as he applied the balm.

The feel of it on his skin was amazing. Relief seeped into his body, replacing the aches and pains with a delicious tingling.

"It took four men to carry the krax from where it lay to the kitchen. Though it looked frightening on the platform next to you, it wasn't until folks came close to it that they saw the true size of the beast. What you did seems more impossible now than when I first heard it."

"You were amazing, Father. I'm so sorry I doubted you."

He waved it away. "There is nothing to apologize for, Lina. I will always stand for you."

Alina's lips went taut. She leaned in and touched her forehead to her father's. He put a hand on her shoulder, slathering balm on it as he did. He pulled his hand away at once and used a leaf to dab at it, smearing it about as he did. They both laughed.

It was heartwarming to see them together. It was a relationship he greatly envied, never having experienced such closeness with a parent before. Gralan had been the closest thing to a father he'd ever had, and he'd had only the barest taste of it before it was torn from him.

Enor turned back to him, applying more balm and covering it with large banda leaves as he went. When Enor finished, Dashin was clad in the thick leaves. His short pants had been rolled up to accommodate them, and some were tucked into his waistband. Even his head sported them so that only his hands, feet, eyes, and mouth were leafless.

"How am I going to train like this?" Dashin asked, his body going numb.

"You are going to get some sleep and let the balm work," Enor announced.

"I can't afford to," Dashin said, trying to get up but not managing it. He was too exhausted to move now, and the balm had made his body numb and unresponsive. But there were only three days left. The thought of sleeping one of them away was frightening.

"I am the healer in this tribe, and so long as you are one of us, your health is my concern," he said sternly. "I won't have you stumbling out there half-asleep, numb and injured, so you fall to the forest floor again."

He opened his mouth to argue, but Enor glared at him, and he closed it.

"At least a half-day's rest for both of you," he declared, fixing Alina with a similar glare, which she did not dispute. "Then only light duty after that, no lanyards for the rest of the day, and another course of balm this evening."

The tantalizing prospect of sleep swam into his mind. Enor was right. He was in no shape to train today. He could barely keep his eyes open.

Enor helped him to bed. As he lay down, Dashin let out a moan of pleasure, so great was the sensation. Pritha leapt up onto the bed next to him and nestled up against his body, burrowing in against the leaves, her little nose twitching at the odd smell.

"Dashin, thank you for saving Alina," Enor said, choking back emotion.

Dashin nodded. "Thank you for everything, too," he replied, waving his leaf-clad arms.

Enor opened his mouth to say more, but then squeezed his arm instead.

Dashin closed his eyes, reveling in the sensation of the balm on his skin and the feel of the bed beneath him. He meant to open them again, but didn't manage it. Sleep took him, a deep, dreamless sleep.

Dashin awoke, coming out from a thick fog. It was hot, and daylight filled the room. Outside, he heard voices and activity on the platform. Last night's events swam up in his mind, and he reached for the kitten at his side. He was shocked to find her gone. He sat up with a groan, looking around the room.

There was no sign of her. Fear gripped him. Could someone have taken her as he slept? Visions of Hedrick or someone stealing in and taking the kitten overwhelmed him. Or maybe the kitten had wandered off into the forest?

Growing increasingly frantic, he reached for her through the connection they shared. There was an immediate clatter from the outer room, and Pritha tore through the curtain and leapt onto the bed with him, pressing her back against him, her hair on end. She was shaking and terrified, filled with a dread she felt but could not see or name. His fear had passed through their link and drawn her to him.

He took a breath, forcing his heart to slow. A moment later, so did hers. Rigin came in with Matse close behind her, looking guilty. Rigin explained Pritha had woken up and wandered about the hut, investigating, and Matse had been feeding her and keeping her company.

Dashin could see Matse was upset. She was hiding behind Rigin, clinging to her pant leg and looking down, like she'd done something wrong. Dashin softened. "Matse, it's fine. You did nothing wrong. I was only worried when I woke up and didn't see Pritha. I thought perhaps she'd gotten lost in the forest."

The little girl looked up, still holding onto Rigin's pant leg.

"I think Pritha may still be hungry," Dashin said. "I wonder if you wouldn't mind feeding her for me?" he asked, fixing the girl with a smile.

Her face broke out into a tentative grin, her eyes sparkling with delight. She nodded meekly and then ran back into the common room.

He looked up at Rigin, his eyes questioning the decision, and she gave him a short nod, assuring him with the motion that she would be nearby. He looked at Pritha, holding the image of Matse and dried meat in his mind. Pritha spun and raced from the room in pursuit.

Chapter 35

Alina raced through the trees, scrambling to stay ahead of the creature. Her lanyards lashed out as she strove to escape. But try as she might, she could feel its hot breath on her back. It crashed in the forest behind her. Her heart pounded in her chest, the forest dark and unfamiliar. The beast lunged and grabbed her leg. She screamed.

She sat up, her eyes wide, panting wildly, soaked in sweat. Hurza and Kani were in her room, Hurza's hand on her leg. "It was just a dream," Hurza said, leaning over her.

Alina's heart pounded as she took in her friends and surroundings. A dream. It was a dream. She let the words seep into her. She looked up at her friends, seeing their concern. "Thanks," she said, scooting to sit with her back against the wall.

Kani stepped into the common room and returned a moment later. "Drink this," she said, handing her a cup of water.

Alina swallowed it, the warm water soothing her. Judging from the light and the heat, it was near midday. She'd slept away the morning and yet still felt exhausted. Her sleep had been restless, filled with anxiety and the feeling of being chased by a terrible beast cloaked in shadow.

She exhaled, her pulse slowing, and took a deep breath.

"You look a mess," Hurza said.

Alina blinked up at Hurza, surprised at the statement. She was on the verge of explaining pointedly how she'd had other things on her mind when she saw the smile on her friend's lips and the glint in her eye. A laugh bubbled up in her chest, pent-up tension ebbing as her friends joined in.

"You looked ready to bite off my nose," Hurza said, laughing.

"I nearly did," Alina agreed.

"You should comb your hair. There are twigs in it," Kani offered, trying to be helpful and not having followed Hurza's sarcasm.

Alina looked at Hurza, and they both burst out laughing.

"What?" Kani asked. "What's so funny?" she pressed, which only made Hurza and Alina laugh all the harder. "Fine," she huffed, crossing her arms.

"Sorry, Kani," Alina said. "It's just that twigs in my hair are the least of my problems at the moment."

"Oh," she said, smiling now that she understood.

Having her friends here in her room chased away the remaining tendrils of the nightmare. She was lucky to have them in her life. It would have been hard to grow up without them.

"You were amazing last night," Kani said, gushing.

"You had the heart of a raging stoda out there," Hurza agreed

"I thought my arm would fall off," Kani began. "It was the longest vote we've ever had. I didn't understand what your father was doing until it was over and everyone was saying you'd won. I was so worried, and then I was so happy. And then Dashin pulled out the krax kitten, and I thought I would die," she finished, breathless.

"Did Dashin really fight the krax with his hands?" Hurza asked, leaning in.

"It was the most terrifying thing I've ever seen." Alina shivered, images of the horrifying episode flashing into her mind.

"And, he did it to protect you," Kani added, her eyes sparkling with the notion.

"Yes," Alina replied, looking up at her friends. "He'd just fallen from the canopy. He was battered and could barely stand, and yet he pushed ahead of me to meet the beast."

"He said he thought he was going to die and was just holding on so you could get to safety," Kani added, always the romantic. Alina could see how this story captured her imagination. And seeing the tale through her friend's eyes made it all the more magical for her, too.

"Yes, he was surprised to have survived. His only wish had been to delay the beast to save me."

Kani sighed. "With a heart like that, I suppose it doesn't matter if he looks odd," she mused.

Alina laughed, and Hurza slapped Kani on the shoulder.

"What?" she said, annoyed. Seeing Alina's face, she flushed. "Oh, I'm sorry."

Alina laughed and crinkled her eyes. "He did look odd to me at first, too. But that seems ages ago. I no longer see the oddness in him."

"Really?" Kani said, her eyes wide.

Alina laughed. "Really."

They sat in silence for a moment.

"I've never seen Hedrick so mad," Hurza said.

Alina exhaled. She'd seen the parade of emotions on Hedrick's face during the evening. Annoyance, irritation, anger, fear, fury, and then a fierce determination, which scared her most of all. "He's just one of my problems," Alina said.

"One of *our* problems," Hurza corrected her.

Alina smiled at her friends. "Thank you, yes, one of our problems."

"Any ideas for the *trial of the forest*?" Hurza asked.

Alina explained how Dashin had moved the egg to the forest floor and how he was planning to use it as shelter. She was surprised that in all the training and excitement, she had forgotten to mention this to her friends. They were excited to hear that another trial seemed achievable.

"That only leaves the trial of the trees," Kani said.

Alina looked at Hurza. "Any luck getting Aor to chase?"

"Not yet," she said, "but I'm still working on it."

"How are you doing it?" Kani asked, leaning forward.

"He's been strange of late, asking my advice on things he never has before." She narrowed her eyes and looked at Alina, who tried to put on an innocent face.

"I thought so," Hurza spat. "What did you tell him?"

"Nothing," Alina said, putting up her hands. "I only mentioned when we were speaking that perhaps he should consult you. That if he did, he might be surprised."

"Really?" Hurza said, blushing.

Alina nodded. "Honest."

Hurza bit her lip, emotion welling within her, something Alina had rarely witnessed in her friend. "Thanks," she said. It was as earnest and naked a statement as she'd ever heard from her.

"Of course," Alina said. She realized in that moment she'd let go of the idea of Aor. It was an idea formed by others, one that had never truly fit. With the development of genuine feelings for Dashin, she now saw that a life with Aor would not have suited either of them. She was happy for her friend. Aor had been Hurza's dream since childhood, one she'd been careful of late not to speak of for fear of hurting Alina's feelings, but one she knew still burned bright. That they would be good for each other, she had no doubt.

"You are seeing Aor?" Kani asked, wide-eyed.

"We are not yet officially *walking,* but we have been talking," she said, crinkling her eyes.

"No luck with the chase?" Alina asked again to confirm.

"Not yet, but since a direct appeal did not work, I've changed approaches," she smiled.

"What are you doing?" Kani asked, unable to imagine any other approaches.

"Oh, isn't it amazing how Drur is in the trees?" she said, mooning. "He moves so elegantly," she sighed. "It's obvious why he's the ideal chaser," she gave another sigh, putting a hand on her chest as she did, and looking off into the trees.

Alina burst out laughing.

Kani was aghast. "You like Drur?" she said, her face drawn, anxious.

"Oh, relax," Hurza said. "I'm not after Drur. He's all yours. I'm trying to make Aor a bit jealous, so he'll consider chasing."

"Oh," Kani said, relieved. "I didn't say he was mine," she protested.

Both Hurza and Alina laughed, and Kani gave them a small smile and a giggle.

"Do you think it will work?" Alina asked.

Hurza shrugged. "Perhaps, but he's stubborn. It may not. I'll keep working on him, though."

Hurza said they had to see to their chores, and Alina thanked them for coming by and for their help and support, choking up as she did. Hurza waved it away, and Kani squeezed her hand before they left.

Alina got up. She was sore from last night. Glancing off branches as she'd raced after Dashin had left her with bruises of her own. She got up, brushed her hair, and smiled as her comb came away with twigs. After washing her face, she scrubbed at the bits of mud and blood still on her arms. She grabbed her pack and walked over to the central platform.

At midday, the place was awash with villagers. All of them were intent on discussing last night's events with her in depth. She politely answered questions as she made her way to the kitchen and began stuffing food, water, and towels into her pack. By the time she was done, a ring of villagers were arguing about the results of the vote, pressing her for details as they did. She excused herself, telling them that she had to look in on Dashin. They grudgingly let her go.

She hurried away and stopped as she reached Rigin's hut. Rigin was standing outside the hut, peering into it, tears rolling down her cheeks. Alina's heart sank, fearing that something terrible had happened to Dashin. She called out to her as she raced over. Rigin turned and put her fingers to her lips. Alina went quiet as she walked up, her eyes probing for the cause of her distress.

Rigin motioned her over and pointed into the hut. Alina sidled up to her and looked within. Matse was sitting at the little table with Pritha in her lap, petting her and feeding her pieces of dried meat from the little bowl on the table. It was an endearing scene, but she'd seen this last night.

She gave Rigin a questioning look. Rigin pointed again, and Alina turned back to the scene. She watched as Matse fed her a few more pieces and was about to shrug when Matse leaned over and cupped a hand over Pritha's ear and whispered something into it. The kitten turned to her and looked up at her as though considering what the girl had just said. Alina felt a shiver run down her spine as tears of her own welled up in the corners of her eyes.

"She's been doing it for some time now," Rigin whispered to her.

"Does Dashin know?" Alina asked.

She shook her head.

Alina patted her shoulder and strode through the common room, ignoring Matse and Pritha as she went. She felt Pritha's eyes on her, which made her shiver, but Matse didn't look up.

Dashin was seated on the bed, trying to peel the dried banda leaves off his body, wincing as he did.

"What are you doing?" she asked, perplexed.

"I was too sore to make it to the cistern and thought I'd try peeling them."

"Never mind that. Come see this," she said, motioning him to the curtained doorway.

He stood up stiffly and walked over.

"What is it?" he asked.

She put her fingers to his lips and then parted the curtain a sliver, pointing. He peered through it, smiling as he saw Matse and Pritha at the table and Rigin watching from the door. He started to turn back toward Alina, but she pointed again to the table, and they waited together until Matse did it again, her little mouth whispering something to the kitten. It was a much longer secret this time. When she was done, Pritha turned to her and rubbed her head against Matse's chest. The little girl giggled and gave her the tiniest of hugs as Pritha continued to rub herself against her arms.

She could see tears in Dashin's eyes now. She let the curtain fall, stepped back to the bed, and sat down. He joined her.

He was too choked up to speak, his lip trembling with emotion.

She also felt full from the moment, her feelings toward the creature shifting within her. She'd been angry at the *melding* and then resigned to enduring it. She'd resented the kitten for making everything so much more difficult and jeopardizing their chances in the trials. But now she saw the kitten differently. There was something about it she'd been closed to last night, something Dashin had sensed and tried to communicate to her, something she'd been unwilling to hear.

She squeezed his hand. "This is a good thing."

He nodded, his lips tight. She took a deep breath. "Are you up to moving through the forest a bit?"

He paused, rolling his shoulders and wincing. "I think it would do me some good to move."

They stepped out into the common room, and Matse's face fell as she assumed Dashin would be taking Pritha.

"Matse," Dashin said, kneeling down next to the table and stroking the kitten's head with his fingers. "Alina and I have to go out for a time, and I don't have anyone to watch Pritha while I'm away. Is that something you could do for me?" he asked.

The girl nodded, beaming at him and giving Pritha a gentle hug as she did. Dashin went quiet for a moment. It seemed he was communicating with the cat. It sat up straight and put a paw on the table, as though to jump away and follow, but then cocked its head and looked from the bowl to the girl, the hut, and back to Dashin a few times before it settled down. It turned from Dashin, as though annoyed. He moved to meet its eyes, but it turned away again, ignoring him.

Alina suppressed a chuckle, and Dashin looked up at her and rolled his eyes, which made the chuckle find its way from her after all. He stood and walked out onto the platform.

"Children are the same everywhere," Rigin said, patting his arm and chuckling.

Alina helped him wash the remaining banda leaves from his body. Her fingers remembered the days and nights when she'd first touched this skin, running a wet towel over it to ease the fever. Those days seemed a lifetime ago.

Rigin came from the hut with fresh clothes. Dashin changed into them as Alina and Rigin discussed the activity in the village. The arguing bothered Alina. She did not like to see her village so. Rigin told her not to worry, that change always brought about disagreements, and that things would right themselves with time. She urged Alina to focus on the trials and leave the village to her and her father.

Alina was surprised at this. She had never noticed Rigin taking an active part in village politics, but she sensed that there was a lot she'd never been aware of. She'd always assumed those making the most noise were those who shaped things, but perhaps that was not always true.

"Where are we going?" Dashin asked when they'd gone a short distance from the village.

"I thought we could go to your egg and get it ready for the trial," she said.

"We're going to climb all the way down there and then back up again?" he said, stopping. They hadn't brought lanyards, heeding her father's instructions.

"Yes, if you're up to it?"

He paused, about to refuse. She could already see the words on his lips, but then he bit them back. "I was just thinking of suggesting that," he lied, and she felt warm inside. She was touched that he would do this without hesitation, even though it was apparent it would cost him. She nodded and turned away.

They made their way down, taking their time and picking their way to the forest floor, moving diagonally toward the egg. The descent was easy at this pace, and Alina had him wait a few times to rest as she collected herbs to clean the egg and get it smelling fresher. If he was going to spend a day and night in there, it needed more cleaning than what they'd done lowering it.

When they reached the egg, it was much as they'd left it, which was heartening. They spent time scrubbing the inside with the towels and water she'd brought, taking short breaks to ensure the forest was still safe. She soaped up the inside and then crushed herbs into the water she'd brought to rinse it with. When at last they were done, it was far more agreeable inside.

"What do you think?" she asked.

"It smells so much better now," he said. "I imagined it would be an unpleasant day and night, but now I'm looking forward to sleeping away the trial in here. It will be the most restful trial of them all, I'm sure."

His words frightened her. "Dashin, you must still be careful. As you've seen, the forest floor is a dangerous place. Do not take it lightly."

"I won't," he assured her, his eyes serious now. She exhaled and nodded.

He secured the pod again, jamming sticks in a groove to force the egg closed. They made their way up into the trees a short distance, and she took out the food she'd brought.

"Is there any news from your mother?" he asked.

She shook her head. "Nothing yet," she said. It was starting to worry her, though she tried to push those thoughts away. She'd often had to do so in her youth. Her mother's schedule was filled with unforeseen things. A *hazard of her gift* was the way her mother described it. She looked off into the trees, and Dashin let it go, which she appreciated.

"Where was Solvan?" Alina asked, as it occurred to her that she'd never seen the children apart.

"Rigin said that he's become very popular. This morning, children came to get him, eager to hear my stories."

Alina choked on the bite she was trying to swallow. She giggled. "Your stories?"

Dashin looked annoyed. "I have no idea what stories he's been making up, but I suspect that breathing fire when I'm angry is only the tip of this mountain."

Alina laughed and nudged him with her shoulder. "You are a thing of mystery that inhabits a world of mortals, Dashin," she said, forcing an even tone, but when he narrowed his eyes and looked at her, she burst out laughing. And the more annoyed he looked, the harder she laughed until, at last, he joined her, and they laughed until they cried.

Chapter 36

They spent the next day in the forest, rebuilding Dashin's conditioning as his body recovered. Enor's balm was a blessing, and slathering it on twice a day, coupled with rest, did wonders.

He was moving well with his lanyards again. It was a far cry from a TreePerson, but far better than how he moved with the regular lanyards. The rubber had peeled away from the fingers on those, which made them even less useful for Dashin. He dreaded having to use them, even on the short trips to and from the cache. He fell often as their cups slipped from the branches they held, which certainly helped maintain the illusion that he was hopeless in the forest for those who witnessed him using them.

Pritha was annoyed that he'd spent the day away from her. She'd glued herself to him and then complained again the next morning when they'd set out. He sensed Pritha enjoyed being catered to by Matse, but she would have preferred Dashin do so as well.

The evening meal had been strained. Arguments and discord had filled the air. Dashin regretted bringing this into the tribe. He'd left the meal early, appetite gone, hoping his absence might lessen the tension.

He sat in Sneva's room, petting Pritha. She was upset they'd left the meal with so much of the meat uneaten, images of semi-full platters of food winking in and out of his thoughts.

Rigin stepped into the room. "I brought you some food," she said, putting a tray down on the little table in the room and taking the chair.

"Thanks," he said, sliding the platter onto the bed. Pritha jumped from his lap and dug in. "I felt our presence was making things more difficult," he said, petting her lightly as she ate.

"Change is difficult for most people. For some, it is a mountain that feels impossible to climb," she said.

"I'm sorry to have brought such strife to the village," he began, but she reached over and put her fingers on his lips.

"Dashin, you did no such thing," she replied forcefully. "We are lucky to have you, even if some do not yet know it."

Her tone took him by surprise.

She held his eyes. "You've done more for us than you know. You've taken Solvan and Matse into your heart. Both were struggling before you came, and both are thriving now. You saved Alina's life and have accomplished impossible things. You are truly a gift from the SkyGods. I thank them every day for sending you, and I pray to them every night to keep you safe."

Dashin swallowed, shocked by the force of the declaration.

"Thank you. I don't know what to say. I have never had much of a home before. The home you've accepted me into is more than I could have wished for."

She crinkled her eyes at him. "Take off your shirt, and I'll apply balm to your back while you eat something. You'd best hurry or Pritha will have it cleaned off before you get a bite."

Dashin snagged a stuffed banda leaf and bit into it, awakening the hunger that had lain dormant during the evening meal.

"You need to eat and rest so you can be your best for the remaining trials."

"Thanks," he said, pulling off his shirt as he chewed. She set to work, her hands gentle and efficient. By the time he and Pritha had eaten their fill, he was covered in leaves again. The warmth he felt from her dispelled the tension he'd picked up from the village, and he drifted off to sleep with Pritha snoring against him.

Morning had become Dashin's favorite time of the day. The coolness on his body. The hint of night blossoms lingering in the air. Birds greeting the day in song. And the endless possibilities of what the day might bring. He stepped onto the platform outside Rigin's hut, filling his lungs with the crisp air.

A full night's restful sleep had done wonders for his body and outlook. This was their last day of training, and he was anxious to be underway. Pritha, on the other hand, was anxious for him to stay. She showed her displeasure, sitting with her back to him as Matse fed her.

Alina arrived, and they left together. She set up another course, and Dashin spent the morning traversing it, being chased by her and then by Hurza and Kani when they stopped by. He was getting better at following the markings and spotting the baskets. He would never evade a TreePerson intent on catching him, but perhaps with a significant lead... Alina seemed hopeful they might be able to arrange one, though she didn't want him to rely on it. She urged him to treat the course as though the chaser was right behind him all the time, breathing down his neck.

Whenever they broke to drink water or eat, he would check in with Pritha. It was the most amazing thing to be able to close his eyes and reach through this connection and feel her mind. As soon as he reached for her, she sensed him.

She began sending him mental pictures, and paired with her feelings, they formed a basic language. An image of the platform outside Rigin's hut, looking down toward the cache, was a question as to whether he was coming home soon. He saw that image often. He would reply with images of the forest to indicate he was still out, or pictures of the village from below to indicate he was on his way.

An image of a full bowl of dried meat indicated that she was eating, or about to eat, or hoping to eat. An empty bowl indicated that she'd recently eaten. Images of branches and sunshine signified rest or naptime. He would often become so engrossed in exploring this connection that Alina would have to nudge his shoulder to get his attention.

"What does the *melding* feel like?" she asked him as the two of them sat eating stuffed banda leaves at midday.

"It is similar to the *touching* in that you can sense the other person," he said. "But it's more immediate, like it's part of your own mind."

"Can I see?" she asked.

It had not occurred to him she might be able to do that. He grinned. "Sure," he said. "I don't know if it will work, but we can try."

She took a breath and reached for him, closing her eyes. He did the same, and a moment later, she stepped into his mind. The warmth of her mind in his was delightful, and he felt her lean into him, perhaps sensing the thought.

"It's strange," she said, her voice tentative next to him. "It's as though there's a new room with a doorway in it that leads into darkness."

"I was just thinking that," he lied.

She chuckled and pinched him.

"Ouch," he said, rubbing his arm.

He took a breath and reached for Pritha. He felt her awareness bloom within his mind. Alina gasped next to him. He sensed Pritha's curiosity at the change in him. She sent him a picture of the cache, and he replied with a picture of the forest, letting her know he wasn't coming yet. She sent a picture of an empty bowl, then one with branches, and then one with children playing.

Alina giggled next to him. He sensed Alina's delight as well as Pritha's probing. Then Pritha sent a picture of Alina sitting at the evening meal, and he sensed it was a question. Dashin responded with a picture of Alina in the trees, wearing her lanyards, as a reply. Alina giggled again. Dashin let the connection go, and Alina pulled away, opening her eyes. They were sparkling with excitement.

"That is a wondrous thing, Dashin. I had no idea she could communicate so well."

"Oh, the pictures were her idea, but did you get her emotions too?"

"Yes, I sensed them as well."

The rest of the day was tiring, but Dashin felt so much more at ease in the trees, even with Alina giving him less of a lead. He'd almost managed to make it back before her on one occasion.

As evening approached, they fetched up together on a branch to finish off their water. Dashin checked on Pritha, and Alina listened in as he did. Having experienced it earlier, she was eager to do so again, asking questions about the texture of it and his own experience that he was unable to answer. Though to be fair, he'd been unable to explain his feelings about a great number of things Alina had asked him about over their time together.

Pritha was preoccupied and wasn't communicating. A variety of emotions washed across the link. Concentration. Excitement. Frustration. Pleasure. Dashin couldn't make sense of them. Alina shifted beside him, her hand light on his shoulder as he sensed her confusion. He reached for Pritha's senses. The common room in Rigin's hut appeared. The image had the oddness he'd noted before. Colors were muted, but the details were sharp. The woven floor matting stood out crisp and clear. Alina gasped and leaned in.

A piece of string darted by, and Pritha leapt for it, her paws pinning it momentarily before it was pulled away. She spun around and pounced, pinning the string again, a thrill running through her as she did. Matse came into view, giggling delightedly, as she pulled on the string and tossed the end of it behind Pritha. Dashin could smell the herbs in Matse's hair along with the scent of the child herself. There were so many components to it that it was impossible to tease them out. Rigin was cutting something on the counter and speaking. It was difficult to make out the words, the impact from Pritha's leaping about muffling them.

Dashin pulled back and leaned up against the trunk of the branch he was on. He opened his eyes. He was so pleased to see Pritha enjoying herself and to see the changes in Matse.

Alina let go of his shoulder, moved to the branch next to him, and leaned against the same trunk so her shoulder brushed his. "Her senses are so rich. They almost make up for yours," she said with a chuckle.

"Hey," he said, chuckling himself.

She grew serious beside him. "You will be careful tomorrow, won't you?"

"I will. Straight down to the pod, and then I'll lock myself in and sleep and eat the day away. It will be like the spa."

Alina turned her head to look at him. "What is this *spa*?" she asked, her mouth forming the Ancaran word with difficulty.

"Oh, it's a place on Ancara where people go to relax."

"They need a special place to relax?" she laughed.

Dashin laughed too. The thought seemed strange now. "Yes, apparently so."

"You lived on a strange world, Amani. No pictures of the trees in your mind. No village life. Living under the earth. And now special places to relax." She nudged his shoulder, glancing at him.

The twinkle in her eye tugged at his heart, inciting a wave of emotion. As difficult as his time on Ndesa had been, these had also been the best days of his life. He had gained so much, and his connection with Alina was the thing he cherished most of all.

"Alina, if somehow I don't..." he began, searching for words to express what she meant to him.

Alina gasped, her fingers flying to his lips, her eyes intent on his.

He stopped speaking.

"Do not speak those words," she said, her face taut. "You must see the trial's success in your mind and feel it in your heart, Amani. Do you hear me?"

He swallowed and nodded.

She took her fingers from his lips, her eyes holding his for several moments more, to ensure he had truly heard her.

He exhaled, trying to let go of his doubts.

She crinkled her eyes at him. "Let's see how ready you are. See that branch over there?"

Dashin turned to look in the direction she was pointing, and she pushed him off the branch. He fell to the one below and caught it with one hand, his lanyards flapping about him as he grunted.

"See if you can catch me, ground person," she dared him, laughing as she dove over him into the trees. Her lanyard made an impossible grab, and she swung at right-angles to her throw, her pack narrowly missing a large limb as she did.

Dashin scrambled back up onto his branch, untangled his lanyards, and leapt after her. She led him on a chase through the forest, moving up and down, side to side, laughing as she did. "I'll race you to the cache," she cried as she sped away.

Dashin tore after her. He let his mind relax, letting the motion of the trees come to him. Letting the paths reveal themselves. Searching for the *TruePath* before him. As he moved, she swooped by him again and again, taunting him, trying to distract him. It upset his rhythm a few times and forced him to exert physical effort to recapture it, but he pressed on. The closer he got to the cache, the more focused he became, so that her efforts to distract him no longer broke his composure. When at last he had the cache in view, he surged ahead, pulling hard on his lanyards and launching himself toward it and then repeating the gesture, accelerating, accelerating, putting caution aside.

Alina squealed behind him as she saw him surge past. Her taunting stopped, and he heard her grunt and exert herself as she raced to catch him. He heard her rhythm pick up. Her breathing grew more labored. He smiled, driving himself forward. He almost reached the platform before her. Somehow, she just managed to drop down a moment before he did. But just a moment, the thought he'd nearly outpaced her filled him with pride. She bent over, hands on her knees, panting.

"That was unexpected," she gasped, fighting to catch her breath. She was about to add something else when a sudden pain brought Dashin to his knees. His head throbbed, and a wave of nausea washed over him.

Alina was next to him in an instant, her hand on his back. "Amani, what is it?" she cried.

The world spun around him, and he felt terror and rage well up within him. It was Pritha. Something was wrong. Very wrong. He opened his eyes. "It's Pritha," he managed to choke out. "Something is going on in the village. Go," he said. "I'll follow."

She hesitated for a moment, looking at him until he nodded to her. She turned and leapt into the trees, moving fast toward the village. Dashin stood up and took a deep breath. He picked up his regular lanyards and wrapped them around his waist. He wasn't going to chance those now. He leapt after her, moving to the village on foot. He had no idea what was happening, but as he neared the village, he could hear screaming, a lot of screaming. His heart sank.

He tumbled to the platform outside Rigin's hut and threw his lanyards behind the cistern, dropping those around his waist next to the door before racing to the central platform. He flew over the bridges, his feet light, finding his footing without effort. As he reached the platform, the entire village was standing there, and he could hear Pritha hissing and screeching madly. Almost everyone was taller than him, so he couldn't see beyond them. He climbed onto the kitchen's counter and looked over their heads toward the children's area, where Matse sat with Pritha in her lap.

The kitten's ears were back on her head, her fur standing on end. She was hissing and screeching at two young girls, Aras' daughters, Dashin thought. The two girls were near the end of a branch facing Pritha before them. They were crying and shaking. Matse was frozen, hunched over the kitten, her face ashen, her body trembling.

Many villagers held spears, poised to throw them. But at the moment, Pritha was too close to Matse. It seemed they were waiting for the cat to spring. The branch the children were on was slight. With the three of them already on it, it prevented an adult from using it. And the other branches around them were all slight for an adult.

Aras was in the netting beneath his daughters, pleading with them to jump, but they were both frozen, too frightened to move. There was shouting and chaos on the platform. Gamoc, the slightest of the young adults, was crawling on a thin branch above them, making his way toward them with his flint knife in his teeth.

Dashin's heart pounded in his chest. His head throbbed, and Pritha's rage and fear made it difficult to think. He couldn't imagine her doing this. How could he have misjudged her so?

He looked for Alina, and she was at the tables where the evening dishes had been laid out. She picked up several of the stones they used to keep the salted banda leaves from blowing away. Then she pushed her way through the crowd to the edge of the platform.

Dashin closed his eyes, trying to reach Pritha to calm her. All he sensed were primal hunting instincts, her body poised to pounce. Pressure was rising within her, and he sensed it about to happen. He took a breath and reached for her senses. The branch snapped into view in his mind, the suddenness of it almost making him lose his footing. Pritha was looking at the children. He could see the terror on their faces now.

She was looking at their knees, which was an odd thing for her to be focused on, Dashin thought. He couldn't make sense of it until he saw movement in the leafy brush of the tree behind them.

He opened his eyes and started yelling. "The brush, the leaves." Villagers turned to him, and Alina, who'd been about to throw, heard his voice and turned as well. "There's something in the brush," Dashin shouted, pointing at the tree.

Alina spun, saw the tree he pointed to, and threw in a single motion. The stone sailed right at the children. Before it had reached them, another was in the air, and a third was in her hand. The first stone whizzed by the youngest girl and hit something in the brush beyond her with a wet thud.

The brush exploded as a huge tree lizard sprang from it and darted toward the children. A nerape. Dashin had heard tales of these creatures and how they were known to snatch children from the edge of a village and flee into the forest with them. It was as long as an adult TreePerson, though much thinner. It had jaws full of needle-like teeth and sharp, curved claws that dug into the wood as it skittered along the branch.

It leapt for the branch with the girls, its jaws snapping at the youngest girl as the second stone caught it in the shoulder. The blow knocked it off balance just enough that the powerful jaws missed the arm it sought and found only air. The girl screamed and bumped into her sister, who lost her footing, and both of them tumbled into the netting below. Aras was on them immediately.

The nerape, having lost its first target, raced along the limb toward Matse, its beady eyes intent on the frozen girl, ignoring the tiny kitten in her lap. Pritha sprang forward toward the creature, and Dashin's heart skidded to a halt. The nerape opened its jaws to meet her, but the kitten slipped beneath them and latched onto its throat, her sharp teeth piercing the leathery hide. The creature howled, thrashing on the branch, claws gripping wood, trying to shake the kitten free. It swiped a clawed foot at the kitten and ripped it from its throat, tearing out a piece of hide as it did so. Pritha was thrown into the air, and Dashin's stomach twisted in knots.

The nerape spun in place as another stone caught it, and a spear grazed it. A flurry of spears filled the air as the creature scrambled away. It leapt back into the brush from which it had emerged and fled through the forest, the sound of rustling branches fading as it went. The village erupted in cries of relief and astonishment. Nyan jumped into the netting to join Aras and her girls. Dashin ran to the edge of the platform and dove into the netting where he'd seen Pritha thrown. The huge claw had thrown her the length of the platform.

Somewhere behind him, Alina was calling his name. He cast about in the dim evening light, looking for Pritha, fearing she might have been thrown clear of the netting and fallen to the forest floor. She was still a kitten and a krax who had no instinct for the trees.

He couldn't find her anywhere. A growing sense of dread settled within him as he searched in vain. Alina joined him, followed soon after by other villagers.

His bottom lip trembled as he reached the end of the netting and peered over the edge into the forest below, praying she'd caught a branch or been wedged in the crook of some tree.

"Can you sense her?" Alina asked.

In his fear for her, he'd forgotten their link. He closed his eyes, took a breath, and felt Alina touch his shoulder as he reached for Pritha. The link was still there, which was encouraging, though it was weak. He couldn't touch her mind or her senses, but he was certain she was still alive.

He opened his eyes and saw that Alina knew it too. She dropped from the netting and ran about below it. Dashin followed, but she was much faster and lighter, racing along the branches, treading lightly so as not to disturb them unduly. Dashin moved cautiously, worried his greater mass might bend the branch that held the kitten and send her tumbling.

"Over here!" Alina shouted.

Dashin ran over to her and arrived as Alina was lifting the little body from the lodra nest she'd crashed into. The rodents had scattered, likely aghast that it was raining krax. Alina looked her over for wounds, her hands probing Pritha's body as Dashin waited, his fingers brushing her furry head.

"I don't see any blood," Alina announced. "And none of the bones appear to be out of place."

Dashin took Pritha in his arms, and as he did, she stirred. His heart raced at the feel of her. She blinked open her eyes and looked up at him, then at Alina, and yawned, shrugging a shoulder as she did. Dashin could see it was tender, though it seemed to move well enough.

Dashin closed his eyes and reached for her, and Alina touched his shoulder. The kitten sent them a picture of a bowl full of dried meat.

Previous tensions were put aside for the evening meal, everyone keenly aware of the horror they had narrowly averted. The men climbed out into the children's area and made short work of thinning the brush before sitting down to eat. It was a task they did routinely, but one which had been left too long this time.

Pritha ate her fill of dried meat. Matse whispered into Pritha's ear in a voice he could barely make out, apologizing for doubting her. Pritha's bowl never ran empty. Eager little hands came from tables around the platform throughout the meal to add to it. Even Aras' daughters came. The eldest shyly asked Matse to thank Pritha for her. Pritha sat happily in Dashin's lap as he stroked her, and Matse whispered how proud she was of her. The words she spoke tonight were the first Dashin had heard from the girl.

Pritha accepted her tribute with grace. She was not one to hold a grudge, it seemed.

Chapter 37

Alina stole across the central platform in the dark. Morning was still only a promise, the birds still fast asleep in their nests. She crossed the bridges, her feet finding them without thought. Lamplight spilled from the doorway to Rigin's hut.

"I can't imagine I'll need this much food," Dashin's voice said from within.

She slipped in through the doorway and found all the occupants already gathered in the common room. Rigin had arrayed a huge mound of food on the table. Dashin was shaking his head as he held Pritha in his lap, his hand petting her as he looked at the food. He glanced at Pritha as she put a paw on his hand and stared up at him.

"Yes, I realize you'd like us to take it all," he said, chuckling.

Matse and Solvan, sharing a chair across the table, giggled.

"You will be gone an entire day and night, Dashin, and tomorrow is the *trial of the trees*. You'll need your strength," Rigin said, pushing the mound toward him.

Alina took the empty chair. "You should take it. We've all seen you eat."

Dashin's face lit up when he saw her. She drank it in, feeling the knot in her stomach loosen a touch.

"Oh," he said, "Solvan, can you fetch my lanyards? They are behind the cistern. I want to take those too."

Solvan slid from the chair and tore outside. Matse jumped down and raced after him. Solvan retrieved his new lanyards, and Matse brought in the regular lanyards he'd left on the platform last night.

"Thanks," he said, smiling at them both and rubbing their heads.

He rolled up his new lanyards and stuffed them into the bottom of the beautiful leather pack at his feet. Alina had seen the pack before. That Rigin had given Dashin her late son's pack was no surprise, though it warmed her heart to see it.

"Did you get any sleep?" Alina asked as he added some large water gourds to the pack.

"Not much," he said, stowing the food on top. "I couldn't settle after almost losing Pritha. Though she slept just fine," he chided, looking down at the kitten.

She yawned and ate the piece of dried meat Matse offered her.

"How about you?" Dashin asked, looking across at her.

She shook her head. "Me neither."

She turned as she heard voices outside. Hurza and Kani stepped into the room.

"It seems everyone is here to wish you luck, Dashin," Hurza said, with a grin.

"Thanks. I appreciate it. And thank you both for all your help with my training," he said.

They both waved it away, but were pleased at his words.

"Are you taking Pritha?" Kani asked, looking at the kitten in his lap.

"Yes, for the *trial of the forest*. After last night, she hasn't left my side. I think she senses my anxiety."

"How are you carrying her?" Kani asked.

"I've just been putting her in my tunic, above my belt."

Kani shook her head. She turned and left the hut, her footsteps a light patter on the bridge.

"What?" Dashin asked.

Hurza shrugged. "I think she's gone to get her tree swaddle."

"Her what?"

"It will be simpler for her to show you," Hurza said.

Moments later, Kani arrived with a blanket-looking device with straps. "I used to carry my baby brother in this when I did chores. Stand up," she said, walking over to him.

He did, and she draped the straps over his shoulders and then around his waist. She adjusted the straps until the harness was snug over Dashin's chest and stomach.

"Normally, the legs protrude from these holes at the bottom of the pocket," Kani said, opening it and adding a towel to the bottom to block the holes and provide padding.

Dashin scooped up Pritha and slid her into it. The kitten's eyes widened as it sniffed the fabric. He moved around testing it. It held Pritha securely, and he would even be able to use his lanyards with it, something he couldn't have done with her loose in his tunic.

"This is great," Dashin said. "Thanks, this will make things so much easier."

The first of the morning birds sang out. A chill ran down Alina's spine.

"The village will be gathering on the platform at sunrise to see you off," Hurza said. "We'll see you there," she said, moving to the door. She stopped, looked at Kani, and cleared her throat when Kani failed to get the message.

Kani, who'd been watching Dashin with Pritha, looked at Hurza confused for a moment until Hurza made a motion with her head. "Oh, yes," Kani said, walking backward toward the door. "We'll see you there."

The two girls left, muttering as they went.

"Perhaps we should go see to the morning meal," Rigin said, looking at both Solvan and Matse, neither of whom seemed thrilled at the suggestion. Solvan grumbled as he squirmed in the chair, taking his time to comply.

Dashin turned to the two children. He reached across and took their small hands in each of his.

They turned and looked at him, their anxious eyes searching his face.

"I feel lucky to have met both of you," he said. "Growing up, I was the only child in my family. I always dreamed of having siblings. I'd like to think of you both that way if you'll allow it," he said.

Solvan's bottom lip trembled, and he nodded, unable to trust himself to speak. Matse squeezed his hand so hard her little fingers went pale.

Dashin turned to Rigin, who was dabbing at something in her eye. "I cannot say how much..." he began, but she stepped forward, put her fingers on his lips, and leaned in, touching her forehead to his. Dashin's own lip trembled as she did.

Rigin pulled away and turned to the children. "Come on, let's see to the morning meal before we're all blubbering," she said, pulling them from their chair and pushing them ahead of her. She turned at the door, glanced at Dashin, and touched her forehead with her fingertips before she left.

Dashin turned to Alina. "I just..."

She put her fingers on his lips. "Don't you dare," she said, laughing. "You'll have me blubbering too."

He grinned at her.

"Just promise me you'll be careful and come back," she said, holding his eyes.

"I will," he said.

She cupped his cheek and kissed him. There was no prelude, no leaning or intense eye contact, the way she'd always imagined a first kiss ought to be. Instead, she'd felt compelled in the moment with a need so primal it was akin to breathing.

His body tensed against her at the unexpected contact, but he relaxed and leaned in to meet her lips with his own. The kiss was such a simple physical act, but her heart took flight, a wild nuxat leaping from its nest and flying free in the forest, reveling in the moment.

The kiss began as a child in the trees, clumsy and with more enthusiasm than grace. Neither of them had experience, but they found the way of it together, their mouths inventing a song that soon had them soaring.

Breathless, she pulled back, her body awash in wonder, and smiled. But his lips reached for hers again, refusing to let it end. She giggled at his eagerness, his ardor sending another wave of warmth through her. She added her other hand to his face, cradling his face between her hands as they kissed. His skin was hot on her fingertips, his breath soft on her cheek. His skin had that salty, earthy scent she felt must be what Ancara smelled of. His fingers found her upper arms, their light touch sending delicious tingling through her body.

She knew how dangerous the next trials would be. The past few days had reminded her how tenuous one's hold on life was. Surely, the SkyGods would see the love they shared and intercede for them, see them through the coming days.

Her breathing grew shallow, and she felt tears pooling in the corners of her eyes. She pulled her lips away, putting the fingers of one hand on his lips and feeling the moisture of their kiss upon them. She leaned in, touching her forehead against his. And somehow, though she'd not intended to, she slipped into his mind.

"That was beyond words," she felt him say as he sensed her within. The space was bright, and his spirit soared, mirroring her own feelings so perfectly it took her breath away. Had she not touched his joy, she could not have believed that its depth could match her own.

"It was a surprise," he sent.

"I'm sorry, the feeling came upon me suddenly," she replied.

"Amani, you don't have to apologize. I've been dreaming of this moment for many nights."

"Oh, really?" she sent, chuckling to herself and yet feeling giddy at his words, for she had spent time herself imagining the moment.

She felt a shyness bloom within him as his thoughts of her swam to the surface. It stirred her to see how precious she was to him. This was the first true connection he'd ever had with another, his first real friendship, his first real love. She swallowed at the enormity of it within him, fresh tears pooling in her eyes.

She reached and cradled his face in her hands again, letting him see her own feelings for him now. Revealing herself to him, opening her heart so he would know that though she'd grown up surrounded by love, she had never known a love such as this one. That she treasured it and would fight to protect it.

He sent her a picture of a bowl of dried meat? She wrinkled her forehead at the sight and then giggled as she heard the soft cry from the tree swaddle on his chest.

"Sorry," he said, opening his eyes and petting the small head peeking out at them, a curious expression on its face.

Alina reached over and scratched behind an ear, the first time she'd done so, and the kitten pressed against her hand and purred. She softened, recognizing that this new mind within Dashin's, the being that now shared his life, might also share hers. She leaned forward and touched her forehead to its furry head.

"You were a hero last night," she said. "You have the heart of your mother."

The kitten purred, a long rumbling sound followed by an odd, vocalized cry, as though answering her. They both laughed.

The sound of Solvan's distinctive footsteps sounded on the hut's platform, and they turned to the door as he appeared.

"Dashin, they sent me to fetch you," he said.

The village gathered on the platform as the sun sliced through the trees. The first rays were in the branches above them, and the birds were filling the forest with song. Fodrick explained the rules. Dashin was to spend the entire day and night on the forest floor. Someone would be watching from above. If he left the forest floor before he was called, he would forfeit the trial. He asked Dashin if he understood the rules, and Dashin answered that he did.

Then, as sunlight touched the platform, Drur led the way into the trees. Dashin, wearing his regular lanyards, followed him. It was painful to watch him pick his way through the trees with those lanyards. The rubber had worn away from the fingers in the cups to such an extent that he could no longer trust them to bear his weight. He walked through the forest, using those lanyards only for support as he went.

Drur was frustrated at the sluggish pace, sitting some distance away and shaking his head as he waited. She heard muttering around her, villagers concerned with how little Dashin had learned in his time there and worrying about what this would mean for the *trial of the trees.*

When at last Dashin was out of sight, she exhaled. This trial was in his hands now. She touched her fingertips to her forehead, as did many on the platform. She turned to Hurza and Kani, who were standing next to her, and they nodded anxiously. It was time to turn their thoughts to the *trial of the trees.*

The counter in the common room of Alina's parents' hut was covered with bowls of various sizes. The entire area was dusted in nut flour with drizzles of thick syrup randomly splattered about.

Alina had first created the treats she fashioned for her *becoming* feast. Since then, she'd prepared them for every *becoming,* offering the treats to villagers during the *trial of the trees.*

She'd sweetened the nut flour with the syrup she'd made by boiling the sap of silas trees down until the mixture grew thick and sweet. She'd mixed the syrup with the flour and added berries. She cooked the treats on a smoldering brazier until they softened and the flour baked. Then she glazed them in syrup and set them aside to cool on trays. Each one sat upon a tiny circle cut from a sugared banda leaf.

She was covered in flour, her hands sticky with syrup, when Hurza and Kani arrived.

"Oh, those look great!" Kani exclaimed, reaching for one. She had the largest sweet tooth in the village. She popped it into her mouth and chewed the candied confection with delight, closing her eyes and moaning. "Those are delicious, the best you've ever made," she said, reaching for another.

"Don't eat them all," Alina admonished, wiping the sweat from her brow with a forearm.

Hurza reached for one.

"No, not those," Alina said, grabbing Hurza's wrist with a syrupy hand.

Hurza pulled her arm back, annoyed, and grabbed a wet towel to wipe off the syrup.

"Those are the doctored ones," Alina said. "There are soapstone shavings in the flour."

"Oh," Hurza said, leaning in to study them. "How do you tell them apart?"

"They are all on that tray for now, but I've made a small nick in the banda leaves too," she said, pointing at one of them.

"Ah," Hurza said, bending over the tray to study them.

"How long do you think it will take for them to have an effect?" Kani asked.

"Shouldn't be long. Perhaps halfway through the trial?" Alina mused. "It will depend on how many the person has. How active they are and what else is in their stomach, I imagine. My father uses it in cases where a person's digestion does not flow normally. It works quickly."

"We have something too," Hurza said proudly, pulling a necklace carefully from the bag at her waist.

Alina frowned. It was a necklace of wooden beads on a string, each bead about the size of a fingertip. She wiped her brow with a forearm. "How will that help?" she asked.

Both Hurza and Kani were beaming, enjoying her confusion.

"I'm going to get the chaser to wear it," Hurza announced.

Alina peered at it, not following.

"The beads are filled with borka juice," Kani blurted, unable to contain her excitement.

Hurza glared at her, annoyed at having been robbed of the reveal. She turned to Alina. "We hollowed out the beads, ran the string through them, sealed one end of each bead with wax, filled them with borka juice, and then sealed the open end with wax too."

Alina studied the necklace as Hurza held it out for her to see. It was exquisite work, obviously much of it Kani's handiwork.

"I made the beads," Kani announced.

"How does it work?" Alina asked, marveling at it.

Hurza brushed the beads with a finger. "The midday sun will soften the wax, and racing through the trees should jostle it enough that the wax seals will fall away and begin oozing borka juice over the wearer's chest."

Alina's eyes opened, and she chuckled, realizing the implication. It might not matter who was chasing. If the juice numbed their chest and perhaps their hands as they rubbed at it or handled the necklace, it would make it very difficult for them to use their lanyards effectively.

"There's not a lot of juice," Alina mused, peering at it.

"No," Hurza admitted. "Not enough to numb someone's arms, but there should be enough to slow them down a bit."

Alina swallowed. That they had worked on this together for her and come up with such an ingenious idea touched her. She dipped her hand in a bowl of water, rubbed her hands together, and dried them on a towel before reaching out and running her fingers lightly over the marvel.

"Thank you both. It's perfect," she said, seeing the relief her words brought to their faces. "I imagine you could get Aor to wear it, but what if the chaser is Drur?" Alina asked.

"Leave it to me," Hurza said. "I'll find a way." She crinkled her eyes.

Alina smiled. "I would imagine this will come as a surprise to the wearer," Alina said, a glint in her eye. All three girls broke out laughing.

"What is all this noise?" a voice called from outside the hut, a soft tread on the platform outside.

Alina's heart leapt at the sound, and she ran toward the door as her mother stepped into the common room. She hugged her fiercely, then pulled back and pressed her forehead against her mother's. They stood together for a moment, a warmth flowing through her body she had sorely missed. There were tears in her eyes again as a flood of emotion rose within her, threatening to overwhelm her. She swallowed, opening her eyes to look at her mother.

Her mother was smiling but seemed exhausted. Her face was gaunt and drawn. She staggered a bit, and Alina helped her to a chair. "What is it?" Alina asked, concerned.

"It's been a challenging time. Could I get a little food and water?" she asked. Alina grabbed a tray of sweets, and her mother waved them away. "I need a proper meal first," she said, with a smile. Kani and Hurza ran from the hut.

"Are you hurt?" Alina asked, taking the chair next to her.

"No, nothing like that," her mother assured her. "My sessions of *sight* were so intense they held me in their grip for days. I did not manage to leave the cave and never made it to Karita. I was released from one session only to find Iodra had eaten my food. I had to forage for what I could find after that. I have not had a proper meal in some time."

"What did you see?" Alina whispered, holding her breath and pouring water into a cup from the pitcher on the table.

"So many things, more paths in these few days than I have seen in my entire life." She took a breath. "How many days are left until the *trial of the forest*?" she asked, after draining the cup and offering it to Alina for more.

Alina stopped, the cup in her hand. "The *trial of the forest* started this morning. Dashin is there now," she said, holding her mother's eyes.

The remaining color from her mother's face drained away. "He passed the *trial of the hunt*?" she asked. "The vision was so strange I could not make sense of it. There was a large krax in my visions, but I don't understand what it means and how the symbol figures into things. Was it a strange hunt?"

Alina bit her lip, so much welling up within her. "Dashin killed the krax," she said, fighting back tears. "He put himself between it and me to save my life. That was the hunt."

Her mother sat stunned as Alina raced through a quick overview of the details. She clutched Alina's hand, devastated by the thought that she had almost lost her daughter. Her face teared up, and she leaned in, pressing her forehead against Alina's. "I'm so sorry, daughter," she said. "I meant to be here to help you carry this. It should not have fallen on you."

Alina could not speak.

A flurry of feet sounded on the platform outside. Hurza and Kani hurried in with her father. Rigin, who had Solvan and Matse in tow, stepped in behind them, the common room growing crowded with bodies.

Her father knelt next to her mother and took her face in his hands, touching his forehead to hers so delicately it took Alina's breath away. She saw the depth of feeling they had for one another with new eyes now, imagining how she would feel in a similar situation with Dashin.

Hurza and Kani pushed the laden trays on the table before her mother. Her father pulled away and urged her to eat, taking the chair next to her and pushing her favorite dishes toward her.

Everyone waited patiently as her mother ate. She was soon full, too soon, it being obvious to everyone that her stomach had shrunk in her absence. Alina's father, seeing her pace slow, pushed the trays away. "You can eat more later," he said. "Let your body see to what you have already eaten first."

She nodded, drinking water to wash it down. She looked around the room at the people. "I had no idea we were so far along in the trials," she said, as though needing to explain.

"It is fine. Dashin managed the *trial of the hunt*," her father said.

"A krax," her mother mused. "I can't imagine."

Her father smiled. "Yes, and not just any krax. It was the largest I've ever seen. It took four men to carry it."

Her mother touched her fingertips to her forehead, which occasioned the same response from everyone else in the room.

"I saw it in my vision. I imagined it a symbol of sorts," she said, shaking her head. "It was so confusing, I didn't imagine it to be a real event. There was also this odd little krax, crying in the background. It was such an odd vision."

"Yes," her father said, clearing his throat. "There is also a kitten. Dashin has *melded* with it."

Her mother's eyes opened wide. She gaped at him and then looked around the room, taking the measure of the faces before her. "This is a new experience for me. I am not often the one who is in the dark," she said with a chuckle, which eased the mounting tension. She took Alina's hand and squeezed it. It felt like her mother had finally arrived, that the lightness she always carried had only just caught up with her.

"How is Dashin doing?" she asked.

"He has a plan for the *trial of the forest*," Alina said. "He moved the egg he arrived in to the forest floor and will be staying in there throughout."

Her mother nodded. "And the *trial of the trees*?"

Alina showed her mother the treats. Her mother took one as Alina explained how she'd doctored some of them. Everyone laughed at the thought of what effect they would have. Her father reached over and squeezed her shoulder, apparently pleased she'd applied things she'd learned from him to the task. Hurza and Kani explained the necklace. Her parents and Rigin leaned in to study it, with two little heads peering in from the doorway, attempting to catch a glimpse of it.

"How is he in the trees?" her mother asked.

"He's quite good," Alina announced. Hurza and Kani both spoke up in agreement.

"He won't outrun a determined chaser," Alina said. "But we've tried to keep his skill a secret. We hope it will make the chaser underestimate him and give him a large lead. And, with the treats and necklace, he stands a chance."

"Did you see the results?" her father asked her mother. Everyone leaned in.

"There were too many paths, though many terrible ones fell away in the past few days, perhaps due to the *trial of the hunt*. Terrible things are coming this way. Things I dare not even speak of. Much depends on Dashin's *becoming*. It is *important* for all of us."

She looked at her father. "Do you think Fodrick would stop the trials and accept him if I spoke to him?"

He considered it and then shook his head. "I don't think so. The village is split on the matter. Though I think Fodrick wants Dashin to succeed, I believe he feels the only way the village will accept him is if Dashin prevails in the trials."

Chapter 38

Dashin picked his way through the canopy. He tried to keep his thoughts on the task at hand rather than all the things that could go wrong on the forest floor. He did believe that with the pod, this would be the simplest of the trials, but his body was still tense with anticipation and nerves.

His regular lanyards were useless at this point, so he used them more for effect than for help. He felt the eyes on his back as he started out, the muttering arising behind him as the village watched him pick his way forward. If feigned incompetence in the trees was the goal, he was certainly meeting it.

When he reached Drur, Dashin smiled at him as he walked past. The young man shook his head. Dashin continued on, descending toward his pod, taking his time as he went. He'd gone quite some distance before he heard Drur take to the trees behind him. Dashin looked up, and the young man floated down through the trees effortlessly. His body drifted down in his wake, his lanyards flashing around him, each cast perfect. In a few moments, he alit next to Dashin and sat down regarding him, his eyes impassive.

Dashin swallowed. The sight of Drur had unsettled him. He turned and continued on. Alina, Hurza, and Kani were fast. He'd imagined Drur would be a bit faster, but he'd been unprepared for this. Alina had mentioned they were trying to get Aor to chase. He hoped they'd succeeded.

As he neared the pod, Dashin sat in the trees above it, observing the forest floor just as Alina had taught him. He saw a few birds hopping about on the ground, and a rodent scurried from one bush to another. Things seemed pretty safe. He waited a few more moments until he was confident it was safe before dropping to the forest floor. The soft earth felt strange beneath his feet, his mind adjusting to the lack of motion.

Now that he was on the ground, he would have to stay here until tomorrow morning. This suited him fine. He'd hardly slept last night. The pod's soft crash seats called to him.

He looked up. Drur had stopped in the trees above him and was taking off his pack and settling in. Dashin smiled. He would be a fair bit more comfortable down here.

As he made his way to the pod, Pritha poked her head out of the tree swaddle and sniffed the air. She hadn't moved on the entire trip down, snoring against him during the descent. She studied the pod as he pulled the sticks from the door latch, and the door yawned open.

She wrinkled her nose at the stale air. They hadn't removed all the filth in their cleaning, for there was still a hint of it beneath the smell of herbs. He climbed inside and pulled the door closed, using the previously rigged bit of rope to leave a gap to allow fresh air to enter.

Pritha was eager to explore. He pulled her from the swaddle and put her down on the floor, and she made a circuit of the pod, sniffing at every crack and storage compartment before jumping up onto a crash seat. He closed his eyes and reached for her, sending pictures of the pod, then nighttime, and then morning again, hoping she would understand they would be spending the day and night there. She sent back a picture of a bowl of dried meat. He smiled and shook his head. Apparently, what they were doing concerned her less than food.

He sat down on the empty crash seat and opened his pack, and there on top, he found a rolled-up banda leaf with only dried meat in it. It seemed Rigin had packed for both of them. He put it on the seat next to Pritha and unrolled it to reveal the meal. Pritha licked her lips, ate the entire thing, and then licked away every trace of meat from the leaf.

Dashin ate a few of the regular stuffed banda leaves and washed them down with a swig of water. He poured some water into his hand and let Pritha drink from it. When they were done, he stretched out on his crash seat, intent on a much-needed nap. As he settled into it, he shuddered at the memory of climbing into this seat as the ship around him was being destroyed. So much had happened since then. Those memories belonged to someone else.

He closed his eyes and sent Pritha an image of the trees and sunshine, her naptime image. A moment later, she was curled up on his chest, her little body soft and warm on him. The air was cool, but welcome after the climb down. A moment later, they were both snoring.

It was well after midday when Dashin blinked awake from a deep, dreamless fog. He reached for Pritha. She fussed as he pet her, but settled as he scratched behind her ear. It was hot in the pod, and the air had grown stale again. He sat up, moving Pritha to the empty crash seat. She mewed a complaint, one he'd learned meant she was only mildly annoyed. He glanced out the windows. Nothing moved in the forest around them. Above in the trees, he could make out a makeshift nest of branches with a leg, Drur's he assumed, protruding from one side. It seemed his watcher had made himself comfortable.

Dashin checked the surroundings again and opened the door wide, letting in fresh air. Pritha stretched, yawned, sniffed the air, and then bounded over to him to glance outside, her eyes peering into the foliage around them and the forest beyond.

"What do you sense?" he asked her, closing his eyes. He reached for her senses, and a moment later, the scene came alive for him. The forest was crisp and sharp, and it was awash in a language of scents he couldn't discern. Pritha didn't seem at all alarmed and was instead reveling in scents she had known before her ascent into the trees.

He mused about the cenote and how cool the water was. How nice it would be to take a quick dip in it. From here, it wasn't far, though, because of the trial, he would have to travel on the ground. He went through the steps in his mind. He'd lock up Pritha in the pod, dash over to the cenote, take a dip in it, and rush back. It was midday, most creatures were bedded down, and if he hurried, he could be back in a flash.

Pritha yowled, getting his attention. He turned to her. She was unhappy. Her eyes narrowed, and the fur on her neck stood up. He closed his eyes and reached for her. She sent him a picture of him locking her in the pod with a strong sense of displeasure. He was shocked. He hadn't felt her in his mind, but apparently, she was privy to his thoughts without his awareness of it. He wondered how often she listened or if she sensed all his thoughts. His mind was becoming a crowded place, with people stopping by regularly, and now with others perhaps in residence.

"I wasn't serious," he tried to convey to her, sending her a picture of the two of them together in the pod. She sent him a picture of a bowl of dried meat. He smiled. It seemed fair compensation. He opened the bag, fished out another banda leaf of dried meat, and unrolled it on Pritha's crash seat.

She ate hers as he finished two more of the rolled banda leaves. He looked at the remaining food, and it didn't seem quite as excessive now. He was just about to close the door again when Pritha bounded over to him and sniffed sharply, turning her head from side to side and then peering intently into the forest. Dashin reached for her sight. He saw a shadow moving through the forest. It was coming this way.

Dashin pulled the door closed, securing it with the rope as he did. He peered through the window. Pritha perched on the top of the crash seat, stretched out with her head next to his.

A male stoda strode into the ferns near the pod. It paused, lifting its head and sniffing the air. It turned its head from side to side, momentarily confused. But, after a few moments, it moved forward and dipped its large head into a patch of ferns, and with a quick shake of its head, it ripped a clump of them from the earth, exposing glistening bulbous roots.

It took the stalks, near the roots, in its teeth and shook them, scattering dirt from the roots onto the ground. It sniffed the air once again before dipping its head down to shear the roots with its teeth, lifting its head and crunching them with delight. It made short work of those roots and repeated this same process for the rest of the ferns in the patch around the pod.

The boar was not as large as the one Dashin and Alina had seen with the herd, but as it neared the pod, Dashin saw its muscles rippling beneath the thick hide. It was a younger male that had likely yet to attract a herd, but it was in its prime and confident enough not to have been overly concerned with the strange smells. As it approached, Dashin instinctively held his breath. Pritha stood at his shoulder, her eyes fixed on the beast beyond the window, her hair standing up, her muscles bunched.

Dashin glanced up into the trees, and he could just make out Drur's head leaning out over the nest, looking down. The boar sidled up against the pod, its coarse hide rubbing against the outside, the sound louder on the inside. It pulled up ferns from beneath it, jostling the pod as it did. Dashin reached out and grabbed both the wall and the top of the crash seat next to Pritha to steady himself. He heard her claws grip the seat.

The pod rocked as the stoda rooted beneath it. The creature was just beyond the window. It grunted as it took huge gouges out of the earth with those deadly tusks. It was a fearsome animal, and Dashin shivered at the thought of having to face such a beast armed with a pointy stick. He felt a wave of gratitude for Enor, who had somehow made his ordeal with the krax count so he would not have to hunt such a beast alone.

The stoda, having eaten all the ferns around the pod, was now aggressively trying to get at those beneath it. It pushed and shoved, but the pod was stuck in the groove formed beneath it. The stoda dipped a shoulder near the ground and bore up, rolling the pod free. Dashin lurched within, trying to remain upright, his pulse racing as the pod rolled over. He fell onto the door. Pritha came loose with a screech and tumbled down onto him.

As they lay there in near darkness, with most of the windows pressed into the dirt, the stoda uprooted the remaining ferns. Dashin stroked Pritha's fur, trying to keep her calm, even as his own anxiety grew. The pod was now upside down, with his back against the door and the crash seats on the ceiling. There was no way to open the door in this orientation. Thoughts of being stuck in here in the dark as they consumed their oxygen supply flashed through his mind. And if people were forced to help free him, it would result in his failing the *trial of the forest*.

The boar, having churned up the earth and eaten all the ferns, left. Dashin heard its footsteps receding at a trot. Dashin put Pritha down and looked at the dirt through the windows beneath him. There was only the tiniest sliver of daylight in the corner of one window to dispel the gloom within the pod. He stood up and tried to rock the pod, seeking to roll it back, but it barely budged at his efforts. He had a sinking feeling and looked down at Pritha, who studied him with a curious expression.

"I'm thinking," he said to the cat.

She walked over and perched on the pack that had fallen to the ceiling, which was now the floor. He took a breath and sat down, trying to see the problem as Gralan had taught him. What were the facts? They were upside down. The pod was too heavy to budge from the inside. He couldn't get outside help. He didn't have any tools that could act on the pod from the outside. There was no way he could break through the thick, hardened glass window, the ceramic walls, or the graphite tiles on the exterior. He sighed, frustrated. He didn't have a friendly stoda he could ask to roll them over. Things didn't look good.

He exhaled, and Pritha meowed. He turned to her. "I know," he said.

"Maybe I just need more force," he said to her.

He got up and, standing against one side of the pod, threw himself against the far side as forcefully as he could. The pod rocked slightly before returning to its original position. He repeated the motion several times, but he gave up, realizing he was creating a new groove in the earth for the pod to settle into.

I'm just going to go down there and sleep, he remembered saying to Alina. *It will be the easiest trial of all*, he'd said. The words bubbled up in his mind, and he sat down with a thud, panting from the effort. He rubbed his shoulder where he'd been slamming it into the wall.

Think. There had to be some way to right the pod. Thoughts of hopelessness and failure drifted up, but he pushed them away. He kept working at it, letting himself consider every impossible idea he could think of in the hopes it would spur something, anything that might be practical. Pritha crept into his lap and curled up there. He reached down and scratched behind an ear.

They didn't have enough mass or distance to throw it inside the pod to overcome the enormous relative weight of the pod or the groove in the soft soil. Every solution he thought of required some external force acting on the pod. It required him to have some footing or purchase outside the pod.

He stopped. He felt his heart rate pick up as the thought came to him. He held it delicately for a moment as he teased the edges of it. As it withstood his initial scrutiny, he grew hopeful and allowed himself to explore it. The door. It wasn't a fixed part of the pod. It could move. If he untied the rope and stood on the door and lifted the pod as high as he could and then rolled the pod to one side and leaped onto the wall, it would provide more force than he'd been able to exert so far. Would it be enough?

The door was roughly his height and width. Lying on a crash seat, it hinged at his knees and followed the curved surface of the pod, ending behind his head. If he stood on the end that opened, he could perhaps lift the pod away from it, essentially opening the pod away from the door instead of opening the door.

He tried to work out the math, but he didn't have enough data on the mass of the pod, the likely distance he could raise it, or the planet's gravity. And in any event, it wasn't like he was trying to compare alternatives. This idea was all he had.

It was going to be incredibly strenuous. Lowering the pod to the ground with mechanical advantage had taken all his strength. He would only have one or two attempts at this, and any failed attempt would further settle the pod into the groove forming beneath it.

He pushed his pack to the far end of the pod and put Pritha upon it. He closed his eyes and tried to convey what he was about to do, but quickly gave up and instead sent her a picture of her gripping the pack with her claws. She was confused, but it was the best he could do.

He untied the rope and shuffled back to the edge of the door. The pod was egg-shaped. He was at the fat end of the egg, where one might most easily balance it if they were to try standing it on end.

He took a few deep breaths, driving oxygen into his muscles in preparation, and adjusted himself to spread the weight of the pod across his shoulders. It was incredibly heavy, but before he could lose heart, he pressed up with his legs. It hardly moved, his knees straining at their limit. He reached down, put his hands on his knees, and pushed with both his arms and legs.

It budged slowly, his legs shaking as he pressed up, the weight unbearable. He felt on the brink of tearing something, but somehow he was able to straighten and then lock his legs.

Grunting and panting, he reached up and put his hands on the floor above his head. The door was only halfway open. He was not going to get it any higher. He practiced the motion in his mind. The strain was so great, he knew there would only be one attempt. The muscles in his shoulders and neck screamed. He gave up trying to determine the optimum motion and instead shifted his weight toward the side he wanted the pod to move.

The pod began to roll. He waited, hoping it would continue rolling, but it stopped, so that he stood tilted at an angle, still wedged between the pod and the door. There was only one thing left to try. He let the pod collapse and threw himself to that side of the pod. The pod teetered for a moment as the door crashed closed. Dashin feared it would roll back to where it had just been, but instead, the impact crushed the lip of the new groove, and it rolled back to its former groove and original position.

The door flew open, throwing wet dirt and fern fronds into the air. Some of it rained down inside the pod, covering them both. Pritha, who was now clinging to the foot of the crash seat, mewled in protest. There was the musky smell of stoda in the air.

Dashin whooped as he lay sprawled across both crash seats. The feeling of dread vanished, leaving him exhilarated. He panted, rolling his shoulders to make sure he'd done no serious damage. He got up and looked outside. The clearing was calm. He could see Drur's head above him. Dashin waved, feeling alive. Drur did not wave back.

He swept out the pod as best he could and then went outside. He dug up a few stones and jammed them in the dirt on either side of the pod to prevent future rolling, then he pulled the door partially closed. Feeling elated, he laid down to rest, his heart rate settling slowly. After some fussing, Pritha curled up on his chest.

As the strain ebbed from his body, his parents came to mind. They would have heard by now that his ship was missing and presumed lost. He did not doubt that they would be sad for him. However, his parents had always pursued their own interests, and he sensed they would cope with the loss by focusing on their work. His relations with them had been at arm's length, but they had always wanted the best for him. He'd grown up lonely, but he'd not understood the extent of it until he met TreeFolk here on Ndesa.

He'd found a family of sorts on the Serendipity, and he still missed them. But within this small village, on this primitive world, was the family he'd been looking for his entire life. And he was so close to having it. If he managed tomorrow's *trial of the trees*, it could all come true.

He thought about Alina and the kiss they'd shared. He touched his lips, remembering the feel of her lips on his, the scent of her, and the touch of her breath on his cheek. She had become his world. Those beautiful emerald eyes. That playful smile. No matter what it took tomorrow, he would find a way to win. He would win for himself, for Alina, his Amani, and for Pritha, whose fate was now wrapped up with his.

This trial had been more exciting than he'd planned. But the pod had held up. They were still secure. Surely the rest of the trial would pass uneventfully. In the meantime, he would spend time thinking about the next trial.

Chapter 39

He'd been staring at the items he'd brought along, trying to come up with some ruse for the *trial of the trees*. So far, he hadn't had any workable ideas, and Pritha had long since tired of this game of looking at objects.

He had a bag of Alina's tokens from her *becoming*, a bag of borka nuts with the husks on them, a bag of crollan he'd gathered on a trip to the cenote, some bits of rope, and a few tools he'd brought along in his pack. He'd imagined he'd have some flash of insight, but so far he'd made no real progress.

He knew the village valued ingenuity, but they'd been holding *becomings* for a great many generations. The rules had evolved to cover obvious ploys. Alina had told him she had some ideas she was working on, which was encouraging, but he wanted to contribute something.

He picked up one of the tokens, turning it over in his hand in the fading light. He studied the swirls and marks on the back put there by the chief. He wondered whether it had been Hedrick or Fodrick who'd been the chief during Alina's *becoming*. It was an intricate pattern, and Alina had mentioned it was often tied to patterns in the wood grain. So even if he had the time, the tools, and the skill, it would be impossible to forge whatever new pattern was on the tokens for his *becoming* onto these older ones.

He flipped them over and looked at the corsol on this particular token. It was a reasonable likeness of the monkey-like creature. He wondered who the artist was.

He picked up the crollan, hefting the bag. He'd imagined slathering branches with it. But Alina had put that ruse to rest. It would take an enormous quantity of the material to cover enough branches to make a basket unreachable. With the tiny amount he'd collected, it would only be a nuisance for the chaser even if they happened upon it. It was not worth the time it would take to deploy.

Likewise with the borka husks. He couldn't think of a way to use it effectively, short of grappling with the chaser. And his chances of catching a chaser were essentially zero. Seeing Drur in the trees put an end to any thought of outmaneuvering a TreePerson. Although having faced Alina, Hurza, and Kani in the trees had not imparted any hope of doing so.

Was it possible to set up some type of trap with the rope and some trees? He'd read of such traps but didn't have any idea of how to go about setting one up, and even had he known how, he could not think of a way to ensure a chaser would happen on it. He would be following a different path than they would. He still struggled to find his own *TruePath*. He couldn't imagine what the *TruePath* would be like for Drur or Aor.

There was also the matter of a dish for the feast. But for that one, he had an idea. He couldn't hope to come up with a dish on his own, never having cooked anything in his life. But he had something in the pod that might help. It would be risky but perhaps worth it.

Dashin's stomach growled. Pritha opened an eye and looked up at him.

"Should we have something to eat?" he asked her.

She sat up and licked her lips.

He pulled over his pack, pulled out another banda leaf with dried meat in it, and unrolled it on the empty bed. Pritha hopped over and began to eat it, chewing the meat to extract the flavor before swallowing it.

This surprised him. He'd imagined she would gobble it up, but she seemed to enjoy savoring the food. He wondered if this was a natural condition for krax or something she'd acquired from the *melding*.

Dashin ate a few of his rolled-up banda leaves, relishing the nut paste, dried fruit, and meat within. As he ate, he watched Pritha finish hers and then lick the banda leaf clean. Her tongue made the leaf wet so that it stuck to the bed.

Dashin remembered how the leaves clung to him when Enor applied them over the balm. He peeled the leaf Pritha had just cleaned from the bed where it was stuck and rubbed it between his fingers. It was a tough leaf and very fibrous.

He swallowed the last of his banda roll and took a drink from his water gourd, giving some to Pritha as well. He felt the urge to relieve himself and looked out the windows into the growing gloom. It would soon be night. Once he was certain the surroundings were safe, he opened the door and stepped outside. Pritha joined him, lifting her head and sniffing.

"Stay close," he said to the cat, who ignored him.

He took a few steps from the door and relieved himself. When he finished and turned around, Pritha was gone. He ran to the door, looked within the pod, and then around the periphery, but she was nowhere to be seen. He looked down for some trace of her in the soft earth and saw tiny footprints leading off into the forest.

"Pritha," he hissed, trying to call her back without attracting other creatures.

He listened, but there was no answer. There was a sudden flurry of activity in the bushes at some distance in line with the footprints, followed by a loud screeching sound. He ran toward it, his heart pounding as he drew the flint knife on his belt.

He hadn't covered ten paces when Pritha appeared before him with a fat bird in her mouth. "Pritha," he said. "I told you to stay by the pod."

She strode past him as though he hadn't said a word and climbed into the pod with the bird. Dashin followed her in and pulled the door closed, tying off the rope to leave it ajar a crack to let the cool air in.

"What were you thinking?" Dashin asked, taking the bed next to her.

Pritha ignored him, ripping at the feathers and skin as she tore into the bird. She was making a mess. Guts and feathers were being strewn about the pod, and if it continued much longer, the entire interior would be coated in both.

"Here, let me help," Dashin said, reaching for the bird.

Pritha pulled it away and fixed him with a hard stare.

He closed his eyes and reached for her. He touched her mind and sent her images of him removing the feathers, gutting the bird, and then handing it back to her. She seemed to consider this, apparently wondering why he'd want the guts and feathers, but willing to part with both since he'd shared his dried meat with her.

He rolled his eyes and then opened them. He took the bird from Pritha. It was still warm. He took out his knife and plucked and skinned it. He'd never done either, and it took him some time to find a reasonable way to do it, but he was able to separate the meat from the less edible parts of the bird. He gave the meat to Pritha, who dug into it. He gathered up the rest and tossed it outside.

Pritha stopped eating to watch as he tossed *his portion* outside. She fixed him an odd look and then resumed tearing flesh from the bird. Once she'd eaten all but a tiny bit of meat from it, she nudged the carcass across the seat, offering it to him.

"No thanks, I'm not *that* hungry," he replied, pushing it back.

She cocked her head to one side, regarding him, and then leaned down again and resumed stripping the last bits from it.

Dashin tried to ignore her as she sucked and licked at it. Trying to think about tomorrow's trial or what Alina might be doing now, or anything but the sound of Pritha working the carcass.

When she was at last finished, she pushed it off the bed and began cleaning her paws and face. Dashin poured some water into his hand and let her use it to clean herself. Once done, she curled up on the bed and was soon snoring. Dashin took the carcass and threw it out the door.

The evening air cooled as night approached. It would be a long night for Drur above, Dashin thought with a smile. He would have to remain vigilant while Dashin slept in comfort. He stretched out on the bed next to Pritha. He worked out the soreness in his shoulders, closed his eyes, and was soon asleep.

He woke to find Pritha alert and standing on his chest, looking up through the window into the darkness above them. He blinked his eyes open, trying to discern what she was looking at. He closed his eyes and reached for her senses, and through them, he saw Drur in the trees above them speaking with someone obscured by branches.

Dashin sat up, opened the door, and closed his eyes again, reaching for Pritha's senses. They were speaking too faintly to make out the words, but they were arguing. Drur was agitated. As Dashin strained to hear, the other figure leaned in. It was Hedrick.

Dashin was fully awake now. He had no idea what was going on, but whatever this was, it wasn't good. Hedrick was yelling at Drur, who was looking away. Then it grew quiet. Drur remained where he was. Hedrick dropped toward the pod.

Dashin watched him come, his features growing clearer as he drew closer. Hedrick was wearing a pack and lanyards.

He stopped just above the forest floor and shed his pack. He reached into it, pulled out a handful of something dark, and tossed it into the ferns near the pod. He reached into the pack again, grabbed more, and tossed it on the other side of the pod.

"What are you doing?" Dashin yelled up at him.

Hedrick didn't respond. He kept throwing whatever it was into the uprooted ferns. Whatever it was made a thick, thumping sound as it hit the ground. When he'd emptied his pack, he glared at Dashin before climbing back up to Drur. He spoke sternly to the lad, who sat mute, looking off, then climbed away and was soon out of sight.

Dashin opened the door and ran outside, searching the uprooted ferns the stoda had left behind for what Hedrick had been throwing. He had a terrible hunch as he crawled through the freshly churned dirt, feeling about blindly. Pritha raced by him and stopped nearby, sniffing at something. Dashin crawled over to her and reached for the dark mass she was sniffing. He picked it up. It was as he feared. Meat. It was meat. All around him, Hedrick had seeded the area with rotting meat. Whether this was meat left over from the krax he'd fought a few days ago, or from some new kill, he had no idea. He threw the slab as far as he could from the pod and turned around.

Could he find them all? And even if he did, what would he do with them? Carry them away? The idea of running through the forest at night with armfuls of meat didn't sound like one of his better ideas. The only alternative was to lock the door and ride out the night. He sensed it would soon be horrific out here in the ferns. The smell would draw every predator downwind of the pod.

He picked up Pritha, who seemed fascinated by the meat, and hurried back to the pod. He was nearing the door when he saw them, an entire pack of turga near the door to the pod. Three of the beasts were eating bits of meat they'd found in the ferns, but the largest of the pack stood with its eyes on him as two others sidled up next to it.

Hedrick must have been dropping bits of meat on the forest floor as he'd approached, leading the predators here. There wouldn't be any waiting involved after all.

Dashin crept toward the door. His body trembled, and though the night air was cool, this trembling was visceral. Pritha was alert in his arms, her body bunched against his chest, her muscles coiled. He prayed she wouldn't do anything to precipitate things. The alpha had its eyes on Dashin and watched as he approached. The other two moved off to the sides, cutting off any escape. He moved slowly toward the pod, counting on them to wait until they were in position before falling on him.

Two other turgas joined the alpha, coming up on either side to replace the two on his flanks. He felt the pod at his back. He groped for the door with his free hand, the other clinging to Pritha, who was hissing. Barely any moonlight made it through the canopy to the forest floor. The darkness was no obstacle for Pritha, but there was no way he was going to close his eyes to reach for her senses. He was close, so close.

The turgas sprang for him in unison. He screamed as he fell inside, tossing Pritha behind him and reaching for the rope. He managed to grab it and yanked down hard as he jerked his feet inside. The door swung down and slammed into the neck of the alpha, who narrowly missed taking Dashin's leg. The thick neck barely felt the impact from the door. The teeth snapped as it fought to burrow into the pod. An army of jaws snapped just beyond the door.

Dashin scrambled to keep his legs free of the jaws, putting one foot and then the other on the walls on either side of the door. He hung from the rope, applying as much force to it as his mass would allow. It wasn't enough. The creature was stronger and was pushing its way in. Another joined it, wedging its head into the crack. The two beasts pressed against the door, lifting him from the floor. Frantic, he sought purchase and moved his feet to the ceiling, where he could bring more strength to bear.

He planted his feet and held the rope fast as he straightened his legs and pushed, straining to squeeze the door closed against their bodies. The second turga yelped and pulled free of the door, the pressure having driven it out. This also stopped the advance of the alpha, who wriggled beneath him now, trying to reach him, teeth snapping a hand's breadth from his back.

The pressure on his arms and legs was enormous. The beast was huge and all muscle. Its breath was foul. Hot saliva spattered onto his back. His arms strained to hold the rope against the heavily muscled beast. He felt the rope slipping, and as he reached up to get a better grip, the alpha wriggled in. Its nose brushed his back, sending a bolt of fear through him. Chemicals flooded his bloodstream. His heart thundered in his chest. He groaned and pulled with every remaining shred of strength he had.

How could Hedrick hate him this much? Fodrick had told him the story of what had happened to his previous village. Had it changed him so much as to warrant this? What threat could Dashin possibly be to him? He was going to die horribly? For what?

The rope continued to slip through his sweaty hands. He kept having to readjust his grip, fighting to hold on. He cried out as his arms shook and his hands burned from the effort. His grip was failing. He visualized the position of his flint knife on his belt and the motion it would take to free it. He would not go easy. He would fight until the end. The snarling beyond the door grew as the creatures outside somehow sensed the change.

The wet muzzle struck his back. The recurved teeth snagged his tunic. The alpha tugged fiercely at it, shaking its head to and fro. Dashin held on, his legs shaking now too, from the intense effort.

And then there was a flash as something glanced off him and landed on the alpha's head. There was a deafening screech. The alpha thrashed even more vigorously as Dashin fought to hold on. Pritha, it was Pritha. He couldn't see her, but the action behind him was vicious, snapping jaws, screeching krax, and hot liquid on his back. He couldn't let go, lest the other turgas join the fray. They were snarling and snapping just beyond the door, claws scratching at its surface.

Dashin's tunic came free as the pressure on the rope turned into insistent jerks. A furry ball of fury churned behind him, its body bumping into his back repeatedly as it unleashed mayhem and pain. The alpha writhed, pulling back, fighting to get free, it seemed. He couldn't be sure, but as the rope slipped in his hands from a sharp tug, he felt the creature yank itself mostly free.

Oh no, Pritha. Dashin was terrified it would take Pritha with it. He yelled for Pritha, reaching for her with his mind, pleading with her to stay. He heard one last screech as she leapt away. The alpha tore itself free of the door, which slammed closed. Dashin secured it with shaking hands.

Pritha screamed in defiance, her voice deafening in the tiny space. Her hair was on end, her eyes wild in the gloom. He pulled her to him, cradling her as his shaking hands ran over her body. Somehow, despite the fierce battle, she had sustained no significant damage he could find. Perhaps the turga pinned and prone had been unable to find enough purchase to reach her.

He sat up and looked out the window for the turgas, but they were gone. He laid down, shaking, holding Pritha to his chest. Her tiny, insistent heartbeat slowed. He was covered in sweat and completely spent from the extreme effort. Once he stopped shaking, he could not keep his eyes open.

Chapter 40

There may have been other predators in the ferns that night, but if they came, Dashin never knew. It was light when he awoke, and the sight brought tears to his eyes. The trial was over. He looked outside, and it seemed safe. He opened the door and filled his lungs with the cool morning air. He was alive. Somehow, they'd survived what he'd imagined would be the simplest of the trials.

Only one remained. Today would decide it all.

He looked up, and Drur was waving at him. He waved back.

He pulled out the rest of their food, and he and Pritha finished it all. Not a crumb was left. He packed his belongings and retrieved a storage case from a compartment in the pod, trying to work out the route he would need to take from here. If he could find his way there, it would help with his dish for the feast. He also fished out an empty water bottle and added it to his pack. With his pack full, he put on the tree swaddle, tucked Pritha into it, and touched his forehead to the kitten's.

"We did it, girl," he said.

She rubbed her head against his.

He stepped out, closed the door, and jammed sticks into the mechanism to keep it closed. He put on his useless lanyards and climbed up to Drur without using them.

Dashin no longer cared what people thought of him. After last night, he wasn't going to plead with people to like him anymore. Hedrick had tried to kill him. Drur had watched. If they were coming for him, he wasn't going to make it easy for any of them.

Drur was decidedly uncomfortable as Dashin reached him. He seemed to be searching for something to say.

"Did I pass this trial?" Dashin asked, his tone flat.

Drur nodded. "Yes, you fulfilled the requirements," he replied sheepishly.

"There were a few rules I wasn't advised of," Dashin said, his eyes on Drur.

Drur looked away, unable to meet Dashin's. "I was not a part of that," he spat.

"You sat there and watched it happen," Dashin replied, angry.

Drur blushed, his skin a dark emerald. He nodded. "I'm sorry," he said, looking away.

"Are you?"

Drur looked back. "I am. More than you know."

The words were sincere, and they took Dashin by surprise. There'd been an argument in the trees last night. Drur was newly *of the tribe*. Hedrick had been chief and still held much power. What could Drur have done? But something didn't add up.

"Why did you argue with Hedrick?"

Drur was shocked that Dashin could have heard. He swallowed. "We had words."

"Why?"

"He wanted my silence on the matter," he said, his eyes even.

"Did he get it?"

"He did," Drur said without apology.

"In trade for what?" Dashin asked, disgusted.

"For my sister," Drur answered, his eyes hard.

Dashin wasn't aware Drur had a sister. "You have a sister?"

"I will not speak of this with you," Drur said, gathering his things.

Dashin regretted having come to a hasty conclusion, sensing that Drur was struggling with the decision. Perhaps he'd misjudged him.

Drur adjusted his lanyards and then turned to Dashin. "Whether you believe this or not, I am glad you survived the trial. Though others did not wish it, I hoped you would prevail."

"Well, you'll get a chance to beat me in the next trial," Dashin said.

"No," Drur replied, "I decided last night that I would not be the chaser. I agreed to say nothing of Hedrick's being here last night and to deny it if you brought it up, but I will do nothing further to stand in your way."

Dashin was stunned. The further declaration that Drur would deny what had happened made him angry. But then Dashin realized Drur had offered this to warn him Hedrick intended to discredit his word before the tribe, should Dashin try to expose him. He searched Drur's face for any sign of falsehood but found none. The lad's face was set, at peace with his words.

He took a breath. He didn't know the details, but he could see Drur felt trapped. "Listen," Dashin said. "I'm sorry to have accused you without knowing your side of the story. If I somehow manage to prevail today, I would like us to be friends."

Drur smiled. "I would like that, Dashin." Then his face growing sad, he added. "Though seeing you move through the forest, I can't imagine how you could succeed in the next trial, even without me chasing."

"Perhaps I will surprise you."

"I hope so," Drur said.

"Why don't you go back to the village? You're much faster than I am, and I'm sure you're hungry. I know the way. I'll be along soon."

"Are you certain?" Drur asked, glancing up eagerly through the trees.

"I am," Dashin said.

Drur nodded and then leapt into the trees. Dashin watched him sail away, marveling at his grace. Dashin sensed how much Drur enjoyed it, his love for movement evident in every lanyard swing.

Dashin climbed up, moving away from the village as he ascended, needing to make a stop before returning.

He stopped when he reached the canopy. He sat down on a thick bough and wedged his pack between two stout branches. He fished out his water gourd, drank some, and gave some to Pritha.

She lapped up the water and then looked at him.

"This is either going to be a brilliant idea," he said. "Or, it's going to be the stupidest thing I've ever done."

She looked up at him, twitching her nose as though she was concerned it might be the latter.

Dashin looked over at the tree a short distance away with the mirha nest in it. He took a breath. He pulled out the storage container from the pod and snapped it open to reveal the emergency space suit. He rubbed the fabric between his fingers. It seemed too thin to provide sufficient protection, but they'd claimed the material would resist any puncture. He sighed. He was about to find out.

He took off the tree swaddle and nestled Pritha behind his pack. He closed his eyes and sent her an image of her staying there as he moved away. She sent him several images of him carrying her, but he insisted, and after a time, she relented. He opened his eyes, and she was looking away, studying some far-off tree. He rolled his eyes.

He donned the space suit, ensuring the wrist and ankle seals were secure, before donning the helmet. It was hot inside, and without tanks or even a rebreather, it was going to get stuffy in here fast. He tied a length of rope around his waist and hung the water bottle from it.

He sent Pritha another reminder to stay here. She didn't acknowledge him. When he opened his eyes, she was grooming herself.

He moved toward the hive. The rubber soles of his boots gripped the branches, but over the past moon, he'd gotten used to the feel of wood beneath his bare feet. It felt odd now to be wearing boots, his toes searching but not finding the bark.

The limited visibility of his visor forced him to rely on the images of the *trees to be* in his mind for his feet to find purchase. He steadied himself with his hands on nearby limbs as he slid along the branch.

As he neared the hive, his motion in the trees was enough to jostle it and alarm the creatures within. A growing swarm of mirha collected outside, zipping about in random patterns, looking for the source of the disturbance. Growing increasingly concerned, he missed a step and grabbed the branch the hive was on to catch himself. The impact shook the hive. An instant later, the entire swarm of angry insects was on him. His visor grew dark with their bodies, and he felt them crawling across his suit. Each of the fat insects was about the length of his finger. Their fat, furry, blue-black bodies were filled with a toxin he had no desire ever to feel again. Their buzzing was deafening even inside the suit.

He held his breath, awaiting the excruciating pain. His heart pounded in his chest as he felt hundreds of points pressing against his flesh. He closed his eyes and prayed the engineered fabric lived up to its hype. After a few moments, he let out a breath. So far, their stingers were proving ineffective.

He felt Pritha's alarm, and he sensed she was on the verge of rushing to him. He calmed himself and sent an image of her sitting in the swaddle. He tried to communicate that he was safe and would come back soon. She was unhappy with the response but acquiesced.

He wiped a glove across the visor and glimpsed his surroundings before it was covered again. The air was hot and becoming stale. Sweat ran down his face and body. As he stood there blind, perched on a branch, and covered with the insects, this no longer seemed like a brilliant idea. But there was no turning back. He shuffled toward the nest again, feeling his way blindly with his feet on one branch and his hands on the other, until he felt the hive with his glove. Okay, now what?

With the swarm on him, it was likely there were no creatures left in the hive. He reached up and broke the hive in two. He had the bottom half in his hand while the top half was still attached to the branch. He leaned against the branch with his shoulder and wiped his visor again with his free hand, being careful not to drop the half he held.

The half in his hand was filled with nectar. The upper half contained one large insect. If these insects were like Ancaran sand wasps, this creature would be their queen. He leaned his chest against the branch to stabilize himself and fished the large insect from the nest. The swarm grew even more frantic. He peeked again, wiping his visor with his forearm. The large insect had small, misshapen wings and seemed lethargic. He threw it off into space, watching it fall. It landed in some branches far below.

He held his breath and waited for a beat. Most of the swarm dove toward the queen, surrounding her. Finally, he could see again. There were still many angry insects crawling over him, but the majority of the swarm had chased the queen. He peeled the bottom half of the hive away from the large head-sized blob of nectar, and when he had it cleaned, he pulled the empty water bottle from the rope at his waist and stuffed it in there, being careful to keep any of the insects from crawling inside. It took some time, and there were plenty of insects around him, but not enough that he had to wipe his visor.

When he'd filled the large bottle to the brim, he screwed the top back onto the bottle and hung it from the rope on his waist.

He took a circuitous path back to Pritha, stopping several times along the way to brush insects from his suit. They followed him and attacked him repeatedly, but their efforts flagged as time passed. Over time, they left to rejoin the others. He headed back toward Pritha, and when he was close enough for her to see him, he had her inspect him as he turned slowly around. He closed his eyes and looked over his suit through her vision. When he was convinced he was free of insects, he made it the rest of the way to her. He checked the seals on his wrists and ankles before removing the suit.

He was soaked. He removed the glove with the thick blob of nectar on it first, turning it inside-out to preserve it. Then he removed the helmet and the rest of the suit, stowing them back in the storage container. After placing the glove with the nectar and the nectar-laden water bottle on top of the suit, he snapped the lid shut and sat down next to Pritha to catch his breath. She wrinkled her nose at the smell of him, sweat mixed with fear, mixed with the antiseptic smell of the suit. He closed his eyes, and she sent him a picture of him washing by the cistern of Rigin's hut. It seemed like a great idea to him, too.

Though he wanted to sit and rest, he knew they would be wondering where he was. He didn't know when the *trial of the trees* was to begin. But they would likely be worried now that he hadn't arrived. This stop had taken more time than he'd planned.

At least he had his good lanyards with him. He put them on, piled everything else in the pack, and slipped on the tree swaddle. Pritha complained at the smell of him again. He ignored her. He launched himself into the trees and made his way back toward the village. It felt good to be moving through the trees again. His shoulders were sore from the encounters with the stoda and the turgas, but they loosened up as he went.

He would make it to the cache, drop off his lanyards, and then make it the rest of the way to the village with the useless lanyards. He looked up, and it was nearing midday. He couldn't wait to get back, wash up, get something to eat, and maybe even take a nap before the *trial of the trees*.

Chapter 41

Alina paced along the edge of the platform, waiting for Dashin and Drur to return. She hadn't slept at all, the many things that could have gone wrong parading through her mind. Several times she reached for him with her senses despite the distance, yearning to feel the touch of his mind and forcing herself to imagine she could sense him, secure and asleep.

She'd been here since well before dawn, unable to lie in bed one moment more. It was still quiet in the village when Aor approached. He was carrying his spear, apparently just coming off guard duty.

"How are you doing?" he asked.

She shrugged, continuing to look out into the trees.

He seemed about to continue on, but stopped and came to stand next to her, looking out into the forest with her.

"It must be good news," he said.

Alina turned to him, confused.

Aor motioned into the forest with his chin. "If anything bad had happened, Drur would have come back already."

She choked back a sob, pressing her lips together to contain the emotion that rose within her. Aor was right. If Dashin had been killed, Drur would have come back. If he'd been injured or had failed the trial, they both would have been back. That there'd been no news eased the terror that had been building within her. *It would be fine*, she told herself.

"Thanks," she said, dabbing at her eyes.

They stood in silence, listening to the breeze rustle the leaves. The calm before the forest woke, a time she'd always loved, now seemed oppressive as she waited for morning.

"It was more than duty, wasn't it?" Aor asked without looking at her.

She tensed at the question. Clearly, he'd noticed the change in her. She gave up pretending, not that she believed she could have, even had she tried. "Yes," she said.

"I'm sad for you," he said. "I've grown to respect him."

She turned to look at him, wondering if he was serious. She saw sadness in his eyes as well as concern for her.

"He would be good for our village," she said.

"Perhaps," Aor replied. "But it is not to be. Even if he manages to pass the *trial of the forest*, he'll never pass the *trial of the trees*."

Alina exhaled. She looked back out into the forest. "Thank you," she said.

She felt Aor turn to her. "For what?"

She shrugged. "For caring enough to share your concern."

He put his hand on her arm and squeezed it, then turned from her and walked across the platform.

She swallowed, the lump in her throat making it difficult to do so. *He's alive,* she told herself, *and it's almost dawn.* She glanced up into the canopy, where the first rays of sun were just now touching the topmost leaves. Her heart soared. Tears flowed down her cheeks, and she bit her bottom lip.

She felt footsteps on the platform. Glancing over her shoulder, she saw her mother approaching. The cistern of emotions within her brimmed over, and a flood of tears spilled down her cheeks.

Her mother strode over and wrapped her arms around her. "Oh, Lina, that's it. Let it out," she whispered into her ear, stroking her hair and pulling her close.

Hurza and Kani arrived and rushed over as well. All three pressed against her, their heads touching hers. She stood there with them until the torrent within eased and then abated. The morning light kissed the branches above them as the birds announced the day.

"The sun will soon reach the forest floor," her mother said.

Alina sniffled and nodded, trying to compose herself. The rest of the village would soon be on the platform to await the results, and she didn't want to look like a blubbering child. Kani ran to the kitchen and fetched a wet towel for her. Alina took it and wiped her face.

As the village gathered, her mother and friends looked into the forest. Alina took some deep breaths, composing herself.

"There was no news during the night," Rigin said, joining them.

Alina nodded. It was a hopeful sign. She could tell Rigin hadn't slept either. Her eyes were tired, her face tense with worry. Solvan and Matse clung to either side of her. The children peered off into the trees, Solvan subdued and quiet, Matse mumbling softly to herself.

Her father bustled up. He was carrying his medical bags. Alina looked from him to the forest, fearing he had heard something awful and was coming to provide medical care. Had Drur reached him, not wanting to alert the village? Was Dashin injured?

Seeing her mounting panic, he spoke. "It's just in case, Lina. No one has called for me." He held her eyes until his words dulled the dread that had sprung within her.

She closed her eyes and took a breath, calming herself. Why was the morning taking so long? She watched as the sun's rays moved down through the forest. It was taking ages.

Finally, someone in the village said that the sun had surely reached the ground.

Alina closed her eyes and imagined how long it might take Dashin to emerge from the pod, gather his things, and climb back up to her. He would be using the regular lanyards, carrying gear, and Pritha, so the climb would be slow. Interminably slow.

"Can you eat something?" her mother asked.

Alina shook her head. Her stomach was one large knot.

Villagers chatted nervously in groups behind her, their tension making her even more uncomfortable. Her mother rubbed her back.

A covey of birds took flight from the forest below, rising through the trees. They were coming. She held her breath, her heart swelling with hope. She peered into the forest, squinting to catch a glimpse of them, and then she saw Drur moving toward them. She grinned, but the grin didn't last. Drur was moving fast, too fast for Dashin to be following.

What could it mean? She looked at her mother,

"Don't jump to conclusions," she said. "Let's wait to hear from Drur. He'll be here in a moment, and then we'll know."

"Why isn't Dashin with him?" she asked, searching the forest behind Drur.

Her mother took her chin and turned her head to her. "We don't know anything, yet. Drur does not seem agitated. Let's wait to hear," she repeated.

Alina swallowed, her lips taut, her heart pounding. She closed her eyes, took a breath, and turned back to the forest.

Drur raced toward them and then alit, featherlight, onto the platform as a hundred questions met him. Alina held her breath. He raised his hand, and the platform went still.

"Dashin prevailed," he began. The questions resurfaced so that he had to hold up his hand again.

"He asked me to come ahead. He's climbing behind me and should be here soon."

Alina exhaled, and her mother squeezed her hand.

"Did the trial go well?" Fodrick asked.

Drur shook his head. "It was a challenging trial," he replied, wiping his brow.

Drur's mother pushed some of the villagers aside and took her son by the arm. "He's been out all day and night and has just arrived. Let the boy eat and drink something before he tells the tale," she said. She pulled him to a table she had set up with food and pressed him to eat, standing guard over him.

Alina was dying to know the details, and she could see the rest of the village wanted them as well. She looked out into the forest as Drur ate, watching for any sign of Dashin.

Drur ate sparingly, only finishing one large slab of nutbread and taking a few sips of water before he declared himself ready, and his mother reluctantly stepped back. The villagers sat down on the platform around him to hear the tale. Hedrick, for some reason, seemed ill at ease, looking from Drur to the forest and back repeatedly. It was odd behavior even for him, and something about it made her skin crawl.

Drur cleared his throat and began by explaining that somehow Dashin had managed to move the egg he'd arrived in to the forest floor and had used it as his shelter. There was some discussion about the egg's size since most of the village had not seen it. They wanted to know how heavy it might be, and then the discussion devolved around how he might have gotten it to the forest floor. Fodrick asked Drur to continue with the tale and to leave discussions of the egg for later.

Drur mentioned the morning had gone uneventfully but that after midday, a male stoda had arrived and pushed the egg over while it was rooting for fern bulbs. The egg had rolled over, trapping Dashin within it. There was a collective gasp at this, everyone hanging on Drur's words. He explained that he could see the egg shaking subtly, but it seemed incredibly heavy, and Dashin could not right it. Drur had been certain this would signal the end of the trial, and he was preparing to return to the village for help, assuming it would take ten men to right it. But then, somehow, Dashin had lifted the egg from the ground by himself and flipped it over. Drur had been stunned to see it, and had he not witnessed it himself, he would never have believed such a thing possible.

The hair on the back of Alina's neck was standing on end, her skin tingling at the tale. She'd helped Dashin move that egg to the ground. It was so heavy she couldn't imagine how he could have managed it alone. He must have been desperate. She couldn't wait to see him.

The crowd discussed the matter, arguing about the feat, some disputing Drur's account of the scale of it, while others marveled at yet another mysterious accomplishment.

"There is more," Drur announced, looking at Hedrick.

There was something there. Hedrick had been involved somehow. She was sure of it now. Hedrick narrowed his eyes, and they stared at each other for a moment. Drur turned away and looked at the village. Alina could see from the looks villagers gave each other that others had noted the exchange.

"In the middle of the night, while Dashin was outside the egg to..." he paused for a moment, "investigating something," he said, leaving the thought unfinished, "he was set upon by a pack of turgas."

Alina's heart sank. A pack of those terrible creatures. She was frozen. What was he doing outside the pod at night? He'd sworn to her that he would stay inside. And, surely if he'd been set upon by a pack of the creatures and survived, he would be gravely injured. How could Drur have let him climb alone?

The village was in an uproar, unable to make sense of this news. But it went quiet again as Drur continued. "He managed somehow to fight them all off."

"Did he have a weapon? He was not allowed to take a weapon," Hedrick spat. His face darkened, and he grew angry.

Drur turned to him. "From what I could see, he used his hands."

"That's impossible," Hedrick sputtered. "One man facing a pack of turgas with his hands. You expect us to believe that?" he demanded, his hands balled into fists, rage on his face. Alina had never seen him thus, nor, she imagined, had anyone else, judging from the looks on the faces around her.

"I can't control what folk believe. But I give you all my word on it." Drur answered, looking hard at Hedrick, daring him to contradict him.

Hedrick looked away, fuming, his lips a thin line.

Alina wanted to scream. What were they talking about? Where was Dashin? Why did Drur leave him alone in the forest?

The muttering arose again, and Alina walked back over to the platform's edge. She couldn't bear to hear any more of the terrible things he'd endured or to try to decipher the mysterious exchange going on between Hedrick and Drur. She needed to see Dashin for herself, to lay her eyes on him and wrap her arms around him to assure herself that he was whole. Her parents, friends, Rigin, and her wards joined her, all of them waiting silently for Dashin.

Alina turned to Hurza. "Did you manage to convince Aor to chase?" she asked, desperate.

Hurza shook her head. "I'm sorry. I tried everything I could think of."

Alina nodded, reached over, and squeezed her friend's hand. If Hurza said she'd tried everything, then Alina was confident she'd done so.

They waited much longer than it would have taken for Dashin to climb from the ground several times over, even laden or injured. Fodrick came over to them. "We're going to organize a party to go out and search for him."

The words took her by surprise, and she felt her knees go soft, the world tilting away from her. Only her mother's hand on her back kept her standing. Alina bit her lip and nodded, her body beginning to tremble.

"Over there!" someone yelled.

All heads turned to Narat, who was pointing into the forest. They followed his finger, and she spotted Dashin walking through the trees, dragging his old lanyards behind him. Alina tried to leap into the trees, but Fodrick held her arm. She looked down, unable to understand why her body would not move. Seeing the hand, she turned, confused.

"He must reach the platform without help for the *trial of the forest* to complete successfully," he said.

She almost burst out crying at his kindness. She might have ruined everything. Fodrick had saved them. She nodded and put her hand on his. He squeezed her arm before moving back to the center of the platform.

Dashin looked beyond exhausted, but appeared to be whole. His tunic was ripped and tattered, part of it hanging open from one shoulder. His hair dripped rivulets onto his face. What could have taken him this long, given he didn't seem injured? How had he survived a pack of turgas without a scratch? She fidgeted in place, willing him forward, needing him to reach her.

As he stepped onto the platform, a cheer went up. It wasn't unanimous nor jubilant. Alina crashed into him, wrapping her arms around him. He was haggard and panting, though it was not yet midday. What was left of his tunic was soaked through.

Once the uneven cheer subsided, Fodrick spoke. "Drur has informed us that you prevailed in the *trial of the forest*, Dashin. And, from what we heard, it was a true test of valor. Remarkably, only one trial remains. Unfortunately, that trial begins at midday."

Everyone looked up, Alina craning up without releasing him to do so as well. Midday was almost upon them. Her heart sank.

"I suggest you eat and drink something. The horn will sound soon to begin the trial."

How had it gotten so late? Alina could have sworn there was still loads of time before midday. She had to pull herself together. While Dashin had been fighting for his life, she had been worrying. She had too much to do in the moments remaining before the trial.

She touched her forehead to his. The familiar feeling brought tears to her eyes, but she pushed it aside. How could he have gotten caught outside the egg at night, *looking around*, as Drur had put it? She was angry, but that would have to wait.

"How are you, Amani?" she asked, her hands on him, needing the heat of his body and the beating heart in his chest to convince herself he was truly here. She could feel the eyes of the tribe upon her, but in this moment, it was only a leaf on the wind to her.

"Better now," he said, trying on a weary smile.

She nodded. "Get cleaned up and get something to eat. I have things to do here. We were not able to get Aor to chase, so you'll have to fly since it will be Drur who chases," she said.

"I don't think so," he replied.

"What are you talking about?"

"Drur told me he wouldn't chase."

She stopped, unable to imagine such a conversation.

"Are you certain?" she asked, wondering if the heat had touched him.

"I think so."

She grinned, squeezing his hands. "That is wonderful news. Quickly, go get cleaned up. I'll tell the others."

Dashin left for Rigin's hut with Rigin and her wards in tow. Alina ran over to her parents and friends. "Dashin says that Drur told him he would not chase."

"What?" Hurza said. "Why would Drur say such a thing?"

"I don't know, but maybe you could find out. There may still be time to make sure it is Aor."

Hurza beamed at her and raced away.

Alina took a breath. "Kani, can you help me? We have sweets to see to."

Chapter 42

Dashin's heart pounded in his chest. Somehow, he'd imagined he'd have more time before the next trial. His dream of a nap evaporated, but at least he'd get to wash up and grab a bite to eat.

"Do you mind feeding Pritha?" he asked Matse, who was close at hand.

She nodded, eager arms reaching toward him as he pulled Pritha from the swaddle. She hugged the kitten to her, and Pritha rubbed her head against the girl's cheek.

"I'll make you something to eat, too," Rigin said, following Matse into the hut.

Solvan helped him shed his pack. Dashin removed the swaddle, his belt, and his soaked tunic.

The lad's eyes went wide as he held the tunic in his hands. The back was in tatters, the tunic held together by a few remaining threads. "Drur said you fought off a pack of turgas with your hands," he stammered.

Dashin was startled by the question. Apparently, Drur had shared some of the tale. "Yes, it was something like that," Dashin replied. "Though it was really Pritha who fought them off."

"That is so *round*," the boy exclaimed.

"What else did Drur say?" Dashin asked as he filled a bucket from the cistern and dumped it over himself. The water sluiced over his skin. It was deliciously cool and refreshing. He refilled the bucket and began soaping up. Solvan took a second soapstone and scrubbed his back.

Solvan related the tale. Dashin noted there was no mention of Hedrick or the meat. It brought to mind the argument and the cryptic statement about Drur's mysterious sister.

Dashin rinsed himself clean and stepped into Sneva's room to change into fresh clothes. Solvan brought in his belt and all the bags he had hung from it. Dashin slipped the belt around his waist and reaffixed the bags to it. He didn't know if his idea for the trial would work, but it was worth a try.

He stepped into the common room. Rigin laid out a huge plate of food.

"If I eat all of that, I won't be able to walk, let alone use my lanyards," Dashin said, chuckling as he reached for a banda roll.

"Eat what you want," Rigin replied, filling the cup next to him with water.

Matse, seated next to him, had Pritha on her lap and was feeding the kitten pieces of dried meat and dried fruit from her open hand. Pritha had not been partial to dried fruit before, but she seemed to have developed a taste for it and was eating it as well as the meat.

"Oh, Rigin, I wonder if you could help me with something?" Dashin asked, remembering the feast.

"Of course, Dashin, anything," she replied, taking the chair next to him.

"I understand it is customary for successful candidates to present a dish at the feast," he said, chewing.

She nodded. "Dashin, no one expects..." she began.

"I know," he said, cutting off the reply. "Alina explained everyone would be so surprised that I prevailed that they'd be happy with a handful of nuts."

Rigin chuckled.

"But if I happen to prevail," he said, and he saw Rigin about to object. "I mean *when* I prevail." She smiled at the correction. "I would like to offer something special."

"I can prepare something if you like," she said.

"That would be wonderful. I collected an ingredient on my way up from the ground," he said.

She waved it away. "That is not necessary. I have everything I need here."

"Perhaps, but I'd like to contribute."

"Of course," she said, humoring him.

"Solvan, can you fetch my pack?"

The boy bounded out and returned a moment later, dragging the pack behind him by a strap.

Dashin reached inside and undid the snaps to the storage container. He retrieved the glove and handed it to Rigin. She looked at it, the glove wet in her hand, wrinkling her nose, confused at what it might be.

Dashin took it from her and turned it right-side out, revealing the fist-sized blob of mirha nectar.

Rigin inhaled sharply. "How did you find an empty nest with this much fresh nectar still within it?" she asked, her eyes alight.

"Oh, the nest wasn't empty," Dashin replied, finishing the banda roll he was eating and washing it down with water.

"I don't understand. Weren't the mirha upset?"

He nodded. "Yes, they were very upset," he said playfully.

She looked him over, searching for signs of stings. Finding none, she touched her fingertips to her forehead. "This is a treasure beyond words," she said, handling the glove with reverence. "Most of us have never tasted such a thing. It will be the talk of the village for some time," she said, beaming.

"Is there enough?" he asked, surprised she seemed so delighted by what he'd imagined to be a modest amount of nectar. He'd planned on surprising her with the bottle, but her delight had taken him off guard.

She nodded enthusiastically. "Of course, this is an amazing bounty. There will be plenty for everyone."

"Oh," he said, reaching into the storage container and extracting the large water bottle. He plopped it down onto the table with a thud. "In case there's not enough, I brought extra."

She gasped and touched her fingertips to her forehead again, then laughed, studying the strange, transparent container and its priceless bounty. She turned to him and touched his cheek with her fingers.

"You truly are a gift from the SkyGods," she said, her voice serious and her eyes soft.

Her touch and her words warmed him to his core.

Outside, a horn sounded.

They turned to look.

"That is the first horn," Rigin said, her smile fading. "The trial will begin on the third sounding of the horn." She pulled his head to hers and pressed her forehead to his. He felt her warmth flow into him. There were no words to express how grateful he felt in that moment.

She pulled back. "I am very proud of you, Dashin. You have no idea what you mean to us. You must complete this final trial," she urged him, her eyes willing it to be so.

He swallowed, overwhelmed by emotion. He turned and looked at the two small faces looking up at him, and was so choked up he did not trust himself to speak. He nodded and stood up. He turned to ask Matse if she would see to Pritha, but she nodded before he could ask.

He stepped out onto the platform and picked up the worn lanyards. One last time, he said to himself, fastening them to his arms and taking a deep breath. The others followed him as he walked to the platform. The horn sounded for a second time.

As they arrived on the platform, the entire village was there awaiting the final trial. A heated discussion was in progress around Drur, with Fodrick, Hedrick, and Aor clustered close around him and Marna, Enor, and others looking on.

"What is going on?" Dashin asked, joining Alina, Hurza, and Kani near the edge of the platform.

"It seems you were right. Drur has elected not to chase," Alina said, her eyes glued to the proceedings.

She turned to him, only just realizing he'd joined them. "How are you feeling?" she asked, looking him over, her hands sliding over his arms and shoulders.

"A little tired, but some food and a change of clothes have done wonders," he lied, putting on a smile. The ordeal of the trial of the forest had not been the recuperative rest he'd imagined. The trial had taxed his body and robbed him of sleep. And the stop to collect nectar had further depleted his reserves. The thought of attempting the *trial of the trees* now was daunting.

"Why were you outside the egg?" she asked, an annoyed expression on her face.

Her friends and the others nearby were watching him. "I think the tale should wait until after the trial," he said, holding her eyes and trying to convey that he did not want to share the details with everyone else listening.

She narrowed her eyes and then let it go. "You're right, we need to remain focused on this trial." She looked him over again. "Are you certain you're fine? It took you ages to climb up from the ground. Fodrick was about to send people to find you."

"I'm fine. I had to make a stop on the way up. It took more time than I expected."

"What?" she glared. "What kind of stop could you have made that was more important than the coming trial?"

He swallowed. "I'm sorry, I didn't think it would take as long as it did."

She seemed about to press him, but she let that go as well. "I'm sorry," she said. "I'm just anxious. Do you remember everything we went over? How to find the baskets. How to find the *TruePath*. What markings to look for..."

"I remember," he said, turning her to him and pressing his forehead to hers.

She bit her lip and closed her eyes, and he felt the warm link between them. A moment later, she was in his mind.

"I was so frightened when I heard," she sent. *"How could you have ventured outside?"*

"You must promise not to say anything about it," he urged her.

He felt her stiffen against him, confused. She asked him why, her mind unable to grasp what could have happened to cause him to leave the pod.

He reached down, found her hands, and squeezed them. He sent her images of Hedrick in the trees, throwing things down around the pod, and felt her lean in as he showed her that he'd gone outside to see what it was and found meat, and then turned to find the turgas already there. She stiffened, growing furious, and began to pull away. He could see her mind planning to confront Hedrick. He pulled her hands to him and held her still.

"No, please don't," he sent.

"But, Dashin, that's not..."

"Please," he sent. *"The tribe is already split. If I..."* he began and then corrected himself. *"When I succeed, we will need to heal the rift. Confronting Hedrick right now*

will only further divide us and postpone things, which will give him time to maneuver. We can deal with this after the trial. Also, he has something over Drur that he plans to use if I confront him."

He could feel her hesitate, her fury still burning within her.

"You must keep it to yourself for now," he sent. *"In the end, it helped us. Because of Hedrick, Drur has chosen not to chase. That's good news, right?"*

He felt her soften. *"The image you sent of the turgas was so much more terrifying than I imagined. How did you manage to survive such a thing without a scratch?"*

"I was lucky enough to hold them off, and then Pritha attacked the alpha and drove them off."

"Pritha?" Alina sent, unable to believe it.

"It was like the nerape, only more so," he replied.

Alina pulled away and turned to Matse, who was holding the kitten. Alina leaned in and pressed her forehead against the furry head. "Thank you, Pritha," she whispered. "I owe you a plateful of dried meat," she said, pulling back and looking into her eyes. Pritha looked from her to Dashin, cocking her head as she did. Dashin closed his eyes and sent an image of a large platter of dried meat. When he opened his eyes, Pritha was licking her lips.

The horn sounded for the third time.

Fodrick looked over and called for Dashin.

Dashin looked at those gathered around him. They wished him good luck. He smiled at them. He closed his eyes, touching Pritha's mind and sending her an image of her remaining with Matse. Pritha protested, sending him the image of the tree swaddle, which he ignored, resending the picture of Matse. When he opened his eyes, she had her head turned and was pointedly ignoring him. He sighed and smiled at those around him again and then walked across the platform to join Fodrick.

"There's been a change," Fodrick said. "Drur has injured his shoulder," he said, not believing it. "He will not be able to chase you."

"I'm sorry to hear that," Dashin said, nodding at Drur, thanking him with his eyes.

Drur held his eyes and nodded back.

"Aor will be chasing," Fodrick continued. "Once you take to the trees, Aor will wait until we can no longer see you before beginning to chase. You understand that if he returns to the platform with all his tokens before you do, you will fail the trial. If you return first but do not have all the tokens, you will also fail."

Dashin nodded his understanding.

"In that case, you can begin whenever you are ready."

Dashin took a breath and unfurled his lanyards, letting them dangle from his wrists. He turned and nodded to Alina, who offered him an encouraging smile.

He threw a lanyard into the trees, and it grabbed onto a branch, but he knew that its grip was uncertain, so he jumped into the trees and began running along, using them only for show. He heard muttering behind him, but he ignored it. He followed the markings on the trees until they diverged from the direction of the cache and then turned toward it. The race was on now, and his blood was pumping.

Chapter 43

Alina was furious as she watched Dashin run into the trees. She could not believe that Hedrick could have done such a thing. She bit her lip and glared over at him as he stood arguing with Fodrick and Aor.

She exhaled. Dashin was right. She had to focus on this trial. Last night's foul deed could wait.

"Are you alright?" Hurza asked at her elbow.

Alina took a deep breath. "Yes, something happened last night that made Drur change his mind about chasing."

"What happened?" Kani asked.

"It's too long a story," Alina answered, shaking her head.

"How did you learn it?" Hurza asked, confused.

Alina swallowed. There wasn't time to explain everything she'd learned to her friends. She bit her lip.

"You *touched* his mind," Hurza said, her face coming to the realization. "Just now, when you were touching foreheads. You were upset. He was telling you what happened."

Alina nodded. Very little passed Hurza's notice.

Kani frowned. "You can do that?" She shuddered, likely remembering her experience with Alina's touch. "I didn't see it."

"I don't have time to explain," Alina said. "We have to get to work on Aor. Hedrick will have pressed him to hurry. We need to delay him as much as possible."

Her mother and father stepped up.

"It is worse than we thought," her mother said.

"Hedrick laid the course himself this morning, and Aor helped him."

"What?" Hurza spat. "How can it be that the chaser has already seen the course?"

Marna shrugged. "Fodrick was upset, but Hedrick is livid and will not listen. Fodrick was unable to get him to see reason and finally relented."

"Why would he allow that?" Kani asked, frowning.

"I don't think Fodrick imagines it will make a difference who chases," her mother said, turning to Kani. "I think he's merely trying to keep the village from coming apart over this."

"I have never seen the village in such an uproar," her father said. "Neighbors who've known each other their entire lives, arguing as though they were not friends."

Aor stepped away from the crowd and rolled his shoulders as he moved to the edge of the platform, getting ready to chase. He seemed eager to have it behind him and was getting ready to leave. Alina's heart sank. Normally, they would have more time, but he seemed about to leave.

"Hurza, Kani, can you get the sweets and the necklace? I'll try and delay Aor," she said, hurrying forward. Behind her, she heard her friends racing away.

She stopped next to Aor.

"My mother tells me that you helped lay the course."

He turned to her, then looked away, and shrugged.

"How could you be a part of this?"

"It doesn't matter who chases," he said, turning back, a defeated look on his face.

His words didn't make any sense. How could it not matter? He already knew the course, where every basket lay, and the exact path between each. "What do you mean?"

He shrugged, biting his lip. "The course will be impossible for him. It is the most challenging course we've ever laid. Most of the baskets are located in the uppermost canopy. He'll never be able to reach them." Aor seemed repulsed by the fact.

Her knees threatened to give out. The upper branches had the slightest of branches. They would never support his weight. If the baskets were up there, this course would be impossible for him.

"How can you go along with this?" she asked, with disgust.

"I didn't choose to chase. Drur refused," he spat, angry.

"But you laid the course."

"Yes, I know. But look behind us," he said, turning and indicating the heated arguments dotting the platform. "These trials are tearing the village apart. They need to end."

"And you've decided *how* they must end?" she asked, her eyes narrowed.

"No. I didn't decide any of this. I'm doing my duty, just like you," he said, referencing her earlier words to him. "I didn't have a choice in this."

She flushed, feeling hope slipping away. Could Dashin find some way to reach those baskets? She had to believe he would find a way. She had to buy him time.

"At least give him a real lead," she said, hoping to buy Dashin as much time as possible.

"Why?" he asked. "It won't make a difference."

"Perhaps not for Dashin, but it will make a difference to them," she said, indicating the villagers behind them. "If Dashin loses, those supporting him will be sad and perhaps bitter. They may understand that you had no say in laying the course, but they will remember how much of a lead you gave him. If they feel that you were hasty in this, you may lose the respect of those you would one day govern."

Her words hit him, and he swallowed, looking down for a moment. He nodded. "You're right. It may make a difference in how people see the loss." His lips twisted in distaste, then he looked at Alina. "I don't have anything personally against him."

She blinked. "You don't?"

"No, he stepped in front of a krax for you. He doesn't deserve to lose like this. But I have to trust that my grandfather, who has seen things I have no concept of and who has given his life in service to this tribe, knows of what he speaks when he says that Dashin will be a disaster for us."

"What do you think?"

"I don't know," Aor said, looking off into the trees. He sighed and then shrugged. "Like you explained to me not too long ago, I am bound to do my duty whether I understand it or not."

Alina had no answer to that.

Hurza and Kani ran up with the sweets. Hurza was wearing the necklace. Alina exchanged looks with them, noting the section of doctored treats on Hurza's tray.

"Kani, perhaps you could take some of those treats to the villagers. It may soothe some tempers," Alina said.

Kani turned and began making the rounds with her tray.

"Your treats look wonderful, Alina," Hurza said, admiring them. "They seem even better than usual."

"Yes, I'm happy with them," Alina said loudly. "The berries were especially succulent this time," she said, plucking one and eating it.

Alina took the tray, freeing Hurza's hands.

Hurza took one and ate it, praising it as she did. Aor was distracted, looking over the platform, apparently trying to decide how long to wait.

"Do you want one?" Hurza said, picking one of the doctored treats up and offering it to Aor on the notched banda leaf.

"My stomach is too tense for food," he said, waving it away.

"Perhaps this will settle your stomach," she said, holding it out.

He seemed to consider it and was about to agree, but then changed his mind and shook his head.

"Here," she said, biting off half of it and chewing it, making appreciative noises, and then swallowing. "Try a small piece," she offered, putting it in his mouth. He chewed it absently and then frowned as he swallowed it.

"Have you changed the recipe for these?" he asked, turning to Alina.

"A little, as I said, the berries were exceptional this time."

"Here, try one more," Hurza said, pushing one toward him and placing the entire thing in his mouth as he opened it.

He chewed it, the slight frown returning before he swallowed it.

"Another?" Hurza offered, but Aor shook his head. His lips puckered as his mouth worked to swallow what remained of it.

Alina took the platter from Hurza. "I'll see if others want some," she said, giving Hurza time with Aor. She threw a large banda leaf over the doctored treats and offered the others to those nearby so she could listen in.

"I have something for you," Hurza said.

There was a pause. Alina glanced over. Aor appeared distracted.

"Did you not hear me?" Hurza said, her tone bringing Aor's head instantly around to her.

"Sorry?" he replied.

"I made you something, but if you're too distracted..."

"No, sorry, what is it?"

She pulled the necklace carefully from her neck.

"A necklace?" he said, sounding disappointed. Alina choked back a laugh.

"Well, if that's how you feel about it," Hurza huffed and put it back around her neck.

"No, I mean, it's nice. You made that for me?"

"I did. And it was a lot of work, I'll have you know."

"Thank you, Hurza," he said.

"Are you sure?"

"I'm sure."

She paused as though considering it. Alina lost track of the people taking treats from her tray.

Hurza placed the necklace around his neck. "There, that looks good on you."

He grinned at her.

"Oh, wait," she said as though she'd had an afterthought. "You'll lose it in the trees." She lifted the end, slipped it inside his tunic, and patted it against his chest. "Take good care of it," she said, crinkling her eyes.

"I will," he said.

"Do you want another treat?" she asked.

Aor shook his head, pursing his lips as though there was a lingering taste he didn't enjoy.

Hedrick stormed over. "What are you waiting for?" he barked at Aor.

Aor turned and leapt into the trees, moving fast.

Chapter 44

Dashin ran toward the cache, leaping from branch to branch, dragging his lanyards behind him as he went. As he reached it, he tore the old lanyards from his arms, fumbling with them in his haste. He bit his lip as he strapped on his new lanyards, making certain the straps on his forearms were extra tight. He'd be pressing these today, and he didn't want them slipping off.

He checked to make sure the bags at his waist were secure. He took two quick steps and dropped from the platform into the branches below. His first lanyard throw yielded an awkward grip and threw him off-balance, but within a few swings, he'd regained the feel of them and was moving swiftly through the forest. His blood was pumping, a sense of urgency driving him on.

He reached the course markings, spying them above as he swung below where the branches were stouter. It felt good to be moving. The nervous flutters in his stomach dissipated now that he was in motion.

The detour to the cache had used up valuable time. He wasn't sure how much of a delay Aor was going to give him. Things had been heated on the platform when he left. Hedrick might already have had Aor begin the chase. He listened for any sound behind him in the trees.

He thought back to Hedrick and the meat. He tried to reconcile those actions with the trauma Fodrick had shared with him. Dashin couldn't imagine the emotional weight one might carry on returning to one's village and finding everyone they had loved dead or dying. And then to realize everyone was dead due to a decision they'd made. It did, in some sense, explain the deep fear of repeating such a mistake, but it seemed to have become a blind obsession. Deliberately attempting to have Dashin killed. Coercing Drur with threats to his sister. These actions seemed well beyond reason.

He was so distracted by these thoughts he almost missed one of the course markings. He realized he wasn't seeing his *TruePath*. He could hear Alina's voice in his mind. *You're making mistakes. Your path is forced and awkward. You're missing opportunities.*

He forced himself to relax. He pushed other thoughts from his mind so he could seek the path ahead. Just like they'd practiced so many times before, he let his mind find the path while keeping track of the forest above, looking for the splotches of red, marking the course.

He felt a jolt of excitement when he saw the red hash mark on a trunk, signaling the first basket. He climbed up to it, swiveling his head, searching for it. He spun around once and then twice, unable to locate it. He checked the hash mark again, and it was indeed there. He made a wide circle around the hash mark, wondering if it might be farther afield, but he still couldn't locate it. He looked up and down without luck.

He looked on, and he could see red marks continuing on, indicating he was indeed on the course. Only there was no basket here. How could that be? Dread settled in his chest, panic building within. Aor would soon be in the trees, and he hadn't even found a single basket.

He looked up to gauge the sun's position in the sky, and his heart sank. The basket was at the very top of the canopy, well beyond his reach.

Who laid this course? he wondered. A moment later, the answer came to him. It had to be Hedrick. The course had been laid out to make it impossible for him, specifically. TreeFolk, who were much lighter, might reach the basket with effort, but the branches were much too slight up there for him.

Fury boiled within him as he glared at the basket. He took a breath, trying to imagine how he might reach it. He climbed up as high as the branches would allow. The footing grew precarious, and the branches he clung to swayed wildly beneath him. He glanced up at the basket, which still lay several body lengths above. The branch he was on snapped. He tumbled through the canopy, snapping more of the thin branches before he reached one stout enough to arrest his fall. He tried again and again with the same results. Finally, he sat down, dejected, staring up at the unattainable basket.

All the training and effort he'd put in, the fight with the krax, the struggle with the turgas. After all that, this was how it was going to end. He would fail this trial not because he'd been outraced but because someone had rigged the trial against him. Someone who was determined to keep him from succeeding, whatever the cost.

He contemplated what failure would mean, seeing himself cast out of the tribe, he and Pritha banished to the forest, cut off from the only home he'd really known and from those he'd come to love. The idea was crushing.

He listened for Aor, imagining the smug look on his face when he arrived to find him sitting here. Just sitting here. Aor would no doubt slip up there without effort, take a token, and whisk away, perhaps offering some snide barb in parting.

He gritted his teeth. He wouldn't just sit here and wait. There had to be something he could try. He shimmied up as high as he could, studying the basket and canopy above. He grabbed the branch next to him and another behind him for support, which quelled the swaying a bit. Then it hit him. If he bunched many branches together, they would form a combined structure of sorts that might support him.

How much time had he wasted fruitlessly climbing and falling and then sitting there bemoaning his situation? He stopped and listened, fearing Aor was already upon him, but thankfully, the forest was still quiet. He swept as many branches as he could reach into a tight bundle with his arms and wrapped his legs around them, essentially building a thick wooden rope from many individual pieces of canopy twine.

He shimmied up this bundle of branches, using his arms to pull and his legs to push as he kept them bunched against him. He managed, in this fashion, to get within a body length of the basket, but then the bunch grew so thin he could go no farther.

Now what? he wondered, his eyes on the basket above. Could he use his lanyard to bring the basket to him? It was directly above him. If he tipped it from here, he'd end up dumping the tokens into the forest. He'd have to come at it from the side, he reasoned, to give the branch the basket was on room to move. If he was careful, a gentle lanyard throw could snag the branch, allowing him to pull it to him. Then what? He was running out of arms. How would he get the token?

One step at a time, he told himself. He repositioned himself, shimmying down again and getting another group of branches together at some distance from the basket and shimmying up again, trying to calm his mounting nerves as time slipped by. Once he was in position, he freed up one arm, holding all the bunched-up branches with his legs and the other arm.

He used his free arm to untangle his lanyard from the jumble of branches it was caught in. He cursed to himself as it snagged. *Oh, you gnarled branch*, he chuckled at how quaint cursing in Ndesan was. It was nothing compared to cursing in Ancaran.

He took a deep breath and forced himself to stop yanking at it and slow down. After a few careful motions, it unsnagged and hung free. He tossed the lanyard toward the branch with the basket, keeping the toss light so as not to overly disturb it. The lanyard cup glanced off the branch. He pulled it back and tried again. On the third toss, he managed to snag the branch.

He held his breath as the basket rocked back and forth, but then it settled, and he pulled it carefully to him. It crept toward him, but he'd pulled the lanyard back as far as his arm would go. Gripping the lanyard with his teeth, he adjusted his grip and then pulled some more while keeping the grip compressed with his remaining fingers so the cup stayed latched on the branch. He repeated the maneuver until the basket was next to his head. Leaning forward, he gripped the edge of the basket with his teeth, holding it there until he could reach into it with a few fingers to retrieve a token.

Once he had it, he took the token in his teeth and let his lanyard slip slowly through a few fingers, until the basket returned to its original position. It had been an awkward series of steps. His legs were shaking from the strain of keeping the branches compressed enough to hold him in position as twigs and knots on those branches dug into his skin.

He shimmied back down until he found solid footing, then opened the bag on his belt and placed the token inside. The effort had been exhausting, and the thought of having to repeat this multiple times was daunting. He had no doubt now where the other baskets would be. He thought of an Ancaran curse for Hedrick, which seemed appropriate to the situation.

He dove into the trees, resuming his transit along the course. This trial was going to be even harder than he'd imagined. There was no way he would have enough time to repeat this process five more times to collect all the tokens before Aor caught and passed him. Even though it would take Aor more time to retrieve a token from a basket on this course, he would still be so much faster than Dashin.

He had to find some way to slow Aor down. As he raced along toward the second basket, he sifted through possible ideas. Finding the second basket was much easier. Once he saw the two hash marks on the tree, all he had to do was look all the way up into the upper canopy to spot it. He repeated the process he'd worked out on the first basket, slipped another token into his bag, and continued on.

When he got to the third basket, he removed the twine from his soapstone bag. The twine cinched it closed and kept it fastened to his belt. He let the stone and bag fall into the trees and kept just the length of twine, which he tied around his wrist. Once he'd retrieved the token using the same technique he'd devised, he tied the basket tree, which was still bent over, to a nearby branch not in the bunch supporting him. He fashioned a slip knot and then inserted a small twig in it to act as a trigger. He held his breath as he slowly let go of the precarious knot, praying it would hold. The branch still bent over drew the knot tight, the twig he'd inserted flexing under the strain.

It seemed like it would snap and come loose at any moment. He dared not even breathe as he shimmied back down away from it, his eyes glued to it the entire time. Once the twig snapped and the knot came undone, the two branches would fly apart. The basket would snap back, past its original position, which would surely launch the token from it into the forest. He willed it to hold as he crept away from it. The idea of having to chase that token and replace it should it come loose prematurely made him shudder. Keeping his tense steps as light as possible, so as not to disturb the upper canopy, he stole away until he was confident enough to use his lanyards again and continue.

If Aor jostled either tree and the basket flung the remaining token into the forest, Dashin would not technically have removed the token himself. He felt the ploy was likely well within the spirit of the rules. After all, placing the baskets so high in the canopy seemed a significant bending of the rules in itself.

With any luck, it would fall to the forest floor, though that seemed unlikely given the amount of foliage up here. It might happen, and even if it didn't, it might take some time for Aor to find it. Time Dashin desperately needed.

It was a gamble. Setting up the ruse had taken a lot of time. As he passed the next red splotch on the course, he heard Aor moving fast through the trees behind him, each lanyard toss closely followed by another. The sound lit a fire inside Dashin's chest, and he sped on, moving as fast as he could manage while listening to the sounds behind him, eager to hear if his ruse worked.

His heart sank as Aor paused and then seemed to resume his chase with only a heartbeat of delay. Dashin feared Aor had either seen the trap and avoided it or come up the far side and taken the token without springing it. All that effort, it seemed, had been wasted.

He was berating himself for having wasted so much precious time on it when he heard it spring. He stopped and listened to the wonderful music of something falling through the forest. He willed it on, as it ricocheted from branch to branch, the sound falling away. The clatter, however, stopped somewhere far below them. He prayed it was wedged well out of sight.

Irate Ndesan curses reached his ears, music for his soul. He grinned and continued on. Behind him, he heard the sounds of Aor dropping down into the forest.

The fourth basket was especially challenging, and Dashin struggled with it, having to reposition himself several times before he managed to secure the token. Whatever time he'd gained on Aor, he might have lost on this basket. But, since he'd spent so much time here, he decided to gamble and try out his banda leaf idea. He remained in that awkward position and worked at the basket, though his mind urged him to just race. But he pulled materials from the various bags at his waist, and using his teeth, his fingers, his chin, and anything else he could bring to bear, he performed the delicate work.

By the time he'd finished, Aor was loud in the trees, gaining on him. Dashin dropped down to resume the course. He'd just reached the lower canopy when Aor swept into view far above him. Dashin was going to leap off, but he couldn't take his eyes off how effortlessly Aor managed the upper canopy, sailing through the thin branches. Aor paused for a moment. Dashin imagined he was making certain this basket did not have a trap attached to it. Then, as he went to climb up to the basket, the lanyard he was using for support came loose, and he lost his footing on the thin branch on which he stood.

Aor tumbled toward Dashin, his lanyards lashing out as he fell, but they kept coming loose as they reached for targets. Dashin saw the stunned expression on Aor's face as he plummeted toward him.

Aor's shoulder caught a branch, and it spun his body around so the back of his head smacked hard against the trunk of a tree. His body went slack. His body was moving fast now, falling uncontrollably, glancing off branches as it came, growing larger as it fell toward him.

Dashin ran through the lower canopy toward Aor's falling body. He dove for it but just missed it as it flew by. But as he grabbed for it, he somehow managed to snag one of Aor's lanyards. The lanyard went taut with Aor's weight and pulled Dashin to his knees and then dragged him off the branch he was on, taking him along in its wake. Dashin caught a limb with his hips, the impact driving the air from him as he doubled up his hands on the lanyard. The lanyard stretched, threatening to snap, under the terrible force. Dashin held on, grinding his teeth at the strain.

It held. Aor slowed, and then bounced up and down a few times before settling. Dashin pulled him up by the lanyard and laid him out on the branch next to him, fearing he was seriously hurt or worse. The blow to the back of the head had made a sickening sound. Dashin imagined how his own fall must have looked to Alina.

He propped him up against a trunk and looked him over. The wound on the back of his head was bleeding. Dashin's hands came away wet, but the skull seemed intact, which was the limit of Dashin's diagnostic range.

Aor was wearing some kind of necklace that had oozed into his shirt, soaking it. When Dashin touched the shirt with his finger, he recognized the familiar tingle of borka juice. It seemed the juice might have numbed his chest and affected his ability to use the lanyards. That Dashin had been below him and in a position to stop this fall seemed improbable. And yet Dashin was standing here today due to a long series of unlikely events. He shuddered at the thought of what might have happened to Aor had Dashin not been here.

Aor blinked his eyes open. He glanced around, wincing and trying to focus his eyes as though he had no idea where he was. He frowned and squinted, his eyes finally coming to rest on Dashin.

"How do you feel?" Dashin asked, studying his eyes. He remembered doctors looking in his eyes when he'd taken a blow to the head during combat training on Ancara, though what they'd been looking at he didn't know.

Aor looked around, trying to make sense of what he was seeing. He tried to stand up but groaned and reached for his head.

"You fell. You took a blow to the head and were knocked unconscious," Dashin explained.

Aor reached behind his head with his fingertips, and they came away wet with blood.

"It doesn't look too deep," Dashin said. "Can you move your hands and feet?"

"Why?" Aor asked, wiggling his fingers and toes.

"I don't know. I've heard doctors in my tribe ask that after a bad impact. I think it's a good sign if you can move them."

Aor laughed. "I would be alarmed if I could not." He looked up and gasped as he saw how far away the upper canopy was.

"I fell all the way down here?" he said, still looking up, his eyes wide.

"Not exactly," Dashin said.

Aor glanced at him, frowning.

"You were still falling when you reached here. I caught you."

Aor stared at him. "You caught me?"

"Well, I saw you falling, and I ran over and tried to catch you, but I missed you as you flew by. But somehow I managed to grab your lanyard," he said, pointing at the broken branches below.

Aor glanced below, his eyes wide, and then turned back to Dashin. "You stopped my fall with my lanyard?" he said, emphasizing the last word.

"I'm guessing if you move that arm," Dashin said, indicating the one tied to the lanyard he'd grabbed, "your muscles will confirm my account."

Aor lifted the arm and winced. He probed it with fingers from the opposite hand. Dashin didn't doubt all the muscles in Aor's arm would be incredibly tender from the strain they'd just been subjected to.

"Why..." Aor began, staring at Dashin, unable to complete the sentence.

Dashin shrugged. "You'd have done the same thing for me," he said.

Aor laughed. "No, I wouldn't have."

Dashin laughed too. "I didn't think you would. But I like to think one day you might."

Aor considered this, looking at him strangely, as though he'd only just met him. "Perhaps one day," he said slowly.

"What happens now?" Aor asked, rolling his shoulder.

"What do you mean?" Dashin said.

"I'm not sure I should continue chasing you, given that you just saved my life."

Dashin thought about it for a moment. Could this be the end? Had he just won the trial? Then he thought of Hedrick and the arguments over the *trial of the hunt*. He shook his head. "I don't think your grandfather will allow you to forfeit."

Aor sighed and glanced away for a moment. "No, I think you're right."

"So, I think we'll have to continue the trial," Dashin said, shrugging.

"Are you sure? I just caught up to you. I'm much faster than you."

"Yes, but you still don't have the token above us. And there are only two baskets left. I think I have a chance."

"I don't think so," Aor said, shaking his head. "Do you want me to pretend to chase you?"

Dashin shook his head. "No, you have to chase me. That way, if someone asks you, you can say you did your best."

"I don't understand. Why would you do this?"

"I want to earn the right to be *of the tribe.* I don't want to win and then hear people saying behind my back that if they'd been chasing, I wouldn't have made it."

"You could lose," Aor said, letting the words sit.

"Yes, I realize that," Dashin said. "Oh, and for the same reason, could we keep this incident between us until after the trial is resolved?"

"I don't understand you, Dashin," Aor said, his eyes on him.

"I get that a lot," Dashin said with a laugh. He adjusted his lanyards, a knot in his stomach, wondering himself what it was he was doing and why he didn't just come to some kind of arrangement.

"Good luck," Aor said, meeting his eyes. Dashin saw a measure of respect there he hadn't noted before, which made him feel better about this decision.

"Good luck to you, too," Dashin said. "Oh, and you may want to remove the necklace," he said. "It's dripping borka juice on your chest. It's probably why you couldn't arrest your fall."

"Oh, itchy silas fabric," he said, making Dashin grin at the curse.

"It was Hurza," Aor said, shaking his head.

"Ah, yes, she can be very crafty," Dashin replied, remembering her chasing him and anticipating his every move.

Aor took it off, smiling as he did. He slipped it into a bag at his waist. He removed his tunic, rubbing the remaining liquid from his chest with a sleeve. He passed the shirt through his belt so the dry part was against his back and the part with the borka juice hung beyond the belt, away from his skin.

"I'm certain she only intended for it to slow you down," Dashin said. "She'll be devastated to hear it almost killed you."

Aor looked up at him, his face drawn. "You can't tell her," Aor pleaded with him.

"Of course," Dashin replied, surprised at the force of the reaction.

"Let's just say a branch in the upper canopy broke as I was racing," he said, thinking through the tale they should tell.

"That should be believable. Perhaps I was overconfident," he continued, imagining the story. "And, I can tell her I found the necklace annoying and that it slowed me down, which she'll enjoy."

Dashin warmed to Aor. They'd never truly spoken before, but his concern for Hurza in this moment touched him, and he felt a rare kinship with him. He hoped one day they could be friends.

Aor's stomach grumbled unpleasantly.

"What was that?" Dashin said, surprised at how loud it was.

"I think Alina and Hurza put something in the treats they fed me," he said, holding his stomach. He chuckled. "It seems you may end up with a lead after all."

Dashin smiled. "So long as you do your best."

"I will. Now you'd best be off. I feel an urgency I would rather deal with in private."

Dashin laughed and leapt into the trees.

Chapter 45

Alina stood on the edge of the platform, looking off into the forest. She could not settle her mind even as her mother rubbed her back in the way that had always worked in the past. She felt her life, not just Dashin's, hung in the balance. And while he was out there fighting for his life, she stood here powerless.

Nearby, Rigin kept her own vigil with Solvan and Matse at her side. Pritha was restless in Matse's arms, mewing into the forest, the little girl whispering continually into her ear as she pet her.

Hurza walked up. "You definitely used enough soapstone," she said, holding her stomach. She'd already made a few trips to the cleansing hut.

"I'm sorry," Alina said, looking at her friend.

Hurza gave her a weak smile. "I am thinking of the many things you will do for me in return," she said, crinkling her eyes.

Alina squeezed her shoulder.

"Lina, listen," her father whispered, leaning toward her.

She turned to him, and he indicated the platform with a short nod of his head.

Alina glanced around, and it was quiet, everyone looking out into the forest. She looked back at her father, confused.

"It's quiet," he said, smiling.

She looked to her mother, who was smiling, and then to Kani and Hurza, who also seemed confused.

"No one is arguing," her mother offered, a glint in her eye.

A warmth bloomed within her. They were right. The continuous arguments of the past days had dissipated. That had to be good news! Villagers stood in small groups, whispering with concerned looks as they awaited the trial's conclusion. Hedrick stood alone, gazing from the village to the trees and back, his eyes furtive and unsure.

"Those under Hedrick's influence have grown fewer," her father confirmed. "After the *trial of the forest*, many villagers have rethought their positions. It seems the wind blows from the mountains now."

She pressed her lips together, emotion swelling within her. She blinked her eyes, trying to keep the mist from them. There was hope. The heart of the village was with them now. Now that her father had mentioned it, she could see it in the faces of those who waited with her. She nodded to her parents, hope tugging at the corners of her mouth.

She turned again to the forest, trying to imagine where Dashin might be on the course now. But she could not see the shape of it in her mind. Had he found a way to reach the baskets in the upper canopy? It seemed an impossible problem, but his mind was a wonder when faced with such puzzles. She told herself again that he would find a way. She crossed her arms, giving her anxious fingers somewhere to be.

The treats were working. The half-treat Hurza ate had already sent her running to the cleansing hut. Aor had eaten three times the amount. Surely that would slow him down. And there was the necklace, too. At the very least, it would be irritating enough to force him to stop, take it off, and clean the juice from his body.

And they'd been able to delay Aor some at the onset, though not as much as she'd hoped. She prayed all these things would give Dashin time to find a way to reach those baskets and make it back. She forced herself to imagine that Dashin had solved the basket problems and was now comfortably ahead and racing back to her.

Pritha screeched and thrashed in Matse's arms. Alina reached over and snatched the little body from Matse before it could dive off into the forest. She pulled it to her and cradled it against her as Pritha squirmed in her grasp, crying loudly as though in terrible pain.

Alina felt a cold shiver of dread run through her. Her heart raced, terrified at what this might mean. She held the kitten close, trying to calm her. Pritha's heart was pounding in her chest as she thrashed in her grip. Something bad had happened. Alina could feel it as she cradled the kitten, holding it close. Pritha squirmed in her arms, trying to free herself, before she settled and her panic eased.

Matse's body trembled against Rigin, her eyes fixed on Pritha as she mumbled unintelligibly.

Perhaps it had only been a close call? Or perhaps it had been a fall Dashin had managed to control? She studied Pritha. The kitten's eyes were closed, but moving rapidly beneath the lids.

Chapter 46

Dashin flew through the forest. He'd been pleased to hear Aor gasp behind him as he'd left. Apparently, Dashin's abilities in the forest were a surprise to him. Perhaps he should have seemed less able? It was too late to change that. It was a race now. Dashin pressed ahead, trying to take advantage of his lead. Judging by the sound he'd heard and the look on Aor's face, he hoped the lead might be substantial.

There were still two baskets to go. He had a chance, but had to be smooth and find his *TruePath*. He couldn't afford any mistakes. He felt confident he'd done the right thing with Aor. He'd been so lucky to have been there. Had Aor been seriously injured, or worse, his *becoming* would have been tarnished by the events surrounding it. He couldn't imagine Fodrick, let alone Hedrick, forgiving him for it.

Had he been stupid in asking Aor to continue the chase and give his best? He had no doubt Alina would be furious with him for it, but he was sure Hedrick would exploit any hint of deviation from a traditional chase. He would undoubtedly ask Aor if he had let him win and would seize on any hesitation. He needed this campaign against him to be done and for his victory to be unequivocal.

The fifth basket went smoothly. He'd refined his technique, and though he was faster at gathering this token, he knew Aor would be faster still. He slipped the token into his bag and flew on.

He could hear Aor in the trees behind him now. Something different and odd about his rhythm reminded him of Solvan. He listened to it and realized every other lanyard pull seemed weaker, as though he was favoring one side of his body. It must have been either the fall or the strain on his arm from Dashin arresting it.

As Aor paused, having reached the fifth basket, Dashin threw caution to the wind and pulled as hard as he could on his lanyards. He was moving faster than he ever had, accelerating with each pull until it felt like flight in a skimmer on Ancara.

The branches were a blur as he wove through them. His heart pounded from both the effort and the fear that he would slam into a branch and either injure himself too severely to continue or worse. He swallowed as the memory of Aor's body tumbling through the trees flashed through his mind. He pushed it away and focused on the path ahead.

He was moving so fast he almost missed the six hashmarks indicating the final basket. He pulled back hard on his rear lanyard, feeling it stretch behind him as he lost momentum, and then threw the forward lanyard above him and released the rear one once he had come to a stop. The rear lanyard shot forward, snapping toward him, and he flicked his wrist, sending it up into the trees to latch onto a branch. The movement had been so sudden and instinctual that he stood there gaping at how smooth and natural it had felt.

He wished Alina might have seen it, imagining how excited she would have been. He shook himself and clambered up to the basket, chiding himself for losing even a moment, daydreaming.

He snatched the last token as Aor showed up. He was climbing back down when Aor soared up past him to snatch his in a few heartbeats.

Dashin bit his lip at how unfair this course was. But it wasn't Aor's fault. Dashin dove into the trees, flying now, surging forward. He ignored the course markings now. He had all the tokens, and he knew where the village lay. All he had to do was get to the platform first. It was a pure race now with all the baskets behind them.

He had a moment of regret at having urged Aor to chase, for it was clear Aor had taken it to heart. He was above him and moving fast, the odd rhythm he'd heard earlier smoothing out. Dashin told himself to ignore him and to focus instead on going as fast as he could. He pulled and pulled, accelerating with each pull. His lanyards grew so taut with each swing he feared they would snap. He selected the thickest branches and trunks he could find so that they could withstand the intense force he was exerting on them as he raced toward the platform.

The villagers were shouting, their figures growing in size as he neared them. He lost track of Aor, so focused was he on the platform. His lungs were like a bellows, panting furiously at the effort. His arms and shoulders screamed at the taxing strain. His legs and abdomen twisted and reached hard with every pull to squeeze as much forward motion out of every action as possible.

In the final pull, he threw his lanyards as far forward as possible, aiming at a huge trunk near the children's play area, and managed to latch onto it before pulling with everything he had. The play area was wide open, with only the sparsest of foliage by design. There were no substantial branches beyond the one at the edge he'd latched onto that would take his weight. Dashin knew that Aor would skirt it, like the villagers always did. He gambled that if pulled hard enough, he might be able to shoot his body right through the entire span and onto the platform.

He pulled with every last remaining shred of strength he had left, taking his lanyards to their very breaking point, and launched himself. He narrowly missed colliding with the tree he'd latched onto, managing somehow to twist in the air and miss the trunk, the bark scratching his cheek as he flew by.

The twisting turned him in the air so that he was tumbling now, coming in as an uncontrolled ball of limbs and lanyards. There was shouting on the platform as people scrambled. Crashing onto the platform, he rolled across it as villagers leapt out of the way. He slammed into the kitchen pantry area with a clatter as bags of nut flour, waxed bags of dried meat, baskets of berries, and cooking pots fell on him.

He dug his way out, looking behind him, straining to find Aor. Aor stood on the platform's edge, looking worriedly toward him.

"Aor was first!" Hedrick exclaimed, running to Aor. "The candidate lost!"

Chapter 47

Breathless, Alina stood watching on the platform as Dashin raced toward her. She clung to Pritha, who was frozen against her, her claws sharp through Alina's shirt, her tiny heart pounding against her arm.

Aor was in the trees above and dropping fast toward the platform. It had become a true race, with both of them giving their all. She had never seen Dashin move so fast. She couldn't believe her eyes. He was holding his own, but only narrowly managing to avoid branches and trunks as he hurtled on. Every motion was forced and desperate as he drove in a straight line for her rather than searching for a smoother path.

People on the platform were shouting. Their communal voice urged Dashin on, the tribe in the trees with him now. Their support washed over her, feeding her own need for him to win.

Every fiber of her willed Dashin forward, drawing him to her. Her heart sank as she saw him miscalculate. He'd continued straight for her when he should have altered course to avoid the children's area. A collective gasp swelled around her as villagers saw the error. He would be forced to stop and skirt the area. She glanced up. Aor was coming fast. He would reach the platform before Dashin could make such a detour.

It had been so close. Despair welled up as her world began to crumble around her. Her knees grew weak. She felt dizzy and had to take a step to remain standing.

Pritha's claws dug into her arm as the crowd gasped. She glanced up, looking to Aor to see if perhaps something had happened to hamper his progress. But he was flying through the trees and nearing the platform. She looked back to Dashin and was shocked to see him still barreling toward the platform. He had not altered course at all. Instead, he had accelerated.

She didn't understand what he was doing. He had to be aware now that there were no branches beyond the one he was currently reaching for. Every eye was fixed on him as he grabbed the trunk on the outer edge of the children's area with both lanyards and pulled with enormous force. It dawned on her that he was attempting to span the entire distance in one leap. It was at least five body lengths, a distance far beyond anything she'd ever seen anyone attempt.

She heard a huge intake of breath from those around her, as though the tribe itself was taking the leap with him, filling its lungs for the immense effort. It seemed an impossible distance to cover. The platform went quiet, people holding their breath as Dashin launched himself into the air, sailing high above the children's area.

Alina's heart made the leap, bound with him as he soared. Every muscle in his body reached for the platform. It seemed uncertain he would find it until the very last instant when he caught the edge of the matting and crashed into it. His body bounced up from the impact and rolled right by her.

People in his path darted aside, narrowly avoiding the flurry of arms, legs, and flailing lanyards as he bounced and rolled across the platform and slammed into the kitchen pantry.

Her heart soared, and she turned to look for Aor. Her hopes dashed as she saw him standing on the platform with Hedrick, proclaiming victory. The villagers looked at one another. It seemed everyone had been watching Dashin, and no one, aside from Hedrick, had noted Aor's arrival.

Had Aor truly arrived first?

She rushed to Dashin. As she neared him, Pritha leapt from her arms and landed on his chest, knocking him back into the strewn kitchen supplies. Pritha nipped his nose, demanding his attention. She threw her head back and mewled loudly at him, her cry both angry and plaintive. He stroked her as she brought her head down, fixing him with a stare and continuing to complain.

Alina joined him, adding her cries to the mix. "Why did you attempt that leap? You could have been killed," she admonished.

"Is it true that Aor arrived first?" he asked, ignoring her.

"I don't know," she said, probing him with her fingers as she checked for broken bones.

"Ow," he said as she poked a shoulder.

"Are you hurt?"

"I strained it, catching something," he said.

"What?" she asked, reaching for it again.

He pulled back. "It's fine. Let's go see what's happening," he said, getting up, taking her hand, and pulling her along. As they pushed their way through the crowd, he pet Pritha absently. She'd latched onto his shoulder and was rubbing her neck against his.

"The arrivals were too close to say for certain," her father argued.

"Did you see Aor alight?" Hedrick demanded.

Her father squirmed. "Not the exact moment, but close enough to it."

"I saw them both," Hedrick announced defiantly.

Alina doubted it was true, and she could see the uncertainty in the faces of the others. She felt the knot in her stomach, which had loosened with Dashin's arrival, tighten again. Dashin squeezed her hand, his touch reassuring. She leaned against him, her body needing the assurance that he was truly here.

The argument spread, and Alina was stunned to find that all voices, aside from Hedrick's, were speaking in support of Dashin.

Aor looked at Dashin, his eyes filled with what seemed like regret or some sort of apology. The sight surprised her, and she looked to Dashin, who seemed to acknowledge it.

She couldn't understand how this could be. Hurza caught her eye, an inquisitive look on her face, apparently having also noticed the exchange.

She wanted to ask Dashin about it, but Fodrick held up his hand, and she turned to see what he would say, not daring to breathe, willing words of acceptance onto his lips.

"Aor, did you note Dashin's position when you alit?"

Aor paused. He seemed to be weighing his answer. She feared he was thinking about confirming Hedrick's assertion. But his eyes seemed conflicted, as though the answer was costing him something. Finally, he spoke. "No, I'm sorry," he said, looking at Dashin again. "I was moving fast and had my eyes on the platform. However, I did hear a commotion and screaming as I alit."

"There," her father announced, "he heard Dashin striking the platform as he alit. Which would mean that Dashin was already upon it."

The crowd hurried to agree, muttering support for the argument.

"It proves no such thing. People were screaming throughout the trial. I saw them both and Aor alit first," Hedrick declared.

Alina felt fury burning within her, certain he'd seen no such thing. From where he'd been standing, he could not have seen them both at once.

The arguments resumed. It seemed everyone, save one, was now taking Dashin's side. She looked up at him, and his lip was trembling at seeing the faces of all the villagers pleading his case.

"Let us vote on it," Arras demanded.

"No, there is no voting on this," Hedrick spat. "Our traditions are clear. The candidate must arrive *before* the chaser. In this case, the candidate has failed."

"We can't be considering failing Dashin after everything he's been through," someone said.

"This *becoming* was unlike any other. Surely he deserves..." another began.

The arguing continued. The trials were meant to prepare candidates for life in the tribe, not to exclude them based on some technicality, many argued. Chasers in the past always pushed the candidates. They didn't try to eliminate them unduly, others argued. But Hedrick stuck to the rules and could not be persuaded from them.

Fodrick put up his hand. He turned to his wife. "What do our rules say on this matter?"

"I am not aware of a similar situation occurring before. Past trials have always been decisive. There is no provision for the chief to rule in such cases," she said, her face concerned.

"That seems shortsighted," Fodrick said, scratching his chin. He sighed. "Then let us follow the rules."

Alina gripped Dashin's hand, the words sending a shiver of fear through her. Dashin looked ahead, impassive. How could he greet such a pronouncement with so little outward emotion? She was beside herself with worry.

"Dashin, will you present your tokens?" Fodrick asked him, putting out his hand.

Dashin pulled the bag from his belt, removed the tokens, and handed them to Fodrick.

The crowd leaned forward, their heads maneuvering to count them. Alina did so as well. All six tokens were there. How he'd managed to retrieve them from the upper canopy was a mystery, but he'd somehow found a way. In all the excitement, she hadn't even thought to ask him.

Fodrick studied each token, and when he was confident that all of them were there and correct, he announced. "All these tokens are valid!"

A cautious cheer rippled through the crowd.

"Aor," Fodrick said, "please present yours."

Aor came forward and put the tokens he'd already taken from his bag into his father's hand. He gave Dashin another regretful look, as he did.

What was going on between Aor and Dashin? She squeezed Dashin's hand, trying to catch his eyes, but he continued to look forward, ignoring her. There was definitely something.

There were six tokens as well, which surprised no one. Fodrick flipped through them, giving them a cursory glance. The chaser would, of course, have valid tokens. The crowd began to mutter again, warming up to resume its protest, when Fodrick stopped on one token and lifted it to study it. A small smile tugged at the corners of his mouth as he did. Everyone noticed, and the muttering stopped.

"Aor, it appears that one of your tokens is not valid," Fodrick said, holding the token up. He peered at it, puzzled, and turned to Dashin.

"What is that strange symbol in the corner of this token?" he asked.

"It's supposed to be my smiling face," Dashin said. "I'm not much of an artist."

"It looks more like a corsol," Fodrick replied, grinning.

Dashin shrugged.

Alina was upset. She didn't know what was going on. What could this mean? She leaned in. "What is going on?" she whispered.

He squeezed her hand.

She took a breath, trying to calm her nerves.

"So, he scratched something on a token. That does not count," Hedrick announced.

"You are correct," Fodrick said. "Had he just scratched something on one of the tokens in the basket, it would not count. But this is not one of those tokens. This is another token altogether."

"What?" Aor said, leaning forward to see it. "There was only one token left in all the baskets."

"Taking more than one token from a basket is also against the rules," Hedrick declared. "Either way, it eliminates him."

Fodrick turned to Dashin. "That is true, Dashin," he said sadly. "Did you replace the other token in the basket with this one?"

Alina's heart sank. She'd been so clear and had gone over the rules with him many times. There had to be another explanation. She gripped his hand, willing it so.

"No, I only removed one token from the basket," Dashin said. "Though I am a little clumsy, and I was admiring one of Alina's tokens from her *becoming* at the time. I might have dropped it in the basket by accident."

Alina's mind raced ahead. There was no rule against adding tokens to a basket. Candidates sometimes did that, but the chaser would then sort through them, and Aor had said there had only been one token.

Fodrick turned to Aor. "Could you have missed the other token?" he asked. "Which basket was it?"

Fodrick glanced at the token. "The fourth."

Aor looked at Dashin. "No, there was only one token in that basket."

"Dashin, do you dispute this?"

"I do," he said. "I think if you get that basket, you'll find there's another token in there."

Dashin's body was tense, but somehow it held no sense of the defeat that now faced him. She wanted to turn him to her and wring the tale from him so as to understand what was going through his mind.

Fodrick sighed. "We need someone other than Aor or Dashin to get that basket," he announced.

Drur jumped up. "I'll get it!"

Fodrick frowned. "I see your shoulder is feeling better."

Drur swallowed. "Yes, thanks. It feels much better."

Fodrick nodded. Drur ran off to fetch his lanyards. Moments later, he raced away on the course.

"While we're waiting, I would like to share something," Aor said, shifting uncomfortably the way he did when he had something important to say.

His father turned to him and nodded.

"I do not understand why Dashin hasn't spoken of what happened on the course or why he asked me to remain silent on the matter. But I find that I can no longer do so."

Everyone was confused now. Alina hated this. What was going on, and why wasn't Dashin filling her in?

"I'm sorry, Dashin," he said.

Dashin shrugged in reply.

She tugged at his hand, trying to get his attention, and noted, with alarm, the traces of dried blood on his forearm. She turned his arm toward her, searching for the source, and was about to press him on it when Aor continued.

"I had an accident on the course," he began. "I took a nasty fall."

Her father jumped up and started forward, but Aor held up his hand. "I'm fine. I have some bruises I'll feel for a few days, but otherwise, I think I'm fine." Her father sat back down, reluctant to take Aor's word for it but willing to let Aor tell his tale for now. She had no doubt Aor would get examined later.

"I was in the very upper canopy when I misjudged a branch."

Alina could see the looks of surprise on the faces of the other villagers. She knew why he'd been in the upper canopy, even if it made no sense to them.

"My lanyards got tangled around me," he said, choosing his words.

There was something odd about the way he looked off to the side as he said this. He was lying. Hurza met her eyes and arched an eyebrow, having noticed it too. Alina shrugged in response. She looked at Dashin, but he was looking at Aor and would not meet her eyes.

"I fell and hit my head and lost consciousness."

Now, everyone was riveted on Aor. An uncontrolled fall? How had he survived such a thing and still managed to complete the course?

"The SkyGods were there today," he said, taking a breath and looking out over the villagers. "For Dashin was in the lower canopy, having just finished the basket I was approaching, and as I fell toward him, he raced to meet me and caught my lanyard as I fell by him and stopped my fall."

All sound on the platform was swallowed up by those last words. Everyone sat stunned, trying to imagine such a thing. How could someone intercept a person falling through the trees, grab a lanyard, and stop such a fall from such a height?

Dashin was strong, but this feat was beyond anything she imagined possible. She stared at Dashin in awe that he would have reacted without thought to save the person who would, in effect, be sending him to die. She could not find words or thoughts to express the enormity of the gesture.

Around her, people touched their foreheads with their fingertips. She reached up and did the same, for it seemed the only possible response.

"After saving me, he helped me recover and then made me promise that I would do my best to chase him despite having saved my life. And, though I am not sure that I arrived before he did," he paused here, letting the words sit. "I do not think that it should matter, for I would not have arrived at all if he had not risked his life to save mine. In light of that, what can the exact moment each of us arrived matter?"

Fodrick had gone ashen at the tale, and he pulled Aor to him. Milena joined them. His parents held him tight, both of them turning to fix Dashin with gazes that everyone understood.

Alina looked over at Hedrick, who'd been silent throughout the tale. He stood there frozen, his mouth agape, a horrified look on his face. His face was so pale it seemed he might pass out. He blinked as though he'd been far away and only just now returned. He turned and fled from the platform.

"Oh," she heard her mother say, behind her.

Alina turned to see her eyes follow Hedrick from the platform.

Drur appeared, dropping to the platform with a basket.

Drur was angry. "I have never seen a course such as this one," he said. "Every basket was at the very top of the canopy. I can't imagine how Dashin managed to reach any of those. I struggled to do so myself."

Everyone turned in search of Hedrick, their faces hard as they did, but he was gone.

Drur handed the basket to Fodrick, shaking his head sadly at Dashin as he did.

Alina's nerves were frazzled. Was this never going to end? She'd been certain after Dashin's statement that they would find the other token, and this would all be finally over.

"Was there anything in it when you got there?" Fodrick asked.

Drur shook his head. "No, it was as you see it."

Fodrick turned to Dashin.

"I'm sorry, but the rules do not allow you to take more than one token from the basket," Fodrick said, holding the empty basket.

"I did not take more than one," Dashin said. He seemed confident, which was confusing. She looked around, and everyone else seemed equally confused.

Fodrick sighed, "Dashin, you'll have to speak more plainly."

Dashin pointed at the basket. "The other token is still there," he said.

Fodrick turned it over so that the inside was plainly visible to everyone, to show that it was indeed empty, but as he did, something caught his eye, and he reached into the basket and picked at the bottom. He grabbed the corner of what seemed to be a banda leaf and peeled it away, and as he did so, the lost token magically appeared, still in the basket.

There was a collective gasp of delight, and the crowd erupted in cheers. The villagers stomped their feet so aggressively on the platform that the entire platform shook.

Fodrick beamed out over the crowd. "It seems we will be having a feast after all."

Chapter 48

Dashin received congratulations from every member of the tribe, save one. Each of them came forward in turn to clasp his forearm in the traditional gesture of acceptance. Each clasp stilled Dashin's shaking arm, so overwhelmed was he by all that had happened to bring him to this moment. Aside from his short time on the Serendipity, he'd never truly belonged to a family before. And the realization that he was now part of one made it difficult for him to do more than nod as each person greeted him formally.

The greetings from Aor and Drur were especially meaningful, as he'd already shared something personal with both of them. It choked him up to see his own desire for friendship mirrored in their eyes.

Hurza mentioned how pleased she was that Dashin had taken her teachings to heart, crinkling her eyes. Kani shook her head and nudged her, and Hurza giggled in response before gushing at how well Alina's treats had worked, holding her stomach and explaining how she'd had to take one herself. She'd been thrilled at the success of her necklace, Aor having explained to her that it'd been so annoying that it'd slowed him down significantly and probably been the deciding factor. Her excitement warmed Dashin's heart, and he'd managed to say he was certain it had indeed been the case.

Fodrick and Milena thanked him for their son's life. Milena spoke the words for both when Fodrick could not get them from his lips.

Marna and Enor also came together, arm in arm, beaming. Though neither said it in so many words, the emotion behind their words made it clear to Dashin that they considered him part of their family and not just their tribe.

Rigin didn't say anything at all. She just clasped his forearm and leaned in, touching her forehead to his. They stood like this for many moments before she pulled back and looked into his eyes. In his short time here, she had become the only true mother he'd ever known, and he tried to convey it in his gaze. She smiled and wiped a tear from his cheek.

Solvan and Matse were not *of the tribe* and, as such, could not officially greet him, but Dashin knelt before them anyway. He greeted each in turn, taking their tiny forearms in his hand as their little fingers gripped his own. He leaned in and touched foreheads with each of them. The greeting was insufficient for Solvan, who threw his arms around Dashin's neck and hugged him fiercely before he could rise. A moment later, Matse joined in, and they stayed thus until both of Dashin's shoulders were wet with their tears. As Dashin was about to pull away, Matse leaned in, hugging him so tight that her hands went pale. She leaned forward and whispered "Dashin" into his ear. Dashin hugged her back, holding her firmly against him until she let go.

Throughout the ceremony, Alina stood a pace behind him and to the side. She held Pritha in her arms, the kitten snoring, spent from the tensions of the day. Alina sniffled throughout the ceremony, apparently as overwhelmed as he was.

When only she remained, he turned to her, and she leaned in. A moment later, she was in his mind.

"How are you, Amani?" she sent, her thoughts soft and warm.

"I feel numb," he replied. *"As though I were floating in a warm cenote."*

"I was so angry with you on the platform earlier."

"I'm sorry, I knew you had so many questions, but there was too much to explain, and I didn't know how things would end."

He could feel the flurry of emotions and thoughts within her, all of them pressing to be shared. He waited, but he felt her push them away. *"Congratulations on your becoming, Dashin,"* she sent instead. *"I accept you as being of my tribe."* Her formal acceptance meant so much more than all the others he'd received, and he finally dared to accept that he had now found a home. Tears pushed their way from his eyes like a spring from the earth.

"Thank you, Amani," he replied, grateful that she was in his mind and could already feel his heart, for he could not have found the words.

They stayed together thus, their minds comforted in the feel of each other, as though a part of them had been absent and only just recovered. Dashin was enjoying the deep peace and joy when Alina sent him the image of a platter of dried meat. The image jarred him. *"What?"*

"That was not me," she sent, giggling.

"Someone has not forgotten my earlier promise for a heaping platter," she said, pulling back. Dashin opened his eyes to see her looking into the kitten's golden eyes. Pritha licked her lips.

The platform around him was astir with people rushing about making preparations for the feast. Dashin had been eager to help, but Marna and Rigin informed him that it was customary for candidates to relax and chat among themselves during preparations. Since he was the only candidate, he sat with Alina and Pritha, neither of whom had left his side since he'd crashed into the platform.

Now that the ceremony was behind them, the many questions Alina had suppressed bubbled up to the surface. He explained how he'd managed to reach the upper canopy, going through the details several times as she questioned him until she could picture it. She pressed him on how the idea had occurred to him, and she was unsatisfied with his answers, but moved on to her other questions.

She asked about the incident with Aor, needing him to explain the fall multiple times until he admitted the borka juice's role in the fall, and the pieces fell into place. She was annoyed with him for the lie, until he explained that Aor had been insistent he not mention it in order to protect Hurza. Aor and Hurza were working together in the kitchen now, both of them glowing. When Alina turned and saw them, she nodded, agreeing to keep the secret, too.

She asked him about the banda leaf, and he told her he'd gotten the idea from Pritha in the pod, licking a banda leaf. He told her everything he'd felt, everything he'd thought, her questions probing and guiding him until she was satisfied that she'd explored both the *trial of the forest* and the *trial of the trees* fully. When the pointed questions and probes concluded, he felt as though he'd just been through a rigorous Ancaran exam with an eager intern.

"You'll have to present your handful of nuts at the feast," Alina said, chuckling. "I told you no one would care about your dish," she motioned to the people bustling about, chatting excitedly. "Your *becoming* will be the talk of the tribe for some time," she said proudly.

"Oh, I have a dish," Dashin said. Given the grilling he'd just received about why he'd left his pod at night to wander about picking up meat, his decision to go in search of mirha nectar wasn't a topic he was eager to broach.

"When did you have time to create a dish and prepare it?" she said, frowning.

"Well, Rigin helped with the preparation," he admitted.

"So, Rigin created the dish for you?" she asked.

"Not really. It was my idea."

"Dashin, I've seen you stuff your banda leaves. Trust me, folks will prefer the nuts," she chuckled, crinkling her eyes.

"Hey, my leaves taste great," he argued.

"It's clear from the way you eat them that you believe that," she said, nudging him with a shoulder.

He pushed that aside. "Well, I think they may like this dish," he replied, deciding now that she would have to wait for the surprise with the others. This way, he would also avoid having to discuss the risks he took in acquiring it.

"Oh, I'm sorry," she said, still chuckling. "Tell me," she prompted.

"No, you'll just have to wait with everyone else," he said, pursing his lips in mock annoyance.

She giggled, delighted. "You are a man of many mysteries, Amani," she said, squeezing his arm and leaning into him.

The tables were piled with food. Everyone was seated, except for Hedrick, who hadn't been seen since leaving the platform after hearing of Aor's fall. The villagers were talking animatedly, recounting bits of his *becoming*. Hearing his trials spoken of, it seemed impossible that he was the one who had lived it. The tales seemed so fantastic, he felt certain they belonged to another.

Pritha had found a place in Matse's lap, to the girl's delight. Dashin had handed Solvan his lanyards after the ceremony for the boy to hold and show others if he so chose. The boy had instantly drawn a crowd of children about him. Dashin heard him explain how he'd had a hand in their creation, which was technically true. It warmed his heart to see Solvan in the center of his peers, no longer an outsider among them. Now he sat at the table, his hands stroking the lanyards, his eyes filled with dreams. Marna and Enor were also at his table, and Alina, of course, was still glued to him, which completed this perfect picture.

Fodrick stood up, and everyone quieted.

"This past moon cycle has been a difficult one. I have never seen such deep divisions within our tribe." His tone was serious, formal.

There was some regretful muttering, but he continued over it.

"I fault no one for their opinions or actions. I trust that everyone was acting in the best interests of the tribe as they saw it." He let the words lie, perhaps wanting them to be true for everyone.

Dashin thought his words were particularly poignant given that his father was absent. But he seemed to be trying to heal things, and it warmed Dashin's heart. He hadn't considered what Fodrick might be feeling for his father, who was out there, somewhere, alone now. It was a feeling Dashin knew well, and it touched him in a way he had not expected.

"Dashin is *of the tribe* now, and though I see from your faces that I do not have to say the words, any ill feelings anyone might have had toward him before need to be cast on the wind now." He looked around until he was satisfied his words had been heard and then continued. "Dashin, it is customary for candidates to offer up a dish at the feast. In your case, I think we can all make an..."

"Oh, I have one," Dashin interrupted.

"A dish for the feast?" Fodrick blinked. "You created a dish?"

"Yes, sort of."

"You believed you would prevail?" Fodrick asked, stunned.

Dashin shrugged. "Well, let's say I hoped I would and I wanted to be prepared."

Fodrick laughed out loud, and others joined in. Dashin didn't know whether to feel flattered or offended.

"Let me guess," Fodrick said, stemming his laughter. "While you were fighting the pack of turgas with your bare hands, you took a moment to climb into the sky to slice a piece of the moon off and turn into a dish?"

The laughter grew, and Dashin got caught up in it, chuckling along.

When it died down, Fodrick turned to him. "I'm sorry, Dashin. We've all seen you eat and..." Milena smacked him in the calf. He looked down at her, and she gave him a hard stare. He swallowed and grew more serious. "My wife is right as usual. We should take your efforts seriously. Please present your dish."

Dashin jumped up, as did Rigin, and they ran to her hut, muttering and laughter in their wake.

"Were you able to make anything with the nectar?" he asked as they neared the door.

"Dashin, the nectar is so treasured that it is never mixed with anything. It is a dish unto itself. All I did was portion it into cups and added flowers for garnish."

They stepped into the common room, and she lifted the towel she had over a tray of cups. Inside each was a modest spoonful of nectar with tiny flowers to one side.

"I had much more nectar than that," Dashin said, feeling terrible. The portions seemed so meager. He turned to protest.

Rigin put her fingers on his lips, smiling. She picked up a small, smooth stick from a pile on the tray and took the tiniest bit of nectar on the end of it. She lifted it to his mouth, and as he opened it, she put it on his tongue. His entire mouth woke up, and his tongue tingled in the most delicious way imaginable. He couldn't believe how such a tiny amount could produce such a glorious effect. His whole body woke, and he felt a warm glow spread throughout.

"This is amazing," he said, beaming with delight.

Rigin smiled at him.

"What will we do with the rest?" he wondered, looking at the jar.

"Dashin, this is a treasure beyond imagining. TreeFolk will trade much for even the tiniest amount."

"I should give it to the tribe," he said, excited.

Rigin cupped his face, beaming at him. "If that is your wish, of course, you could. But this is a big decision. Wait on it before you decide. There may be other things you want to do with it."

Dashin couldn't imagine what else he might do with it, but he nodded. "Will it keep?" he worried.

Rigin nodded. "The nectar keeps very well, which is why it is still edible when an abandoned nest is found. In that magical container of yours, I would think it would last a great many sun cycles."

Dashin was excited now and so eager that when he grabbed the tray, all the cups slid across it, jostling each other as they slid toward the edge.

Rigin put her hand on the edge of it to still them, chuckling as she did, "Why don't I carry it to the platform and you present it?"

"What do I say?"

"You don't have to say anything," she replied, crinkling her eyes. "We'll just walk around the tables, and you put one of these cups and some sticks down on each."

And that is what they did. By the time Dashin placed the final cup, many fingertips had already found foreheads, and the platform was dead quiet.

Dashin sat down, and even Alina, who'd been chatting nonstop since the ceremony, had no words.

The silence went on until Milena nudged Fodrick, who stood again. He opened his mouth to speak several times, but no words came out. Finally, he began, "Dashin, when I jested earlier about you taking a slice from the moon, I had no idea that you'd done so."

He paused, reaching an arm toward the forest. "How you managed to find this much fresh nectar I cannot understand. And yet I find I cannot understand how you managed any of your trials, so why should this be different?" he said with a chuckle.

"Few of us have ever tried this, though our songs speak of it. So as you can see, we are all eager to do so. Thank you for this gift. It is gratefully received."

Fodrick sat down, reached in, took a tiny amount on one of the sticks, and put it on his tongue. As he did so, other villagers did the same, and parents then carefully fed tiny bits of it to their children.

Rigin gave a stick to Solvan and two to Matse before taking one for herself. Matse held one of the sticks for Pritha, who had just finished the enormous platter of dried meat Alina had given her. The kitten sniffed it and tasted it with the tip of her tongue. Then she shook her head, wiping her face with her paws before fixing her eyes on the stick again and licking every remaining bit of nectar from it. Everyone at the table chuckled.

Alina turned to him, "Amani, I cannot..." she began.

"Is this better than nuts?" he grinned at her.

She leaned in and touched her forehead to his, the warmth of her regard washing over him. Then she grinned and picked up a stick.

"Excuse me for a moment," he said, standing. Behind him, everyone was so fixated on the treasure before them that no one saw him leave.

Chapter 49

Dashin found Hedrick in the grove, sitting in the dark, mumbling to himself with his head in his hands. He looked small and anguished in a way that reminded Dashin of the many nights in his youth when he'd lain in the dark bemoaning his lot.

He walked over and sat on the opposite end of the bench from Hedrick. The older man didn't notice him at first, but then, sensing his presence, he looked over and groaned.

"I do not mean to disturb you," Dashin began, "but I think we should speak."

Hedrick's shoulders slumped further. "Of course," he said, without looking at Dashin. He took a deep breath and sighed. "This day would not be complete without the SkyGods providing the finishing blow. Say what you must."

Dashin didn't understand this despair. Hedrick had merely lost an argument. An argument that would have cost Dashin his life. Rage boiled within him. Angry words filled his mind, seeking the river to his mouth. He bit them back, taking a breath and turning his thoughts back to the tribe and, in particular, Aor and Fodrick, who both loved this man. During the preparations for the feast, he'd heard Hedrick's name several times in concerned tones. They had found him in the grove, but he'd refused to speak to anyone. Even Aor had come back, shaking his head as he spoke to Fodrick.

"I am *of the tribe* now," Dashin announced.

"Yes, I gathered from all the cheering," Hedrick sneered.

Dashin bristled, pushing down the anger that threatened to overtake him. He took another breath. "I would put behind us that which has passed," he said, his voice devoid of emotion.

The words shocked Hedrick, and his head came up. He turned to look at Dashin, his eyes searching for some trace of falsehood or ruse. Dashin remained impassive, returning the stare.

After a pause, Hedrick spoke, "Why would you do such a thing?"

"I'm not doing it for you. After last night, there were a great many things I wanted to do," he replied, a touch of anger creeping through.

Hedrick turned away and nodded.

Dashin exhaled. "But the village needs you. Your family needs you."

"You would have us go on as though nothing happened between us?" Hedrick said, not believing the words.

"I don't imagine we'll be friends, but I would like the village to move beyond this."

"Dashin, I think everyone would be better off without me," he said, his tone defeated.

Those words scared Dashin, who was uncertain what they meant but certain they did not bode well.

"People have already moved on and are speaking together again," Dashin said, trying to sound hopeful. "Fodrick made it clear to everyone that they were to put things behind them. I'm sure people will be happy to have you back."

"You don't understand, Dashin," he replied, his shoulders slumping again.

Dashin sensed the pain inside the man. A great shadow intent on swallowing him. "You're right, I don't," Dashin said, inviting him to speak.

Hedrick sighed and could not bring himself to break the silence stretching between them. Instead, he retreated inward again.

"Fodrick told me something of the story of your village," Dashin prompted.

Those words brought Hedrick's head around, his face confused.

"He didn't share all the details, of course," Dashin said. "But he wanted me to know why you were so protective of this tribe and why the *becoming* was an especially sensitive point for you."

Hedrick sat with his mouth open for a moment, then he asked Dashin to relate what he knew of the story. Dashin complied, telling the tale as he remembered it, how Hedrick had made a poor decision for a *becoming* and that this person had come back with others and killed everyone, leaving Fodrick on the brink of death.

Hedrick listened to the tale, and when Dashin was done, he nodded. "That is the rough shape of it." He sighed. "Though it is only the tip of the story."

Dashin waited, sensing that Hedrick's torment was near the surface now. If he could help him speak it, perhaps the speaking might draw it from his soul and release it into the night where such things lived.

"I am fortune's fool, Dashin," he said.

It sounded like a preamble. Dashin waited for the thread he could see unraveling within.

"When I was young, younger than Aor is now, I was touched with the *sight*," he began.

Dashin gasped.

"Yes," Hedrick said, nodding at Dashin's outburst. "I'm sure most of the other villagers would find that as surprising as you do."

He paused, gathering his thoughts. "My gift was slight, not like Marna's. I had dreams from time to time that showed me things that might be. I had no control over these dreams, no understanding of them, and lacked the discipline or guidance to attempt to divine their meaning."

He was looking into the trees now, remembering a time long ago, the tale unfolding haltingly.

"I saw the woman who was to be my wife in such a dream, long before I met her. She lived in a neighboring village, and when I met her, I could scarcely believe my eyes. I took it as a sign that I should pursue her, which I did, and she eventually *chose* me. That was the happiest day of my life. Then my sons were born, filling our lives with joy." The creases in his face eased for a moment, and a lightness touched his features as he recalled these memories. The lightness ebbed as he continued. "From time to time, I saw things that helped me gain influence and status within the tribe. I never asked myself how I should act on the information the SkyGods offered me."

He glanced up at the stars, his eyes sad, reproachful. Dashin's skin tingled at the foreboding tone of Hedrick's words.

"I began to believe I deserved these dreams. When I became chief, I had attained all I could have dreamed of. Things were fine for a time, but then my dreams grew dark. I would awaken from nightmares of death, which I knew to be of my doing, though I could not find the source. And, as days passed, they plagued me. Whereas I had helpful dreams once or twice a sun cycle before, now the nightmares came several times each moon cycle. To rid myself of the nightmares, I stopped sleeping, except when I was so exhausted that my sleep was free of dreams. As you've heard, my nightmares came true. All those I loved, except for Fodrick, died, essentially at my hand."

He paused, looking off into the forest.

"The only good thing was that after that day I lost my *sight*, and from then on sleep for me has been mercifully dreamless. I thought the SkyGods had taken pity on me and turned from me, leaving me to carry the scars of my failure."

"You have the shape of our travels beyond my dead tribe, though not the details," he said, pausing, his mind adrift for a moment. "After many sun cycles, we came to this tribe, and I built a life here for my son. I tried to put aside the horrors of my past for him so that he might have a life beyond it, even if that terrible day still lived on within me. In time, he married and had a son, and Aor was a seed of joy in the cold soil of my heart."

Hedrick's words were flowing now, the dam having burst within him. He spoke without trying to shape the words, letting them rise naked from his heart to tumble into the world.

"Aor became the reason I arose from my bed in the morning and the last thing I considered before I closed my eyes at night. And that was what my life had become until the day you arrived in our village."

Hedrick's face lit up as he spoke of Aor. Dashin dared not breathe, now that they had reached the brink.

"The night you arrived, I had a feeling of fear I could not shake. I argued with Marna, and when she expressed that she had seen your arrival in her *sight* when she was but a girl, the thought terrified me. I feared the SkyGods were again turning their gaze upon me and those near me."

"That night I dreamed. It was the first dream I'd had since the day those I loved died. In my dream, you were standing over Aor, who lay dead at your feet, your hands covered in his blood."

Dashin could not breathe. The thought was appalling. No wonder Hedrick had been terrified of having him in the village. What might Dashin have done when faced with a dream of someone standing over Alina, covered in her blood?

"I would never..." Dashin stammered.

"I know that now, Dashin," Hedrick said miserably. His entire body shook as deep sobs escaped his lips, the following words tumbling out between them. "It was me who nearly killed him. Aor almost died because of me. The SkyGods have again made me their fool."

"I don't understand," Dashin said.

The sobbing ebbed, and Hedrick continued. "As Aor told the tale of his fall and how you caught him, I saw the truth of my dream. When I glanced at your hands and saw Aor's blood upon them from the fall, I recognized the pattern of blood on your arms from my dream."

He turned to Dashin, his face horrified. "You were not killing Aor in my dream. You were saving his life. And, had I not pressed matters as I have, he would never have been in danger. Had I not forced Drur to forgo chasing, Aor would never have been in the trees. I put him there, and had you not risked your life to save him, Aor would now be dead, by my hand."

Dashin could think of nothing to say. In Hedrick's place, would he have acted differently? He couldn't imagine that there was anything he would not do to protect Alina.

"So you see, Dashin, all of this was my folly. I cannot find a way to atone for what I've done to you or to express my gratitude for the life of Aor." He was crying now, tears streaming down his face, the conclusion of his tale having broken the barrier within him that held them in check.

Dashin sat with him as he cried, gazing at the man he'd come to hate. Dashin had come to the grove reluctantly. He'd come to find some way to make peace with Hedrick for the good of the tribe, but somehow he'd also found peace for himself. He dabbed at his own eyes with a sleeve.

Eventually, Hedrick's tears stopped flowing, and they sat in silence as nightbirds called to each other and the breeze dried their eyes.

Dashin exhaled a long breath. "Thank you for trusting me with your tale. I find that on hearing it, I cannot fault you for your actions. And the anger and resentment I have toward you is only a sapling now instead of the tree it was earlier."

"How can that be?" Hedrick asked, shaking his head.

"You caught me on a good day," Dashin said with a laugh.

Hedrick snorted, the laugh catching him by surprise. He wiped his face on his sleeve. "Dashin, I have no words to express how grateful I am to you for this. If there's anything..."

"There is actually," Dashin said, with a grin.

"I see," Hedrick said, surprised but willing to hear the terms.

"Everyone in the tribe has accepted me formally already. You are the only one who hasn't. I would like to make it official in front of the tribe."

Hedrick nodded, smiling weakly, spent from the day. "I would be honored."

"There are two more things."

Hedrick nodded.

"I do not need to know the details, but whatever hold you have over Drur and his sister, you need to resolve it and release him from it."

Hedrick flushed and looked down. "Of course, I intended to do as much. I regret having done that. There is no excuse for it."

Dashin nodded, content it would be settled.

"The final request is that you allow me to share what happened here with Alina. I'll ask her not to mention it to anyone else, but she will likely learn of it from me whether I want her to or not." He didn't elaborate on how that might come about. "I would like your permission to share it, so I don't have to try to keep it from her."

"Yes, you have it."

"Good. Are you ready to rejoin the tribe?" Dashin asked, tired from the ordeal.

Hedrick nodded. "Waiting will not make this easier," he said.

"It seems the feast is still going strong. That will make it easier. And there may still be some of my dish for you to try."

Chapter 50

Dashin drifted up from a dream filled with lush greenery. He'd been swinging through the branches with Alina, laughing as the sun lit up the forest. Blinking his eyes open, he glanced up at the window. It was still dark outside. The moon had left the sky, but the sun had not yet kissed the upper canopy. A cool breeze swept into the room, carrying with it the scent of night blossoms and causing the hut to sway softly beneath him. He pulled the blanket up under his chin. In the distance, a night-bird called out, and nearby, he could just make out the faint scurrying of lodra in the trees.

This was his forest now, his home. He tried to imprint every detail of it in his mind. He grinned. It seemed his new home had even displaced the dreams of sand and stone of his youth and replaced them with dreams of verdure.

Yawning, he rubbed the sleep from his eyes, shaking off the last tendrils of the dream. He was still exhausted but too excited to sleep anymore. It had been late when the feast broke up. Folks had lingered on the platform long after everything had been put away. The new moon was high in the sky when they'd made their way to their beds.

There'd been an awkward moment when Dashin and Hedrick arrived from the grove, but Hedrick's formal acceptance of Dashin resulted in thunderous slapping of the platform, which had quickly dispelled it. The looks he'd received from Fodrick and Aor had warmed his heart.

Alina had been angry with him at first, unable to understand how he could have forgiven Hedrick. It wasn't until they sat together later that night and he told her Hedrick's story that she understood. She had grown very quiet after that, perhaps seeing her own past interactions with Hedrick in a new light.

Dashin arose and stepped onto the hut's platform to wash his face. The world looked so different today. The persistent tension of the past month was behind him. The sheer joy of being *of the tribe* made him smile every time he thought of it. He stepped inside and looked in on the children, their small bodies curled up on their sleeping pallets. Matse had her arm over Pritha, and Solvan had his over Dashin's lanyards. Dashin knelt next to the children, watching them sleep, their tiny bodies so delicate.

He put his forearm next to Solvan. It was the same size as his thigh, and Matse's wrists were the size of a few of Dashin's fingers put together. Pritha opened an eye and looked up at him. He pet her, and she turned her head so he could reach behind her ear. He gave her ear a scratch, and he felt her touch his mind. He closed his eyes, and he saw a picture of a bowl of dried meat. How she could still be hungry was beyond him, given the quantity of food she was consuming. Although she was growing rapidly and was already twice the size she'd been when he found her. Dashin smiled and sent her an image of her sleeping with Matse. Pritha considered this and responded with the sleeping picture. He opened his eyes, and she'd burrowed her head into the crook of Matse's neck.

Dashin drank a glass of water in the common room and went back to his room. He opened his tool bag and dug through the supplies he had left over from his work on his lanyards. There was quite a bit of rubber left over from the lengths he'd cut off to shorten them. There might be enough there for what he had in mind. He slit the lengths open, separating the harder interior core from the external rubber sheath.

He was trying to be quiet, but he must have made more noise than he'd intended for Rigin stepped into his room with a lamp.

"Dashin, do you need light?" she asked. "Is it not too dark to work?"

"Oh, thanks. I didn't mean to wake you."

She waved it away. "I was awake, thinking of last night's meal," she said, squeezing his shoulder and then sitting on the bed next to the table.

"What is it you're doing?" she asked, curious at all the bits and pieces he had scattered on the table.

He explained it to her, and she gasped. "Is such a thing possible?"

"I don't know, but I thought I'd try. Though I could use some help with gluing some of these pieces together and sewing some leather supports at either end and..." He paused, looking at the supplies. "Actually, I need help making most of it. I just have the idea for it."

She hurried from the room and returned with two large baskets filled with her leatherworking tools. Dashin moved everything to the floor to give them space to work. They worked on it together until well after the morning birds had sung their songs. The village was slow to wake after the long feast. The platform remained quiet long after it should have been bustling.

Dashin was trying it on when Alina came in, yawning. She stopped just inside the door, looking at the mess covering the floor. "What in the world are you two doing?" she asked, chuckling, as she picked her way over to the chair and moved the stuff that was on it to the table so she could sit.

"What do you think?" Dashin asked, slipping the rubber sleeve up his forearm and over his elbow. He flexed it. The sleeve felt much better now. The leather cuffs along the top and bottom of the sleeve secured both ends, with straps allowing for adjustment. Within the sleeve, they'd added the strips of harder inner core from the lanyards. It was firm yet comfortable, and support increased the further it flexed.

"Why are you making a sleeve for your arm?" Alina asked, concerned. "Did you injure it?"

"No, my arm's fine. I have something else in mind," he grinned.

Alina chuckled. "You are a man of mystery, Amani."

"Yes, I am," he said, grinning.

He slipped off the sleeve and turned to Rigin. "I think it's ready to try out," he said.

Rigin jumped up from the floor and hurried from the room.

"Are you going to let me in on the secret?" Alina asked.

"That would take away the mystery, wouldn't it?"

She picked up a stray piece of rubber from the table and threw it at him. He grinned, and she narrowed her eyes. He put up his hands. "Just one more moment," he assured her.

Rigin led Solvan, who was still half asleep and looking even more disheveled than normal, into the room. Dashin stood up, walked to the chair, and took Alina's hand. He moved her to the bed and sat down next to her. Alina's eyes grew wide with excitement, apparently having caught on to where things were going.

Solvan blinked wearily and yawned. As his eyes found Dashin, his face lit up. "Your lanyards are in my room," he said, turning to go get them, thinking that Dashin was calling him to ask for them.

"No, Solvan, I don't need the lanyards," he said.

The boy turned to him, noticing all eyes on him. He squirmed, and Dashin saw the look in his eyes, the little mind going over the events of last night, wondering what he might have said or done to warrant this.

Dashin chuckled. "No, you're not in any trouble. I was wondering if you could help me with something Rigin and I are working on. We need someone to try it, and you came to mind."

He was beaming now, so excited to be a part of whatever this was.

"This is so *round*," he exclaimed, hopping in place.

"Can you sit here for a moment?" Dashin asked, indicating the chair.

Solvan bounced over to the chair and hopped onto it, giggling.

"I want to try this on your leg," Dashin said, indicating the sleeve. "Can you pull your pant leg up for me?"

Solvan reached down and pulled up the pant leg on his good leg.

"No, the other one," Dashin said.

Solvan frowned and then blushed, embarrassed by the attention to that leg. The look pained Dashin, and he bit his lip. What taunts the boy must have endured. How vulnerable he seemed in this moment, with the people he looked up to most in the world focused on his infirmity.

But the boy reached down and pulled up his pant leg, exposing the joint he always kept covered. He turned his trusting eyes to Dashin's, his breathing faster now.

Dashin slipped the sleeve over his foot, having to maneuver it over the extremity, which had atrophied and twisted from the uneven use. Dashin pulled it up over the knee and secured it in place with the straps. The sleeve fit very well, Dashin's forearm indeed being a good proxy for Solvan's thigh.

Solvan was excited but confused. He looked from face to face, eager to be let in on the secret. "Can you take a few steps with it?" Dashin asked him.

Solvan eased out of the chair and walked across the room, dragging his damaged leg as he did.

"No, I'd like you to walk on it, if possible."

Solvan was unsure what Dashin meant, but he put a bit of weight on the leg and was stunned when it spring back. His eyes went wide, and he pushed against it and hobbled across the floor on it, pressing more and more against it as he did. It was an awkward gait at first. His foot was unused to bearing any weight, and with it turned to one side, it would take some work. But he was much more mobile.

The boy's eyes were wide with shock as he stared down at it.

"It will take some time to get used to it, and we'll have to work your foot several times a day to restore the muscles. But I think it might allow you to regain use of your leg over time."

Solvan broke down and cried, embarrassed by the tears but unable to stem them.

"Come here," Dashin called, taking the young boy in his arms. "It's okay to be overwhelmed."

Solvan buried his head in Dashin's shoulder.

"I cried many times when Alina was training me," he said to the boy.

Solvan looked up, not believing this could be true. He sniffled and looked into Dashin's eyes.

"Ask her," Dashin prodded.

Solvan looked across at Alina, and she nodded. "Yes, he cried often and like a baby. It was embarrassing for him."

Solvan made a series of small choking sounds, his sobbing slowing. He looked wide-eyed at Dashin for confirmation.

Dashin arched an eyebrow. "I didn't cry *that* much."

"Oh, it was terrible how much he cried. Almost every day. I didn't think it would ever stop," she said, looking right at Solvan.

He snorted and then began laughing at the thought. He laughed so hard he could hardly breathe as he leaned into Dashin. Dashin held him against his chest, feeling his heart beat against his ribs.

When at last the laughter subsided, Dashin said, "You will need to practice with this if you are to train for your *becoming* one day."

The words had only just left his lips when the boy stopped breathing and fixed him with a gaze so intent that it shocked Dashin. It was clear he'd never dared believe this would be possible for him. He put his small arms around Dashin and hugged him fiercely.

"Ow, I'm still sore from yesterday," Dashin teased. "You are crushing me with those arms." Solvan relaxed his grip a bit but kept hugging Dashin.

It broke Dashin's heart to sense the pain the child had endured. And, despite that, he always had a smile for everyone. He was determined to make good on the promise. Someday, he swore to himself, Solvan would be *of the tribe*.

"I want you to practice with it," he said, pulling Solvan away to look into his eyes. "You must learn to use it and show me every day what progress you are making. Can you do that?"

Solvan nodded, smiling now as he sniffled and wiped his eyes with his sleeve.

"Now go and practice," Dashin said.

Solvan jumped from the chair and hobbled from the room. They could hear him showing Matse in the other room, the little girl slapping the floor. A few moments later, Solvan's feet thundered on the bridge, running hard for the platform.

Alina turned his head and placed her forehead to his. Rigin stepped out of the room. He went to say something, but she put her fingers on his lips. They sat like that for a long time.

Chapter 51

Alina awoke as songbirds greeted the morning. She stretched, delighting in the lingering kiss of an undisturbed night's sleep. She sat up and yawned. It seemed impossible that the *trial of the forest* had been only a handful of days ago. The morning that Dashin left for the forest floor seemed a lifetime ago. The transformation in the village itself since that morning was dramatic. The rhythms of village life had reasserted themselves, only now they included her Amani. She never tired of saying it, grinning as she thought of his smiling face.

She washed up and hurried to the platform, eager to see him. She greeted the villagers she passed on her way, all of them having smiles for her these days. As she neared the platform, she heard the thumping of Solvan. She smiled as the platform came into view, and she saw him running from one end of it and back, the rhythm of his gait sounding better each day. Both Rigin and Dashin had been massaging his foot, Solvan biting down to stop from crying out as they did.

Pritha was chasing him this morning, and when he got to the end of the platform, she would turn and have him chase her. She could have outpaced him, but she seemed to enjoy the game, thrilled to either chase or be chased. Matse sat on the platform's edge, looking on and slapping the matting encouragingly each time they passed her.

"How did you sleep, Amani?" Dashin asked, bringing her a slab of nutbread with just the right amount of nut paste and berries.

"Wonderfully," she said, taking the bread and touching her forehead to his. She felt a tingle run through her as she did. That she had someone to share that with daily, without worrying that they might be sent out to die at any moment, was something she was just beginning to get used to.

"What chores are we doing today?" he asked, grinning.

"I think you're gathering silas pods today," she said. "Aor and the others will be here soon," she said, crinkling her eyes, happy that her friends had taken to him.

"I'll be working with Hurza and Kani," she said, taking a bite of nutbread. "We'll be spinning the silas fiber we've processed and discussing your shortcomings, I presume," she said, chewing and giggling.

"My shortcomings?" he chuckled.

"Oh, not just yours. I'm certain Aor and Drur will figure into it too, though I imagine your shortcomings will occupy the bulk of the time," she crinkled her eyes.

"Well, perhaps then us boys will have to discuss your shortcomings too," Dashin ventured, grinning.

"Then that should be a very quick conversation," she chuckled.

"Yes, I'm afraid I'll have nothing at all to share," Dashin said, his eyes sparkling.

His words and the look he gave her made her knees weak, and she leaned in and wrapped her arms around him, tears welling up in the corners of her eyes. She pulled away a moment later and dabbed at her eyes.

"Are the two of you still hanging on each other?" Hurza teased as she arrived with the others.

Her friends greeted her and Dashin. They all ate a bite together before setting off for the day. Dashin waved at her as he donned his pack and joined the others. She watched them go, her heart full of joy.

"Are you coming to help, or do you plan on mooning there all day?" Hurza quipped behind her.

"I haven't decided yet," Alina said with a giggle as she turned to her friends.

The day passed pleasantly, the sunlight chasing them around the platform in the grove as they hugged the shade while they worked. The boys joined them laden with silas pods, and the talk, as they worked, was soft and light.

Her family had officially moved to Rigin's table. They'd been taking their meals there for so long now that others with children had taken their former table. The talk filling the platform during the evening meal was pleasant. Alina let it wash over her, savoring the feel of it on her ears.

So, she missed it at first when the talk grew serious at her table.

"When do you think that might be?" Dashin asked.

"There is no way to know, Dashin," her mother answered.

"What?" Alina asked. "I'm sorry, what are we talking about?"

Her mother looked away.

"I was asking your mother what she saw when she was away, and she mentioned that there are challenges ahead."

Alina swallowed. Her mother was uncomfortable with the subject. She tried to remember her mother's words. She'd spoken of *terrible things* coming, things she *dare not speak of yet.* The memory of her words sent a shiver through her.

"Solvan, how is your foot doing?" Enor asked, changing the subject.

Solvan plopped his dirty foot up onto the table next to the food.

Rigin pushed it off, tickling him as she did. "You can show Enor your foot once we've all finished with our food."

Solvan giggled madly as she tickled him.

Alina grinned, looking out over the tables at the faces of her village. Hurza, seated next to Aor, teased him about something to his delight as his parents looked on, smiling next to them. Hedrick sat at the table, eating quietly and amiably, seldom venturing a word. The proud fern that had stood tall and towered above others in their village had bent its head, making room for others to find the light reaching down through the trees.

Though Kani was not yet sitting with Drur, she'd seen them working together on tasks throughout the day. It seemed many moments presented themselves where Kani required help with something she could have done alone. And, in those moments, Drur was somehow always at hand.

Over the past moon cycle, Rigin and the children had effectively become family. Rigin had treated Alina like a daughter in her mother's absence, saying things through her eyes and gestures that revealed that she'd understood things going on within her before Alina had realized them herself.

The children hung on her now like the siblings she'd never had. Matse insisted now that Alina be the one to cut her hair, and Solvan kept her apprised of each day's progress with his new brace. The dream of having children still lingered within her, called to her, and yet...

Her parents were, as ever, perfect together, happy to be reunited, though she knew her mother's visions troubled them both. Her mother had no doubt shared more of what she'd seen with her father, finding room upon his shoulders to place some of the cares and worries she carried.

It was a relationship that she had only glimpsed, as though through thick foliage, but that she'd envied and despaired of ever knowing. And, somehow, impossibly, the SkyGods had cast a ball of fire from the sky directly into her heart. Her very own love sat next to her, laughing now and chatting. He was warm, and giving, and brave, and yet still vulnerable, and amazingly now, *of her tribe,* and *of her heart.*

After the evening meal, she took Dashin to sit in the tree she'd found with branches that were just right. His was just a touch higher than hers, so that when they sat on them with their backs to the smooth trunk, their shoulders touched and their heads lay next to each other.

They discussed the day, rambling through it, enjoying the simple act of sharing time together. When the conversation slowed, Dashin brought up the exchange he'd had with her mother during the evening meal.

"Your mother is uncomfortable speaking of her *sight*," Dashin said.

"Yes, it has always been so."

"Is she afraid that speaking of it may change the outcome?"

She gasped, shocked. She leaned forward and turned so she could see his eyes. She couldn't understand how he could have grasped so easily what her mother had had to explain to her countless times. She'd pestered her mother regarding her *sight* since childhood, puzzled at why her mother could not change events to shape the things she saw.

"Has she explained this to you?" she asked, wondering when they might have discussed this without her.

"No, it seemed obvious," he replied.

She bit her lip and almost pushed him off his branch. She sat back in a huff.

"What?" he asked, sensing her tension.

"Nothing," she answered curtly.

She felt him swallow, and the action was so endearing she had to chuckle.

"Did I say something?" he asked, apparently still worried.

"No," she lied, no longer needing to discuss it.

She looked up at the stars above them. "What is it like to fly among the GodLights?"

He looked up. "It's cold and dark up there."

"Is it not warm with the sun in the sky?"

"No, there's no air up there, and you feel the warmth of the sun through the air."

"That's silly," she replied. "Everyone knows that air is cool. One feels it at once when the wind blows."

"You have a point there," he replied.

She sensed that he'd merely let her win the argument, his warm heart more concerned with her than any need to be right. She leaned in and kissed him.

Acknowledgements

Until I started working on this novel, I only skimmed acknowledgments in books I read. Somehow, I imagined books sprang fully-formed from the author's mind and that those mentioned were incidental.

I've learned while bringing this book to life that nothing could be further from the truth. Like our TreeKeepers, it took a village to turn a crude idea into the work you now hold. I've been blessed to have been surrounded by so many who gave so much to help shape it.

Janis has been there from the first page and provided support and insights throughout. However, once I finished my first draft and naively believed I had a novel, it was my army of beta readers that was responsible for helping me shade in the world and characters and find the best story. They helped me polish that lump of coal into something that shines in comparison.

In particular, I want to thank Amy Jensen and Sophia Heath, both of whom have been there since the earliest draft and have read every iteration since. The decision to include them at the last minute in a full roster was the best one I could have made. Stephanie Moore and Margie Sarsfield were also a tremendous help in reviewing later drafts and making editing passes of their own. My other beta readers: Kristen Martin, Margaret Herndon, Nerissa Draeger, Nolan James, Taylyn Anderson, Leah Parkhurst, Alyssa Thomsen, Natalie Potell, Mandy Bartmess, Zephanasia Lewis, Mindy Thompson, Kathleen Fossum, and Alyssa Blackmon all contributed valuable feedback and suggestions. Many of the above were also involved in giving feedback on the cover design and blurb, an odyssey in itself.

Finally, my long-running book group, coming up on thirty years, has been a terrific source of support, as have my local writing groups, in both Cupertino and Mountain View.

Thanks to everyone above and to anyone I might have left out.

About the author

David Pariseau has always dreamed of writing novels. He even tried it a few times amid life's obligations and detours. This book and those that follow are the culmination of that dream.

David lives in the Bay Area in California with his wife Janis and his writing partner Coco, who's been invaluable in fleshing out Pritha's details, though he still doesn't understand why she had to be a cat and not a Shih-Tzu.

David can be contacted via his author website or links (below)

www.dkp-books.com

@david.pariseau.author   Instagram

@david.pariseau.author   TikTok

We live in an age where thousands of books are published daily. Reviews, especially for self-published authors, make all the difference. So, if you have a moment, please leave a review wherever you read them.

Thanks.

Book 2 of the Ndesa series
Songs of Flint
www.dkp-books.com

They just wanted a simple life.
It was not to be…

Dashin has found the family he dreamed of. Life is nearly everything he hoped it might be. But while Alina is thrilled to have him by her side, she grapples with what this means for the future.

When a mysterious disease arises that preys on seers, anxiety ripples through the village. Unease turns to dread as grim news reaches them of a scourge that stalks the treetops and might see their entire world undone.

If they are to avoid disaster, the tribe must find a way to stand against an implacable force. As visions have foreseen, Dashin, Alina and Pritha are thrust into the center of the coming storm. But visions are muddled, most of them dire, and time is running out.

Book Two of Ndesa series

SONGS OF FLINT

David Pariseau